PURPOSE OF EVASION

PURPOSE OF EVASION

GREG DINALLO

ST. MARTIN'S PRESS

NEW YORK

DESIGN BY BARBARA M. BACHMAN

Map by Gerald C. Nash

Library of Congress Cataloging-in-Publication Data

Dinallo, Gregory S.
   Purpose of evasion / Greg Dinallo.
     p. cm.
   ISBN 0-312-04331-7
   I. Title.
  PS3554.I46P87   1990
   813'.54—dc20   89-78020
                                                         CIP

First Edition

10 9 8 7 6 5 4 3 2 1

FOR MY WIFE, GLORIA

AN INDIVIDUAL, EXCEPT FOR THE
PRESIDENT, ELECTED OR APPOINTED
TO AN OFFICE OF HONOR OR PROFIT IN
THE CIVIL SERVICE OR UNIFORMED
SERVICES, SHALL TAKE THE
FOLLOWING OATH:

"I, _____, DO SOLEMNLY SWEAR (OR
AFFIRM) THAT I WILL SUPPORT AND
DEFEND THE CONSTITUTION OF THE
UNITED STATES AGAINST ALL
ENEMIES, FOREIGN AND DOMESTIC;
THAT I WILL BEAR TRUE FAITH AND
ALLEGIANCES TO THE SAME; THAT I
TAKE THIS OBLIGATION FREELY,
WITHOUT ANY MENTAL RESERVATION
OR PURPOSE OF EVASION; AND THAT I
WILL WELL AND FAITHFULLY
DISCHARGE THE DUTIES OF THE
OFFICE ON WHICH I AM ABOUT
TO ENTER.
SO HELP ME GOD."

—5 U.S. CODE ANNOTATED
SEC. 3331

PREFACE

J U N E   1 4 ,   1 9 8 5—terrorists hijack a TWA jetliner: an American serviceman is executed; thirty-nine other Americans are held hostage for seventeen days.

December 27, 1985—terrorists attack the Rome airport: twenty people are killed; five of them, Americans.

April 2, 1986—a terrorist bomb explodes aboard a TWA 727 en route from Rome to Athens: four Americans are killed.

April 4, 1986—terrorists bomb La Belle Club, a West Berlin disco: two American servicemen are killed.

April 5, 1986—a U.S. spy satellite intercepts a cable from the Libyan People's Bureau in East Berlin to Tripoli. The president, citing it as proof that Libya sanctioned the bombing, decides to retaliate.

April 14, 1986—U.S. Air Force F-111 bombers from Lakenheath, England, and U.S. Navy A-6 Intruders from carriers in the Gulf of Sidra attack Libya.

The result: military facilities in Tripoli and Benghazi are destroyed. Colonel Muammar el-Qaddafi's compound is hit, but he is unharmed. Two F-111 bombers are hit by Libyan missiles. One is destroyed. Its crew is lost.

In the aftermath many questions were asked, the most incisive being: Why use F-111s based in England—a 5,800-mile, 14-hour round trip, requiring many inflight refuelings—when A-6 Intruders, based on carriers 200 miles from Libya's shores, could have been used exclusively?

The official answer: To showcase military hardware and coordination skills, proving to Americans and the world that years of increased defense expenditures had paid off.

All that is history. What follows is fiction.

ACKNOWLEDGMENTS

FOR TECHNICAL INFORMATION about the F-111 bomber, and the raid on Libya, I am indebted to the 27th Tactical Fighter Wing at Cannon Air Force Base, New Mexico, and especially to the following U.S. Air Force personnel: Major Richard E. Brown, who has logged in excess of 4,000 hours at the controls of F-111s, more than any other aviator; Master Sergeant Gregory Weigl, crew chief; and Technical Sergeant Rhett Blevins, weapons specialist—all of whom at one time or another served with F-111 squadrons based in England.

I would also like to thank Major Ronald Fuchs and Captain Marie K. Yancey of the Air Force Public Affairs Division for directing me to the above-mentioned experts.

Furthermore, with regard to submarine sequences, it is important to acknowledge the extremely high level of technical literature published by the U.S. Naval Institute, as well as the counsel of those experts whose request for anonymity must be honored.

Along with my thanks, I offer apologies to all for technical embellishments or errata that were dictated by the drama and the need to blend fact with fiction.

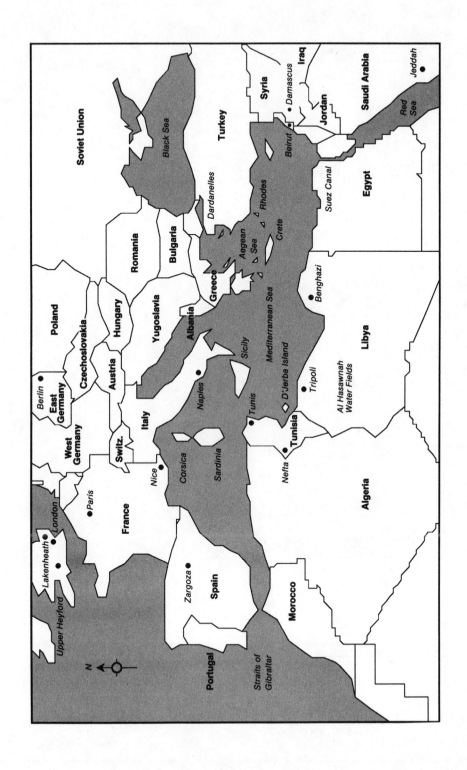

PROLOGUE

KATIFA'S skin was flawless. Bassam had no doubt of it as he caressed her, his fingertips gliding gently over her smooth flesh, which had the sheen of translucent amber. Not a freckle, not a blemish, not a single needle mark had he found—which was strange since the prescription for insulin was in her name.

Bassam had no doubt of that either.

About a week ago, a contact at the Turk Hospital pharmacy where it had been filled showed it to him. And though Katifa's fiery beauty stirred Bassam's passion, it was the medication that aroused his suspicion.

He immediately set out to satisfy both.

That afternoon, following a day of classes at Beirut University College, where she taught political science and Bassam taught economics, Katifa had hurried across the parking lot and got into her car.

The old Mercedes sedan refused to start.

Bassam just happened to be passing by and offered to help. He opened the hood and jiggled a few wires.

"Try it now," he said in a confident tone.

Katifa turned the key and held it; still nothing.

"You've found me out," Bassam joked with self-deprecating charm. "Fuel economy was my worst subject." Then, after appropriate tinkering and head scratching, he deftly replaced the rotor he had removed from the vehicle's distributor a short time earlier.

The engine kicked over.

Katifa beamed.

And as Bassam had planned, he soon spent an evening exploring Katifa's supple body, paying special attention to the smooth expanse of her thighs and flat plane of her abdomen, sites where insulin was most commonly injected. Now he knew just *how* flawless her skin was, and his suspicion had intensified.

"You should go," she said in her husky voice as they lay tangled in the sheets, sharing a cigarette.

"I'm crushed," he replied with a mischievous grin, stroking the line of peach fuzz that rose from her pelvis like wispy strokes of Japanese calligraphy.

"I have papers to grade," she said, moaning as the tip of his finger found its mark. "And so do you," she went on in a futile plea.

When Bassam finally left, he circled the block in his car and parked down the street from her apartment on Tamar Mallat, savoring the smell of her while he waited.

About an hour later, a garage beneath one of the white stucco buildings opened and Katifa's old Mercedes drove into the darkness. Bassam kept his headlights off and tailed her through Beirut's twisting streets to the hospital pharmacy on De Mazraa, where she picked up a package.

Katifa was driving north on Mar Elias when a reflection from Bassam's windshield flickered in her mirror. It was just a twinkle. There and gone in an instant. Katifa wasn't sure what she had seen. She turned at the next corner, parked, and shut off her lights. Thirty seconds later Bassam drove past. The streets ahead were deserted. Not a vehicle or pedestrian in sight. He realized what Katifa had done and came round the block, which put him behind the Mercedes when it pulled out again. Katifa detoured through the low-income Sunni district of Al Zarif to the intersection of Rue H. Daoud and Patriarche Hoyek on the Green Line, separating the city's Muslim and Christian sectors. She went through the checkpoint without incident and took Avenue Charles Helou to the coastal motorway that snaked north along the rugged coast, skirting the boiling surf below.

Forty minutes later Katifa drove onto the unkempt grounds of a rundown estate. Weeds sprouted from cracks in the marble fountains and filled the spaces between the rococo letters of a sign that proclaimed: CASINO DU LIBAN.

The once grand gaming palace stood alone on a promontory above the sea. A mix of Middle Eastern architecture and Louis XIV decor, the abandoned casino was a casualty of the decades of warfare that had destroyed Beirut; that had turned a sun-drenched playground for socialites into a war-torn battleground for terrorists.

Katifa parked beneath the casino's arched portico. Bassam stopped outside the gate and watched as she left her car, carrying the package from the pharmacy; then he proceeded on foot down the long approach road.

Katifa slipped into the soaring entrance hall that led to the main gaming room. The tables where countless fortunes had been won and lost were shrouded in darkness and dust. Katifa hurried between them, seized by an impulse to spin one of the roulette wheels; but her reflection, rippling across the darkly mirrored walls like a dozen consciences, warned against it, warned that to succumb to the temptation would somehow tarnish her.

At the far end of the gaming room, where crates of weapons and ammunition and drums of plastic explosive were stockpiled, a gilded staircase rose majestically between immense chandeliers. Katifa climbed the steps to the second floor, negotiated a maze of marble corridors, and knocked on a carved wooden door.

Dark eyes peered through a slit that had been crudely hacked in the richly textured paneling.

Katifa's brother, an intense young man named Rashid, threw the dead bolt and let her in. He slung his machine pistol over his shoulder, took the package, and gave it to Hasan, his second in command.

Hasan left the room and went downstairs through the gaming room to an exterior gangway that led to a marina directly behind the casino. A Soviet-made Zhuk-class gunboat was waiting in one of the slips, where the yachts of Greek shipping magnates and Arab potentates had once been berthed. All markings had been stripped from the vessel's hull. No national flag flew from her mast. Several heavily armed sentries stood on the deck. They wore civilian clothes, their heads swathed in checkered kaffiyehs. One took the package from Hasan and signaled the helmsman with a wave. The rust-stained gunboat pulled away and sped into the night.

In the room on the second floor of the casino, Rashid listened until the sound of the engine had faded, then glanced at his watch. "What happened?" he asked, his impatience growing as Katifa pulled a cigarette from a pack of Gaulois with her lips and lit it.

"I was followed," she finally replied, the smoke coming from her nose and mouth. "I went through Al Zarif to make sure I lost him."

Rashid's face tightened. He led her to a window, peering through a slit in the boards nailed over it.

"You didn't," he said in a tense voice.

Katifa's eyes narrowed to see a shadow moving across the grounds below. The glow from a window washed over the man's face, revealing his features.

"Bassam . . . you bastard," she hissed bitterly.

"You know him?"

"Yes, from school," she replied, trying to hide the embarrassment she felt. "We're . . . colleagues."

Rashid saw the evasive flicker in his sister's eyes. "You've been fucking a shetan," he said, pegging Bassam for a spy, possibly a CIA operative, which he was. "He's been making inquiries at every pharmacy in the city."

What Rashid didn't know was that several weeks before, CIA had been informed that a terrorist leader had been treated at the Turk Hospital private clinic for diabetic shock—unofficially, no name, no records—and Bassam had been checking out all new prescriptions for insulin.

Rashid gathered men from other rooms in the casino. Like him they were young and lean, with eyes that blazed with intensity— the offspring of Palestinians deported from Jordan who had sought refuge in Beirut amid the warring Druze, Amal, and Shiite militias, with whom they shared a hatred for the United States and Israel. Despite it, Palestinians were unwelcome in Beirut and had been without power since Yasser Arafat was expelled in 1982. They would have been long forgotten if not for the series of bombings, hijackings, and kidnappings that captured world attention. Yet it wasn't the PLO that had orchestrated them, but a radical PLO splinter group called the Fatah Revolutionary Council.

Now Rashid and his band of FRC guerrillas fanned out into Casino du Liban's marble corridors and stairwells in search of the intruder. All were armed. Several carried Skorpions, the ultralight, easily concealed submachine gun long favored by the PLO.

Bassam had crossed the darkened gaming room and was climbing the sweeping staircase, his hand wrapped around the grip of a pistol. He reached the top, moved slowly down a corridor, and had started up some steps to a landing when the marble tread beneath his foot creaked. He froze and cursed silently, deciding to leave while he still could, and report his discovery. But a shadow was stretching slowly across the floor in the corridor behind him. He glanced about for a way to avoid an encounter. The soft whisk of denim up ahead told him he was trapped. He holstered his weapon, inching his way back toward the corner, his eyes glued to the shadow, which grew longer and longer. His fingers slipped a knife from his pocket and opened it, skillfully masking the click of the blade as it locked in place. He waited until the last possible instant, until the terrorist's lithe silhouette was about to turn toward him with his Skorpion. Then swiftly, instinctively, Bassam clamped a hand over his mouth, yanked his head back sharply, and drove the long blade upward into the soft flesh just behind his chin. It pierced his tongue, went through the roof of his mouth, and darted into the base of his brain. He died instantly without making a sound.

Bassam set the body aside, then retraced his steps through the corridors and down the staircase. He was crossing the gaming room when a half-dozen guerrillas sprang from the pitch blackness. Gun muzzles poked into him from every angle. They were muscling him between the tables when an anguished cry echoed through the casino. Several of the Palestinians dashed up the staircase to the source of the chilling wail. They found Katifa in the corridor, kneeling over Rashid's body. His eyes were glazed. His head lay in a small halo of black blood that had spilled from the puncture beneath his chin.

W H I L E Katifa cradled her brother's corpse in the corridor at Casino du Liban, the Soviet-made gunboat was cutting swiftly through Mediterranean blackness. A short, stocky man with wary eyes and an iron will sat in one of the cabins opening the package that Katifa had delivered to the pier.

He removed two boxes of pharmaceuticals.

One contained disposable syringes, the other a supply of insulin. His mouth was dry and his hands trembled, making it more difficult to peel the wrapper from the syringe. The laser-honed needle glistened as he brought it to the vial and pierced the blue polypropylene seal. He withdrew precisely 25 ccs of the milky fluid, flicked the syringe several times with a fingernail, then depressed the plunger until a few drops of insulin spurted from the needle.

His thumb and forefinger pulled a thickness of abdomen from under his shirt and he deftly slid the needle beneath the skin.

Then the Fatah Revolutionary Council's radical founder, the mastermind of international terrorism who had vowed to fight to the last man if that's what it took for Palestinians to reclaim their homeland, cursed his poor health and shot the insulin into his flesh. His name was Sabri Banna but he was known to the world as Abu Nidal.

He had just withdrawn the needle when the phone in the cabin sounded. Nidal answered it and was informed by his radioman that Hasan was calling on the ship-to-shore radio. The news of Rashid's death filled the terrorist leader with anger and sadness. He ordered the gunboat to return to Casino du Liban.

Katifa and Hasan were waiting on the dock when the vessel pulled into one of the slips.

The insulin had worked its magic. Nidal leapt onto the dock and hurried to Katifa's side, embracing her emotionally. "I'm sorry," he said, his eyes welling.

Katifa didn't reply. She couldn't. She just broke down and, sobbing in Nidal's arms, remembered another day eighteen years ago when he had comforted her. The horrid memory was a blur of screaming people, gunfire, and helicopters.

That was in 1967.

Egypt had closed the Suez Canal to Israeli shipping and the Six-Day War was in full swing. Ram Allah, an ancient city on the West Bank, was the center of Palestinian resistance. Katifa's father, Abu Issa Kharuz, was the settlement's leader. Days of bloody fighting with Israeli troops forced him to consider evacuating. He polled his two young protégés; Abu Nidal was vehemently opposed; Yasser Arafat sided with his mentor. Decision made, helicopters were called in. While Issa Kharuz and Nidal resisted the advancing Israelis, Arafat loaded the women and children. Nidal made it aboard the last helicopter; Katifa's father didn't. It lifted off in a hail of gunfire that killed him.

Now Katifa watched as her brother's body was loaded onto the gunboat; then she and Nidal followed Hasan up the gangway into the casino. He led the way to a darkened Greek-style amphitheater opposite the gaming room. Towering Ionic columns circled the stage where spectacular shows had once dazzled jet-setters. And there, hanging naked from an ornate trapezelike apparatus that had been used to lower bare-breasted showgirls to the stage, was

Bassam. His ankles were tied and he had been hoisted into the air upside down.

Hasan handed Abu Nidal a knife. Bassam's knife.

"Who are you working for?" Nidal asked.

Bassam didn't respond.

"Who?" Nidal shouted, grabbing his hair and yanking his face up toward him. "Who is he?"

"An American. He works at the embassy—in the communications section," Bassam finally replied weakly, using information he'd been instructed to reveal should such a situation arise. "I . . . I don't know his name."

With a sudden slash of the blade, Abu Nidal cut off the clump of hair. Bassam yelped in fright. The stocky terrorist circled him, then suddenly stuck the blade, just the first half-inch of razor-sharp steel, into the flesh below Bassam's rib cage.

He let out a short scream.

"His name," Nidal commanded, flicking his wrist, causing the puncture in Bassam's flesh to widen.

"I don't know!" Bassam screamed in pain, blinded by the halogen atop a whirring videotape camera manned by one of the terrorists. He was crouched next to Katifa, who stared unflinchingly at the blood running over Bassam's back, which still bore the marks of her passion.

"Do you know what happens next?" Nidal asked menacingly. "Have you ever seen a man skinned alive?"

Bassam was writhing in agony, blinking at the blood that covered his face and dripped to the floor.

"Only his name can save you," Abu Nidal prodded, flicking the blade.

"Fitz . . . Fitz-gerald," Bassam whimpered. "Thomas Fitzgerald."

Abu Nidal smiled thinly; then, following Arabic tradition that a blood relative exact vengeance, he turned to Katifa and offered her the weapon that had killed her brother.

She lowered her eyes, declining. "No, no, it is your right, Abu-habib," she said emotionally, paying tribute to Nidal. Though the prefix Abu, which means father in Arabic, is often used informally as a gesture of respect, it had special meaning for Katifa; and she had purposely added the suffix, beloved, to acknowledge that, having raised her and Rashid since their father's death eighteen years ago, Abu Nidal had more than earned the right to avenge his adopted son's death. She saw the pride and acceptance in

Nidal's eyes, then hugged him and hurried from the amphitheater.

When Katifa was out of sight, Nidal held the blade against
Bassam's torso while Hasan and one of the others spun him slowly
on the trapezelike apparatus until a shallow incision completely
girdled his waist.

"No! No! God, no! I told you! I told you!" Bassam howled; but
his shrieks of pain and protest were for naught, as the two Palestinians pushed their fingers into the bloody slit and grasped his
flesh tightly.

On the ground floor of the casino, Katifa was crossing the main
gaming room when a piercing scream echoed off the mirrors,
raising her pores.

THE AIR WAS ALIVE with the cool, salty bite of the
sea as Tom Fitzgerald left his apartment on Rue du Caire in the
once fashionable Hamra quarter of West Beirut, wishing he could
walk to his office as he once had. Indeed, the U.S. Embassy on
Avenue de Paris was a short distance away. Fitzgerald was listed
as communications officer; but his real title was CIA chief of
station. He waved to some neighborhood children on their way
to school, then crossed to the beige Honda that he had recently
begun driving to work.

Suddenly, a van came out of an alley and stopped next to him,
almost pinning him against the car.

Fitzgerald knew what was about to happen; knew the horrid
nightmare was about to swallow him. He turned to run but a
young Palestinian leapt from the van, blocking his way. He reversed direction and ran into another, who pressed a gun to his
temple and ordered him into the van. But Fitzgerald had long
ago decided that capture wasn't an acceptable option, that if the
moment ever came, he would escape or die trying. He slapped
the pistol aside, drove an elbow into the Palestinian behind him,
and ran, expecting the searing sting of bullets to follow; but a
third Palestinian appeared and drove the butt of a rifle into his
solar plexus. The three terrorists dragged him into the van, slammed
the door, and drove off.

No more than fifteen seconds had elapsed.

LATER THAT WEEK in Washington, D.C., a body-guard assigned to Director of Central Intelligence William Kiley left the DCI's home on the old Rockefeller estate on Foxhall Road to retrieve the *Washington Post*. As he did each morning before delivering the newspaper to his boss, he carefully checked it for explosive devices. This was standard security procedure.

Today the bodyguard found a package. It contained a videotape cassette. A Polaroid photograph of a haggard Thomas Fitzgerald was taped to the slipcase, announcing that he had been kidnapped —*not* by Abu Nidal's Fatah Revolutionary Council, but by Hezbollah, a fanatical, pro-Iranian terrorist group.

The DCI's face was ashen when he finished viewing the video-tape of Bassam's torture and death. He sat in stunned silence for several moments before his eyes drifted to the Polaroid of Fitzgerald. The chilling implication that his longtime colleague and friend could suffer the same fate horrified him.

This was the second time in as many months that Kiley had been personally burned by terrorists. The first, the discovery that two former CIA agents had set up and equipped numerous ter-rorist training camps in Libya, still tormented him.

"Goddamned animals," the DCI whispered hoarsely, seething with hatred. "They turned the worst of my people, now they kidnapped the best."

And that was the moment he went over the edge; there were no rules anymore, no cost too great, no person too valuable. What-ever it took, Bill Kiley would find a way to satisfy his hunger for vengeance.

Book One

A PEOPLE THAT EATS

IMPORTED FOOD

CANNOT BE FREE.

—COLONEL

MUAMMAR

EL-QADDAFI

1

L I B Y A, six months later.

Monday, March 31, 1986.

Not a blade of grass, not a single plant, bush, or tree, nothing but burnt sienna sand stretched for miles across this wind-burnished landscape—nothing except a concrete pipeline that slithered over the dunes like an immense, sunbathing rattlesnake.

The infernal stillness was soon broken by the rising whisk of rotors. A Libyan Air Force helicopter came streaking low over the Sahara, sunlight reflecting off its windshield like a flashing strobe.

Saddam Moncrieff sat next to the pilot, staring at the endless miles of concrete pipe that passed directly beneath him, contemplating a problem. A hydrologist of international repute, the pensive Saudi had engineered a plan to solve Libya's serious water shortage, a shortage compounded by the high salt content of rainfed wells, the nation's only source. Even in Tripoli, tap water had become barely drinkable.

Subterranean aquifers discovered beneath the Sahara by American geologists searching for oil were the key to Moncrieff's plan: hundreds of wells drilled in the desert would pump 200 million cubic feet of water a day, twice OPEC's daily output of oil, through 2,500 miles of pipeline to Libya's thirsty cities.

The sections of concrete pipe, each 13 feet in diameter and weighing 73 tons, were manufactured round the clock at a modern desert complex; and Moncrieff's aerial survey of wellheads and pipeline had confirmed that the project was right on schedule. Despite it, Libya's Great Man-Made River Project was in jeopardy. The subterranean reservoirs were drying up. By the time the $20 billion undertaking was completed, there would be little if any water to pump through it; and the Saudi had just determined beyond doubt that the cause was a dam that had diverted its source—a dam built several years before in neighboring Tunisia.

Contrary to popular conception, Tunisia had plenty of water, as did neighboring Algeria and Morocco. The mountain ranges of the northern Maghreb—where ski resorts remain open well into April—were a copious watershed, supplying a string of oases that ran south to the city of Nefta. Here, hundreds of natural springs were funneled into an east-flowing tributary. It eventually drained deep into thirsty salt lakes, creating underground rivers that for eons had flowed hundreds of miles beneath the Sahara into Libya, feeding the subterranean Jabal Al Hasawnah water fields.

But Nefta Dam had blocked this tributary. Now, where there had been nothing, an immense, glass-smooth lake encircled by lush palm forests, olive groves, and fields of barley stretched to the horizon. Unfortunately, though a boon to Tunisia's economy, the dam had cut off the supply of water to Libya's reservoirs.

That was Moncrieff's problem; that and the fact that he was on his way to meet with Colonel Muammar el-Qaddafi to decide how to deal with it.

The sun was burning through a light mist as the helicopter came in over the desert and landed at the Bab al Azziziya Barracks south of downtown Tripoli.

Moncrieff was ushered into the boldly patterned tent that served as Qaddafi's personal domicile, joining the colonel, his chief of staff, General Younis, and several economic and industrial advisers.

Qaddafi wore a bulletproof vest and maroon beret embroidered with the Insignia of Islam. He sat on the edge of a desk beneath the soaring fabric and harsh fluorescents, digesting Moncrieff's report.

Ten years before, Qaddafi, the son of an illiterate Bedouin shepherd, had cut a shrewd deal with the Ivy League presidents of Western oil companies. The money provided free housing, education, and medical care for his people. But the lack of water threatened his vision for Libya's future.

When Moncrieff and the members of Qaddafi's staff were seated and had ceased to murmur among themselves, the Libyan leader looked up and broke the stillness. "We're going into Tunisia," he said quietly.

A stunned silence fell over the group.

A look flicked between Moncrieff and Younis.

The general was a short man with rigid posture that suited his title. "Send a military force across the border?" he finally asked, wary of Qaddafi's impulsive bent for invading his neighbors. An attack on the Tunisian city of Gafsa in 1980 and the current war with Chad, a demoralizing struggle over a worthless strip of desert, were its most recent manifestations. True, the lack of water was arguably a more noble and justifiable motive but, as the general knew, Tunisia was a far more formidable adversary.

"We have no choice," Qaddafi replied, going on to remind his staff that relations between the two nations were strained and that it would be unrealistic to expect even a staunch ally, let alone Tunisia, to destroy a multibillion dollar investment. "I suggest an air strike, carried out at night by bombers flying below radar at supersonic speed," Qaddafi concluded. "In a matter of minutes that dam would be a pile of rubble; and it would be over before Tunisian Air Defense knew it had even happened, let alone who did it."

Younis's face stiffened with grave concern.

"You don't agree?" Qaddafi challenged.

"On the contrary," the general replied. "Unfortunately, we don't have aircraft capable of it."

Qaddafi's eyes narrowed, forcing vertical creases deep into his forehead. After a moment, he removed a thick, soft-cover volume from a bookcase behind his desk.

The Military Balance was published annually by the International Institute for Strategic Studies in London. It quantitatively assessed the armed forces of more than 140 countries. The colonel relied on it to keep informed of the strength of enemies and allies alike, the latter with an eye to purchasing military hardware. He turned to the section where the Libyan Air Force was inventoried:

BOMBERS:	6	TU-22
INTERCEPTORS:	26	MIRAGE F-1ED, 4 F-1BD
	131	MIG-23 FLOGGER
	49	MIG-25 FOXBAT A
	49	MIG-21, 12 25U
GROUND ATTACK	45	MIRAGE 5D/DE, 13 5DD
FIGHTERS:	14	MIRAGE F-1AD
	44	MIG-23BM FLOGGER F

14   MIG-23U
90   SU-20/22 FITTER E/F/J

The list further enumerated helicopters, transports, and trainers. Qaddafi pointed to the total. "We have five hundred and forty-four combat aircraft," he intoned. "None are capable of flying this mission?"

"Four hundred and fifty-one are inoperable, sir," Younis said gently, citing a statistic in the report Qaddafi was conveniently ignoring. "We are woefully short of maintenance technicians, and spare parts. Only our SU-22s are—"

"Well, what about them?" Qaddafi challenged, zeroing in on the mainstay of his air force.

"A defensive weapon, nothing more," Younis explained. "Even in broad daylight it can barely—"

"We've spent billions, *billions*, and still can't take out an unprotected dam?" Qaddafi bellowed.

"Not at night. Not at supersonic speed. Not below radar. Not in Tunisia without getting caught, sir," Younis replied evenly. "No."

Qaddafi ran a hand through his wiry hair, pondering the problem. "The Soviets will never sell us these aircraft," he concluded sharply. "They're worried we're defaulting on the five billion we already owe them."

Moncrieff had been quietly observing and analyzing. "Moscow isn't the only source," he said calmly after a long silence.

Qaddafi's eyes shifted to the Saudi. "Where else?"

"Washington," Moncrieff replied softly.

Younis looked stunned.

The colonel concealed his surprise, his large head tilting back at the familiar cocky angle. He had no doubt Moncrieff was serious. He knew the Saudi could make things happen; that he had powerful international connections; that he was different, privileged.

The Saudi prince had been educated in Switzerland and France as well as the London School of Economics, where he had honed his exceptional analytical skills. Indeed, Moncrieff had been the first to realize that finding a solution for the lack of water, not milking the abundance of oil, was the key to economic growth in the Middle East. It was a theory that had brought him to the Massachusetts Institute of Technology, where he received a doctorate in hydrology.

"I'd be happy to explore the matter, sir," Moncrieff said coolly.

"What would they want in exchange? My head?" Qaddafi cracked, knowing he had nothing that could induce the United States to give supersonic bombers to him, the financier of international terrorism.

"No, sir," Moncrieff replied, not daring to laugh. "I'm quite certain acceptable currency can be acquired. However, delicate linkages would be involved. I'd need your help to secure them."

"For example?"

"A meeting with Chairman Arafat would be essential—a private meeting."

Qaddafi was considering it when the swish of a tent flap behind him broke his concentration.

An aide-de-camp entered and delivered a communiqué. "From the People's Bureau in Rome, sir."

Qaddafi took the envelope, broke the seal, and removed a cable, which read:

WE HAVE AN EVENT PLANNED THAT WILL PLEASE YOU.

The colonel looked up, smiling, and announced, "It seems our friends in Rome plan to celebrate Easter with a bang." Then he went to his desk to make a phone call.

Younis took Moncrieff aside. "These bombers—you understand, they must, *must* have electro-optical guidance," he sternly warned, referring to the state-of-the-art system that allows a pilot to locate his target at supersonic speed in total darkness and destroy it with bombs that home on a laser frequency.

"It's called Pave Tack," Moncrieff replied.

2

THE GENERAL DYNAMICS F-111 had Pave Tack. It had APQ 144 forward-looking attack radar, ASQ 133 digital fire control, and APQ 138 terrain-following radar.

The F-111 had everything; and Major Walter Shepherd, United States Air Force, lived to fly it.

An airborne stiletto, Shepherd thought, the first time he saw the bomber's crisp edges, long, pointed snout, and swept-back wings. He knew it was a hot aircraft, one whose performance far outstripped its nickname; sure, the Aardvark was a bomber—a bomber with the speed and agility of a supersonic fighter.

The instrumentation was dazzling: navigation computer screen at left, Pave Tack radar at right joined by rows of flight systems gauges, topped by HUD, the heads up display system that projects data onto the canopy, allowing the pilot to keep his eye on the target while the weapons systems officer destroys it.

Walt Shepherd knew every square inch of his plane, every rivet, wire, computer chip, and data readout; his name was stenciled on the nose gear door. The United States government may have paid General Dynamics $67 million for it—but it was *his* plane.

Sixteen years ago, he was a twenty-two-year-old second lieutenant fresh out of flight school when he started flying them. Assigned to a special squadron during the last years of the Vietnam War, Shepherd flew dozens of F-111 missions. Indeed, while many protested and avoided service, Walt Shepherd was flying an untested bomber in combat, and counted himself lucky to have the opportunity. Military service was a family tradition—God, love of country, a strong national defense were its guiding principles. An Eagle Scout by age fourteen, he delivered newspapers with dedication and sang with the Friendship Church choir. Like many towns in the southwestern pocket of Oklahoma, towns with names like Granite, Sentinel, and Victory, Friendship's economy was dependent on nearby Altus Air Force Base. As a teenager, Shepherd spent many afternoons watching military jets taking off; and despite his gentle nature, their thundering roar stirred something in him, something primal and raw that bonded with his unquestioning sense of duty, giving rise to a powerful yearning for combat.

Officially, Major Shepherd flew with the 253rd squadron of the 27th Tactical Fighter Wing at Cannon AFB in New Mexico. Three years ago in a TAC reshuffle, he came east to fly a routine operational readiness inspection. A clever and resourceful thinker with a flair for tactical innovation, Shepherd proved so adept at playing the enemy and penetrating radar defenses with his F-111 that he was assigned to the Pentagon to document his expertise and develop training programs. He had since been temporarily stationed at Andrews Air Force Base in Maryland, just outside Washington, D.C.

On this cold, crystal clear morning, he was in the kitchen of his home on Ashwood Circle, a wooded cul-de-sac in the officers' family housing sector, helping his two-year-old into a snowsuit.

"Come on, Jeffrey, hold still," Shepherd admonished in his easy drawl, finally getting it zipped up.

"Bathroom," the squirming child protested, clutching his crotch with mittened hands. "Bathroom."

Shepherd let out a sigh. "Take him, will you?" he asked Laura, who had bounded into the kitchen, donning a parka.

The thirteen-year-old took one look at her heavily bundled brother and presented Shepherd with an open palm.

"Two bucks," she said with a grin.

"Fifty cents."

"Hold out for a dollar," her mother chimed in, fighting a roll of plastic wrap, one eye on the small television atop the counter tuned to the "Today Show."

"Steph," Shepherd protested.

The phone rang. Shepherd answered it. "Congressman Gutherie's office," he said, handing it to Stephanie.

She wiggled her brows in anticipation, making him laugh, and moved aside with the phone. A bright, ingenuously sexy woman, at thirty-seven Stephanie Shepherd still had the freshness of the University of Denver journalism student who had caught Walt's eye at an Air Force Academy mixer nearly twenty years ago.

"Wish we were going with you, Daddy," Laura pouted, glancing at her father's luggage next to the door.

"Me too," Shepherd said warmly, "but you know—"

"Yeah, I know, I can't miss school."

"I'll miss *you*, princess."

"You're going to miss the finals too," Laura said, referring to her upcoming gymnastics competition. She was standing next to the television when Willard Scott's folksy weather report segued to an update of the morning's top news stories.

"A terrorist bomb exploded aboard a TWA 727 jetliner en route from Rome to Athens, yesterday," the newsreader somberly reported. "Authorities said those responsible are believed to be supported by, if not actual agents of, Libyan strongman Muammar el-Qaddafi. The explosion tore a hole in the fuselage, killing four American passengers who were sucked out of the plane, and fell fifteen thousand feet to their deaths."

Laura turned to her father, her face a bewildered mask. "How can people do things like that?"

"They're uncivilized, sweetheart," Shepherd gently explained, turning off the television. "They don't play by the rules the way we do."

The child nodded sadly, a dozen questions in her eyes, then she took Jeffrey's hand and headed for the bathroom.

"The interview's set for this afternoon," Stephanie announced brightly, hanging up the phone. She worked as a reporter for the *Capitol Flyer*, the base newspaper, and Andrews was in the congressman's district.

"I hope he voted for the ERA," Shepherd teased.

A horn beeped outside. Their faces tightened apprehensively. They looked at each other for a long moment, then kissed.

"Something else you're going to miss," Stephanie whispered as their lips parted.

"You bet; twenty years with a sex-crazed journalist isn't the sort of thing that just slips a man's mind."

"Walt," she admonished gently, unable to suppress a girlish giggle. "I meant our anniversary."

"I know," he said more seriously. "We'll do something special as soon as you come to England."

They were still embracing when the children returned and the horn beeped again. Shepherd kissed and hugged each of them, then hefted the luggage and went out the kitchen door to the air force van in the driveway.

AN HOUR LATER, Major Shepherd and his weapons systems officer, Captain Al Brancato, were at their lockers in the squadron life support room, donning flight suits, helmets, and inflatable G-suit harnesses that girdled their legs and torsos; then they strode down the flight line to a khaki and brown camouflage-patterned F-111F bomber. It had low visibility markings with black stencils. The tail code read: CC-179.

TAC had finally finished the reshuffle and they had been transferred to the 48th Tactical Fighter Wing based at Lakenheath Royal Air Force Base in England.

Brancato was a gregarious man whose taut physique shaped his flight suit. Like most aviators, he adhered to a fitness program of aerobic exercise and workouts in the squadron weight room, where a sign cautioned: THE FORCE IS WITH YOU LIKE IT OR NOT. Gravity was the force, and aviators who flew high performance aircraft viewed G-induced loss of consciousness as a lethal adversary. Well-developed musculature acted as a natural G-suit, augmenting the inflatable harness to raise G-tolerance and prevent GLC.

For the last eight years, Brancato had been Shepherd's alter ego and wizzo. The latter in more ways than one.

"Name the island that has a quarter of a million less inhabitants today than it did a hundred years ago."

"Ireland," Shepherd answered hesitantly.

"Not bad. . . . The American who had a long association with the Soviet Union as businessman and ambassador?"

"Armand Hammer."

"Averill Harriman. Hammer was never ambassador."

"You going to do this all the way to the U.K.?"

"Just for that, which famous composer poured ice water over his head to stimulate his brain?"

"Elton John," Shepherd cracked, as they stowed their luggage on a rack in the weapons bay, empty because the plane was flown "clean," without ordnance, on deployment flights. The crew chief, who for three years had overseen 179's maintenance with customary fervor, hadn't been transferred to England and he watched wistfully as the two aviators did their inspection, then slipped beneath the gullwing canopies into side-by-side red leather couches.

After forty-five minutes of systems checks and engine warm-up procedures, Shepherd radioed for clearance. "Andrews tower, Viper-Two ready to roll."

"Viper?" Stephanie had asked when they first dated, thinking there was nothing at all venomous about him. "It certainly doesn't suit you."

"Well," he replied, glancing skyward, "you have to understand I'm different up there."

She hadn't understood; indeed, she still didn't. Despite being blessed with that rare combination of guts, skill, and judgment found in the best fighter jocks, killing was out of character for Walt Shepherd; conversely, call sign Viper had no trouble handling it.

Shepherd started the F-111 down the west runway; 30 seconds later, the sleek F model, hottest of the 111 series, was banking over Chesapeake Bay. Soon it was at 30,000 feet, streaking through the atmosphere at 750 MPH. The wings were at 16 degrees, standard for takeoff and climb. Shepherd set the indicator stop at 52, advanced the throttles, and eased back the handle in the sidewall; the wings swept at a rate of 10 degrees per second and the F-111 bolted forward.

"Yeah," Brancato hooted as the acceleration slammed him back into his seat; it was a kick every time.

Speed was now Mach 1.75; precisely 1,250 MPH.

Shepherd guided the plane into a GAT-assigned commercial air corridor and engaged the autopilot; then he and Brancato settled in for the long haul.

Two hours later, the sleek bomber was 2,400 miles out over the Atlantic, 1,300 miles from its destination. Unlike practice missions, deployment flights had no tactical objective. Once on autopilot, aviators were essentially passengers in a supersonic taxi. Brancato passed the time reading, his nose buried in a biography of Churchill. Shepherd monitored the avionics.

"Mind watching the store for a while?" Shepherd asked, as he removed a palm-sized cassette recorder from a pocket in the leg of his flight suit and clicked it on. Years ago, the first time he and Stephanie were apart, he had wooed her via cassette, and he had been using it to keep in touch with home ever since: from Vietnam, the Philippines, wherever he was stationed without her.

"Thursday, three April," he began in his easy drawl. "Real pretty up here, babe. We left the Grand Banks behind about an hour ago. Advance report for touchdown is rain and more rain. Sounds like we're talking weather for ducks. Speaking of water, Al thought you should know that Beethoven used to pour ice water over his—" He paused, catching Brancato signaling to the multi systems display. "He's waving at me like a matador. Not Beethoven, Al. Be talking to you soon."

"Three bogies coming off the deck at a hundred miles," Brancato said, eyes riveted to the MSD screen, where three blips had penetrated the radar envelope.

Far below and to the northeast, a Redfleet Surface Action Group was cruising the waters of the North Atlantic: four submarines, three cruisers, and six destroyers in escort of the Kiev-class carrier *Minsk*.

A radar operator in the *Minsk*'s attack center had picked up the F-111's signal. Its speed indicated he was tracking a military jet. The chance to observe American military aircraft wasn't taken lightly.

Three Yak-36 VTOL interceptors had been scrambled. They were far from the cutting edge of technology. But advanced Soviet interceptors hadn't been engineered to withstand the stress of catapult launches and arrester-hook landings like their American counterparts, and the vertical-takeoff-and-landing Forgers were the only aircraft deployed on Redfleet carriers.

In the F-111's cockpit, Shepherd was intently studying the three blips on his radar screen. "Nothing coming back on the IFF," he observed. Identification friend or foe transponders were carried on all NATO aircraft; radar blips not accompanied by an IFF symbol were considered hostile. "Have to be Forgers," he concluded. "Under or over? What do you say?"

"We have twenty angels on their ceiling," Brancato replied, suggesting they climb to avoid contact.

"Going to be tight," Shepherd said.

He pulled back on the stick, putting the F-111 into a climb. The Forger's ceiling was 41,000 feet, the F-111's 60,000. At a rate of climb of 3,592 feet per minute, the F-111 would reach clear air in 3 minutes 10 seconds. The F-111 kept streaking upward through the blinding whiteness. The beeps from the radar detector were coming faster. The altimeter had just ticked 37,000 when they blended into a screech.

"Three bogies dead ahead fifteen miles," Brancato announced. "We're not going to make it."

At a combined closing speed of 40 miles a minute, the 15-mile gap closed in just over 20 seconds.

The two lead Forgers split at the last instant and screamed past; one above, followed an eyeblink later by the second below. The passes were dangerously close.

The F-111 shuddered and bounced, emitting loud, thumping protests as it slammed into the vortex of turbulent air that spiraled off the Forgers.

"Crazy bastards," Brancato growled.

"Six months on a carrier'll do it to you."

The third Forger was still 10 miles away, closing on the F-111's nose from below.

"I got a lock on the trailer," Brancato said, which meant the F-111's computerized attack radar system was targeted on the approaching Forger. It was a warning, a game of one-upmanship, a deadly way of making a point. Hell, the Russian had it coming.

"Squirm, turkey, squirm," Shepherd drawled, at the thought of the Soviet pilot's radar detector letting him know that, but for an aversion to starting World War III and a clean plane, he and Brancato would have blown him out of the skies.

They had no way of knowing that the Russian was a kid; that his wingmen had purposely set him up for an initiation, fully expecting *he* would get the "treatment" for their harassment of the F-111. Unfortunately, the treatment had an effect his wingmen hadn't anticipated. The novice pilot froze in the cockpit, his eyes wide with terror at the thought of his young life being ended by one of the Sidewinder missiles he imagined hung from the hardpoints beneath the F-111's wings.

"What the hell?" Shepherd exclaimed, realizing the planes were on a collision course, seconds from impact.

He turned hard right, executing the standard avoidance maneuver, expecting the Russian to do the same. He didn't. Instead, he panicked and turned left across the F-111's path, just beneath its nose.

The Forger's wingtip slashed into the underside of the bomber's fuselage just forward of the cockpit. A hailstorm of metal fragments filled the air as the wingtip disintegrated and the Forger continued past. Several of the projectiles punctured the F-111's skin. One tore through the left sidewall beneath the auxiliary gauge panel and slammed into Brancato's right shoulder.

"Al? Al?" Shepherd shouted, over the piercing whistle of rushing air as the cockpit depressurized.

Brancato groaned in pain. His hand clutched the blood-soaked shoulder of his flight suit. A crimson splash was creeping up the side of the canopy, turning it into a garish stained-glass window that gave a red glow to the cockpit.

Shepherd scanned the instrument panel: the master caution light was full on; the left engine tachometer was surging erratically, indicating the whirling turbine had ingested metal fragments; the utility pressure gauge had dropped to well below 1,000 psi, which meant the hydraulic system that deployed landing gear and activated speed brakes was also damaged.

Shepherd shut the malfunctioning engine down, pushed his oxygen mask bayonets tight into the receivers, then did the same to Brancato's. "Al? Come on, Alfredo, talk to me!"

"I don't know, I feel real weird," Brancato muttered. "Better head home."

"We're past the PNR," Shepherd replied, making reference to the point of no return, which meant they were closer to England than the United States. "Hang in there," he said. He thumbed the radio transmit button and began broadcasting. "Four-eight TAC? This is Viper-Two. Four-eight TAC, this is Viper-Two. I have an in-flight emergency. Do you read?"

"This is Four-eight TAC," Lakenheath tower replied. "Affirmative, Viper-Two. Go ahead."

"Harassed and struck in midair by hostile aircraft. Assume Soviet Forger. My wizzo's injured. We have frag penetration in the capsule; left engine and utility pump are out. ETA nineteen-thirty zulu."

"Copy, Viper-Two. You have an immediate CTL. Repeat, immediate CTL. We'll monitor."

The three Forgers were nowhere in sight now.

Shepherd brought the wings forward to 16 degrees and set the throttle of the working engine to cruise speed; then he engaged the autopilot and unzipped Brancato's flight suit, peeling it away from the wound. "How're you doing?"

"Nothing a dish of fettuccine wouldn't cure," Brancato growled, fighting the pain.

Shepherd removed his squadron scarf, folded it into a thick wad, and pressed it against the bloody puncture. "That one *T* or two?"

"Huh?"

"How many *T*s in fettuccine?"

"Two, dammit. You going to do this all the way in?"

"Yeah. Somebody once told me it's impossible for a Sicilian to die while he's talking."

"God." Brancato groaned, adjusting his position in the flight couch.

"That big *G* or little *g*?"

3

THAT SAME MORNING in Washington, D.C., while shock waves from the bombing of the TWA jetliner reverberated round the world, armored limousines converged on the White House. They snaked between the concrete barricades, depositing solemn passengers at the South Portico.

The hastily convened group sat with the president in the cabinet room as he read a memorandum. It listed the names, hometowns, and ages of the four Americans who had been killed. One was a fourteen-month-old child. The president's lips tightened in anger; then, he set down the memo and looked up at his advisers.

"Is this Qaddafi's work?" he asked softly.

"We can't prove he gave the order, sir," National Security Adviser Kenneth Lancaster said, "but we know he did."

"I think it's time to consider an air strike against Libya," the secretary of state chimed in.

"Not in my book," the chairman of the Joint Chiefs said firmly. "I'm going on record right now as opposed to any military response to terrorism. Frankly, I'm far more interested in talking about the Soviets," he went on, chafing over the incident with the Forgers.

"As you very well know, Admiral," the secretary of state lectured, "a protest has been filed and I expect an apology will be forthcoming. The incident has been overshadowed by these events and I suggest it remain so."

"I agree," the president said. "This is no time to take a hard line with Moscow over an accident."

"Yes, sir," the CJC replied dutifully. "But I respectfully submit we have no justification for attacking Libya."

"What we *have* is a nasty problem," Lancaster said. "Anyone care to suggest how we solve it?"

"With a pistol, Ken," CIA's Kiley replied coldly. The pressure had become intolerable of late, intensified by the fact that, despite

CIA's vast resources, Beirut station chief Tom Fitzgerald had vanished without a trace.

"That would put us in violation of twelve-three," the secretary of state warned, referring to Executive Order 12333, which forbids sanctioning assassinations.

"Forget twelve-three," Kiley said. "An attack on Qaddafi's nerve center couldn't be construed as an assassination even if it *did* kill the son of a bitch."

The president thought it ironic that the civilians were in favor of using force and the military opposed. "It seems we have no proof Qaddafi gave the order. Is that right?"

"Yes, sir," Lancaster replied, tamping his pipe. "Furthermore, the antiterrorist people in Rome and Athens have announced their investigation isn't focused on Libyans."

"Which means Qaddafi's going to get away with it," Kiley retorted, angrily. "We should bomb his Muslim ass right out of North Africa." He saw the president grimace and added, "As Machiavelli once so wisely advised, 'Never do an enemy a small injury.' "

"Well, no one would like to get him more than I," the president said. "But first, I want evidence, *hard* evidence that Libya is behind these terrorist acts."

"You'll have it, sir," Kiley replied, then he turned to an aide seated behind him, one of many who ringed the walls of the conference room, providing documents and data to their bosses. "That KH-11 we have parked over Poland—how fast can we adjust its orbit?"

Keyhole number eleven was a spy satellite equipped with an ultrasophisticated electro-optical surveillance system a hundred times more sensitive to energy in the infrared and visible light spectrums than state-of-the-art film or video cameras. It also had formidable signals intelligence capability and could intercept a broad range of electronic data: radio, telephone, video, and cable transmissions in the VHF, UHF, and microwave bands, among them.

An intense, physically compact man with military bearing stood in response to the DCI's query and crossed to the table carrying a red binder. A Vietnam ace and charter member of a top-secret Special Forces unit formed after the failed Iran hostage rescue mission, Air Force Colonel Richard Larkin possessed the cool fatalism men who have often faced death acquire. The surge of terrorism had gotten him assigned to the White House as a consultant on antiterrorism; but in truth he worked for Bill Kiley.

Colonel Larkin set the binder on the table and found the section he wanted. "Three days, sir," he replied in a resonant voice that emphasized the hard Ohio vowels.

"Good," Kiley said. "Have them park it right over Qaddafi's tent. We're talking cast-iron coverage. He won't be able to get a hard-on without us knowing it."

SEVERAL DAYS after meeting with Muammar el-Qaddafi, Saddam Moncrieff flew to Tunis, 300 miles northwest of Tripoli, taking a taxi to PLO Worldwide Headquarters.

Despite the grandiose title, it turned out to be a series of cramped offices in a shabby building near the university quarter. The Saudi was thoroughly searched by PLO guards, then driven to Yasser Arafat's private residence. The nineteenth-century seaside villa was on a cul-de-sac several miles northeast of the city, near Carthage. The chairman of the Palestinian Liberation Organization had been living here since his expulsion from Beirut.

Now, in a sparsely furnished sitting room adjacent to a courtyard where several stunted pines rustled, the man with the large features and scraggly beard, who had made the checkered kaffiyeh a symbol of the Palestinian cause, listened intently as Moncrieff laid out a proposal that involved the PLO, Libya, and the United States. "The net result," Moncrieff concluded, "would be a homeland for Palestinians in Libya."

Arafat's eyes widened with resentment. Despite being scattered throughout the Middle East and North Africa, despite decentralized leadership, despite being oppressed and demoralized, Palestinians had never lost sight of their goal. "Are you suggesting we relinquish our claim to Palestine?" Arafat asked incredulously.

"On the contrary," Moncrieff replied, having purposely provoked him to make the distinction. "I believe this could go a long way to securing it."

Arafat's eyes softened with curiosity. "How so?"

"Think of it as a sanctuary; a territory, if you will, where you could gather your people and infuse them with a renewed sense of hope and purpose."

Arafat mused as the implication dawned on him. He had long ago admitted, if only to himself, that the Israelis would never willingly grant Palestinians any degree of sovereignty. Indeed, they had recently begun resettling Soviet Jews throughout the West Bank and Gaza Strip. "An *unoccupied* territory—"

"Yes, sir, precisely."

"Free of Israeli scrutiny," Arafat went on, becoming more intrigued with what he was envisioning. "One where, if I understand your thinking correctly, Palestinians and their leaders could regroup and launch an all-out effort to reclaim their homeland."

"I'd say your view coincides with mine, sir, yes."

Arafat settled back in his chair and spooned some honey into a cup of tea. The idea had merit, he thought. Divide and conquer was the oldest tactic in the book; and for decades, the Israelis had confined Palestinians to territories in southern Lebanon, the West Bank, and the Gaza Strip, which their forces occupied—territories that were thousands of miles from Tunis, where the PLO leadership had been exiled. Four frustrating years of it, not to mention *decades* as the titular head of a nonexistent nation, had convinced Arafat that reunification was vital. "I think it's worth exploring," he said after a long silence. "What does Qaddafi want? Or should I be asking, how much?" he added with a knowing smile.

"No, he's not interested in money; but he would very much like to acquire certain 'currency' which you've amassed per Article Seventeen of the *Intifada*."

Arafat stiffened as Moncrieff expected he would. The *Intifada* was the PLO manifesto, a top-secret document that after decades of impulsive warfare and rhetoric had precisely defined the movement's goals and tactics, and given the Palestinian uprising its name. Only PLO leaders were privy to its contents.

"I proofed the first drafts, sir," Moncrieff explained. "I met the author when I was at MIT; actually, I knew her quite well."

"Then you also know Abu Nidal controls the currency you're after, not I."

"That's why I came to you first."

"Abu Nidal is no longer a member of the PLO. I've no power over him," Arafat declared, splaying his hands resignedly. "To be blunt, you don't stand a chance."

"They said that about the Zionists in forty-eight," Moncrieff replied, risking the insult to win his respect. He knew that the Palestinians' hatred of their archenemy was tempered by grudging admiration. The Zionists had pulled it off—*they* had a homeland.

Arafat studied Moncrieff's eyes, gauging his intent. It was a guileless challenge, a forthright peering into one's soul in the Arab manner. Then the PLO chairman's expression softened, and he pulled himself from the chair. "We'll take a walk," he said genially. "And I will tell you what you're up against with Abu Nidal."

Arafat slipped through the arched doors into the courtyard and strolled off into the night with Moncrieff at his side. Two bodyguards appeared from the shadows and followed them across the pale gray marble. "It's a horrid story," Arafat began. "A story that would make a smart man abandon the idea. Of course, there's always the fool who would find it encouraging."

IN WASHINGTON, D.C., the meeting with the president broke up just before noon. Colonel Larkin avoided the postmortem sessions in the White House corridors and drove to the Pentagon, just south of Arlington Cemetery, to initiate redeployment of the spy satellite.

Not gifted, not born to lead, Larkin grew up in a family where compassion went unrewarded and ruthlessness triumphed. He developed a tenacious, can-do mentality in an effort to satisfy the harsh standards. It was Larkin, deemed too small to play football, who starred on his college team, who won the hand-to-hand combat competition in survival training camp, who after being shot down and captured while strafing a North Vietnamese supply convoy in his F-4 Phantom, escaped from a POW camp and survived months in enemy-infested jungles, fighting his way back to American lines.

"What's going on?" he asked his secretary as he entered his office in the Pentagon's basement, where Special Forces personnel were inconspicuously housed.

"What isn't?" she replied, brandishing a stack of phone messages.

"I need satellite tracking first."

She was reaching for the phone when it rang. "Colonel Larkin's office? Hold on please." She covered the mouthpiece and said, "Mister Moncrieff."

Larkin's eyes widened with curiosity, then he reached across the desk and scooped up the phone.

"Moncrieff," he said, brightening. "It's been a while. What's going on?"

"I'm having breakfast," the Saudi replied, though it was evening at Arafat's villa. "I had an insatiable craving for scrambled eggs and bacon."

Larkin's eyes flickered knowingly at the remark. "Coming right up," he said, hitting the hold button. "Put this on the scrambler, will you?" he said to his secretary. Then he headed down the long corridor toward his office, reflecting on the blustery autumn morning in Boston when he recruited Moncrieff.

That was five years ago.

The Saudi was writing his doctoral dissertation at MIT at the time. He was walking across the campus alone when the precise man with the short, neatly combed hair and dark suit, whom he thought bore a striking resemblance to former Secretary of State Alexander Haig, approached.

"I represent some people who are very interested in your work," Larkin began after introducing himself. "You have a minute to chat?"

"Yes, sir, I do; but I'm afraid there wouldn't be much point in it," Moncrieff replied, having assumed Larkin was a corporate recruiter. "I've decided to go into business for myself and haven't been interviewing."

"Yes, I know," Larkin said, privy to a CIA background check that informed him Moncrieff planned to return to Saudi Arabia and open his own consulting firm. "Have you ever considered working for the U.S. government?" he asked, showing him his identification.

"I can't say I have, sir, no," the young Saudi replied somewhat curiously. His English was impeccable, with a mild British inflection imparted by years of schooling in the United Kingdom. "I'm not an American citizen."

"Not a requirement. Talent and intelligence are the criteria. I'd say you're more than qualified."

"So is everyone else at MIT."

"They won't have your positioning. Your work will be a natural entrée to situations we'd like to observe."

"Observe—"

"Right. No assignments. You do business and tell us what you've seen or overheard along the way."

"May I think it over?"

"Of course; discuss it with your family. I've no doubt they'll approve."

Nor did Moncrieff. Born into the Saudi royal family, he knew this was a chance to make his mark within the competitive and staunchly anti-communist family structure. Those who practiced Zakat, a pillar of Islam that obliged Muslims of wealth and social rank to almsgiving and involvement in affairs of state in the spirit of Western noblesse oblige, were well rewarded.

Since acquiring his Ph.D., Moncrieff had been "observing" those drought-stricken nations in Africa and the Middle East where his work had taken him. The political and economic climate, the mind-set of leaders, their state of health and personal happiness were all reported to Larkin; and bright fellow that Moncrieff was, he began seeing opportunities and proposing ways to exploit them.

Now, on this cool, April morning, Larkin entered his office, closed the door and lifted the phone. "Moncrieff—we're clear. What's on your mind?"

"You mean other than the fact that civilization is unraveling at the seams?"

"Tell me about it. This damned bombing's got the president stuck in neutral."

"Yes, rather nasty business, isn't it?"

"Very. The DCI's taking it pretty hard."

"Perhaps I can help the old fellow out."

Larkin brightened and loosened his tie. "You saying you have something on Libya for me?"

"I'm involved in a project with the colonel that might have a connection," Moncrieff replied, encouraged by the anxious tone he detected. "In brief, you invest little and receive a substantial and immediate return."

Larkin's brows went up. "My kind of game. What's the ante?"

"Bombers," Moncrieff replied evenly. "Bombers with Pave Tack."

"Christ," Larkin said, stunned. "What's *his* ante?"

"The hostages."

4

"WHY WOULD WE give bombers to a madman?" Bill Kiley asked incredulously before Larkin could explain.

Now, stunned by the reply, the DCI stared at the Polaroid of Tom Fitzgerald that he kept amid the top-secret folders on his desk, then went to the window.

The director's office was in the southeast corner atop the seven-story, 1-million-square-foot headquarters building that looked out over a forested campus.

Bill Kiley loved Mother K, as insiders affectionately called Langley. Every morning he strode through the lobby, pausing at the south wall to ponder the memorial stars engraved in the richly toned Georgia marble. Each honored a CIA operative who had died in the line of duty. Kiley had known them all, in spirit if not in person, starting in Europe during World War II with the OSS; and it was the hallowed presence of these dedicated men and women that sustained him at these times.

"The hostages," Kiley whispered hoarsely.

"Yes, sir."

Kiley removed his glasses and cleaned them methodically with a handkerchief, taking the time to compose himself. Hostages had brought down one president and now haunted another, a nagging reminder that CIA's vast intelligence resources had been beaten by diverse groups of rag-tag zealots: Islamic Jihad, Hezbollah, Force 17, the Revolutionary Justice Organization, Cells-Omar Mouktar Forces, Lebanese Revolutionary Faction. Each had claimed to have kidnapped at least one hostage. "Bull," Kiley finally growled. "Qaddafi doesn't have them."

"He will."

"All of them?"

Larkin nodded.

"Fitzgerald too?"

"That's the deal."

Kiley's jaw dropped.

"Moncrieff's already cleared it with Libya and the PLO. The bottom line is the Palestinians get a sanctuary in Libya in exchange for the hostages. Qaddafi turns the hostages over to us in exchange for the bombers."

"Christ," Kiley exclaimed, his eyes flashing. "You mean we've been chasing all these factions, and Arafat has had the hostages all along?"

"Nidal, sir," Larkin corrected gently.

"Nidal? How does Moncrieff know that?"

"He mentioned a connection in Beirut, sir."

The DCI seethed. "Fitzgerald's people scoured every sewer and rat hole . . ." He paused, then chortled, starting to savor the idea. "The Israelis will hate our guts for doing it without them. One problem—how do we know Qaddafi won't screw us? How do we know he won't take the bombers and welch on delivering the hostages?"

"Pave Tack is useless without ANITA," Larkin replied. The acronym stood for alpha-numeric input for target acquisition, a transposition key used to program Pave Tack computers to find and identify targets. "You can't enter target data into the computer without it. No hostages, no ANITA."

"Sounds good," Kiley mused, impressed. "But we're not talking guns and bullets for the Ayatollah here. A couple of seventy million dollar bombers can't get lost in OMB's computer. This won't mean a hill of beans until we figure out how to deliver and account for them."

"An air strike is the only way I know, sir."

The DCI nodded pensively. "Two planes downed over Libya —over the Mediterranean," he said, quickly seeing the possibilities. "Sixth Fleet could handle the whole thing," he went on, alluding to carrier-based bombers but a few hundred miles off Libya's shores.

"At the risk of appearing self-serving, we already have air force personnel in place."

"Good point. Who do you have in mind?"

"Paul Applegate," Larkin replied, referring to a longtime air force and Special Forces colleague.

"Applegate," the DCI echoed, recognizing the name. "Lebanon, three years ago." Moncrieff had picked up some intelligence on the terrorist group that had bombed the marine barracks in Beirut. Larkin and Applegate had flown an unconventional air strike on their training camps. "You stuck it to those Shiite bastards."

Larkin nodded, eyes ablaze with the memory.

"What's Major Applegate up to these days?"

"Military intelligence with Third Air."

"U.K.?"

Larkin nodded. "I touched base with him before coming over and took the liberty of bringing him up to speed. The major sends his regards and asked me to tell you he'd be more than tickled to take on Qaddafi."

"Tripoli's a long haul from Piccadilly."

"That's what the air force does, sir," Larkin said with a little smile. "I realize it'll be a bitch cutting the navy out of this."

"We'll give them their own target," the DCI said, undaunted. "Air force gets Tripoli; navy gets Benghazi. The place is overrun with terrorist training camps. It'll take the focus off Tripoli and reinforce the idea that this is nothing more than an antiterrorist strike."

"A *night* strike," Larkin quickly added. "We can't deliver bombers to Qaddafi in broad daylight."

"No problem. Defense has put billions into night-mission avionics and has never used them. They'll jump at the chance to show off their hardware." The DCI paused, his face taut with concern. "You know the president's attitude toward an air strike."

Larkin nodded solemnly. "Well, sir, I'm sure he'd approve the raid if he knew the hostages would be—"

"You bet he would," Kiley interrupted. "But he can't sign a finding on this one. Arms for hostages doesn't bend the law, it breaks it in half."

"How do we explain their release?"

"We claim," Kiley began, assembling the pieces as he went, "that they had been shrewdly hidden in Tripoli—CIA found and rescued them. The air strike was a diversion to get them out."

"That'd work," Larkin said, smiling at his mentor's facile mind. "Maybe we can take that to the president?"

"And State, Defense, the Joint Chiefs, everybody'll have an opinion," Kiley grumbled. "Before you know it, Congress and the media will be into it. We get these hostages out, Colonel, nobody will give a damn how we did it. Let's keep it simple. CIA needs an air strike, CIA provides the president with the incentive to approve it."

"I understand, sir," Larkin said dutifully, reading between the lines.

"Considering the attitude of the Chiefs, we better come up with something that'll get their attention too."

"I'll take care of it personally."

Larkin was on his way to the door when Kiley called out, "Dick?" The colonel turned to see the DCI walking toward him.

"The Company needs this one—*badly*," he said.

Larkin nodded grimly.

"They're torturing him," the DCI went on, referring to Fitzgerald. An emotional timbre, unusual for Kiley, was reflected in his voice. "God knows what they're doing to him. I don't care what it takes."

"I've been proceeding on that basis, sir."

Larkin left the office, went to an adjacent anteroom, and made three phone calls: the first two—to Major Applegate at 3rd Air Force Headquarters on Mildenhall RAFB in England, and to Moncrieff at Arafat's villa in Tunis—confirmed that the project had the DCI's blessing and was operational; the third, to the CIA station chief at the U.S. Consulate in Berlin, laid the groundwork for a plan Larkin had devised to obtain presidential approval for the air strike.

The colonel then drove into the District to a high-rise on Virginia across from George Washington University. He had leased an apartment here years ago after his marriage broke up, and had since lived alone. It was a small, low-maintenance unit that suited his spartan life-style and the transient nature of his work. Among the furnishings were his collection of handguns, a word processor, secure communications equipment, and an exercycle with 9,361 miles on the odometer.

After showering and changing into civilian clothes, he restocked his two-suiter, which was always packed, then drove to Andrews Air Force Base in neighboring Maryland, where he boarded a flight to Germany.

5

T H E   F - 1 1 1 was descending over the Suffolk countryside 10 miles north of London shrouded in darkness when Shepherd thumbed the microphone button.

"Four-eight TAC, this is Viper-Two. This is Viper-Two with in-flight emergency. Request immediate CTL."

"Roger, Viper-Two. Cleared to land on six left," the supervisor of flying in Lakenheath tower replied. The SOF was always a pilot, the duty rotating daily through the wing roster. "Repeat, six left; straight in; winds are two-four-zero at fifteen knots."

"That's a copy, Lakenheath."

"Update your condition, Viper-Two."

"Left engine is shut down; utility pump is down; I've still got my primary; hydraulic system indicators read seven-six-five and falling."

"Roger that," the SOF replied, thinking they might as well have read zero. "Emergency personnel are standing by. I'll take you through the boldface for BAK-12 when you're on short final," he went on, referring to procedures for landing without braking capability.

BAK-12 arresting systems were part of every military runway. They were installed at the approach and departure end overruns; both had to be operating for a runway to be declared open. Like aircraft carriers, the BAK-12 used a cable stretched just above the tarmac to engage an arrester hook and bring the aircraft to a stop.

The F-111 was three miles northeast of Lakenheath when it dropped below the clouds. Shepherd smiled at the sight of the runway lights winking in the mist.

"Coming onto short final, Al," he said to Brancato, who was slumped in his couch, his head against the canopy. "Al? Al, how many *E*'s in Beethoven?"

Brancato grunted unintelligibly.

"Come on, Alfredo, don't die on me now."

"Viper-Two, we have you on short," the SOF said over the radio. "Let's cover the boldface."

"Roger," Shepherd replied, coolly.

"Blow in doors closed."

"Affirm."

"Wing sweep at sixteen."

"Sixteen."

"Emergency extension on gear."

Shepherd pulled the release. Compressed air from an emergency reservoir charged the system at 3,000 psi, blowing down the nose and main landing gear. His eyes darted to the position indicator lamps, which had just come on, informing him both were down and locked.

"Two greens," he reported with relief.

"Verify green," the SOF echoed. "Slats down."

"Affirm."

"Flaps down at twenty-five."

"Flaps down; two-five."

"Tail hook down."

Shepherd reached to the yellow and black striped handle in the corner of the instrument panel and pulled hard. The arrester hook blew down at an angle from a fairing beneath the tail, the trailing end hanging several feet lower than the landing gear. Like many military fighters, not only those deployed on carriers, all F-111s had an arrester hook for emergency landings.

His eyes were riveted to the instrumentation now, monitoring angle of attack, sink rate, and air speed, which he kept at 160 knots—30 ks faster than landing with both engines—as the bomber came in at an angle against the blustery crosswinds. The tail hook touched down first; it dragged along the concrete, sending a rooster tail of blue-purple titanium sparks shooting into the darkness from below the F-111's empennage.

Shepherd set the main gear of the 50,000-pound bomber on the ground with featherlike delicacy, then dropped the nose. The plane began rocketing brakeless down the 10,000-foot runway at 160 knots. It had traveled about 1,000 feet when in an eyeblink —bump-bump-wham!—the tires rolled over the inch-thick, braided steel cable and the arrester hook snagged it. A screaming whine rose from pits on either side of the runway as the cable unspooled from immense reels connected to a centrifugal clutch that absorbed the kinetic energy and brought the plane to a stop.

Ambulances and emergency fire fighting equipment were already racing toward it, their roof flashers sending splashes of colored light across the runway, their headlights serving to illuminate the area as they encircled the bomber.

A flight surgeon and several nurses clambered aboard a hydraulic platform with their equipment. It reached cockpit level just as Shepherd popped the canopies and released Brancato's flight harness; he was pale and unconscious.

The surgeon dove beneath the blood-spattered Plexiglas, and cut away the shoulder of his flight suit, exposing the wound. "Prepare a bag of LRs and give me two grams of Monocid," he said; then, taking the syringe, he shot the antibiotic into Brancato's thigh.

Shepherd assisted in lifting him from the flight couch onto a gurney on the platform. It began descending immediately. One of the nurses wrapped a blood pressure cuff around Brancato's bicep. The other hung a 1,000 cc bag of Lactated Ringers on the gurney, uncapped the IV needle, and slipped it into a vein in his forearm.

The platform bottomed out with a gentle thump.

In one continuous motion, they rolled the gurney off the edge, across the tarmac, and into an ambulance.

Shepherd watched it speed off into the darkness; then he glanced apprehensively at the technicians swarming over his plane.

"Major Shepherd?" a voice called out.

He turned to see two men approaching; one was a master sergeant he correctly assumed was a crew chief; the other, a broad-shouldered fellow with a friendly face and lumbering stride, was an officer.

"We'll have her patched and on the flight line ASAP, sir," the crew chief offered. "Long as you're okay . . ."

"I'm fine. Thanks. I'd like to call my wife."

"There's no need for concern, Major," the officer replied, taking charge. "Andrews has been notified of your status. I'm sure she's been informed," he went on in a high-pitched voice that was poorly matched to his big frame and gregarious demeanor; then he shook

Shepherd's hand and introduced himself. "Major Applegate, military intelligence. I'll be debriefing you."

THAT SAME AFTERNOON in Washington, D.C., Stephanie Shepherd hurried across Independence Avenue toward the Rayburn Office Building, a banal, gargantuan edifice opposite the Capitol. She had trouble finding a parking place and was late.

Representative James Gutherie's office was on the third floor. A nine-term congressman and ranking member of the House Intelligence and Oversight committees, he made two stops on his way to the Hill every morning: the first at Georgetown Rehabilitation Center to see his wife; the second at Holy Trinity R.C. Church on 35th Street to pray for her recovery.

Both avid skiers, the Gutheries first met on a chairlift at Killington. Twenty-five years later, the sport that had brought them together tore them apart. It was a low-speed fall, and there wasn't a scratch on her, but his wife had been in a coma ever since.

The congressman had been a failed Catholic for years. The day the doctors said her recovery was in God's hands, Gutherie went back to church; the day the polls revealed he had fallen behind his opponent, he began praying for *two* miracles.

Stephanie hurried from the elevator and down the endless corridors, long auburn hair flying behind her, turning several male heads in the process, which pleased her.

The congressman's suite was a beehive. Phones rang incessantly. Harried staffers crisscrossed the reception area. The door to Gutherie's office opened and a towering, ruggedly handsome man came toward her.

"Stephanie," Jim Gutherie said, smiling. He hugged her as if they'd been close friends for years, letting his head fill with her perfume.

"Mr. Congressman, good to see you," she replied stiffly as she disengaged. "Sorry I'm late."

"That's what you said the last time," he teased.

"That's not what I hoped you'd remember about me." She had interviewed him during his reelection campaign two years ago, and was feeling more surprised that he had remembered than embarrassed.

"What's somebody who can't make deadlines doing as a re-porter, anyway?"

"Beats me. The pay's an insult, the pressure ages you, and congressmen only remember your faults."

Gutherie broke into a hearty chuckle and showed her into his office. His opponent had been using his work on the Oversight Committee to imply he was antidefense and the congressman wanted to remind his 20,000-plus constituents who lived and worked at Andrews of his votes for military pay hikes and defense appropriations. They were halfway through the interview when his secretary reminded him of an appointment. "VFW luncheon," he said to Stephanie with a facetious scowl. "Wouldn't want to miss one of those."

"It's going to take a lot more than that this time, isn't it?" Stephanie declared, suddenly serious, detecting he had lost his taste for battle.

"Tough one," Gutherie admitted, lowering his guard. "I'll have my secretary get in touch to reschedule." He placed a hand on Stephanie's shoulder and guided her to the door. "Maybe we can do it over lunch?" he suggested, his palm sliding to the small of her back, remaining longer than she thought appropriate.

"I'd love to, Mr. Congressman," she said diplomatically. "But this girl hasn't had lunch since she turned thirty and started splitting her jeans."

Twenty minutes later Stephanie was in her brown Dodge station wagon, heading back to Andrews on I-95, when the WPTZ disc jockey interrupted Bruce Springsteen in midlyric for a news bulletin.

"Harassment of a United States Air Force F-111 bomber by Soviet interceptors resulted in a midair collision over the North Atlantic this morning," the newsreader said. "Fortunately, both planes remained airworthy, and the F-111, on a flight from Andrews Air Force Base to Lakenheath, England, safely reached its destination. However, one member of the two-man crew was seriously injured. Their names are being withheld pending notification of next of kin."

Stephanie's heart raced. The media was always more efficient than the military in these matters and thoughtfully withheld the names of those involved; but the next of kin always knew. Now there were two families ridden with anxiety, instead of one. She rolled down the window, inhaled the cold air, and stepped on the gas.

S H E P H E R D and Major Applegate drove the five miles from Lakenheath to 3rd Air Force Headquarters on Mildenhall RAFB, where the latter's office was located.

"You did a hell of a job, Major," Applegate said, after Shepherd finished briefing him on the encounter with the Soviet Forgers. "One question. How're you feeling?"

"I'm fine," Shepherd grunted, reflecting sadly on Brancato. "I wish I could've splashed the bastard."

"Long time since combat—"

"*Too* long," Shepherd replied, thinking he was one of the lucky ones; he'd seen combat, used his skills. How many highly trained and eager warriors never had? How many feared their careers would pass without a war to fight? Sure, he was proud to serve his country, to preserve peace and deter aggression; but down deep, it was far more satisfying to tackle it head on.

"The point is, the Forty-eighth's been on alert for the last week," Applegate said.

Shepherd looked at him, curiosity building.

"Rumor control says it's Libya."

"Qaddafi's got it coming."

"You're on the mission roster, Major," Applegate said. Then, testing him, because he had to know, he prompted, "Of course, after this, no one would fault you for wanting out."

"All I want is a chance to do my job, sir," Shepherd declared, his tone sharpening.

"Thought you might say that," Applegate mused, concealing that he had his own reasons for wanting Shepherd to remain on the mission roster.

"Hard to do without a wizzo."

"Maybe I can help," Applegate offered, feigning compassion. "Turns out you and Captain Foster are in the same boat. His right-seater bit the dust a couple of days ago—literally. Broke an ankle sliding into home against the Eighty-first TAC. Hell of a game."

"Well, if you need a good first baseman . . ." Shepherd offered, matching his grin.

"We need pilots," Applegate replied, getting back to business. "We're cutting orders to get Foster a new wizzo. We can cut yours at the same time. Be a hell of a lot easier to do now. Once you report to a new CO and his crew chief gets his paws on your one-eleven . . . Think about it. Okay?"

"I have, sir," Shepherd said. "Count me in."

"Good," Applegate enthused, shaking Shepherd's hand. He waited until he had left the office and was well down the corridor before lifting the phone.

THE MILITARY TRANSPORT that had left Andrews that afternoon for Berlin was in a commercial air corridor high over the North Atlantic when Larkin was summoned to the cockpit.

"Call for you, sir," the flight engineer said, handing him the receiver.

"Colonel Larkin speaking."

"Colonel?" his secretary said. "I have Major Applegate on satellite relay."

"Dick? It's A.G.," Applegate said when the connection was made. "I got us a couple of one-elevens."

"Way to go," Larkin enthused.

"All we need is an order to deliver them."

"I'm placing it tonight," Larkin said, ending the call. "You still there?" he prompted his secretary.

"Yes. I have him on the other line," she replied, having anticipated the colonel's request.

Bill Kiley was in his limousine on his way to a meeting in the Pentagon, when Larkin's secretary put the call through to his mobile phone; a fully secured cellular terminal, the STU-III/Dynasec was impervious to eavesdropping or intercept.

"Good work," the DCI said when briefed on the bombers. "You talk to Moncrieff about payment?"

"Yes, sir," Larkin replied, pleased by the praise. "He's making the arrangements as we speak."

6

AN OLD MERCEDES SEDAN raced along Avenue du General de Gaulle atop the palisades of West Beirut past the bombed-out hulks of hotels and high-rises that had once made the city the Riviera of the Middle East; the place where wealthy Arab women worked on topless tans and shopped for French perfume and couture while their men traded oil for tankers and tactical fighters between visits to the gaming tables at Casino du Liban.

Katifa sat behind the wheel, her hair snapping in the wind, her face aglow with the anticipation that had been building since the cable from Saddam Moncrieff arrived the previous evening. She guided the car through the sharp bend at Ras Beyrouth onto Avenue de Paris, past the British and American embassies, and parked on a promontory high above the Mediterranean.

A twisting wooden staircase led to the Bain de l'Aub, the beach at the base of the palisades.

Katifa hurried down the steps and set off across the sand with long, graceful strides. She had gone about a quarter-mile when she saw the stylishly dressed man near a rock jetty up ahead, saw his eyes tracking her, his smile growing in anticipation.

Moncrieff had spent the night at Arafat's villa. After a three-hour flight from Tunis, he had arrived in Beirut late morning, then took a taxi from the airport.

As the Saudi watched the beautiful woman with the silken complexion and model-fine features coming across the sand toward him, he began reflecting on that day in Cambridge five years before, when he had last seen her.

They were graduate students and lovers, living together at MIT at the time. Katifa was dedicated to the Palestinian cause. Moncrieff had sworn to uphold Saudi law, which forbade members of the royal family to marry foreigners; he had also sworn another allegiance, an allegiance he couldn't discuss. They walked the banks of the Charles on that humid Sunday afternoon, knowing it wouldn't work, and said good-bye.

Now the Saudi took a few steps toward her and opened his arms, and Katifa ran into their embrace.

"Moncrieff," she said, leaning back to look at him. "I still can't believe you're here."

"I was concerned you wouldn't come."

"And if I hadn't?" she asked with a smile.

"I would have pursued you relentlessly," he replied with a grin; then, in a more serious tone, he added, "I would have had little choice."

She studied him for a moment, recalling his habit of gently working a conversation to convey that something was on his mind. "This is business, isn't it?"

Moncrieff nodded, offered her a cigarette, and took one himself, glancing about cautiously as he lit them. As he had anticipated when selecting Bain de l'Aub for the meeting, they were alone on the long stretch of sand. "I'm looking for your brother," he finally said.

"Why?" Katifa asked, darkening.

"I have to see Abu Nidal."

"My brother is dead," she said, forthrightly.

"I'm sorry. I didn't know."

"He died for our cause. He's not to be grieved."

"Then I'll tend to business," Moncrieff said, taking the opening. "This meeting with Nidal is of the utmost importance," he began, his tone sharpening as he explained the arms-sanctuary-hostage exchange.

"What makes you think Abu Nidal has the hostages?" Katifa challenged when he had finished, concealing that, like Arafat, she thought the idea had merit.

"Does Article Seventeen ring a bell?"

"I think it might," she replied.

They were in their last year at MIT when Katifa wrote *Intifada* as a tribute to her father. With eloquence and moving emotional fervor, her treatise not only called for the liberation of Palestine, but outlined a strategy to achieve it, a strategy of terror and intimidation designed to force the United States into pressuring Israel to provide a Palestinian homeland.

That summer, she left MIT and returned to Bir Zeit University, where she had done her undergraduate work. Located on Jordan's

west bank fifteen miles from Jerusalem, it was a center of PLO
radicalism. When Katifa's mentor in the political science department read *Intifada*, he knew his protégé had fulfilled her promise.
A high-ranking PLO adviser, he brought the document to Yasser
Arafat's attention; and it was soon adopted as the PLO's official
manifesto. *Intifada* was more than brilliant; it was written by the
daughter of a martyred leader.

Article 17, titled "Human Currency," advocated hostage-taking
and urged the creation of fictitious radical Muslim groups who
would claim responsibility for the kidnappings: a tactic to cause
confusion and deter rescue attempts, a tactic which the ruthless
and cunning Abu Nidal had refined to an art. *He* had kidnapped
them all; not to force the release of political prisoners, not to trade
for money or arms, but to ransom Palestine.

"And if you're wrong about Abu Nidal holding the hostages?"

"I have it on good authority that I'm not," Moncrieff replied,
quietly confident.

"State your source, Mr. Moncrieff," she said, as if challenging
one of her students.

"Chairman Arafat," he said, playing the card.

Her eyes widened at his sagacity. "I had a professor like you
once. No matter how I argued, he always had an answer."

"You didn't learn very much."

"But *he* did."

Moncrieff laughed. "My White House contact has to know," he
said, purposely invoking his sanction.

"He'll have to wait until tonight."

"I'll be here," he said, taking her hand.

They walked along the surf to the staircase and climbed to the
palisades where Katifa's Mercedes was parked, then drove to her
apartment on Tamar Mallat in the Al Fatwa quarter. They spent
the afternoon reliving old times and drinking araki, a sweet local
liqueur distilled from wine. They talked for hours before their
words gave way to desire, before Moncrieff gently pressed his lips
to hers. Katifa had had no interest in having a lover since her
brother's death. The self-denial served as a form of punishment
and emotional insulation; but the Saudi had always been a special
and reassuring presence, and she surrendered willingly.

Soon they lay naked on her bed—Katifa lanquid and adrift in
the sensations that began surging through her like gentle bursts
of current; Moncrieff exploring the planes of her smooth torso,

tending to every square inch of copper velvet, until her flesh quivered and the first explosion broke over her; and as the second rose, he brought their glistening bodies together, timing his entrance to the instant it crested. Katifa gasped at the sudden surge in intensity, lost in the way it used to be and hadn't been since they were last lovers.

THAT EVENING, they drove to the Turk Hospital on De Mazraa, where Katifa picked up a package at the pharmacy. Sporadic flashes of gunfire winked in the darkness as the Mercedes crossed the Green Line at the Patriarche Hoyek checkpoint, heading north on Avenue Charles Helou and up the coastal motorway to Casino du Liban.

A group of Palestinian sentries met the Mercedes at the entrance and escorted Moncrieff and Katifa down the gangway to the dock.

Hasan, the terrorist who had been her brother's lieutenant, signaled with a flashlight that they had arrived. The throb of diesels rose as the gunboat emerged from the blackness and nosed into the slip, slowing with a noisy reversal of its engines. Armed sentries were deployed on deck. Then Abu Nidal came from below, joining Moncrieff, Katifa, and Hasan on the dock. He had been grooming Hasan to assume leadership of the casino-based group, and gestured for him to accompany them as they walked along the rows of empty slips.

"No," Nidal said after Moncrieff had revealed the three-way proposal. The terrorist had listened without comment, his expression noncommittal throughout. "We don't want another territory," he said calmly. "We want our homeland. Nothing more, nothing less."

"I'm aware of that," Moncrieff replied, undaunted. "As I explained, this would be a significant step in that direction. I strongly urge you to consider it."

"I'll say this once," Nidal responded evenly. "The currency you seek will be used to ransom Palestine, not to lease Libyan desert."

"*Unoccupied* Libyan desert," Moncrieff corrected, with the cool detachment of a diplomat brokering a treaty. "A viable alternative to living in police states; an end to violence and the slaughter of your young."

"And the destruction of our homes, and confiscation of property, and demeaning identity cards," Katifa interjected, bitterly rattling off the list of injustices.

"You overlooked curfews and unlawful detention," Moncrieff said gently. "My point is, your people are tired of fighting tanks with stones. It's hard to believe they wouldn't flock to a sanctuary where they could lick their wounds and heal."

"And become soft and complacent," Nidal said in a derisive tone. "It's the inhumanity that drives them."

"Yes, in lieu of leadership. As I understand it, there are those who believe reuniting Palestinians with their leaders is vital to your cause."

"Ah," Nidal said knowingly, his face a haunting mask in the moonlight. "Arafat . . . you've spoken with him, haven't you? Of course you have."

Moncrieff nodded matter-of-factly, unshaken by the challenge. "He views the proposal favorably."

"I'm not surprised. We've often differed on these matters."

"With good reason, I'm sure. But the fact remains that despite your having the currency in hand, neither the Americans nor the Israelis have budged."

"Yes, they're still chasing Hezbollah, aren't they?" he said with a sly smile. "They'll do more than budge when they find out who really has the currency."

"I disagree," Moncrieff said, maintaining his cool demeanor. "It's becoming clear that a strategy based on lawlessness will ultimately fail."

"We think of it as courage," Nidal snapped angrily. "We've fought for forty years and we'll fight for forty more if need be; without the interference of outsiders. And if seven hostages aren't sufficient . . ." He paused, letting the words trail off ominously.

"We'll acquire more," Hasan said intensely, unable to resist finishing his mentor's sentence.

"Abu Nidal is right," Katifa chimed in. Despite thinking the proposal of some value, despite her feelings for Moncrieff, her almost lifelong allegiance to Nidal gave undue weight to his argument. "The Americans and Libyans wouldn't accept inequities. Why should we?"

"For your people. 'A nation's leader should never put his pride before them,'" Moncrieff answered, paraphrasing. "Mohammed." Then, shifting his look to Nidal, he said, "The offer stands. Though I'm not sure for how long. Let me know if you reconsider."

The terrorist glared at him with cold hatred, then broke it off and took Katifa aside. "Binti el-amin," he began, addressing her as My loyal daughter to emphasize his disappointment, "why did you bring this shetan to me?"

"Because I don't presume to speak for Abu Nidal."

His eyes softened in approval, then drifted to his watch. "The Saudi is wrong," he declared in conclusion. "Pragmatism is a poor substitute for passion."

Katifa nodded dutifully and handed him the package of pharmaceuticals.

Nidal went up the gangway into the casino, continuing through the main gaming room to the amphitheater where he entered a backstage room that served as a communications center. A radio operator sat at a console. It was precisely 9:00 P.M. when the radio crackled.

"This is the Exchequer," the caller said, using the code name Nidal had given the Palestinian in charge of the hostages. "This is the Exchequer. Do you read?"

"Yes, go ahead," Nidal replied, taking the phone.

"Your currency is secure," the Exchequer reported as he did daily at this hour, reciting the cipher that meant all was well with the hostages.

"Very well," Nidal said, clearly pleased. He had no questions or instructions to impart and abruptly ended the transmission to minimize the chance of intercept.

AFTER LEAVING CASINO DU LIBAN,
Katifa and Moncrieff drove back to the city in stony silence.

Far from beaten, the Saudi was keenly aware of Katifa's divided loyalties and decided to let her live with the ambivalence for a while before provoking her.

"Arafat was right," he finally said as they entered her apartment and settled on opposite ends of a sofa in the living room. "Nidal is addicted to the violence. The day this is settled, he becomes nothing; a terrorist without a cause."

"He just wants what is best for Palestinians."

"No. That's what your father wanted," Moncrieff replied slyly, baiting her.

"My father?" she asked indignantly. She had often spoken of him when they were students and resented the inference. "What does he have to do with this?"

"If he had lived, Katifa," Moncrieff replied, starting to reel her in, "if he had been captured by the Israelis, what would have happened?"

"They assassinated him," she snapped bitterly.

"Humor me. What if they hadn't?"

"He was respected by both sides. If anyone had a chance to resolve the differences between—"

"Right. *He* would have compromised," Moncrieff interrupted; then he locked his eyes onto hers and pointedly added, "That's why Nidal executed him."

"What?" Katifa leapt from the sofa and hovered over him angrily. "How can you make such an accusation?"

"I have it on good authority."

"Arafat?" she ventured cautiously.

"He was there, was he not?"

"So was I," she retorted, lighting a cigarette.

"He doesn't remember it quite the way you do," Moncrieff said gently. "He told me the story just yesterday; he said that your father and Nidal were holding off the Israelis while Arafat loaded the settlers into a helicopter. As soon as they were aboard, Arafat began firing at the Israelis, pinning them down so that your father and Nidal could run to the helicopter. Nidal managed to get aboard; then the Israelis began firing at it. The pilot panicked and lifted off, leaving your father behind. When Nidal saw he was about to be captured, he went to the door with his machine gun and shot him."

Katifa gasped, unwilling to accept it, the words of angry protest sticking in her throat.

"When Arafat demanded an explanation," Moncrieff continued, "Nidal said he was concerned your father would break under torture and reveal the names of other Palestinian activists. Of course, he told you and your brother that the *Israelis* had killed him."

Katifa was stunned. She turned away like a wounded animal, staring out a window into the darkness. "That is a vicious lie," she finally protested in a dry rasp. "Abu Nidal took us in and raised us as his own children. He was everything to us."

"That's why you never suspected the truth. If Abu Nidal is

so dedicated to your father's principles, why did he turn me down?"

Katifa winced, knowing the Saudi was right. "There would be no currency without Abu Nidal," she replied defensively.

"Granted; but he has served his purpose. It's your fight now; you're the one who must spend it. Where are they, Katifa?" he said forcefully. "Where are the hostages?"

She looked at him for a long moment, the smoke from her cigarette filling the space between them as she decided. "They're not in Beirut."

Moncrieff was stunned. CIA had long believed the hostages were being held somewhere in the southern slums; and he expected Katifa knew the exact location.

"Then where?" he demanded angrily.

Katifa shrugged. "They were brought to Casino du Liban and taken away on Abu Nidal's boat." She paused, deciding. "It was given to him by the Syrians."

"Is that where they are? Syria?"

"No, I don't think so."

"Why not?"

"I've heard Abu Nidal say the shetans could turn the entire Middle East over stone by stone and never find them. No," she went on, anticipating Moncrieff's next question. "It wasn't a figure of speech. Nidal wasn't bragging; he stated it as a simple fact."

"The hostages are under Syrian control," he prompted.

"Yes. It was part of the agreement for Assad's support," Katifa answered, referring to Syria's radical leader.

"Assad can authorize their release?"

"Not without clearing it with Abu Nidal first. There's a Palestinian in charge of the hostages who reports to him daily. He'd know if Assad went around him."

Moncrieff nodded pensively. The more he learned about the hostages' whereabouts the more of a mystery it became. He was thinking he should call Larkin and inform him of the impasse when his eyes came to life with an idea.

"Then Nidal must authorize it."

"Impossible."

"Is that what your father would have said?" the Saudi challenged, knowingly.

7

T H E   S T O R M that had been drenching all of Europe was blowing across the runways in sheets when the military 707 landed at Templehoff, the United States Air Force base in West Berlin.

The time was 5:26 A.M. when Colonel Larkin came down the boarding ramp and cleared passport control.

The CIA station chief in the American consulate on Clayallee had made several arrangements at Larkin's request, ground transportation among them. The Audi sedan was waiting in slot T-44 in the terminal parking lot. The major found the keys under the floor mat, opened the trunk, and removed a rumpled Adidas gym bag. It contained $10,000.

He drove north into the city through the rain that slowed traffic on the Mariendorfer Damm to a crawl.

About an hour and a half later he parked along the S-bahn tracks near the Tiergarten and walked through the flea market to No. 42 Potsdamer, an unkempt row house just west of the city's infamous wall. He rang the buzzer for the street-level flat. Shortly, the security peephole flickered, then the dead bolt clanked.

The woman who opened the door had a tired face that Larkin had once thought attractive; she balanced a baby on her hip. The pocket of her apron sagged with the weight of a pistol.

"Richard?" she said with a warm smile. "I was surprised when I got the message you were coming. Wie geht's?"

"Hanging in there," Larkin replied as she bolted the door and led the way inside. His head filled with the aroma of gun oil and blued-steel that came from crates stacked against the walls of the apartment. He set the gym bag on a table and pushed it toward her.

"If you would," she said, handing Larkin the baby. "He cries if I put him down."

She unzipped the bag, removed the money, and put it in a

drawer. Then she made a phone call, whispering just a few words in German before hanging up.

"He's coming soon," she said. "I'll make some coffee." She went into the kitchen, leaving Larkin holding the child, its tiny fist clenched tightly around a bullet.

LATER THAT MORNING, after meeting with Larkin, a middle-aged man with sad eyes and a wispy mustache crossed the border into East Berlin and spent some time working with a colleague in the cable room of the Libyan People's Bureau on Unter Den Linden.

That evening, the woman went to Kufurstendamm, the hub of West Berlin's notorious nightlife. As always, it was crowded with tourists, prostitutes, and off-duty military personnel. She stood near the entrance to La Belle Club, her foot tapping to the beat of the rock music that boomed from within. It was 12:21 A.M. when she spotted a young, sensitive-looking American soldier hesitating to enter the disco.

"Go ahead. It's a great club. You'll love it," she said. "My husband's in the band."

"It's that obvious I'm new, huh?" the soldier replied with an embarrassed smile.

"No, you just looked a little uncertain."

"Thanks," he said, turning toward the entrance.

"Oh, could you do me a favor?" she asked, holding out a rumpled gym bag. "My husband sweats so much when he plays. He forgot his towels and change of clothes."

"You want me to give that to him?"

"If you would," she replied, gesturing to the baby sleeping peacefully in a canvas carrier slung across her chest. "The music will wake him if I—"

"Sure, no problem," the congenial fellow agreed, taking the bag. "Heavy," he said, somewhat surprised.

"The water. A big Thermos of it," she explained shrewdly. "They take a break about one. Oh, how silly of me," she said as if she had forgotten. "My husband is the drummer."

"The drummer," the soldier repeated with a smile, backing his way into the entrance.

The woman waved and hurried off.

The shy soldier went to a table, ordered a beer, and set the gym bag on the floor behind his chair.

Inside it, amid a few soiled towels, a cheap wind-up alarm clock lay ticking. The plastic lens that covered the face had been removed and a thin, pliable wire affixed with airplane glue to each of the hands. The insulation had been stripped from the tips, exposing about a quarter-inch of copper; one of these prongs had been bent slightly downward to ensure contact would be made when they coincided. As beer flowed and dancers gyrated, the minute hand slowly brought the tips of the two wires closer and closer together.

It was exactly 1:04 A.M. when the young soldier waved the waitress over again.

"Think this set's ever going to end?"

"I sure hope so," she said, leaning over so he could hear her above the music.

His eyes darted shyly to the swell of her breasts, the smooth skin almost brushing his cheek. He was hoping fervently it would and was fantasizing how it might feel when the clock hands moved to within a few ticks of coinciding, and an impatient purple-green spark jumped across the gap between the contacts.

The 9-volt charge surged through the wire and tripped the detonator, which was plugged into a 15-pound chunk of C-4 plastique called Semtex. It was part of a 20-ton shipment of the deadly explosive that one of the renegade CIA agents had procured for Qaddafi. RDX, the main ingredient of the off-white putty, was unmatched in destructive potential save for nuclear weapons.

It erupted in a thunderous explosion.

The music and blinding strobes masked the sound and flash of the blast, but the torn bodies hurtling through the air like dolls left no doubt as to what had happened. Within seconds, La Belle Club was a roaring inferno filled with screaming people.

Scores were injured.

Two American soldiers were killed.

8

THE NEXT MORNING, an entourage of civilian and military advisers assembled at Camp David, the presidential retreat in Maryland's Blue Ridge Mountains.

The president had spent the weekend relaxing. He was dressed casually when he joined them in the library, where, despite the crackle of hand-split logs, a damp chill prevailed.

"Intercepted a few hours ago," Lancaster said, handing him a red folder marked KEYHOLE TOP-SECRET TALENT, the code name given intelligence collected by KH-11 spy satellites. It contained a cable that read:

WE HAVE SOMETHING PLANNED THAT WILL MAKE YOU HAPPY.

"When am I going to get one of these that will make *me* happy?" the president asked, settling in his chair. "I thought we had cast-iron coverage on these people?"

"We do, sir," Kiley replied. "Repositioning that KH-11 really paid off."

"Not for those two soldiers, it didn't!" the president snapped in a rare display of acrimony.

"My apologies, sir," Kiley said, stung by the reply. "I meant we can prove that cable was sent from the People's Bureau in East Berlin to Qaddafi in Tripoli."

The president's posture softened, his head tilting slightly, reconsidering his remarks.

"As was this one," Lancaster said, exhaling a haughty cloud of smoke as he handed him a second cable. Like the others present, the NSA wasn't aware of CIA's involvement in the bombing and believed the cables to be genuine.

AT 1:05 AM AN EVENT OCCURRED.
YOU WILL BE PLEASED WITH THE RESULT.

"That's the exact time the disco was bombed, sir," Kiley said incriminatingly.

"Do we have any proof that *Qaddafi* gave the order?" the president asked.

"I'd say it's implicit, sir," Kiley replied.

"In other words, Bill, we don't have irrefutable evidence that Qaddafi was behind this."

Kiley's lips tightened in a thin red line. "No, sir."

"Be advised," the chairman of the Joint Chiefs said, "the La Belle Club is a hangout for black servicemen. Libya has never targeted minorities. Pick off a cable going in the other direction —an order from Qaddafi saying, 'Bomb a disco tonight'—then come talk to me."

"Dammit," Kiley snapped. "Why do you people always need a Pearl Harbor as an excuse to go to work?"

"Mr. President," the secretary of state began in his ponderous cadence, "we've tried diplomacy, public condemnation, a show of military strength. None have worked. It's time for military *action*."

"We have an interservice strike force on alert," the defense secretary chimed in. "It can be launched on short notice to drop a few hot ones right in Qaddafi's lap."

"Not from any of my aircraft," the CJC retorted. "Not without a smoking gun."

"You already have one," Kiley said emotionally. "Hundreds of them. Two hundred and fifty-three marines! A navy diver murdered in cold blood! A man in a wheelchair thrown into the sea! Innocent travelers gunned down in airports! Blown out of planes! College professors, journalists, *one of my own people* kidnapped and tortured by these animals! Two soldiers blown to bits in a nightclub! How many more? The wrong guns are doing all the smoking! And I'm damned sick of it!"

Kiley's passion drew a taut silence over the room. Twenty seconds passed before the president broke it. "So am I," he said in a voice hoarse from tension. "It's time to make the world smaller for terrorists."

T H A T   A F T E R N O O N a heavy rain was still falling at Mildenhall as a military transport, which had taken off from Berlin's Templehoff an hour and forty minutes earlier, landed.

Colonel Larkin deplaned, cleared customs, and strode in a precise cadence to a gray government sedan parked adjacent to the MAC terminal. He tossed his two-suiter into the backseat and got in next to Major Applegate, who was behind the wheel.

"I hear business in Germany is booming," Applegate said in his high-pitched rasp as he pulled away from the arrivals gate.

"So did the president," Larkin replied with an intensity that set him apart from his affable colleague. "Talk to me about these crews, A.G."

"*Pilots*," Applegate corrected smartly, handing him a file card with two names, one of which was Shepherd. "No wizzos. I figure the fewer personnel involved the better," he went on, explaining he had purposely selected two pilots, assigned to fly the raid on Libya, who had unexpectedly lost their weapons systems officers.

"Assigned to the raid . . ."

"That's the beauty of it."

"What do you have in mind?" Larkin prompted warily. "I mean, have you talked to them about this?"

"Not yet. But it might be worth a shot."

Larkin's expression darkened. "I don't know. There isn't a pilot alive who'd turn his plane over to the enemy without asking a lot of questions."

"We've got some damn good answers."

"What if they don't agree? What if one of them takes his military oath too seriously; refuses to carry out an order that's wrong? That's *illegal*?"

Applegate's prominent brows arched. "Good point. We'd be in deep shit if one of them turned out to be a whistle-blower."

"Bet your ass. This cat gets out of the bag, it makes a beeline right for the oval office."

"There are ways to make sure it doesn't."

"Just one," Larkin said ominously. "Separate these guys from their planes and fly the mission ourselves."

"Sounds like we're talking hardball," Applegate said, the stone-cold expression in Larkin's eyes leaving no doubt as to his intent.

"You have a problem with that?"

"You know better," Applegate replied; then, hunching his bear-like shoulders with uncertainty, he added, "It's just that these guys are air force."

"I don't need to be reminded, A.G.," Larkin said firmly. "The problem is, if we're going to sell the idea that two one-elevens were lost in the raid, we have to release the names of the pilots that went down with them, the *assigned* pilots. And we can't have these guys walking around saying otherwise."

"What about incapacitating them somehow—a fender bender, food poisoning? Then *we* fly the mission, and release phony names and bios."

Larkin shook his head emphatically. "It'll never hold water. The media is going to be all over this thing. They'll want to interview the dead pilots' families. The air force will hold a memorial service. The president will console their wives and kids—"

"Hadn't thought of that," Applegate said, steering around some double-parked vehicles.

"Besides, it's not sure enough. What if one of them gets his gut pumped and shows up on the flight line? We can use phony IDs to cover a couple of nonexistent wizzos but not these guys. We're not dealing with just planes, we're dealing with assigned planes and assigned pilots and we have to account for both."

There was no more to be said on the matter. The scenario demanded stringent security. Extreme measures would be necessary to guarantee it wasn't breached. The slightest chance that the top-secret mission would be revealed, the hostages imperiled, or the government compromised had to be eliminated in advance.

"A couple of details still have to be covered," Applegate said, as he turned off Lincoln Road, parking in front of Building 239. The pedestrian, postwar structure served as headquarters for U.S. 3rd Air Force.

The place was buzzing with activity as the two officers cleared security and climbed a staircase to Applegate's office at the far end of a second-floor corridor. The computer terminal was tied in to Mildenhall's main frame. Larkin turned it on and typed in his security clearance code. The computer responded:

VERIFIED: CLEARED TO TOP SECRET: PROCEED

Next, Larkin accessed the mission file and scrolled through the personnel roster, finding:

PILOT: SHEPHERD, MAJOR WALTER M.
WIZZO: TO BE ASSIGNED

He changed it to read WIZZO: ASSIGNED—ensuring a new weapons systems officer wouldn't appear. He repeated the procedure for the second pilot, then, accessing their personnel files, deleted the name of their commanding officers and inserted his own. This was preventative damage control; any queries from those not privy to the covert subtext, which might threaten the mission, would come to him rather than to 3rd Air Force personnel.

Larkin was about to shut down the computer when something caught his eye. Along with personal information each file also contained a photograph. The images hadn't registered during the data search, but now the colonel's attention was drawn to the engaging smile and thoughtful eyes of Major Walter Shepherd.

Their forthright stare filled Larkin with anxiety. It wasn't the unconventional nature of the mission that troubled him; nor was it what those in the trade called the Nuremberg Syndrome, the specter of Nazi officers executed for carrying out orders they knew to be wrong rather than question them. No, what bothered Larkin was that the men he'd be acting against were on his side.

He had steeled himself against it until now. A few minutes passed before he found the rationale. Yes, he could live with that, he thought, having convinced himself that the two pilots would be called upon to do no more than they had promised the day they were sworn into the military—indeed, no more than what might happen if they flew the mission; no more than Larkin, himself, would do should the need arise—die in the service of their country.

9

THE FOLLOWING MORNING the rain had eased to a steady drizzle when Shepherd awoke in his quarters in the housing provided to newly arrived officers at Lakenheath Royal Air Force Base.

Four days had passed since the encounter with the Soviet Forgers. After being debriefed by Applegate, Shepherd had immediately phoned Stephanie at their home on Andrews Air Force Base in Maryland and assured her he wasn't injured. Having eased her anxieties, he decided not to mention in the same breath that he had been assigned to fly a mission.

Now, after showering and pulling on a jumpsuit, he settled back with a cup of steaming coffee and turned on his cassette recorder.

"Tuesday, eight April. How is my favorite little gymnast doing?" he drawled. "And how's her mommy and brother? I went over to the hospital last night to see Al. He's complaining the pasta isn't al dente, so I figure he's doing okay. It turns out that little sortie with the Russians was just a warm-up. We've got a real live mission on the boards now. It should be history by the time you get this; so should Qaddafi. I'm real sorry about messing up our anniversary, babe. Like I said, we'll make up for it soon as you get here." He paused at a knock and shut off the recorder.

The door was partly open, and he looked up to see a rain-soaked courier standing in the corridor.

"Major Shepherd, sir?"

"You got him, Corporal," Shepherd replied, returning his salute and taking the envelope. "Thanks."

"My pleasure, sir," he said, saluting and hurrying off down the corridor.

Shepherd glanced to the puddle where the corporal had been standing and smiled. Well, they sure named this place right, he thought.

The envelope contained orders, informing Shepherd he had

been transferred to Upper Heyford RAFB, and was to report that afternoon at 17:00 with his F-111.

Upper Heyford, one hundred and forty miles southwest of Lakenheath, was dedicated to the training and deployment of weapons systems officers and ECM technicians. Crews permanently stationed there flew EF111-As, the Electronic Counter-Measures version of the F-111. They escorted the bombers during raids, jamming enemy defense and missile guidance radar.

It was just past 3:00 A.M. at Andrews Air Force Base. Shepherd decided to wait until after arriving in Upper Heyford to call Stephanie about the transfer.

About an hour later, he and Captain Mark Foster, the other wizzo-less pilot, arrived at squadron headquarters.

Square-jawed and blue-eyed with a thick shock of auburn hair, Foster had grown up on a ranch in the Texas hill country.

After processing aircraft and personnel transfer documents, the two pilots spent the rest of the morning plotting turn points for an orientation mission they would fly en route to Upper Heyford—an extended flight that would allow Shepherd to become familiar with the crowded and tightly controlled air corridors that crisscrossed the United Kingdom. When finished, they suited up and went to the flight line.

Shepherd's F-111 had been repaired and had been on active status for several days now. He settled into the cockpit as the air crew hooked up the Dash-60, a pneumatic blower that wound the engines to start speed. At 17,000 RPMs, he lifted the throttles and the turbines came to life. After an hour of routine warm-up procedures and systems checks, he glanced wistfully to the empty seat next to him, and radioed the tower for takeoff clearance.

AFTER ALTERING the two pilots' computer files at Mildenhall, Larkin and Applegate had gone directly to Upper Heyford. With CIA sanction, they took over a hangar in a remote corner of the field. In the next few days the offices and life-support room, which contained the aviators' lockers and gear, were quickly painted and outfitted. A small group of Special Forces personnel—guards, aviators, technicians, clerical staffers—who would play various roles in the scheme to acquire the two F-111 bombers joined them.

"Better find out if either of these guys carries a weapon," Larkin asked when reviewing the details.

"Done," Applegate said proudly; he knew most pilots carried a sidearm only when flying combat, but there were those who carried one whenever they flew. "The Texan carries a thirty-eight. Shepherd flies clean."

"Sequences your targets if nothing else," Larkin mused. It also resulted in the selection of a sniper rifle as a weapon. Fired from a distant and concealed position, it would provide a margin of safety for the marksman and, requiring an imperceptible change of angle between shots, facilitate extremely rapid shooting.

That was three days ago.

Now, in one of the offices, Larkin and Applegate sat on opposite sides of a desk, the parts of a disassembled rifle spread out in front of them.

The Iver Johnson Model 300 was the finest of sniping rifles: a fluted and counterweighted barrel reduced vibration and whip; a short-throw bolt allowed a marksman to fire all four rounds in five seconds; an X9 Leupold scope ensured they would be bull's-eyes.

Applegate had cleaned the IJ3's parts and now, as he assembled them, he checked each for specks of dust or excess oil, making sure the action was working smoothly.

Larkin opened a box of 8.58 mm cartridges and examined them, his wintry eyes making certain that the bullet was properly seated in the case, that the primers were centered, that there were no imperfections that might result in a misfire. He selected four cartridges and handed them to Applegate, who began thumbing them into the magazine.

T H E   R A I N had finally stopped as the two F-111s completed the orientation mission and streaked through swiftly falling darkness, landing side by side on Heyford's north-south runway. At Larkin's request, air traffic control directed them through the maze of taxiways to the remote hangar.

The colonel was waiting on the tarmac when the bombers emerged from the mist and taxied into view. With him were four members of the Special Forces contingent that he and Applegate had assembled: two crew chiefs who would tend to the aircraft, and two guards wearing Air Force Security Police uniforms who would patrol the area.

The crew chiefs guided the planes to a stop, then positioned ladders against the fuselages and assisted the pilots from their cockpits.

Larkin tensed slightly as Shepherd and Foster strode toward him in the darkness, removing their flight helmets. "Hope you'll excuse the lack of drums and bugles," he said genially after introductions had been made.

"President's got to cut the deficit somehow," Shepherd joked.

"We hear he's got other priorities this week, sir," Foster said with a smile.

"And we're keeping them as low pro as possible," Larkin replied brightly, stealing a glance at the pistol on Foster's hip. "You'll hook up with your wizzos and spend a few days getting in the groove. When the red light flashes you'll brief with the EF crews and join the strike force en route."

Larkin led the way toward the hangar. Shepherd and Foster followed him through the personnel door and down a long corridor, entering beneath a narrow balcony that ringed the hangar's second-floor offices.

"LS room's over there," Larkin said, gesturing to the far side of the huge space. He began falling back, his heart pounding in his chest, as they crossed the empty, sound-deadened hangar, which, he and Applegate had reasoned, would not only contain the loud reports but also offer no cover to their targets.

Above and behind them on the darkened balcony, Applegate was waiting with the sniper rifle. He quietly set the forestock on the pipe rail, tuned the telescopic sight, and aligned the first target, the *armed* target; he let the cross hairs drift onto the back of Foster's head, held a breath, and calmly squeezed off the round.

Shepherd heard the sharp crack and whirled at the same instant Foster pitched forward, spinning toward him in a shower of tissue and blood.

Simultaneously, Applegate jacked the IJ3's bolt, made the quick shift in angle that put the cross hairs on Shepherd, and fired again. But in that split second, the unforeseen happened—Foster had spun into the line of fire. The round tore into his back as he passed in front of Shepherd. Larkin was reaching to his shoulder holster when Shepherd, having every reason to believe the colonel was also a target, made a lifesaving dive, knocking him to the ground.

Applegate saw the tangle of arms and legs and held his fire for fear of hitting Larkin, who had drawn his pistol and was fighting furiously to get to his feet. Shepherd saw the flailing weapon and then, their faces inches apart as Larkin broke free and went rolling out from under him, Shepherd saw, not fear and surprise, but determination and intent—*murderous* intent that told him *he*, not the sniper in the balcony, would be Larkin's target. Shepherd kicked Larkin's arm as he came up out of the roll into a firing crouch. The shot went wild. The 9 mm Baretta skittered across the floor.

Shepherd ran for the exit, glimpsing an obscure figure on the darkened balcony above. Applegate fired both remaining shots, but Shepherd had taken away the angle by running directly beneath him, and the rounds missed, chipping into the concrete floor.

Larkin retrieved his weapon and dashed into the corridor. Shepherd had already reached the opposite end and exited into the darkness. He spotted one of the security policemen, assumed he was bona fide, and sought assistance. "Hey! Hey, these guys just—" He bit off the sentence when the SP went for the pistol on his hip. Shepherd still had his flight helmet by the chin strap. He swung it at arm's length. The rock-hard plastic connected with the side of the SP's head. He fell to the ground, writhing in pain.

The flight helmet went bouncing across the tarmac.

Shepherd's eyes darted to the SP's pistol, lying 10 feet away. A lanyard trailed from the handgrip to the holster, which meant Shepherd couldn't just grab the weapon and run. He saw Larkin exiting the hangar and sprinted toward a tanker truck that was parked beyond the two F-111s. Larkin opened fire but, in the darkness, he had little chance of hitting a moving target with a handgun. Shepherd didn't know what was going on, other than that men in air force uniforms had killed Foster and were trying to kill him. Russians? Spies? Terrorists? The last thing that would occur to him was that they were Americans, officers who had fought for their country and were as committed to its defense as he was. The only thing he knew for sure was that he would be dead if he didn't get out of there.

Shepherd climbed into the cab of the tanker, thanking the Almighty that most military vehicles had unkeyed ignitions. He turned the starter switch, slammed the transmission into drive, and roared off into the darkness as Larkin and the SPs approached on the run.

Applegate came out of the hangar an instant after the truck

roared past. He lumbered to his sedan, drove across the tarmac, and pulled to a stop next to Larkin. "Mop up inside," Larkin barked at the SPs. He got in next to Applegate, who floored the accelerator.

The truck had reached the far end of the huge hangar and was turning into an access road that ran alongside it. Shepherd was steering with one hand and fumbling across the dash in search of the headlight switch with the other. He had no knowledge of the base; no idea where wing or security police headquarters were located.

The side view mirror came ablaze with light.

Shepherd glanced to see the sedan in pursuit. His hand finally found the dash switch. The truck's headlights came on, revealing a chainlink fence dead ahead. The gate was closed and padlocked. The truck smashed through it, littering the area with fencing, and came onto an unlighted, two-lane road that wound through the rural Heyford countryside.

The sedan rumbled over the fragments of twisted pipe and chainlink, in pursuit.

Shepherd had the gas pedal to the floor now, but the massive truck wasn't made for speed. The headlights in the mirror were closing fast. They would overtake the lumbering tanker in a matter of seconds. Shepherd waited until the gap had closed, then slammed on the brakes. The truck's huge stoplights came alive in an explosion of crimson light. Smoke spewed from the wheel housings. The tires streaked the macadam with rubber as the tanker shuddered violently to a stop.

As Shepherd expected, the sedan was directly behind him, heading for the massive steel bumper that stretched across the back of the truck, windshield high.

Applegate spun the steering wheel.

The sedan swerved, narrowly missing the truck. It went up on two wheels, traveling the tanker's entire length before coming down with a jarring thump, and sliding sideways across the road in front of the cab.

Applegate had just slammed on the brakes when Larkin saw headlights bearing down on them; bearing down on his side of the car. "He's going to ram us!" he shouted as the car jerked to a stop. Larkin fired his pistol at the truck. Several rounds popped through the windshield, whistling above Shepherd, who was hunched behind the steering wheel.

Applegate stepped on the gas. The car lurched across the road. The onrushing truck clipped the rear fender, spinning the sedan around.

Shepherd kept on going.

Applegate got the car turned around and pursued.

The truck came through a sharp turn. Red lights were flashing up ahead. A spiderweb of cracks radiating from the bulletholes in the windshield picked up the light. Shepherd could hardly see through the pulsing maze, but he heard the rapidly clanging bell. The truck was approaching a railroad crossing—so was a forty-car freight. Shepherd had no idea how close the train was and kept the accelerator to the floor. The truck blasted through the crossing, splintering the gate arm, bouncing over the tracks.

The locomotive was 50 feet from the crossing. The engineer recoiled as the diesel's headlight revealed the truck flashing past. He released the throttle and yanked hard on the emergency brake. A shower of blue-orange sparks exploded from every one of the train's cast-iron wheels. The air filled with the high-pitched screech of grinding steel.

Since this was a rural crossing, the engineer hadn't reduced speed as he would in a town or city. The 175-ton locomotive smashed into the rear of the tanker at full throttle. The tremendous impact knocked the huge truck aside like a toy. It pivoted around and began rolling back toward the tracks. Thousands of gallons of jet fuel were spewing from the buckled tanker.

The pursuing sedan came through the turn. Applegate slammed on the brakes. The sedan screeched to a stop a distance from the crossing, where, despite *its* brakes being locked, the freight was still streaking past, blocking their view.

"Son of a bitch!" Larkin exclaimed, thinking the truck had made it through.

"Come on, come on," Applegate urged the train impatiently, eager to resume the pursuit.

Suddenly, the jet fuel ignited with a loud whomp. Flames shot into the night, high above the passing freight, which continued through and beyond the crossing, finally revealing the conflagration beyond.

The truck was on its side, almost parallel to the tracks, and totally engulfed in flames. The interior of the cab looked like the inside of a blast furnace.

Larkin and Applegate got out of the sedan and stared awestruck at the roaring inferno.

The intense heat kept them at a distance.

Larkin watched one of the fenders turn to a puddle of molten steel. His mind was racing, calculating all the factors: There would be no human remains, he reasoned, nothing to identify *who* had died. Shepherd would be cremated; his flight suit and dogtags would be ashes amid the debris. Furthermore, theft of equipment from military bases was an ever-growing problem. Investigators would have every reason to conclude that the truck and its valuable cargo had been stolen and that it was the thief who had perished in the fire.

While the flames raged, Larkin and Applegate searched the surrounding area, concluding beyond any doubt that Shepherd hadn't been thrown from the cab.

The locomotive had come to a stop more than a mile past the crossing. By the time the engineer and fireman had shaken off the effects of the collision and walked to the burning truck, Larkin and Applegate were long gone.

They drove back to the hangar, joining the two Special Forces SPs who had completed the cleanup. Now, at Larkin's direction, the SPs drove to a darkened corner of the airfield where a new runway was under construction and buried the pilot's body, knowing that the corpse would soon be forever entombed beneath an 18-inch-thick slab of rock-hard concrete laced with reinforcing steel.

Larkin went to his office, thinking that Kiley would really be pleased, and sent a cable that read: BIRDS IN HAND.

It was time to get on with the business of delivering two F-111 supersonic bombers to Muammar el-Qaddafi.

10

T H A T S A M E A F T E R N O O N in Beirut, Katifa sat at a table in the kitchen of her apartment with a package of insulin she had picked up from the pharmacy. She opened the box and lined up the vials on the table.

Moncrieff sat opposite her with a cup of water and a small pitcher of milk. He poured a little into the water and stirred it. Then added a few drops more.

Katifa peeled the wrapper from a syringe, pierced the first vial, and began extracting the insulin.

Moncrieff kept adding drops of milk to the water until the cloudy liquid perfectly matched the density of the insulin, which he was pleased to discover was odorless, sparing him the task of duplicating its scent; then he left the table to make a phone call.

I N T R I P O L I, Muammar el-Qaddafi was in his tent at the barracks compound on As-Sarim Street, sulking over a devastating economic report issued that afternoon by the Libyan secretariat of industry.

The quarterly index stated that once fertile agricultural communities were failing; many factories—producers of ore, textiles, and foodstuffs among them—were shutting down; citizens were complaining that shops and market shelves were bare—all due to the frustrating lack of water.

Qaddafi reflected on his goals; on the dreams of grandeur that drove his ambition to unite the Arab world under the teachings of Islam and to destroy Israel, an ambition that justified his offer of sanctuary to Palestinians. Having helped ease tensions in the Middle East, he would not only gain military hardware but also stature as a statesman—stature he expected would lead to his being hailed as a modern-day Gamal Abdel Nasser, who had been his boyhood hero. The late Egyptian leader had had similar ambitions and had faced similar problems, irrigating his arid land with the Aswan Dam. Despite Qaddafi's desire to emulate him there was no Nile, indeed, not even a single river, in Libya. Now, having found the solution, another nation—an *Islamic* nation—had nullified it. In his most lucid moments Qaddafi attributed the existence of Nefta Dam to a cruel twist of fate, not malicious intent; but when lost in the darkest recesses of his paranoia, he had no doubt it was a Tunisian conspiracy to deny him greatness.

The intercom buzzed several more times before the colonel set aside the report and tapped the button.

"Moncrieff is calling from Beirut," the Bab al Azziziya operator announced.

"Moncrieff," Qaddafi said, brightening, "I can usually count on you for some good news."

"Not today, sir, I'm afraid," the Saudi replied, going on to explain that Abu Nidal had scuttled the plan. "However, with your cooperation I'm quite certain it can be salvaged."

THAT EVENING IN BEIRUT, Abu Nidal's gunboat was approaching Casino du Liban when Qaddafi called on the ship-to-shore radio. The conversation was short, contentious, and ended moments before the boat entered the marina, where Katifa and Hasan were waiting.

"Qaddafi's called a summit," Nidal said, gesturing they come aboard. "He wants to meet with Assad and Arafat in Damascus."

"What about?" Katifa asked nonchalantly as she handed him the package of insulin.

"This sanctuary in Libya," Nidal replied with disgust. "I'm not going. It's a waste of time."

"I agree," Katifa said firmly before adding, "unless that's exactly what Qaddafi wanted to hear."

"What do you mean?" Nidal asked, his curiosity aroused as she had hoped.

"Well, your absence would make it much easier for him to turn the others against you."

"Not Assad. Assad would never turn against me."

"Forgive my boldness," Katifa said gently. "But as a famous Palestinian fighter once said, 'Loyalty taken for granted eventually leads to betrayal.' "

Nidal smiled, taken by her acuity and spunk. He had recognized early on that of the two siblings he had adopted, Katifa was the child of promise. *She* had the first-rate mind and cunning most akin to his own. He reflected for a moment, then shifted his look to his protégé. "Hasan?" he prompted, soliciting an opinion.

"Qaddafi is just trying to assert his power. It would be a sign of weakness to come when he calls."

"I wouldn't be so concerned with appearances, Hasan," Katifa retorted. "Results are what count."

"You sound just like the Saudi," Hasan taunted.

Her eyes flashed with feigned anger. "How dare you compare me to the shetan who created this problem?"

"You're the one who brought him here."

"Enough," Nidal snapped, his eyes darting to Hasan. "She would have been wrong to do otherwise; the decision was mine to make; as is this one." He jerked his head, dismissing him, then turned to Katifa. "I think you're right," he said, his eyes softening with pride. "If I don't protect our interests, who will? Make the arrangements for Damascus."

A short time later, Nidal's gunboat slipped out of the marina and into the night. Hasan was still seething when Katifa went up the gangway and through the casino to her car, taking the coastal motorway back to the city. He followed in his jeep.

The shower was running when Katifa entered her apartment on Tamar Mallat.

Moncrieff was just starting to soap up. The draft that blew through the apartment when Katifa opened the door billowed the shower curtain against his body.

"Katifa?" he called out.

"I'll be there in a moment," she replied.

Hasan had parked around the corner. He slid along the side of the coarsely stuccoed building to a window, peering between the shutter slats. His eyes widened as Katifa removed her dress and slipped out of her bra and panties. He was so intent that his foot dislodged a few small stones, which went tumbling down the hillside.

Katifa was on tiptoes, stretching her lithe body, when she heard the sound. She glanced curiously to the window, then crossed to it. Hasan leaned back into the darkness as her shadow fell across the shutters and she secured the latch, then crossed to the bathroom.

"Hi," she said brightly, as she slipped into the shower with Moncrieff. "Nidal agreed to go. No thanks to Hasan," she added, explaining what had happened.

Moncrieff wrapped his arms around her waist. She arched her back, forcing her pelvis against his, aroused by the needle-fine jets of water that stung her flesh.

Hasan had gone around the building to the entrance and down the corridor to Katifa's apartment. He pulled his knife from its sheath and inserted the point between the door and jamb, quickly slipping the latch.

Moncrieff and Katifa were embracing passionately when Moncrieff felt the shower curtain blow against his torso again. He put his finger to her lips, then pointed to the billowing curtain. "Someone's here," he whispered.

Hasan was crossing to the hall that led to the bathroom when his eyes darted to something familiar. The paper wrapper was lying on the floor next to a wastebasket in which he found several used syringes, one still half-filled with milky fluid. He was examining it when he heard the creak of floorboards and whirled to confront Moncrieff, who was wrapping a towel around his waist as he came down the hall. An instant later Katifa appeared behind him, slipping into a bathrobe.

"Stop him," she exclaimed. "If he gets to Nidal—"

Hasan lunged toward the door. Moncrieff went after him, got a fistful of his hair, and yanked him backwards into the apartment, kicking the door closed. Hasan pulled free and slashed at him with the knife. The Saudi sidestepped, grabbed Hasan's wrist with one hand, and threw a punch with the other.

Katifa recoiled as they tumbled past her to the floor, fighting for control of the knife.

Hasan came out on top and tried to plunge the knife into Moncrieff's chest. The Saudi had both hands wrapped tightly around Hasan's wrist, holding it off. Gradually, Moncrieff twisted it around until the point of the blade was facing Hasan. Moncrieff bent a knee, getting a foot under him for leverage, and tried to roll Hasan over. But the Palestinian's elbow was planted firmly on the floor, securing his position.

Katifa slipped a bare foot behind Hasan's elbow. He sensed what she was about to do and flicked her a horrified glance. Her face turned to stone. She kicked his arm out from under him.

The tremendous pressure Hasan was exerting propelled him suddenly downward. The knife pierced his chest to the hilt.

Moncrieff pushed Hasan's body aside, staggered to his feet, and studied her for a moment, then broke into a thin smile.

"I know," Katifa said. "My father would have been proud of me."

11

THE SNOW-DOTTED HILLS of Scotland's Southern Uplands lay basking in the warmth of a spring morning. Billions of water droplets, swelling until they could no longer cling to the basalt ledges, began plunging to the earth. Soon, a gentle gurgle rose, increasing gradually to a throaty roar as the rivulets formed streams that rushed across the moors. Finally, as they had for millennia past, they came together with thundering fury in a breathtaking cascade at the Falls of Clyde.

From there, the River Clyde flowed northward past Glasgow to the coastal Firth, where vessels steamed south toward the Irish Sea and English Channel, or north into the Atlantic Ocean and Norwegian Sea.

Centuries ago, this access to major sea routes spawned Glasgow's legendary shipyards. More recently, it led the United States Navy to select Holy Loch on the west bank of the Clyde as a submarine base.

The USS *Cavalla*, a Sturgeon-class hunter-killer submarine, was stationed there. Assigned to an ongoing top-secret CIA covert action program, the *Cavalla* was outfitted with a hull-mounted dry deck shelter. The DDS housed a submersible vessel used to deploy the team of navy SEALs who were part of the crew. This highly trained and motivated special warfare unit was skilled in demolition, assassination, and counterinsurgency techniques.

Commander Christian Duryea was the *Cavalla*'s skipper. As a youth, the lanky, blue-eyed son of a New York City fireman dreamed of being a navy pilot; and he was well on his way the day the acceptance letter from Annapolis came. It was during his second year at the academy when he first noticed his vision had deteriorated.

"Twenty-sixty in both eyes, son," the optometrist said a few days later, confirming that Chris would never fly military aircraft. "I'm sorry."

Chris Duryea quickly decided that next to dogfighting, skippering a sub was the most autonomous command the navy offered.

Now, almost twenty years later, he was hovering over his chart table when a cable was delivered to the command center. His eyes went right to the Z prefix, which denoted FLASH priority.

Z172608ZAPR
TOP SECRET
FM: KUBARK
TO: USS CAVALLA
RE: REDEPLOYMENT
AF COLONEL RICHARD LARKIN ARRIVING 9APR. WILL
CONDUCT MISSION BRIEFING. CITE DIRECTOR.

Duryea tugged thoughtfully at an earlobe. Orders usually came via COMSUBLANT, commander of the submarine force in the Atlantic. CITE DIRECTOR meant they had come directly from the DCI. Something big was in the works.

"That's tomorrow," Duryea said to Lieutenant McBride, his executive officer. "Better juice the crew."

THE MORNING after acquiring the F-111s, Larkin boarded a flight at Upper Heyford for Holy Loch. The plane headed northwest over the English countryside to Scotland, arriving at the submarine base just over an hour later. A Royal Navy hovercraft was waiting. The powerful vessel rose up haughtily on its cushion of air, slid down the ramp into the Clyde's oily waters, and whisked him across the immense loch. In less than fifteen minutes it was approaching the concrete refitting pier where the USS *Cavalla* was berthed.

Larkin stepped ashore, carrying a slim aluminum attaché case. He strode beneath the towering cranes used to lower ICBMs into submarine missile hatches and went up the gangway, boarding the *Cavalla*.

A brisk wind came up as Duryea greeted him and led the way down into the command center. "Where we headed?" he asked offhandedly as they came off the ladder.

"Tripoli," Larkin replied flatly.

Duryea's brows went up. "Don't stop now, Colonel," he prompted, intrigued as Larkin knew he would be.

The colonel used the DCI's cover story to explain the mission: the hostages had been shrewdly hidden in Libya. CIA had found and rescued them. The air strike was a diversion to get them out—on the *Cavalla*.

"Why not fly them out?" Duryea wondered.

"One Stinger and it's all over," Larkin replied, referring to the shoulder-mounted mobile missile launcher favored by terrorist groups. He explained that the *Cavalla* would ferry the hostages to the USS *America*, an aircraft carrier based in the Mediterranean with the 6th Fleet. "We're talking need-to-know rules, Commander. Nobody, not Sixth Fleet, Third Air, or Cinclant, knows about this yet," he concluded, the latter an acronym for commander in chief of the Atlantic. "If word got out and it went bust—"

"I understand, Colonel."

"Good. Only after we have the hostages aboard, and only then, will the *America* be notified. By the time we rendezvous, teams of physicians and psychologists will have been flown in to care for them."

Duryea broke into a broad smile, pleased to have the challenge, and went to the electronic chart table, a large horizontal television screen linked to the boat's powerful BC-10 computer. An inventory of surface and undersea charts were stored in its superfast bubble memory. He encoded at the terminal and a highly detailed chart of Tripoli harbor appeared on the screen.

"Right there," Larkin said, indicating a desolate wharf near the Old City. "That's the rendezvous point. The air strike will be keyed to your schedule. I need a guaranteed ETA."

"Five days would be realistic."

"The night of the fourteenth?"

Duryea nodded.

"What about Redfleet surveillance?"

"My specialty." Duryea was a genius at playing underwater hide-and-seek with his Soviet counterparts. It was the one source of pride his humble nature couldn't suppress. "We'll be there."

"So will I," Larkin replied smartly, handing him the attaché he'd brought. It contained ANITA, the key essential to programming Pave Tack computers. "Keep this in your safe. I'll need it when we rendezvous in Tripoli."

"You're going in?" Duryea asked, surprised.

"Four of us. We'll be leaving with you."

"I can't promise you a room with a view," Duryea joked, shaking Larkin's hand. "Good luck, Colonel."

Larkin went to the communications room and sent a cable to Kiley confirming 14 April as the date for the air strike, then left the submarine.

"Cast off," Duryea ordered in a soft, firm voice.

The departing hovercraft was still on the horizon when the *Cavalla*'s deck crew cut loose the hausers that had kept her lashed to the refitting pier. A stiff breeze tore at the lookouts standing on the hydroplanes on either side of the sail. Both wore safety harnesses cabled to the hull as they leaned into field glasses scanning the expanse of green-black water.

Several hours later, the *Cavalla* had left Holy Loch and proceeded down the River Clyde into the choppy Firth.

One hundred miles northwest, a Redfleet submarine was cutting through the North Atlantic's cold depths. The titanium-hulled Alpha routinely tracked U.S. submarines emerging from the Firth of Clyde into North Channel, the turbulent body of water between Scotland's southwest shores and Northern Ireland.

Captain First Rank Aleksandr Solomatin was her skipper. He was thumbing a fresh bowl of tobacco into his meerschaum when sonar notified him they had picked up the *Cavalla*'s signal.

"All ahead full," he ordered, lighting his pipe.

The *starpom* echoed the command.

A blast of steam surged against the turbine blades and the sleek Soviet boat sprinted forward. The blazing 45-knot speed was achieved by its sleek profile and the use of a highly automated liquid-metal–cooled nuclear reactor.

An hour later the *Cavalla* was entering North Channel from the Firth. Duryea stood on the bridge scanning the horizon. "Depth under keel?"

"One eight five, sir," McBride responded smartly.

"Take her down," Duryea said. He took a deep breath of the crisp, salty air and exhaled slowly, savoring it.

"Clear the bridge," he ordered. "Rig for dive."

The whomping claxon joined the hiss of air rushing from ballast tanks. Plumes of water arched gracefully over the sea from the main vents. The bow tilted down sharply, sending water over the submarine's deck in graceful swirls.

"Conn? Sonar," came the voice over the bridge phone.

"Talk to me, Cooperman," Duryea responded.

"Contact bearing one seven three," the *Cavalla*'s sonarman reported, his left hand dancing over the entry panel keyboard, his right rolling the target designation ball, his ears tuned to the syncopated beat in his headphones that came from the twin screws common to all Soviet submarines. "Redfleet boat for sure, skipper."

"Anybody we know?" Duryea wondered.

"She's coated, sir. Squooshes instead of pongs." The unusual echo was produced by the anechoic tiles on the Alpha's hull, which absorbed sonar transmissions.

"That cuts it to Alpha, Mike, Sierra, or Viktor," Duryea replied, knowing all had the new Clusterguard coating. "Can we narrow that?"

Cooperman pushed several buttons on his console, as he studied the patterns tracing across a monitor in the panel in front of him. A high-speed computer printer, built into the surface of the control console above the keyboard, was recording the images on a continuous printout.

Stocky and slow-moving, Marv Cooperman defied the classic profile of a sonar technician. He loathed electronics and wasn't into music or video games, but had infinite patience and an exceptional memory for sounds.

"She's cutting a big hole in the water, sir," he reported. "Forty-four knots. Has to be an Alpha."

"Good going," Duryea enthused. Knowing he was up against the much faster boat would affect the evasive strategy he selected.

In the Alpha's attack center, Captain Solomatin stood in a cloud of pipe smoke, smoothing the coarse beard that concealed his smile. No other submarine in the world could have gotten there in time.

"Keep him on a tight leash," the Russian ordered. Whatever the *Cavalla*'s mission, it would have to get past him to carry it out.

12

A GOLDEN, late morning sun streamed through the curtained windows of Stephanie Shepherd's kitchen.

She was loading the dishwasher when the phone rang.

"Stephanie?" the congressman said in his gregarious rumble. "Jim Gutherie. Glad I got you. Why don't we have lunch and finish that interview?"

"I'm up against a deadline on a story," she fibbed, "but I can drop by your office this afternoon."

"My afternoon's jammed. I'd sure like to knock this off today."

She paused, her lips tightening as she wrestled with the decision. She'd be less than truthful if she denied she was flattered by the congressman's attention; less than truthful if she denied she didn't sometimes feel left out of her husband's life. Oh, she was still madly in love with him; but over the years she'd come to realize that Walt loved his country, the air force, his F-111, and his wife in that order. She didn't really mind, she just longed to be a part of it; to share it; to better understand it and him. Writing for the base newspaper was a less than satisfying attempt to do so. Funny, she thought, the things that made Walt so special to her were the things that got in the way. "Why not, Jim?" she finally replied.

"Good," Gutherie enthused. "Twelve-thirty, Cafe Promenade at the Hay Adams."

Stephanie showered and was wrapping herself in a bath towel when she caught sight of her naked torso in the mirror and poked an accusing fingertip into a ripple of flesh. The first time someone said she and her daughter, Laura, looked like sisters, she was flattered. But down deep, she knew it was because they dressed alike. Stephanie had been living in jeans, sweatshirts, and running shoes, and rarely dressed up anymore. She hated middle age. A harmless lunch would ease the pain of it.

She had just finished dressing and was evaluating the effect when the phone rang again. It was the gymnastics coach at Camp Springs Junior High.

"I'm afraid Laura took a little fall during practice this morning," he said matter-of-factly.

"Oh my . . . Is she all right?"

"She's fine; twisted her wrist when she landed. I think it'd be a good idea to have it X-rayed."

"Of course. Thanks. I'm on my way."

Stephanie called Gutherie's secretary and canceled the luncheon; then, she left Jeffrey at the base day care center, and headed for Camp Springs Junior High.

It had never been any different, she thought. As soon as Walt left, the catastrophes began. It was the children's way of letting him know he was needed. The syndrome was all too common among military families.

A half hour later, Stephanie had picked up Laura and returned to Andrews, driving directly to Malcom Grow Medical Center on Perimeter Road.

The emergency room doctor looked young, she thought. Too young, like a high school debater. He snapped Laura's X-rays in front of a light panel and indicated a gray line on a bone just above her wrist, pronouncing it a hairline fracture of the lower radius.

It wasn't a serious injury, but to a budding gymnast who had been training hard, it was terribly upsetting not to be able to compete.

At home, Laura settled gloomily in the kitchen with a tin of chocolate chip cookies.

"Builds strong bones," Stephanie chided, pouring her a glass of milk.

"I really miss Dad," Laura said wistfully, making circles in the crumbs on the counter.

"Me too. What do you say we call him?"

The teenager's eyes brightened. "Mean it?"

"Of course. The number's in the—" Stephanie cut off the sentence as Laura bolted from the kitchen. "Easy! You'll have a cast on the other wrist," she cautioned, hurrying after her.

Laura quickly found the package of transfer data and read the digits aloud as her mother dialed.

"Forty-eighth TAC," a woman's voice answered.

"May I speak with Major Shepherd, please?"

"Major Shepherd," the woman said, encoding at a keyboard filling her computer screen with names. "I'm sorry but I don't list an extension for him."

"Are you sure? I talked to him last week."

"I'm sorry," the woman said, scrolling through the names again. "Let me transfer you to Personnel."

Personnel had no trouble at all finding him. "Ah," the clerk said, pulling the file up on her screen. "He's right here on my transfer roster."

"He's been transferred?"

"To Upper Heyford. I have the number if you like."

"Of course, please." That's odd, Stephanie thought, as she jotted it down. It wasn't like Walt. He always let her know how to reach him. "Could it be temporary?" she asked, thinking that might be the reason.

"I doubt it. He's got a new CO. According to his file, he reports to a Colonel Richard Larkin now."

Stephanie wrote down the name, hung up, and called Upper Heyford. Informed Major Shepherd wasn't in his quarters, she left a message.

A T   A B O U T the same time 90 miles west of London, the haunting whistle and rhythmic clack of a freight train, snaking through the Buckingham countryside, greeted the early twilight.

Shepherd thought he had died and gone to heaven, which he was surprised to discover smelled like a beer hall. The tangy scent of lager, strong and tart, the way he liked it, filled the air.

He was lying on his stomach, atop a mountain of hops in an open freight car, one of many on their way to a London brewery. As he slowly regained consciousness, his mind filled with confusing flashes of memory: the scream of grinding steel, the pain of brutal, bone-jarring impact, the sting of searing sheets of flame.

His presence on the train was a matter of simple physics and decisive action. For as the locomotive collided with the rear of the tanker truck, knocking it out of its path, the front went pivoting around back toward the tracks. The vehicle came to rest on its side, the cab literally within inches of the passing train. The impact had torn open the driver's door, wrenching it back on its hinges into a nearly horizontal position; and while the flame and smoke from the roaring inferno at the rear of the tanker blocked Larkin and Applegate's view, Shepherd pulled himself out of the cab and climbed onto this "platform." He was spattered with burning fuel; but his flight suit, made of Nomex—the same fireproof material used to outfit astronauts and race drivers—protected him. Despite the pain from the battering he'd taken in the tumbling cab, he was fully conscious and able to think. He had no doubt the men who had tried to kill him were waiting on the other side of the tracks; he also knew, injured and unarmed, he didn't stand a chance on foot. He crouched there staring at the wall of flames shooting up around him, then glanced to the open gondolas rushing past just below and made his decision. The inferno was literally licking at his heels, as he crawled to the edge of the door and jumped.

He landed in one of the gondolas atop a mound of hops. It cushioned the impact, but couldn't overcome the momentum of the train. He clutched desperately at the crumbly cones that offered no handhold and went rocketing into the steel sidewall. His head smashed against it, knocking him unconscious.

Hours later, he was still out cold when British Railway officials, who had been dispatched from London, arrived on the scene, disconnecting the damaged locomotive and detaining its crew for questioning. The train spent the night on a siding, as did Shepherd, who was concealed in one of the forty gondolas. He slipped in and out of consciousness several times, though he had no recollection of it.

The following morning another locomotive and crew were assigned to take the cargo to its destination.

Now, as the freight moved slowly through the countryside, Shepherd was gradually accepting that he was alive. His head pounded. His bruised muscles protested the slightest movement. His mind fought to comprehend what had happened to him. He turned over and struggled to a sitting position. Excruciating pain shot through his battered limbs. Everything began whirling about. He fought the rising nausea and put his head between his legs, which steadied him. Slowly, methodically, he undid the zippers of his G-suit and discarded it. He made his way through the hops to the edge of the open gondola and peered over the side.

The darkened countryside whistled past in a blur.

The right-of-way ran parallel to the A40 motorway. An illuminated sign at an interchange was visible through a break in the trees. The letters were three feet tall but a severe case of double vision prevented Shepherd from reading them. He shook his head, trying to clear it, to no avail. Finally, he covered one eye with his palm and squinted. The jumble of letters merged. For a brief instant he could make out: LONDON 45K. The letters gradually blurred and everything started spinning again. He slumped against the side of the gondola and passed out.

A short time later, he awakened beneath a star-dotted sky. The temperature had plummeted and he was shivering from the dampness and cold.

The piercing sound of an air horn announced that the freight was entering the yards just south of Hackney Wick Stadium on the desolate eastern outskirts of London. The engineer began guiding it through the myriad of signals and switches.

Shepherd crawled to a standing position. Lights from distant buildings looked like tiny balls of illuminated fuzz. The canted roofs of sheet metal warehouses marched into the gritty darkness, blending with the endless acres of rolling stock parked on sidings. Shepherd swung a leg over the side of the gondola and fought to keep his balance while his foot searched frantically in the darkness for the first tread on the ladder. Finally secured, he straddled the edge for a moment, then swung his other leg over and began making his way down.

The train snaked between darkened maintenance sheds, then jerked through a series of switches.

Shepherd lost his grip on the ladder and started falling backward. The train lurched in the opposite direction, propelling him toward the ladder again. He clung to it fiercely, waiting for the freight to slow. An eternity passed before it braked to a 5 MPH crawl.

A flickering light on the other side of the yard pierced the ground fog that draped over the tops of the buildings and boxcars. It caught Shepherd's attention. He could vaguely see several figures gathered around it. Trainmen? Yard workers? A conductor? he wondered, his spirits rising as the ghostly forms seemed to materialize, then vanish in the haze.

Shepherd didn't have the strength to jump. He let go of the ladder and hit the ground hard, rolling across the chunky gravel and tall weeds sprouting between the ties and spurs. His aching body came to rest against the ungiving concrete base of a yard signal. He lay there for a moment gathering his strength, then pulled himself upright and leaned against it, squinting into the darkness to get his bearings.

The light was on the other side of the yard.

Shepherd took several deep breaths and started walking toward it. A sharp ringing rose in his ears. Light reflecting off the landscape of polished steel rails intensified the serpentine pattern, heightening his feeling of vertigo. He began swaying but pressed onward, struggling to maintain his balance.

The flickering light came closer and closer.

It came from a fire in a trash pail just outside an abandoned switchman's shack—a source of warmth for the derelicts huddled around it. One wore a rumpled military surplus officer's cap. The other had a filthy ponytail and was shaking uncontrollably, not from the cold but from heroin withdrawal. He wrapped a tattooed fist around the neck of an empty beer bottle and watched expectantly as Shepherd stumbled toward him.

13

"WHERE IS HASAN?" Abu Nidal asked as he stepped from the gunboat onto the dock at Casino du Liban. The meeting with Qaddafi, Assad, and Arafat was that afternoon; and he had expected Hasan to drive him to Damascus.

Katifa thought Nidal would be flat on his back in his cabin. For two days he had been injecting himself, not with insulin but milky water. She couldn't believe he had held on this long.

"We haven't seen Hasan for days," one of the young terrorists replied with a baffled shrug.

"Not since you chastised him," Katifa responded, feigning she was equally perplexed.

Following the confrontation at her apartment, she and Moncrieff had bound and gagged Hasan's corpse and left it in the trunk of an abandoned car in the Ammal sector, making it appear he had been killed by enemy militia.

Katifa, Nidal, and his bodyguard walked up the gangway and through the casino onto the grounds. They were approaching her car when Nidal stumbled.

"Are you all right?" Katifa asked, alarmed. The words rang true, despite her relief that he was, at last, on the verge of acute ketoacidosis, a condition that occurs when blood cells are forced to burn fat and protein instead of glucose which requires insulin. As a result, the blood becomes saturated with glucose and potentially lethal waste products called ketones.

"I feel lightheaded," Nidal explained, as they steadied him. "It's been like this for several days."

"Are you taking your medication?"

"Of course," the terrorist leader snapped, impatient with his poor health. "It doesn't seem to help."

"Perhaps I should drive you to the clinic?"

"When I return from Damascus. Should Assad and the others learn of my illness, your prophecy might come true."

"If Hasan were here, he could go in your place," she suggested, planting the idea of a substitute.

"Hasan isn't ready yet. He may never be," Nidal replied, his eyes considering the obvious alternative.

"I'd prefer to remain with you," Katifa said, not wanting to appear eager.

"You shall," Nidal said decisively. "Someone has to drive me." Then, iron will supplanting the lack of insulin, he began walking toward her car.

Damascus was 50 miles southeast of Beirut beyond the Bekaa Valley on a flat expanse of Syrian desert. It was well over two hours by car from the casino.

Nidal was sitting alone in the backseat, fighting a rising nausea as the Mercedes crossed the Beirut River and headed south on the Gemayel Motorway, skirting the city.

Katifa glanced often and anxiously to the rearview mirror as she drove. If Abu Nidal prevailed, if he somehow made it to the meeting, he would voice his opposition to the plan, forever destroying it. Her mind raced to find a way to make sure he didn't.

"How is he now?" she prompted the bodyguard sitting next to her, purposely distracting him. The instant the burly fellow turned to check on Nidal, she reached to the dash and turned on the car's heater.

Soon, the warm air coming from the floor vent had Nidal sweating profusely. His tongue thickened, as did his saliva, which was now the consistency of honey.

They had just turned into Rue de Damas, the boulevard that leads to the Damascus Motorway, when the bodyguard felt the air rising. "You have the heater on?"

"No, the control is broken," Katifa lied boldly, jiggling the levers. "It doesn't work when it should and does when it shouldn't."

The bodyguard grunted and rolled down the window.

Abu Nidal leaned forward, letting the breeze blow against his face. But a tingling sensation was already creeping up his legs into his torso; shortly, everything went black and he slumped against the seat.

Katifa saw him in the mirror. "He's lost consciousness," she said with alarm.

The guard glanced back at Nidal. "To the hospital, immediately," he blurted, clearly shaken.

Katifa made a U-turn and drove straight to the Turk Hospital on de Mazarra. By the time they arrived, Abu Nidal was in a severe diabetic coma.

As always, he was admitted under a pseudonym.

After handling the paperwork, Katifa left Nidal with the bodyguard and drove to Damascus.

IT WAS LATE AFTERNOON when Katifa arrived at Hafiz al-Assad's villa; its limestone walls radiated the pale peach tones of fading sunlight. She was shown to an opulent meeting room, where Assad, Muammar el-Qaddafi, Yasser Arafat, and their aides were gathered in front of several large maps of Libya that stood on easels along one wall. On each, various sites for the proposed Palestinian sanctuary had been delineated. After the introductions had been made, they dispensed with the maps and took seats around a conference table.

Katifa began by explaining Abu Nidal's absence.

Arafat lightly drummed his manicured nails on the arm of his chair as he listened. "I'm sorry he's not well," he said when she finished.

"As am I," Assad declared, clearly annoyed. Syria's president had a retiring demeanor that belied his ruthlessness. An inordinately large cranium capped his narrow face. "We certainly can't proceed without him."

"We must," Qaddafi retorted, flicking a veiled glance to Katifa. "I must have a decision today."

"You can have it now," she offered. "Abu Nidal's instructed me to approve the plan on his behalf."

"Then it's settled," Qaddafi said, relieved.

"One moment," Assad countered. He crossed to the wall of limestone arches that framed the windows and looked out over the rugged countryside, deep in thought.

For decades, his confrontational policies had neatly meshed with the Soviet Union's Middle East strategy. Moscow supplied the weapons, Assad the turmoil that kept the United States mired in the struggle between Israel and the Palestinians. Forced to take sides, the Americans appeared anti-Arab, giving the Soviets the Middle East entrée they sought. But Moscow's priorities had changed rapidly. Fueling regional conflicts wasn't high on Mikhail

Gorbachev's agenda. Assad knew that without Soviet backing, the Palestinians would soon become a thorn in *his* side—the hostages more so. And he saw the deal as a graceful way to dump both on Qaddafi. But the scope of the decision made him cautious. He knew of Katifa's lineage; knew she had authored the *Intifada*. He had no reason to doubt she was Abu Nidal's bona fide emissary; indeed, no reason whatsoever to suspect she was conspiring against him; but this was no time for expedience. "No offense," he said to Katifa as he turned from the window. "But I can't approve this without speaking to Abu Nidal."

"The man is incapacitated," Qaddafi protested, his cape whirling about him. "I don't have time for this."

"I agree," Arafat chimed in, getting to his feet. "We've missed too many opportunities." For years he'd been criticized for backing proposals that went nowhere. This one had promise; and now that it had come this far, he was determined it succeed. "You have Abu Nidal's decision," he said to Assad sharply. "Act on it."

"Not without confirmation," the Syrian replied, with the even temper of the fighter pilot he once was.

"This is a delicate linkage," Qaddafi complained, confronting him. "And your foot-dragging is going to—"

"Gentlemen? Gentlemen, please?" Katifa implored in a soothing tone, unshaken by Assad's demand. She and Moncrieff had foreseen the possibility. They also knew that Damascus and Beirut had outdated telephone equipment. The fidelity of transmissions was predictably poor, exacerbated by the fact that the system in war-torn Beirut wasn't well maintained. "Abu Nidal said we were to call him if there were any problems," Katifa went on, jotting the number on a slip of paper that she handed to Assad. "He's in room seven thirty-six. Under an assumed name, of course. Ask for Mr. Bargouthi. Farouk Bargouthi."

Assad went to the phone. Qaddafi picked up an extension.

"Turk Hospital private clinic," the switchboard operator answered after the connection was made.

"I would like to speak to one of your patients, please," Assad said. "A Mister Bargouthi."

"That would be room seven thirty-six," the operator said over the crackle on the line. "Just a moment."

"Yes?" a weak voice said after several rings.

"This is Assad calling. I'm sorry you're not well."

"Thank you, brother. I'm just tired, very tired."

"I'm sure you'll be yourself again soon," Assad said reassuringly. "I won't keep you long. I just wish to verify that Katifa Issa Kharuz speaks on your behalf."

"Yes, of course she does," came the tired reply.

"And you're in favor of this proposal?"

"Yes, yes, fully."

"Thank you, brother. Take care of yourself," Assad said, ending the call.

"I always do," Saddam Moncrieff said to himself with a smile after hanging up the phone in hospital room 736. It had been years since he'd had a complete physical. And several days before, when Katifa warned that someone at the meeting might insist on confirmation from Abu Nidal, the Saudi decided the solution was to check into the Turk Hospital's private clinic and get one. He did so under the name Farouk Bargouthi. Of course, Assad had no idea he had just spoken to Moncrieff, and not Abu Nidal.

In a room on the floor below, the steady drip of an IV alleviating his severe dehydration, the diabetic terrorist leader was sleeping like a baby.

Moncrieff swung his legs over the side of the hospital bed, lifted the phone again, and dialed. "Yes, I would like to send a cable, please?"

Before the meeting adjourned, Katifa suggested that that evening when the Exchequer contacted Casino du Liban, the call be routed to Assad's villa so Assad could give the order to release the hostages. Indeed, she knew that Nidal couldn't contact the Exchequer, though she didn't know why; and, despite the hostages' being under Syrian control, she had correctly assumed that Assad couldn't either.

"Thank you, but that won't be necessary," Assad responded with a thin smile, surprising her. "The Exchequer makes *two* calls each evening."

A L M O S T forty-eight hours had passed since the USS *Cavalla* had put to sea. Proceeding at top speed, 200 meters beneath the surface, the submarine had crossed the Biscay Abyssal Plain and was off the coast of Portugal entering the complex range of trenches just west of the Straits of Gibraltar.

Commander Duryea scooped up the phone in the command center. "Sonar? Conn. Where's Alpha now?"

"Bearing one seven nine, range ten miles," Marv Cooperman reported. The patient sonarman had spent the better part of two days in his electronics-lined cubbyhole, tracking the Redfleet boat on the towed array.

"Stay on him," Duryea said, then whirling to McBride he ordered, "Break out a brit."

The AN-BRT1 was a radio-transmitting buoy that contained a cassette recorder and laser transmitter capable of sending a four-minute message. Transmission could be delayed up to an hour. This meant a submarine could be far from the source of the signal when sent, thereby communicating without revealing its position.

Duryea shrewdly planned to do just the opposite. He drafted a short message and gave it to the radio officer. "Set the timer for max delay," he ordered.

A short time later, the BRT was released through an aft airlock. It rose to the surface and was carried south by the swiftly moving Canaries current.

"Where's the TC?" Duryea asked, referring to the thermocline, a layer of abrupt temperature change between colder bottom and warmer surface currents; it acted as a barrier to active sonar, deflecting outgoing signals and trapping returns from the few that managed to penetrate.

"Three hundred forty meters, sir," McBride replied.

"Okay, let's see what he's made of," Duryea said. "Rig for dive and take her down to four hundred."

The *Cavalla*'s ballast tanks filled, her dive planes angled sharply, the propeller cut a massive vortex in the water, and she headed for the bottom.

The Alpha's sonarman detected the surge in cavitation and change in depth, and then the silence. "We've lost contact, Comrade Captain," he soon reported.

"Thermocline," Solomatin scowled, knowing that pursuit would be futile. Once lost, the *Cavalla* could run in sea trenches undetected. It was up to Redfleet strategic reconnaissance to pick up her trail now.

Cooperman's sonar arrays were strangely, pleasantly silent. "Clear water astern," he reported.

"He's waiting and wondering," Duryea said to McBride firmly. "Come to zero six five. All ahead full."

The *Cavalla* turned hard to port, steam from her reactor driving the twin turbines ever faster. Now, dead-centered on the Straits of Gibraltar, she began proceeding east toward the Mediterranean at top speed.

An hour later, when the BRT transmitted Duryea's message, the swift currents had already swept it more than 15 miles south of the Straits. SSIX, a satellite dedicated to submarine communications—one of five in geosynchronous orbit that made up the fleet satellite communications system—received and re-layed it.

Seconds later, inside a massive concrete blockhouse at Fort Belvoir, Virginia, the ground link where intelligence from spy satellites is gathered, a high-speed printer in the message center came to life.

FM: USS CAVALLA
TO: RTS KEYHOLE/FORT BELVOIR

REQUEST PRIORITY UPDATE COURSE AND
POSITION OF REDFLEET ALPHA.

LAST CONTACT 354012N/072823E. COURSE 015.

A clerk tore the cable from the printer and took it to a tracking room, where pensive technicians sat at rows of consoles, studying their VDT screens.

The RTS prefix stood for real time surveillance. Keyhole series satellites used a charged couple device to provide it. The half-inch-square CCD contained 640,000 pixels that continuously collected and transmitted data—which meant these were real time images.

The technician monitoring the sector of ocean in question was given Duryea's cable. He entered the geographic data on his keyboard, directing the satellite's optical system to the appropriate grid square and coordinates; then he began searching for a specific surface pattern created by a dived submarine's propeller.

Simultaneously, a Soviet EORSAT spy satellite had detected the BRT transmission and sent the data to a similar tracking facility in Pechenga on the Kola Peninsula. The coded message couldn't be deciphered but the signal's geographic coordinates were immediately radioed to the Alpha.

"He's south of the Straits," Solomatin said. He had no way of knowing the signal had come from a BRT and, as Duryea had planned, assumed it came from the *Cavalla*. "Come to zero two zero. All ahead full."

In Fort Belvoir's KH-11 tracking room, the technician reacted to a line of side-by-side swirls that had surfaced from the Alpha's twin props and were tracing across his screen. Though not detectable from ships or planes, the pattern was clearly visible to a high-altitude satellite and had measurable speed and direction. The technician dispatched the following to the *Cavalla*:

FM: RTS KEYHOLE/FORT BELVOIR
TO: USS CAVALLA

SURFACE WAKE DETECTED AT 364504N/065741E.
10 MILES SOUTH STRAITS OF GIBRALTAR.
COURSE 035. SPEED 44 KNOTS.

McBride whistled when he saw it. "He took the bait, sir. He's really cutting a hole in the water."

"Not to mention his throat," Duryea said.

A T   A B O U T the same time in Upper Heyford, the sun hovered low over the English countryside.

A good omen, Larkin thought, as the golden rays streamed through the canopy, warming the cockpit. He dipped a wing, putting the bomber on a heading for the air base, and thumbed the radio transmit button.

"Upper Heyford, this is Viper-Two," he said. "Request clear to land."

"We have you, Viper-Two," the tower replied. "You're CTL on one seven west. Winds are at one three five; ten knots."

"Copy that, Heyford."

The two F-111s circled to side-by-side landings and taxied to the hangar at the far end of the field. Larkin popped the canopy and climbed down from the cockpit. The name on his flight suit read MAJ W. SHEPHERD. All uniform badges and insignia were fastened with Velcro and easily changed.

He and Applegate had test-flown the F-111s several times since Larkin's return from Holy Loch. Special Forces aviators served as their weapons systems officers.

A cable was waiting for them in the office when they got to the hangar. Larkin tore it open, smiled at Moncrieff's message, and handed it to Applegate. It read:

READY TO PROCEED WITH TRANSACTION.

14

S H E P H E R D had been comatose for several days when his eyes finally fluttered open. He was in an unfamiliar bed, an IV sticking into his arm, the suffocating smells of illness filling his head.

Two security guards, making their morning rounds of the train yards, had found him—he was blue from the cold and naked, save for a torn T-shirt and a pair of skivvies. The derelicts had picked him clean: flight suit, boots, watch, dogtags, tape recorder, and wallet.

The guard with the metal chevrons pinned to his black cableknit returned to the security office at the gate, scooped up the phone, and dialed 999, London's toll-free emergency number.

A short time later, a white ambulance, its blue roof flasher glowing eerily in the ground fog, came racing down Leyton Road. The clumsy-looking van went round the eighteen-wheelers queued at the entrance to the yards and across the flyover that bridged the expanse of tracks, continuing to where Shepherd had been found.

Shepherd was taken to The London Hospital on Mile End Road. The dreary buildings of soot-blackened brick were well suited to the tough East End neighborhood, which had been terrorized by Jack the Ripper a century before. Since the end of World War II, Whitechapel's traditionally ethnic population of European Jews had gradually given way to Indians, who were now being supplanted by poverty-level blacks and Pakistanis.

The men's ward was on the second floor of the main building. The glossy white walls had long ago turned a pale nicotine yellow. A single row of lights hung overhead, the illumination dimmed by the dead flies in the bottom of the milk glass globes. Forty beds, separated by clothes lockers, lined the sides of the long, narrow room. A rectangular card at the foot of each bed displayed the patient's name in letters boldly printed with a black marker. Shepherd's name card was blank.

Administrators had no clue to his identity. But that wasn't unusual among the many indigents treated here. Like them, Shepherd was dirty, battered, and unshaven. The fact that he wasn't emaciated or suffering from exposure led them to conclude he was a victim of an all too familiar scenario: New arrivals to the street were constantly being preyed upon by the bands of hardened regulars. The army of homeless that roamed the city was growing at an alarming rate; engineers were becoming almost as common as laborers. Following standard procedure, London's Metropolitan Police had been notified; a check of their missing persons files shed no light on Shepherd's identity.

A nurse making her rounds noticed Shepherd pushing up onto an elbow and hurried to his side.

"Go easy now," she whispered, delighted that he had regained consciousness.

"Where am I?" he wondered feebly.

"In luck is what I'd say," the sprightly woman quipped, before hurrying off to fetch a doctor.

"Can you tell me who you are?" the doctor asked in a gentle singsong cadence as he leaned over Shepherd, examining him. He was a rail-thin Indian with coal-black eyes and a soft smile.

"Walt, Walt Shepherd," Shepherd muttered, his head throbbing. "Major, United States Air Force."

"I see," the young doctor replied with the amused smile of a man accustomed to hearing grandiose claims: Jesus Christ and John Lennon were the most common.

Shepherd heard the skepticism in his tone and slowly recited his serial number, adding, "I'm a pilot."

"Well, you've been with us for several days, Major," the doctor said, beginning to sense that Shepherd's claim might be genuine. He went on to explain how Shepherd got there and that they had been unable to identify him. "I'll be happy to let your people know you're with us, if you'll tell me who to call."

Shepherd just stared at him blankly, suddenly overwhelmed by the terrifying events that started coming back in a chilling rush: a montage of gunfire and blood; of screeching rubber and steel; of bone-crunching collisions and exploding fuel; and of hope, dashed by the cruel shattering of glass against his skull.

"Major Shepherd?" the doctor said, testing his response to the rank. "Major, are you all right?"

"Oh, sorry," Shepherd finally replied, coming out of it. He winced in pain, his hand going to the bandage on his forehead, where he'd been struck by the bottle. "Hurts. It hurts like hell."

"Yes, you've had a rather nasty knock on the head; actually, more than one," the doctor replied in his clipped musical cadence, having treated Shepherd for a severe concussion, scalp lacerations, and minor burns on his hands and face. "Now," he said in a gentle challenge, "you were going to tell me who to call—"

"Applegate," Shepherd finally replied in a dry whisper. "Major Applegate—Lakenheath."

It made perfect sense to call him. Shepherd never saw who shot at him from the balcony and had no reason to think it was Applegate. On the contrary, the major was with military intelligence and had conducted a bona fide debriefing after the incident with the Soviet Forgers. Besides, though Larkin and the others who had attacked him were wearing air force uniforms, it went completely against Shepherd's grain to accept that U.S. military personnel were involved. His unquestioning sense of patriotism wouldn't allow it.

THAT SAME MORNING, five hours before its scheduled launch, the raid on Libya was given the final go-ahead.

In the hangar at Upper Heyford, Larkin and Applegate were in a planning room, reviewing mission data at a map-covered plotting table, when one of the Special Forces clerks informed Applegate he had a call. The major left and crossed the hangar to his office to take it. His eyes widened at the doctor's message, his mind racing to cope with the knowledge that Shepherd was alive.

In The London Hospital, a nurse was at the foot of Shepherd's bed writing his name on the blank card when the doctor returned. "I'm afraid he insists on talking to you, Major," he said, displeased at the idea. "I told him more than once you were in discomfort."

Shepherd nodded and pushed up shakily onto an elbow. His double vision was gone but the moment he sat up, the room started spinning. They lifted him into a wheelchair and took him to the doctor's office.

"Can you identify these men, Major?" Applegate asked after Shepherd had explained what happened.

"Just one of them," Shepherd replied weakly. "His name was Larkin . . . Colonel Larkin."

"Larkin . . ." the heavyset intelligence officer repeated coolly, glad that Shepherd couldn't see the panic in his eyes. "Doesn't ring a bell. You sure they were in the military?"

"They looked and sounded like Americans, but—"

"Americans from Charm School," Applegate interrupted, referring to a Soviet KGB facility that was an exact replica of an American town: Only English was spoken; only American food was served; only American clothing was worn; only KGB agents, being trained to impersonate Americans, lived and worked there. "For all we know that run in with the Forger wasn't an accident," Applegate concluded, shrewdly embellishing the lie. "We'll have you picked up and taken to a military hospital as soon as possible. Meantime, I don't want anyone else to know you're alive. Whoever they are, whatever they're up to, they want you dead. Talk to no one, Major. That means nobody. Not even your wife. They may be watching her; may have tapped her phone trying to get a line on where you're hiding. Got it?"

"I understand, sir," Shepherd replied dutifully.

"Good. Now, put the doc back on," Applegate instructed, going on to impress upon the doctor the need for absolute secrecy and cooperation.

The nurse wheeled Shepherd back to the ward. He fell onto the bed, exhausted. Moments later, she returned carrying his flight suit, name stripe still affixed. It had been washed and folded. His cassette recorder and an envelope were on top of it.

"I think these belong to you, Major," she said, explaining that a comatose derelict several beds down the line was wearing the flight suit over his clothing when brought in the previous evening. The London Hospital's casualty room served the entire East End, and there was no other facility in the area where the derelict, who, like Shepherd, had been found comatose in the train yard, could have been taken.

Shepherd's wallet, credit cards, and identification were gone; but the envelope contained what was left of his cash: $63 and a few British pounds that the derelict, who had assaulted him, hadn't spent before succumbing to a drug overdose.

IN UPPER HEYFORD, Applegate had given the news to Larkin, who shuddered at the implications. "This whole fucking mission's on the bubble," he lamented bitterly, thinking about Fitzgerald and the DCI's emotional mandate.

"No need for it to burst," the big intelligence officer counseled. "Shepherd's just laying there groggy, waiting to be picked up; and we've got people who can handle it."

The two Special Forces guards who had played the role of SPs were given the task. "Kill him and use the same method of disposal," Larkin ordered; then he and Applegate returned to the computerized data that had been prepared for each F-111 crew by mission planning in Lakenheath.

Each package had been tailored to a specific target. It contained reconnaissance photographs; a foldout route book of the flight plan; and a sequential list of fly-to-points: latitude, longitude, elevation, and brief description of each, the last of these being the target itself.

ANITA was used to enter the alphanumeric target data into a computer in mission planning headquarters. Once encoded, the entire program was copied to tape; the cassette was inserted into a mission data loader, which was taken to the aircraft and cabled to an input port left of the nose wheel, adjacent to the com-cord jack; then with the push of a button, the target data was transferred from the MDL to the Pave Tack computer.

This entire operation was handled by mission planning technicians; however, neither they nor the MDL were indispensable. The data could have been entered directly into Pave Tack computers by pilot or wizzo via the nav-data entry panel, an alphanumeric keyboard in the cockpit used routinely to correct and update target information in flight.

Larkin and Applegate completed their data review, suited up, and were soon climbing into their F-111s.

The time was 5:13 P.M. when they took off from Heyford with the EF-111 radar jammers. As they streaked skyward, KC-135 tankers were lumbering into the air from Mildenhall. They rendezvoused over Land's End at the southeasternmost tip of England with twenty-two F-111F bombers from Lakenheath and one E2C Hawkeye.

The latter was the strike control aircraft, a flying radar installation that housed the mission commander and his staff. A saucer-shaped antenna atop the fuselage picked up the transponder signal of every F-111 in the strike force and displayed it on a radar screen. Strict radio silence would be maintained throughout the mission, which meant this was the only contact mission command would have with the bombers.

In precisely 7 hours 11 minutes, the F-111s and their Pave Tack systems, capable of acquiring, tracking, and bombing surface targets at high speed in total darkness, would be doing just that—all but two of them.

15

T H E   T I M E in Washington, D.C., was 12:32 P.M.

Congressman Jim Gutherie had put in a morning's work and was heading across town in his chauffeured car.

A week had passed since the bombing of the West Berlin disco. Rumors of military reprisals had been rampant but Gutherie hadn't given them much credence. A hostile act against another nation would have to be cleared with Congress—with *his* committee—in advance, and no effort had been made to do so. He had spent the weekend with campaign aides, mapping out strategy to reverse his continuing slide in the polls.

For years, his wife had been his most trusted political adviser. Since her accident, it was but one of many things in the congressman's life that had changed. Monday afternoons were another.

The women with whom he spent them were stunningly beautiful, with faces like models, which they sometimes were. Save for fiery tresses and galaxies of freckles sprinkled over her white skin, the redhead was always naked when he arrived. The blond worked in lingerie. Black stockings hugged her endless legs. Garters framed a tuft of golden wool glistening in the shadow of a bottomless teddy. Its bodice skimmed her upright nipples, which were all that kept it from falling.

The idea of being with another woman, while his wife—a passionate sex partner with whom he was still in love—lay in a hospital bed barely alive, tormented him, and he had sought professional guidance.

His committee work and his exposure to top-secret data narrowed the field to a handful of psychiatrists in the District who had the necessary security clearances.

Dr. David Kemper had been recommended by the CIA. His office was in a mansard-roofed structure on Connecticut Avenue. Its separate entrance and exit spared his patients the embarrassment of running into colleagues.

"You know, I'm wired all the time," Gutherie said as one session began. "I jog, I work out. It still takes me hours to fall asleep. I'm not myself."

"Well, what do *you* think it means?" Kemper asked from behind his neat moustache.

"Beats me. I'm still in love with my wife and everything. I mean, I don't even know what that's got to do with it; but lately, I don't know."

"Well, what I hear you saying, Jim," Kemper said with a trace of a smile, "is that you need to get laid."

"Yeah? Yeah, I guess I do."

"Anybody in mind?"

"Sort of."

Six months had passed since Dr. Kemper supported Gutherie's suggestion that he visit the turn-of-the-century townhouse behind the wrought-iron fence in the 2000 block of Decatur Place just north of Dupont Circle.

Now Gutherie lay in an elegantly furnished room, the blond's fingertips tracing over his trembling lips, "lost," as Sister Mary Janice, his eighth-grade teacher once put it, "in the depraved sins of the flesh."

Gutherie's breathing quickened in expectation as the redhead straddled his waist with her freckled thighs, then began sliding slowly backwards, capturing the head of his penis inside her. He shuddered as she continued inching back until her tight wetness consumed him. The soothing sense of security and well-being that Gutherie craved spread over him like a warm blanket.

"Oh, yes," the blond moaned softly, slowly undoing one of the pastel bows on the front of the teddy; soon her pointed breasts were free of it and one of her large nipples was in Gutherie's mouth.

"Oh, yes, yes; do we want to make it happen now?" the redhead prompted in a breathy whisper, segueing into a circular motion astride him.

"Yes. Oh God, yes, yes, now. Make it happen now."

He arched his pelvis, forcing her to grind against it, then began bucking beneath her until he emitted a series of long moans and collapsed into their arms. The congressman was wholly oblivious to the stress of public office and private pain, when suddenly a muffled twitter came from beneath the pile of clothing on the other side of the room.

Gutherie sat up, somewhat disoriented, trying to clear his head. His secretary had strict orders not to beep him at this hour except in an emergency; and she hadn't, not once, in six months. The congressman pulled the bedding around him, then took the phone from the nightstand and called his office. "What is it?" he asked anxiously when his secretary came on the line. "Something happen to my wife?"

"No, sir," she replied. "The White House called."

"The White House?" Gutherie echoed, feeling suddenly out of touch and wondering what was going on.

"You have a meeting with the president at the OEO in half an hour. Twenty-five minutes, now."

As a ranking member of the Intelligence and Oversight committees, Gutherie was often summoned to such meetings, but rarely on short notice.

The time was 3:58 when he arrived at the Old Executive Office Building across the street from the White House. He was ushered to a conference room, where congressional leaders, the secretaries of state and defense, the national security adviser, the CIA director, and the chairman of the Joint Chiefs had assembled.

"As you know," Lancaster began, "the War Powers Act requires, and I quote, 'that the President in every possible instance shall consult with Congress before introducing United States Armed Forces into hostilities,' and that's why you've been invited here today."

The congressmen sat up straighter in their chairs.

The president entered and, reading from typed notes, explained that the recent wave of terrorism had prompted him to authorize preemptive action. Tripoli and Bengahzi were the targets. When he finished reading, he pocketed his notes and left the meeting.

Lancaster presented the intercepted cables as evidence linking Libya to the Berlin disco bombing, then laid out the details of the operation.

"What about civilian casualties?" a senator asked.

"Every effort has been made to minimize collateral damage, sir," the chairman of the joints chiefs replied.

"Where do our allies stand?" another wondered.

"France and Spain have denied us use of their air space," the secretary of state replied.

"Frogs," Kiley muttered bitterly.

"Israel, Canada, and Mrs. Thatcher, of course, are with us," the secretary concluded.

"She better be," a congressman intoned. "She owes us one for the Falklands."

"She owes Qaddafi one for that cop he murdered," Kiley said, referring to Constable Yvonne Fletcher, who was gunned down outside the Libyan People's Bureau in 1984. He didn't remind them that the pistol had been traced to a shipment of weapons procured by renegade CIA agents.

"How much time we have?" Gutherie asked.

"ETA to target is two hours fifty minutes," Lancaster replied boldly, fully anticipating protest.

"Our bombers are in the air?" Gutherie exclaimed.

"Correct," the CJC replied. "F-111s are en route as we speak. Intruders have yet to be launched."

Uneasy glances flicked between the congressmen.

"Now that Congress has been consulted," Gutherie said sardonically, "what if some of us object?"

"The attack can be called off within ten minutes of strike time," the defense secretary replied.

"If that objection is unanimous," Kiley chimed in slyly, knowing the chance for such an accord was zero.

No objections were voiced, let alone a unanimous one. For in truth, none denied that the United States had been pushed to the limit or that the evidence was compelling. But Gutherie and the others *were* wondering: Why at night? When despite popular conception, daylight bombing techniques afforded a much higher degree of accuracy; a fact the Israelis had recently demonstrated by destroying eighteen Syrian missile batteries— against antiaircraft defenses far superior to Libyan installations —without losing a single aircraft. Furthermore, why use F-111s from faraway England? Why not hit *both* targets with carrier-based bombers?

It was pointless to ask now, to cross-examine the president's staff in the tense hours just prior to the strike. The media would do that. Indeed, within hours the litany of thorny questions would be asked.

Only Bill Kiley knew the answers would be lies.

The DCI had been feeling the strain of his years lately but he bristled with energy now. Fitzgerald and the other hostages would soon be delivered from their harrowing nightmare. He had no doubt that the cost, however steep, was more than worth it, and that CIA would get the credit. Victory and vindication. It was so close Kiley could taste it.

16

A LATE-AFTERNOON SIROCCO had subsided to a gentle breeze and by nightfall the temperature in Tripoli had dropped to a humid 81 degrees. The time was 11:16 P.M. on Monday.

At the Bab al Azziziya Barracks, Muammar el-Qaddafi, his wife, and their children went down a staircase into the basement of their porticoed home. The colonel led the way through a long tunnel to an underground garage that housed an armored personnel carrier. The garage was located well beyond the compound's walls to provide Qaddafi with an escape route should his citizens or disloyal military officers one day turn against him.

The vehicle, an all-wheel-drive Transportpanzer, had been manufactured to special order in West Germany by Thyssen-Henschel. Fitted with a cupola-mounted machine gun and eight huge puncture-proof combat tires, the TTP was fully amphibious. The rear troop compartment had been gutted and the interior comfortably outfitted as a mobile home, with a small galley and sleeping quarters. It was stocked with food, water, and clothing.

"Allah has willed this," Qaddafi said, referring to the raid, urging his family to take solace in Islam, which requires submission to the will of God. On another day, or at another hour, he might have reacted with raging anger. Neither his aides nor his wife of eighteen years could predict his mood swings, which ranged from submissiveness to his religion to enthusiastic support of terrorism—of the Islamic Jihad or holy war—in its name.

As soon as Qaddafi and his family were aboard, the Transportpanzer drove off, escorted by an armed military convoy. Its destination was the desert town of Hun, where a new national capital, its future dependent on the water that would one day flow through the Sahara pipelines, was under construction.

The leader of the People's Libyan Arab Jamahiriya sat deep in thought. Although he was the nation's leader, he had retained the rank of colonel and held no formal government office, to emphasize his kinship with the common people of his birth; other than his family, only General Younis and staff members involved in the scheme to acquire the supersonic bombers had been fore-warned; and though Qaddafi had been assured the upcoming raid was designed to "minimize collateral damage," he knew Libyans would die this night and he had agreed to it.

FIFTEEN HUNDRED MILES to the west, the spectral glow from F-111 cockpits streaked through the blackness. The bombers flew in tight RRC formations, one tucked left, right, and beneath each tanker. If detected by defense radars, the return from each radar resolution cell would appear on the screen as one aircraft, not four.

The strike force was approaching the Straits of Gibraltar when the high-speed extensible booms of the Stratotankers began lowering for the second of four refuelings. Minutes later, thousands of gallons of JP-4 fuel had been pumped simultaneously into each bomber.

When refueling was completed, Larkin, Applegate, and the members of the other F-111 crews each ingested a 5-mg amphetamine capsule to ward off drowsiness brought on by the long flight, ensuring they would be at peak sharpness over the target.

About an hour later, the inky blackness was broken by specks of light twinkling in the distance, where the port cities of Tarifa, Spain, and Punta Cires, Morocco, pinch the Straits to a width of 8 nautical miles.

The attack force was now 1,375 miles from Tripoli. ETA to target was 1 hour 42 minutes.

IN THE WATERY DEPTHS BELOW, the USS *Cavalla* was 500 meters beneath the Mediterranean, just off the Libyan coast. The continental shelf is unusually narrow here, extending less than 10 miles from shore before dropping off sharply. This meant the *Cavalla* could make a deep-water approach, minimizing the chance of detection.

To further diminish it, Duryea rode the currents that swirl counterclockwise from Tunisia and Sicily into Tripoli harbor, moving silently into position.

The submarine's interior had been in redlight since sunset, a daily event on dived boats, giving the crew a sense of day and night. It also preserved night vision for periscope surveillance should it surface.

Duryea was hunched over his chart table, his face bathed in the eerie glow from the luminous screen. He scooped up the phone and punched the button labeled Sonar.

"Talk to me, Cooperman—"

"I'm doing a three-sixty now, skipper," the sonarman replied. He was absorbed in the fuschia-colored readouts and the sounds of the sea singing in his headset, while he methodically switched through the various sonar arrays. "Usual surface traffic, nothing else."

"Good. Anything weird turns up, *anything*, I want to know right away."

"Aye-aye, skipper."

"Let's take her up to a hundred and go in," Duryea said to McBride firmly.

The exec relayed the command to the duty officer in the control room, and the planesmen who controlled the boat's depth and angle went to work.

The hiss of high pressure air and the rush of water being forced from the ballast tanks reverberated through the hull. The bow tilted upward, and the *Cavalla* began rising from the depths. She had just leveled off when the BQQ-5 dish in the bow detected another submarine.

Cooperman immediately reported it to the captain.

"One of ours?" Duryea prompted anxiously.

"Beats me, skipper," Cooperman answered, studying the acoustic signature pattern that was tracing across his monitor and printing out, simultaneously, on the console below. "This is going to sound weird but it's like nothing I've ever seen or heard before."

"Nuke? Diesel? Twin screw? Single? Take a shot," Duryea prompted, unsettled by the threat an unidentified submarine represented.

"Twins," Cooperman replied, pressing a key on his console to store the data in the boat's computerized acoustic signature library. "Probably a diesel. I'd put my money on a clunker; a real old one."

"What are the chances this antique is tracking us?"

"Slim and none, skipper. She's way out there," Cooperman replied, pressing a hand against one side of his headset. "She just cut back her engines. My guess is she's surfacing."

"Okay, talk to me if she starts getting nosy." Duryea hung up, swiveled to his keyboard, and encoded a command. A pulsing cursor appeared on the electronic chart table, marking the mystery sub's location. He watched it blinking at him for a moment, then turned to McBride and said, "Let's move into final position."

THE AMERICA'S PROW cleaved through the Mediterranean like Excalibur's blade, the broad flight deck at its hilt broken by silhouettes of A-6 Intruders lurking in the steam that belched from launch catapults. Its air group of eighty-five warplanes could deliver more destructive power than the entire navy in World War II.

In the combat center—a computerized maze of video monitors, Plexiglas charts, and status boards—tense young men, many still in their teens, were about to launch the air strike against Benghazi.

"Ready to launch!" the air boss barked.

On deck, the taxi director, alienlike in green helmet, goggles, earmuffs, and kerchief tied outlaw-style over his nose and mouth, dropped to one knee and thrust his right arm to the black sky.

The pilot of the A-6 in the catapult responded with a thumbs-up and shoved the throttle to the stops. The turbojets seared the pop-up exhaust baffle with blue-orange flame. The bomber strained at the massive steel hook until the engines had built up enough power to keep it out of what fliers call the box—too much speed to stop, too little to become airborne.

The instant launch-pressure had been reached, the catapult operator released the hook.

In less than 2 seconds, 25 tons of exotic metals and electronics were accelerated from a dead stop to 150 miles an hour. The bomber was 60 feet above the water when the Pratt and Whitney turbojets took over and sent the gleaming-white Intruder climbing into the blackness above the Gulf of Sidra.

IN WASHINGTON, D.C., the sun had set, leaving a luminous lilac haze in the sky. The time was 6:47 P.M.

In the oval office, technicians were adjusting lighting and camera positions in preparation for the president's address, which would follow the raid.

The chief executive sat in an anteroom, reviewing the script with his writers while a television makeup artist added some color to his complexion. When he was finished, the president headed for the situation room in the basement, where Kiley, Lancaster, and his other civilian and military advisers had gathered. He had just settled in his chair beneath the presidential seal when the chairman of the Joint Chiefs, who had taken a call, announced, "Intruders are in the air. ETA to target nine minutes fifty-three seconds."

AT OKBA BEN NAFI AIR BASE, a former U.S. Air Force installation on the coast just east of Tripoli, a platoon of infantry ringed hangar 6-South, where the two F-111s would be housed. Once called Wheelus Field, it was the most well equipped and defended of Libya's air bases, hence its selection as the landing site.

Inside the hangar, in an office that had been set up as a command post, General Younis anxiously awaited word that the bombers had arrived. His attention was riveted on an aide who was in communication with air traffic control in the tower.

"SAM batteries are ready, General," one of his officers reported, referring to the antiaircraft missiles that would defend the airport during the raid.

"You checked each and every one?"

"Yes, sir. Guidance radar is off. Only adjusted sixes have been mounted."

"Good. We wouldn't want to blow up our F-111s before we get our hands on them."

Indeed, Younis had been faced with the problem of shooting down two bombers without shooting them down. Antiaircraft fire was required to explain their loss during the raid and couldn't be curtailed; and though Libyan missile defense batteries would be forced to turn off their ground radar to prevent air-to-ground HARM missiles from homing on the signal, greatly diminishing their accuracy, the chance of a lucky hit had to be eliminated. Younis knew that both heat-seeking and radar-homing SAM-6s were fitted with proximity fuses, which detonated just prior to impact, and had ordered them adjusted to maximum sensitivity. This meant they would detonate, not just prior to impact, not even close to impact, but on the slightest detection of the flares and metallic chaff that would be released into the air by each bomber to confuse missile guidance.

IN THE COCKPIT of the lead F-111, the pilot glanced at his flight navigation monitor.

"Thirty miles to target," he announced.

The wizzo grasped the Pave Tack control handle in the sidewall and thumbed one of the buttons. A long cylindrical pod pivoted out of the plane's belly. Its spherical head began scanning the horizon with radar and infrared cameras, using the preprogrammed alphanumeric data to search for its target.

The pilot put the bomber into an attack dive. He leveled off at 500 feet and thumbed the countermeasures release button. Bundles of missile-distracting flares and chaff were ejected into the slipstream from ports beneath the stabilizers.

"One plus thirty," the pilot announced.

The F-111 was slicing through the darkness toward downtown Tripoli at 595 MPH when the wizzo reacted to the image of the Bab Al Azziziya Barracks on his screen. Columns of alphanumeric data flanked the image; one fixed, the other changing rapidly.

"One minute," the pilot said, turning over command of the bomb release mechanism to the Pave Tack computer.

"Target acquired," the wizzo replied, pressing a button that fired a pulsing red laser from the Pave Tack pod to the ground. The pencil-thin beam locked onto the target and began measuring the range, relaying the ever-changing alphanumerics to the Pave Tack computer. "We have a lock," he called out when the target indicator became fixed on Qaddafi's compound.

"Twenty seconds . . . ten . . . five . . . four—"

Electrical impulses activated the ejector feet on the bomb release units below the F-111's wings and, in a programmed sequence, four 2,000-pound GBU-15s were unleashed from the hardpoints.

The pilot punched the throttles to avoid the upcoming explosion. The agile warplane accelerated up and away but the Pave Tack pod, swiveling in its gimballed cradle, kept the laser locked on Qaddafi's compound.

Sensing devices in each bomb began making adjustments in the moveable tail fins. This kept the bombs homing on the laser's frequency, as if they were traveling on a wire stretched between warplane and target.

The time was 1:57 A.M. when the first percussive blast blew out the front wall of Qaddafi's residence.

"Yeah!" the wizzo exclaimed, having no reason to think Qaddafi wouldn't be at home. "Kiss it good-bye!"

IN DOWNTOWN TRIPOLI, in the deluxe Al Kabir Hotel on Al Fat'h Street where the international media was housed, the force of nearby blasts set chandeliers swinging and guests scurrying for cover.

The time was 2:03 A.M.—7:03 P.M. New York time.

On the ninth floor of the Al Kabir, a CBS News correspondent crouched next to the window of his room, talking by phone to anchorman Dan Rather, who had just started his nightly telecast.

"Dan," he reported. "Tripoli is under attack."

IN WASHINGTON, D. C., Congressman Gutherie and his staff were also watching the report on CBS.

"Put your microphone out that window and let us hear it," Rather urged the correspondent in Tripoli.

Sounds of explosions boomed from the television.

"Perfectly timed for the evening news," Gutherie cracked. "Only thing the White House didn't do was list it in *TV Guide*. Must be killing them they couldn't."

ON ANDREWS AIR FORCE BASE in Maryland, Stephanie Shepherd and her children were in the den, surrounded by Walt's air force memorabilia: recruiting posters, photographs of military jets, a large American flag, flying helmets, trophies, and academy citations and awards.

She had finished the Gutherie interview that afternoon by phone and was at her desk working on it—one eye on her word processor, the other on the television news. She stiffened as Dan Rather said: "Informed sources have told CBS News that United States Air Force F-111 bombers based in England are carrying out the surprise attack."

"Come up here with Mommy," Stephanie said to Jeffrey, who was playing with his trucks. "Come on," she coaxed, as she pulled him up onto her lap.

Five days had passed since she and Laura had phoned Walt and learned of his transfer to Upper Heyford. He never called back, and the feeling of not really being part of his life had begun haunting her, though now Stephanie thought she understood why he hadn't called.

HIGH ABOVE THE MEDITERRANEAN near Sicily, 300 miles from Tripoli's laser-slashed skies, the Hawkeye strike-control aircraft was in a holding pattern, monitoring the action on radar. It was out of skin-painting range, which meant pulse-doppler scanning couldn't pick up raw radar returns from the F-111s; only radio transponder signals, using special frequencies not detectable by enemy radar, were being tracked on the screens in the electronics-packed fuselage—alphanumeric data next to each blip denoted tail code, altitude, and air speed.

Radio silence had reduced C3—command, control, communications—to waiting. No signal to commence attack had been given by the mission commander; none would be given to cease. Each crew was on its own; each flew the sequence points to its target, bombed it, and proceeded to a holding area to regroup. All but two.

Colonel Larkin was approaching his target, a military installation in the desert, when he reached to the fuel control panel, lifted the red safety catch, and threw the toggle used to dump fuel.

At the rear of the aircraft, directly beneath the vertical stabilizer and centered between the engine exhausts, the conical fuel mast opened, releasing a burst of JP-4 into the bomber's slipstream.

Larkin flicked the toggle to off; then, capitalizing on a technique called torching, sometimes used by pilots to distract heat-seeking missiles, he hit the afterburners, igniting the fuel, which erupted in a massive fireball a distance behind the F-111. To any of the other crews that might be observing—crews concentrating on high-speed bombing and evasive maneuvering in total darkness —it would appear that one of the bombers had been hit by a surface-to-air missile.

The instant the fuel exploded, Larkin put the F-111 into a steep dive, pulled out at extremely low altitude, and shut off his transponder.

In the Hawkeye, one of the eight radar operators monitoring transponder signals stiffened apprehensively as an F-111 in his sector began losing altitude rapidly. Suddenly, the blip vanished from his screen. "One-eleven down, sir," he reported in a choked voice.

"Tail code?" the mission commander asked, knowing the crew wouldn't have broken radio silence even if able.

"One seven nine, sir."

The MC scanned his computerized roster. "Shepherd."

An operator at an adjacent console winced as a blip vanished from his screen. "Bastards got another one, sir."

Immediately upon acting out their crash scenarios, Larkin and Applegate made sweeping low-level turns onto headings for Okba ben Nafi and walled the throttles.

AT OKBA BEN NAFI AIR BASE, an air traffic controller, keeping a vigil for the F-111s, picked up the raw return on his radar as they came within skin-painting range.

"Two aircraft approaching," he reported to his anxious superiors in the hangar command post.

General Younis lit another cigarette and went outside to see the fast-moving, aerodynamic shapes emerging from the darkness; then, in an eyeblink, two fully armed United States Air Force F-111 attack bombers touched down and roared past in a startling blur.

Younis smiled, nodding to personnel who began rolling back the huge sliding doors. Soon the black needlenose of an F-111 stabbed into the hangar, followed by a second.

Libyan Air Force maintenance and ground crew personnel were waiting for them. They rolled ladders up to the cockpits the instant both bombers were safely inside. Larkin and Applegate popped the canopies and climbed down the ladders, followed by the Special Forces aviators who had acted as their wizzos. Each carried a small gym bag that contained civilian clothes.

"They're all yours, General," Larkin said to Younis, who came forward to greet them.

"You have brought ANITA with you?" the general asked, referring to the Pave Tack programming key.

"On the sub," Larkin replied, not too exhausted to share a little smile with Applegate. "I'll turn them over to Moncrieff soon as the hostages are aboard."

Younis grunted, led the way to the command post office, and

placed a call to Qaddafi at his quarters in Hun. While the general reported the good news, an aide went to another phone, dialed, and handed it to Larkin.

IN TRIPOLI HARBOR, on a desolate wharf where the hostages would be released, Saddam Moncrieff and Katifa Issa Kharuz stood in the darkness, scanning the expanse of choppy water.

That morning they had boarded a regularly scheduled Middle East Airlines flight in Beirut, arriving in Tripoli just before noon. They had spent the remainder of the day at the Bab al Azziziya Barracks, going over details of the exchange with Younis and other members of Qaddafi's military staff.

Now, as a steady breeze blew across the harbor, Moncrieff and Katifa waited. Soon, two vessels—the *Cavalla* and Abu Nidal's gunboat, which was delivering the hostages—would emerge from the foggy blackness and tie up on opposite sides of the narrow wharf; the hostages would walk the short distance between them. They had just spotted the gunboat's running lights streaking toward the wharf when the radiophone that Moncrieff was carrying twittered.

"Yes?" he answered in Arabic.

"Moncrieff, it's Larkin," the colonel said, the exhaustion evident in his voice. "We're here."

"So are the hostages," the Saudi replied, watching the gunboat making its way between two Libyan Navy patrol boats stationed in the harbor.

"Thank God," Larkin replied. "What about the *Cavalla?*"

Moncrieff glanced to the other side of the wharf.

The immense submarine was lurking just beneath the brackish water. Duryea had taken advantage of the fact that Tripoli harbor has some of the highest tides in the world, and moments earlier had quietly slipped into position at periscope/antenna depth. Only the upper head of the boat's main scope was visible. The command center had switched from redlight to blacklight—a condition of total darkness broken only by the dim glow of essential instrumentation—which dilated Duryea's pupils, maximizing his night vision.

The lanky skipper had his face pressed to the eyepiece of the periscope, panning it slowly as he tracked the gunboat across the harbor.

"Take her up," he ordered as the vessel reached the end of the wharf and began pulling into position.

The black water erupted into a tumultuous bubbling as the football-field-long hull began rising.

"Colonel? *Cavalla* just broke the surface," Moncrieff reported as water cascaded off the sub's sail. "It'll be good to see you."

"Tell me about it," Larkin said. "On our way."

Larkin, Applegate, and the two Special Forces aviators quickly exchanged their helmets and flight suits for the civilian clothing in their gym bags in order to maintain the cover scenario Larkin had given Duryea. Then the group piled into an unmarked Libyan Air Force helicopter that wasted no time in lifting off and heading for Tripoli harbor.

IN BEIRUT, on the sixth floor of the Turk Hospital, Abu Nidal's physician sat in his office studying a lab report. It baffled him, as had the previous one—which had prompted his order that the test be repeated. His notorious patient's health was an all-consuming concern and he had waited anxiously for the results. He pondered their implication, then headed down the corridor to one of the VIP suites in the private clinic.

Despite the late hour, Abu Nidal sat propped up against the pillows in his bed, reading reports from terrorist groups around the world that were faxed to Casino du Liban and delivered to the suite daily.

"How are you feeling?" the doctor asked.

"Better. Much better," Nidal replied, delighted at his progress. "It's like a miracle."

"No, it's called insulin," the doctor said with a smile, shaking a finger at his patient admonishingly. "All you have to do is take it regularly."

Abu Nidal's brow furrowed. "I *was* taking it."

"Certainly not as prescribed."

"Yes, of course," Nidal said adamantly.

"You're positive?"

"Yes, yes, absolutely positive. Why?"

"Well," the doctor replied, clearly baffled, "your blood workup found no evidence of it."

"None?"

"That's correct. I ran the tests twice just to be certain. I know it sounds odd but it was as if you hadn't been taking any at all."

"That doesn't make sense. I just started a fresh supply."

"I'd very much like to see one of those vials."

"I'll arrange for it right now," Nidal said, his eyes narrowing in suspicion at an upsetting notion that struck him. He swung his legs over the side of the bed, lifted the phone, and dialed. "Mobile operator, please."

IN TRIPOLI HARBOR, the breeze had died and a taut stillness prevailed. The two vessels flanked the wharf.

Duryea stood on the *Cavalla*'s deck. The team of navy SEALs armed with AR-16 assault rifles was deployed around him.

Directly opposite, heavily armed PLO terrorists, faces concealed by checkered kaffiyehs, lined the rail of the gunboat. The canvas shroud had been peeled from the 14-mm deck gun, which was loaded and manned.

Moncrieff stood alone on the wharf between the two vessels. His nerves crackled with tension as he watched Katifa walk up a gangway onto the gunboat's deck and disappear into the cabin.

Moments later she emerged, leading the hostages. They paraded behind her like a line of obedient schoolboys, uncertain as to their fate.

They were all men—faces gaunt from malnutrition and anxiety; pale from months—and, for some, *years*—of confinement in darkness. Seven men with atrophied muscles and minds who had been deprived of life's sweetness, their hope destroyed by the fear of being forever lost to the forces of political extremism and religious fanaticism. They stood there timidly, heads bowed, staring blankly into the night.

They were close, so close, Duryea thought, as he watched the deckhands roll a gangway into position. So close he could almost touch them. His eyes caught Fitzgerald's and he smiled, nodding reassuringly.

The haggard station chief was just committing his heart to the scenario, just starting to believe that he and the others were actually being released, when the ship-to-shore phone in the cabin behind him buzzed, shattering the tense silence.

It was Abu Nidal calling.

The gunboat captain's eyes filled with panic as they spoke. The instant he hung up, he began shouting in frenzied Arabic at the terrorists on deck. They sprang into action, descending en masse upon the group of hostages, and began roughly pushing and shoving them back into the cabin.

"What are you doing?" Katifa demanded, trying to stop them. "What's going on?"

The captain slammed the transmission into reverse and gunned the engines. The gunboat lurched and roared away from the wharf. "Shoot her!" he shouted, seeing Katifa's interference. "Shoot her!"

Katifa heard him and ran across the deck, intending to dive into the water to escape. One of the terrorists stepped out from behind the cabin, blocking her way, and fired a burst from his Skorpion. The rounds tore into Katifa's body, but her momentum carried her into him.

They both went over the rail into the sea.

Katifa was wracked with searing pain that radiated from each wound like internal flashes of lightning. The plunge into the chilly water had a pleasurable, numbing effect; she went into shock and lay there, floating face down, motionless.

The Palestinian went under and stayed under, fighting to shed the heavy cartridge belts girdling his chest, which were dragging him down.

"No! No, hold your fire!" Duryea shouted, concerned the terrorists would kill the hostages if the SEALs returned the fire.

Moncrieff was already sprinting across the wharf's rough-sawn timbers. He tossed the radiophone aside and dove into the oily water, remaining submerged as he began swimming toward Katifa.

Terrorists on the departing gunboat began spraying the surface with bursts from their Skorpions.

The helicopter carrying Larkin and the others had come in over the Old City, which borders the west end of the harbor. It had circled the wharf and was just touching down when the gunfire broke out. The four Americans piled out of the chopper and dashed up the gangway onto the *Cavalla*'s deck.

"What the fuck happened?" Larkin exploded.

"I don't know!" Duryea shouted over parting bursts from the Skorpions. "Shit just hit the fan!"

"Bastards!" Larkin exclaimed bitterly. "Let's get out of here."

"They your people?" Duryea asked, pointing far across the wharf to the water on the opposite side.

Larkin turned to see Moncrieff and Katifa in the center of a widening pool of blood. The Saudi was struggling to keep her afloat and swim toward the wharf.

"No," the colonel replied coldly, unwilling to risk the time it would take to maneuver the sub into position to rescue them, or to risk that once aboard they would inadvertently blow the cover story he had given Duryea. A hollowness grew in the pit of Larkin's stomach. He couldn't believe it had gone so wrong.

"Cast off!" Duryea shouted to McBride, who was standing on the bridge atop the sail.

The *Cavalla* was already slipping away from the wharf as Duryea, Larkin, and the others scrambled down deck hatches. The black-hulled submarine cut swiftly through the water and vanished in the night.

17

T H E   A I R   S T R I K E   W A S   O V E R.

For eleven and one-half minutes, the early morning silence had been rudely shattered by the thunderous roar of supersonic bombers and earth-shaking explosions, then replaced by the wail of countless sirens.

Flames were raging through the Bab al Azziziya Barracks on As-Sarim Street; dazed and panicked, Libyans were emerging from the rubble that covered downtown streets where the air was ripe with the pungent odor of cordite and death; the crews of F-111s were settling down for the seven-hour return flight to England; the mission commander was conducting an accountability check, confirming that two F-111s had been lost; navy Intruders were landing on the decks of carriers; and network anchormen were just wrapping up their evening broadcasts when the president took his seat behind his desk in the oval office.

"We Americans are slow to anger. We always seek peaceful avenues before resorting to the use of force, and we did . . ." the president said in his smooth, perfectly paced delivery, pausing just long enough before adding, "None succeeded. This raid was a series of strikes against the headquarters, terrorist facilities, and military assets that support Muammar el-Qaddafi's subversive activities. It will not only diminish his capacity to export state-sponsored terrorism, but will also provide him with incentives and reasons to alter his criminal behavior." He paused again, his lips tightening into an angry red line. "I'm sorry to report," he went on gravely, "that two of our aircraft were shot down and four of our brave young men gave their lives in the fight against terrorism. We have done what we had to do. If necessary we shall do it again."

T H A T night in London, two Special Forces agents arrived at The London Hospital on Mile End Road. White uniforms and maroon baseball caps with military insignia identified them as air force medical personnel. They had wasted no time in getting there; but it had taken hours to acquire the proper vehicle, attire, and identification, and several more to drive the 140 miles from Upper Heyford. It was 10:45 P.M. when they approached the nurse's station, pushing a gurney.

"We're here to pick up Major Shepherd," one of them announced genially.

"Oh, my," the nurse replied, glancing to the ID tag clipped to his pocket. "We weren't expecting you at this hour. There's a form you'll have to fill out," she said, hurrying off to fetch it. "I won't be a minute."

A patient, returning from the men's room at the end of the corridor, overheard them. He returned to the dimly lighted ward and crossed to Shepherd's bed.

"Shepherd?" he said, shaking him. "Hey, Shepherd?"

"Uh?" Shepherd awakened from a deep sleep. "Yeah, yeah, what is it?"

"Some people here for you."

"People?" Shepherd wondered groggily, the meaning of it finally dawning on him. "Oh, oh, yeah, thanks."

He pulled himself from the bed, intending to go to the bathroom. His knees buckled slightly and he fell back against the pillows to gather his strength.

The phone at the nurse's station was ringing when the nurse returned with the form. "I'm sorry to keep you waiting," she said, handing it to one of the Special Forces agents as she answered the phone. "Men's ward," she said brightly, wincing at the reply. "I'm sorry, doctor, we're quite understaffed at night, and—Certainly, doctor," she replied, jotting on a pad.

At the far end of the corridor, Shepherd, feeling steadier now, was pushing through a door on his way to the bathroom when he froze in his tracks, recognizing one of the ambulance attendants at the nurse's station. It was the SP he had bashed with his flight helmet the night he escaped from Upper Heyford.

Shepherd had no doubt they had come to kill him; nor that Applegate had sent them. Indeed, as Applegate had ordered, Shepherd had told no one else where he was, not even Stephanie, and now he knew why Applegate had wanted it that way. He leaned back behind the half-open door, closed it slowly, and returned to the ward, his mind racing in search of a way to elude them.

A few minutes later, the agent finished filling out the transfer form and signed it. The nurse was still on the phone. "Be all right if we get Major Shepherd ourselves?" he prompted.

"If you don't mind?" the nurse whispered, covering the mouthpiece. "The patients' names are on the beds. They're fast asleep. Go about it quietly, if you will?"

"No problem."

"Oh, lovely," she said, relieved, gesturing to the set of battered double doors at the end of the corridor. "I'm sorry, doctor. Could you repeat that?"

The agents had no trouble finding Shepherd's bed. One of them removed Shepherd's flight suit from the open locker and folded it. The other positioned the gurney to make the transfer, then peeled back the bed covers and slipped a pistol from his shoulder holster. He had the butt poised to render the sleeping occupant unconscious when he noticed the ponytail flopped across the pillow and recoiled at the sight of the comatose derelict.

"This isn't Shepherd," he said in a tense whisper.

They had Shepherd to thank for it. On returning to the ward, he had exchanged name cards with the derelict who had attacked him; then, he removed his hospital gown and, knowing he would be conspicuous in his flight suit, he put on the shirt and blue jeans that were in the derelict's locker, leaving the flight suit in their place. He slipped out a door at the far end of the ward, made his way to a service entrance, and went down one of the black wrought-iron staircases that led to Mile End Road. A street market filled the median between the east- and west-bound lanes. It was deserted at this hour, the voices haggling over prices silenced, the boxes of merchandise locked away. Shepherd was stumbling toward it when he saw a bus approaching. He waited in the shadows of the curbside shelter and flagged it down.

The conductor thumbed the clumsy ticketing machine that hung at his waist, watching with amusement as the apparently inebriated passenger struggled to climb aboard; the aging fellow's grin turned to a sour scowl as Shepherd stuffed an American dollar into his fist and plunged unsteadily down the aisle into a seat.

About a half hour later, the red double-decker bus had crossed

Stepney and was winding through Poplar. Shepherd was feeling
woozy. He feared passing out in public and falling into the hands
of authorities again. The bus turned into Preston's Road, where
the Isle of Dogs juts boldly into the Thames, bending it sharply.
The street was lined with rundown hotels. Shepherd got off the
bus at the corner. He took a room in the Wolsey, a grim edifice
with crumbling plaster and torn, yellowed curtains, paying cash
in advance. The lumpy mattress felt like a waterbed, and he fell
asleep instantly.

THE FOLLOWING MORNING in Camp
Springs, Maryland, Stephanie Shepherd's station wagon came
down Perimeter Road and turned into Ashwood Circle. She had
driven her daughter to school, then delivered her piece on Congressman Gutherie to the *Capitol Flyer* offices. Unable to sleep
after the reports of the air strike, she had worked late into the
night on the article.

"Mrs. Shepherd?" a man's voice called out softly as she got out
of the station wagon.

Stephanie freed Jeffrey from his seat belt, and turned to see
three air force officers approaching from a government car at the
curb. One was a chaplain.

"Can we give you a hand with those?" he asked, gesturing to
the groceries.

She had seen casualty notification teams knock on other doors;
seen the solemn faces and somber cadence; and she knew before
another word was said that something had happened to her husband.

"Yes. Thank you," she replied evenly, recalling she had promised herself she would respond with dignity and strength should
this moment ever come. She handed them the groceries, scooped
up Jeffrey, and led the way inside. They sat in the den amid the
military memorabilia and toys. Jeffrey began playing with a truck.

Stephanie couldn't imagine the truth, nor could these officers
tell her. Indeed, their emotion was genuine as they reported precisely what 3rd Air Force Command and Pentagon officials believed had happened.

"Your husband died in the service of his country," the chaplain
said.

"Yes, I know," Stephanie replied weakly.

It was a common response. Families of men in combat often subconsciously accept their deaths as inevitable, in defense against the terrible shock.

"His one-eleven was hit by a surface-to-air missile during the raid on Libya," one of the officers said. "We have no reports of the crew ejecting."

"I understand," Stephanie said, his words dispelling any hope that Shepherd might eventually be found alive. She tilted her head thoughtfully, taking small comfort in the knowledge that he had died doing what he loved.

"Major Shepherd's effects will be forwarded as soon as possible," said the other officer. "On behalf of the president and the United States Air Force, we extend our condolences and sympathy."

"Thank you," Stephanie said, voice cracking with emotion. "Thank you very much."

"God bless you," the chaplain said.

Stephanie responded with a fragile smile. She showed them to the door, closed it, and stood there traumatized, fingers knotted, the tears running in a steady stream down her cheeks, the shattering words echoing over and over, "Your husband died in the service of his country; your husband died in the service of; your husband died; died; died; died . . ."

She was pulling a sleeve across her eyes, trying to regain her composure when a toy truck rocketed across the floor, startling her. An instant later Jeffrey came crawling after it. He looked up at her, his head cocked to one side, open-faced and innocent. Her lower lip started to quiver, then the grief overwhelmed her. She slid to the floor numbly and hugged the child to her bosom.

THAT SAME DAY, on London's Isle of Dogs, it was well past noon when Shepherd awoke to the sounds of the bustling waterfront streets below. He dragged his aching body out of bed and down the corridor to the bathroom. His elbow brushed the wall, sending a cascade of peeling paint chips onto the floor like confetti. The face that stared back from the cracked mirror startled him. He had a heavy growth of beard, a small bandage across one side of his forehead, and a purple discoloration on his jaw. He took a cold shower, which invigorated him, then headed for the nearest pub and ordered a roast beef sandwich and a cup of coffee.

The Great Auk's Head on West Ferry was buzzing with the lunchtime crowd of dock workers, aproned market clerks, and seamen. The air strike on Libya was the topic of conversation; and the president of the United States was on the television above the bar, holding a press conference.

Shepherd watched in disbelief as the chief executive announced that he and Captain Foster had died in the raid on Tripoli. Despite the fact that he was alive, that assassins were hunting him down, the president was telling the world that he had died heroically. Shepherd didn't know why; and he still didn't know if those trying to kill him were spies, terrorists, or renegades within his own government; but he was certain that military, diplomatic, and law enforcement officials were to be avoided until he did. Having paid for the hotel, he had $43 in cash and no credit cards. The only people he could trust were unavailable: Brancato in a hospital bed; and Stephanie, 3,500 miles away. Shepherd glanced across the pub at the phone booth, aching to call her, aching to say, "Hi, babe, I'm alive. I love you. I need your help." But he knew how they worked: their phone would be tapped; mail intercepted; family surveilled. Applegate had told him; he just failed to mention that his people would be doing it.

Shepherd sat there, absentmindedly stirring the coffee, searching for a way to contact her safely; and then the pieces began falling into place. Whoever they were, he would appear to play right into their hands; do exactly what they expected; their zeal and professionalism would do the rest. It was a long shot, but the risk factor was low and it was all he had. He finished the sandwich and returned to his hotel room. It was a dump, to be sure, but the sun streaming through the window gave him a good feeling. He took his cassette recorder from a pocket and turned it on.

Book Two

THE UNITED STATES HAS
NOT SWAPPED BOATLOADS
OR PLANELOADS OF
AMERICAN WEAPONS FOR
THE RETURN OF AMERICAN
HOSTAGES.

—RONALD

REAGAN

18

THE TIME WAS 7:16 A.M. Eastern Standard Time.

A maintenance van entered Andrews Air Force Base through the systems command gate just off Allentown Road. The technician behind the wheel wore an identification tag clipped to his breast pocket. It displayed his picture and security clearance, and identified his employer as SOUTHEASTERN BELL but, in truth, the quiet, unassuming fellow worked for Bill Kiley's Company.

The van proceeded down Perimeter Road to a huge windowless building that contained telephone switching equipment for base housing and offices.

The technician left the van, and entered the hardened structure, proceeding through the vast interior to the towering racks of switching equipment that routed incoming international calls. Each was identified by a country dialing code.

Rack 044 handled all calls originating in England.

The technician rolled the track-mounted ladder into position, climbed to a work platform, and opened his attaché case. It contained tools and electronic devices aligned in neat rows. He removed one of the latter from a sealed plastic bag and went about installing it in the panel.

This wasn't a standard bugging device but a unique communications interceptor that was a vital part of a damage control plan hatched by Kiley in the tense hours following the air strike and aborted hostage exchange.

That was more than twelve hours ago.

On leaving Tripoli harbor, the *Cavalla* had joined the 6th Fleet in the Mediterranean beyond Libyan waters.

Larkin disembarked, carrying the aluminum attaché that contained the ANITA codes. He, Applegate, and the two Special Forces agents transferred to the USS *America*, presenting themselves as intelligence operatives brought out of Libya. The failure of the rescue mission meant that "need to know" rules were still in force and no mention was made of the hostages. Larkin went straight to the carrier's communication room, called Kiley on a secure satellite link, and gave him the bad news.

"The hostages . . ." Kiley said as soon as Larkin had finished. "They were all on deck—Fitz was with them." They were statements, not questions.

"Yes, sir," Larkin replied.

"What about a fix on the gunboat's position?"

"Not yet, sir. *Cavalla*'s working on it."

"I need Duryea right away," Kiley ordered.

When the hookup was made, he and Duryea formulated a plan to use the team of navy SEALs aboard the *Cavalla* to rescue the hostages should the gunboat be located.

Soon after, Larkin and Applegate were flown from the carrier to an air base in northern Spain, where they boarded separate military jetliners.

A P P L E G A T E ' S flight to Mildenhall RAFB in England took just under three hours. The two Special Forces agents informed him Shepherd was still on the loose.

Applegate immediately contacted Kiley at CIA headquarters in Langley and briefed him. The DCI decided against including British military and civilian authorities in the manhunt; CIA couldn't very well ask for help in finding a pilot the president had just announced died in the raid on Libya. Instead, a discreet search under Applegate's direction was mounted. He and the two agents wasted no time in leaving for the hospital on Mile End Road in London, where Shepherd had been last seen, a two-hour drive from Mildenhall.

L A R K I N was still high over the choppy Atlantic, several hours from touchdown, unaware of the problem. The dexadrine had done its job too well and he couldn't sleep. The details of the failed mission raced through his mind like an endless videotape replay. It wasn't the fact that he had murdered good men in cold blood that tormented him, but that he had done so and come up empty.

The time was 10:14 A.M. when the flight landed at Andrews.

Larkin cleared customs, went to the longterm lot where he had left his car, and drove directly to Langley for a debriefing session.

"Morning, sir," the colonel said wearily, as he entered the DCI's seventh-floor office.

Kiley was standing at the window, reviewing a copy of Shepherd's personnel file, and didn't respond immediately. "Hello, Dick," he finally said in a subdued tone.

"Tough one to lose, sir."

Kiley nodded glumly. "It gets worse," he replied, going on to explain that Shepherd was still at large.

Larkin paled and fought to maintain his composure.

"Applegate figures he's still somewhere in London. We have a full-court press in the works. According to this we might very well need it," Kiley concluded, indicating Shepherd's file. He turned to a page he had marked and, with grave expression, read, " 'Major Shepherd is a precise and resourceful thinker. Throughout his career he has demonstrated an unusually high aptitude for tactical expertise and innovation—' "

"I'll leave for London immediately," Larkin offered stiffly, anxious to repair the damage.

The DCI shook his head no. "A.G. can handle it."

Larkin nodded numbly. He was certain Kiley knew how badly he wanted to fix it and was purposely denying him the chance as punishment.

"The good news is we had a cable from Duryea. He has a pretty tight fix on that gunboat."

"She hasn't made port," Larkin ventured, the glaze lifting from his eyes. "The hostages are still aboard . . ."

Kiley nodded and allowed himself a little smile. "*Cavalla*'s on an intercept course. Odds are we can come out of this with what we want if we lick this Shepherd thing."

19

"**I LOVE YOU, BABE.** I love you with all my heart," Shepherd said, feeling the words more than he ever had in his entire life.

He clicked off the recorder, rewound the tape, and played back the entire message he had dictated. Satisfied, he rewound the cassette again and removed it from the recorder. That was the easy part. The rest, the things he usually took for granted—a pen, an envelope, postage—were another matter.

He sat in his shabby hotel room, staring out the window at the bustling waterfront streets below until the screech of a boat whistle pulled him out of it; then he slipped the cassette into a pocket of the unfamiliar shirt and went downstairs to the front desk.

The clerk was a rotund woman whose huge bottom hung over the sides of her stool. She was opening mail with an old paring knife she kept handy for the task.

"Excuse me?" Shepherd said. "Would you have an envelope and a pen I could borrow?"

The clerk slit open an envelope and removed the contents. "Know what I always say? Not a borrower or lender be. Now, *leasing* on the other hand . . ."

Shepherd grimaced and reached into his pocket.

"A pound would do nicely," the clerk said, plucking the coin from Shepherd's palm. She handed him a worn ballpoint and resumed slitting open the mail.

"Excuse me, but I think you forgot the envelope."

"Right you are, sir," she said, offering him one of those she had just opened.

"I'm afraid that's already been used," Shepherd said, forcing a smile.

"Oh, right you are again, sir," she said, as if she hadn't noticed. She opened a drawer and removed one of those sickly blue air mail envelopes Europeans favor and handed it to him.

"I'd prefer a more substantial one," Shepherd said, fingering the tissue-thin paper with concern.

"You're a bloody picky one, aren't you?" she whined. "This isn't the Hilton, you know."

"I've noticed," Shepherd retorted, unable to resist. He took the envelope and walked toward the lift, intending to return to his room; but his eyes were drawn to a pay phone on the opposite wall. An overwhelming compulsion surfaced and took hold of him. He knew better, knew it would be a mistake to give in to it, but the temptation grew until he found himself striding boldly toward the phone, sorting through his pocket change; then he paused suddenly, glanced over his shoulder at the desk clerk and changed direction, charging through the lobby and out into the street.

"Piss off," the clerk muttered under her breath, watching him go. She took the knife and slit open another envelope with a flick of her pudgy wrist.

Like many London phone booths, the one on Preston's Road had a royal crown embossed above the entrance and a list of international tariffs and dialing codes on the wall. Shepherd's heart pounded with anticipation as he lifted the receiver and thumbed a one pound coin into the slot. He hesitated momentarily, then sent the second after it with a flick of his thumb and dialed.

Thirty-five hundred miles away, in the telephone switching center at Andrews Air Force Base, the device that CIA had wired into international board 044 kicked in. It intercepted the incoming signal and diverted it to a computer that, prior to the connection being made, screened the number against a list: Shepherd's home and the homes and offices of his friends, military associates, and minister. It took just several hundredths of a second to screen each call. Those that weren't on the list were put through; those that were, were handled differently.

Shepherd leaned against the wall of the crimson booth, listening to the hollow hum of the line. The first ring sent a surge of adrenaline through him.

Steph, it's me, he would say the instant she answered. I'm alive, I love you, I need your help. So what if the phone was tapped? What could they do once he had said it? They couldn't stop him; he would just blurt it out and take his chances.

The phone rang again; and then again and again.

No one answered.

Shepherd had no way of knowing Stephanie was at home; no way of knowing CIA hadn't used a listening device, but one that shunted the call to a phantom extension that would ring forever. Indeed, despite the advantages of eavesdropping, Bill Kiley's foremost priority was to prevent Shepherd from making contact, from revealing he was alive, especially to his wife. Others Shepherd might somehow contact could be manipulated, could be convinced it was a hoax or a crackpot, could somehow be kept at bay until Shepherd could be terminated. That was CIA's strong suit. But not a wife who knew her husband was being screwed by his government; not a *military* wife. No, Kiley had learned from experience they were the most dangerous because their outrage was driven by monumental feelings of betrayal; and whether by lover or bureaucrat, hell, indeed, hath no fury like a woman scorned.

The phone rang more than a dozen times.

Shepherd finally hung up and stood there for a long moment, coping with the crushing disappointment. The thick brass coins clunked into the return cup. He scooped them into his palm, glanced about cautiously, and left the booth.

N O T   F A R   A W A Y on Mile End Road, the street market on the traffic median opposite The London Hospital was in full swing, an international mix of housewives milling about them in search of bargains.

Applegate and the Special Forces agents, dressed in casual civilian clothes, stood among the white canvas kiosks. The M11 motorway from Mildenhall had been backed up and the drive to London had taken somewhat longer than anticipated.

"You sure that's it?" Applegate asked, pointing to the wrought-iron staircase next to the ambulance ramp.

"Positive," one of the agents replied. "He couldn't get to any of the other exits without passing us."

"He took the bus," Applegate said flatly, as his eyes came to rest on a shelter across the street.

"Or a taxi."

"Taxi . . ." Applegate echoed skeptically. "In this neighborhood? At that hour? No way." He stepped off the median without waiting for an answer, snaked between the vehicles that were slowing for the traffic signal on the corner of Turner, and crossed to the shelter where the bus schedule was posted.

The London Hospital was the oldest in the city and served many communities: Whitechapel, Hackney, Deptford, Stepney, Bromley-by-Bow, Millwall, and countless others, which meant this stop functioned as a major hub.

"He could be anywhere," one of the agents announced, catching up.

"What time last night?" Applegate asked.

"Ten fifty-two," the agent replied, referring to a copy of the patient transfer form.

"He must've caught the ten fifty-five," Applegate ventured, giving the bus schedule a quick glance.

They returned to their car and drove a few miles to the London Transport Depot just east of Blackwall Tunnel, where Mile End Road turns into High Street.

Applegate showed his military identification to the dispatcher, and explained he was an intelligence officer, trying to find a man involved in thefts of classified data from RAF bases. He was seen boarding an East End bus the previous evening.

The dispatcher pointed out the conductor who had worked the bus in question, an elderly fellow hunched over a counter, tallying the previous night's fares.

"It's hard to be sure," the conductor said, studying the photo of Shepherd. "But it might've been him. Yes, yes, I think he could be the one."

"The one?" Applegate echoed, gently. "The one who what?"

"Who paid his fare with this," the conductor complained, holding up an American dollar he had set aside. "And he was bloody pissed too, if you ask me."

"You remember where he got off?"

The conductor's face tightened with uncertainty. "There was a time I'd have had it just like that," he replied, dismayed. "My wife says our Yorkie has a keener . . ." He paused, his eyes coming to life, and said, "Isle of Dogs. Yes, Isle of Dogs, it was. Preston's Road."

Applegate went to a phone booth outside the bus depot, removed the yellow pages from the hanger, tucked it under his arm, and returned to the sedan. One of the Special Forces agents compiled a list of hotels and rooming houses while they drove to the Isle of Dogs.

They began with the one nearest the bus stop on Preston's Road, a seedy rooming house on the street that ran along the Isle's western perimeter.

"One of your guests?" Applegate asked, showing the clerk Shepherd's picture. "Checked in last night maybe?"

The weathered fellow shook his head no without taking his eyes off the racing form that was spread across the desk in front of him.

"It might help to look at the picture," Applegate prodded, his patience worn thin by fatigue.

"There's no need," the clerk explained matter-of-factly. "We're bloody empty, save for me and the owner; have been for three days."

Applegate and the agents made stops at two more hotels with similar results. Next on their list was the Wolsey.

SHEPHERD returned to the hotel, hurrying through the lobby to the lift. Dumb; dumb to have chanced calling, he thought as the gate slammed shut and the lift began its rickety ascent. He knew better; knew the tape was his best shot; his safest shot. What had come over him? Why had he weakened? He was entering his room when he realized that the bizarre sequence of events, which had transformed him from cocky, high-tech pilot to vulnerable, survive-by-your-wits fugitive, had shaken his confidence and sense of identity; and that even just listening to Stephanie's voice—to one of the children—would have provided sustenance and the contact with reality he so desperately craved.

He settled in the chair next to the window, set the envelope on the sill, and addressed it to Stephanie. Then he wrapped several lengths of bathroom tissue around the cassette to protect it and also prevent it from puncturing the envelope. The soft padding filled it neatly. Shepherd moistened the flap and was running a fingertip across it when he heard several car doors slam in rapid succession and glanced out the window to the street.

Applegate was walking swiftly from a gray sedan toward the hotel entrance, the two agents at his heels. In the lobby Applegate showed the photograph of Shepherd to the desk clerk.

"Familiar?"

The clerk put her elbows on the counter, her flabby underarms hanging in a catenary to the worn Formica. "Nothing real distinctive about him, is there?" she wondered, solicitously.

Applegate took a ten pound note from his pocket and snapped

it between his thumbs and forefingers. "Yes or no?" he demanded impatiently.

"Room two oh six," the clerk said, snatching the note from Applegate's hand. "Oh, he's here all right," she offered, anticipating the next question.

"How many ways out of here?"

"Main and service," she replied, indicating a second door at the base of the staircase.

The agents remained in the lobby, covering the exits. Applegate took the lift to the second floor.

It groaned to a jerky stop. He slid the gate back just enough to exit, guiding it closed to keep it from slamming. Shepherd's room was at the end of the hallway beyond the stair landing. Applegate drew his pistol, walked to the room, and leaned to the scarred door, listening; then he turned the knob slowly. The latch withdrew with a soft clack and the door opened slightly. Applegate sent it smashing back into the wall in the event Shepherd was behind it. The knob bashed a hole in the plaster.

The room appeared empty.

Applegate entered, glancing about cautiously, peered beneath the bed, then advanced toward a closet. He threw open the door, ready to fire.

Shepherd was outside in the hallway, concealed in the angular space beneath the staircase. As soon as Applegate entered the room, he slipped from his hiding place and hurried to the lift.

Applegate was staring into the empty closet when the gate slammed. He whirled at the sound and ran into the hallway in time to glimpse the lift rising behind the decorative grillework. He stepped quickly to the stairwell, leaned over the rail, and shouted. "Hey! Hey, he's heading for the roof!"

Applegate took off up the staircase, both agents following after him from the lobby below.

Shepherd had sent the lift on its way and returned to the space beneath the staircase. He crouched in the darkened cranny listening to the footsteps approaching; soon they were thundering directly overhead, sending a cascade of dust atop him. He waited until they made the turn on the third floor landing, then he started down the stairs.

The desk clerk was keeping a vigil at the base of the staircase. Shepherd came rocketing past her and made a beeline for her counter.

"Hey! Hey, what the bloody hell are you doing?" she shouted, waddling after him.

He leaned over the counter and snatched the paring knife she used as a letter opener, then charged past her to the street. She lumbered across the lobby to the staircase. "He's down here!" she bellowed through cupped hands. "The bloody creep's down here!"

Applegate and the agents had already realized they'd been duped and reversed direction. They came clambering down the staircase and through the lobby to the street, the clerk padding after them.

Shepherd was at the corner, getting into one of the black taxis that patrolled London's streets like convoys of teeming ants.

Applegate and the agents ran to their car. He opened the door, then paused and slammed it in disgust without getting in. "Son of a bitch!" he shouted, sending a frustrated kick into the front tire, which had been slashed.

The taxi turned the corner and drove off.

"Where to, sir?" the driver asked.

"A post office—a busy one," Shepherd replied, slipping the paring knife into his sock.

"That would be the main off Trafalgar Square," the driver said, selecting not only a busy but also a distant post office. "Tough morning?" he prompted. "I mean it's not every day a chap runs from a hotel and slashes a tire."

"Pardon?" Shepherd said, stiffening. "I'm afraid you're mistaken about that."

"I saw you right here, I did." The driver tapped his rearview mirror.

"Better just pull over and let me out."

"You don't want me to do that, sir, believe me."

"Why not?"

"Because I'd have to tell the police where I dropped you. I could lose my license if I didn't. Of course, they pay for information. Twenty pounds minimum if it works out, and I have a feeling you're worth quite a bit more. Maybe fifty, even a hundred."

"I don't have that much," Shepherd replied, getting the driver's point. "I'll take my chances on the street. Pull over."

"I haven't finished," the driver replied. "How much were you paying in that hotel?"

"Fifteen pounds."

"Well, we know you're not staying there tonight, don't we? Now, I can put quite a lovely roof over your head for ten; you guarantee me two nights and we all make out. See how it works?"

Shepherd nodded warily. "I'll think it over."

"Plenty of time," the driver replied.

A short time later, he had driven the length of the Strand past Charing Cross Station and turned into Duncannon, stopping in front of a Greek revival structure ringed by huge columns of bloated granite.

"Well?" he prompted, turning to Shepherd.

"Where is this place?"

"On the waterfront. Quiet, no one about. I've no doubt you'd find it to your liking, if you follow me?"

Shepherd studied him, wrestling with the decision.

"I'm going that way from here," the driver went on as inducement, concerned he might lose the sale. "I'll wait until you're finished if you like."

Shepherd nodded and turned to get out of the cab.

"That's three pounds fifty," the driver said sharply, resetting the meter.

Shepherd paid him and hurried toward the post office. He was pushing through the door when he saw the taxi's reflection in the glass, saw the driver turn to the microphone next to him, and begin talking.

A sickening chill came over Shepherd. Was the driver reporting in to his dispatcher or to Applegate? Was he just a hustler making a buck any way he could? Or was he one of them, one of Applegate's operatives who had slyly ensnared him? But he had picked the cab from several on the street; could Applegate's people have been driving every one of them? Bet your ass, Shepherd decided. He's in the post office on Trafalgar Square, he imagined the driver saying to Applegate with a smug smile. Come get him.

As Shepherd crossed the lobby, his eyes darted to a newspaper in a nearby trash receptacle. The headline proclaimed U.S. BOMBERS ATTACK LIBYA. His photograph was one of those that accompanied the story. He fetched the paper, using it to shield his face while he waited in the postal queue. It inched forward at an unnervingly slow pace. At least ten minutes passed before he stepped to the window and mailed the cassette.

A light rain was falling when he came out of the post office. The square was a bustle of homeward-bound office workers, scurrying about Nelson's Column beneath umbrellas on their way to the Underground. He scanned their faces warily; not one approached or took notice of him; there was no sign of Applegate or the Special Forces agents as Shepherd hugged the facade of rain-darkened stone and peered round the corner.

The taxi driver was slouched behind the wheel, reading a magazine. There was nothing anxious or vigilant about him; nothing to suggest he was anything other than what he appeared to be, Shepherd thought, dismissing his previous anxiety as paranoia. It might be a week before Stephanie got the tape and could take action; furthermore, he had no credit cards and little cash. Deciding it would be more difficult for Applegate to track him down again if he avoided hotels, he hurried through the rain to the taxi.

"Sorry to be so long," Shepherd apologized as he got in and pulled the door closed after him.

"Does that mean we have a deal?" the driver asked.

"Something you should know, first. Those men were trying to kill me."

"I didn't think they had news of an inheritance," the driver quipped. He put the cab in gear and drove off, the wipers slapping noisily at the windscreen. "By the way, I'm Spencer, Spencer Quait."

"Smith," Shepherd replied. "Walt Smith."

Spencer drove south on Craven to Victoria Embankment, the broad boulevard that snaked along the Thames, then east toward the waterfront into ever-narrowing streets until the stately granite buildings gave way to a russet landscape of abandoned warehouses that lined the approaches to Blackwall Tunnel.

Dusk had fallen by the time the taxi started down a cobbled hill that twisted steeply through thickening fog to an expanse of dilapidated wharves. The decaying timbers rumbled in protest as the taxi proceeded across the dock, stopping next to a lone houseboat lashed to the tarred pilings. The decrepit vessel had a low-slung cabin with canted sidewalls and a rusted pipe rail that ran atop the gunwale. It listed slightly to port, tugging gently at the mildewed hausers, which matched the color of her hull.

"There she is," Spencer said as they got out of the taxi into the rain. "A coat of paint, a tune-up, and I'll sell her for twice what I paid; maybe more. In the meantime, she's all yours."

"You don't live here?"

"Not on your life. I have me a flat in Woolwich. That's on the south bank, just through the tunnel."

Shepherd's head filled with the strong odor of creosoate and salt as he followed Spencer up a rickety gangway that swayed over the brackish water.

The slight cabbie opened the padlock, grasped the paint-encrusted hasp, and slid back the door. His hand found the light switch and turned it. Nothing happened. He grunted in disgust. "I must've thrown the main last time. Don't go way."

He hurried down the gangway and across the dock to an equipment shed that leaned against a power pole, making his way in the darkness to the electrical panel. Shepherd remained on deck until the lights inside the barge came on, then entered cautiously, half expecting to find Applegate waiting for him. He was greeted instead by the bored meow of a battle-scarred tomcat who shouldered past him into the main cabin. It was cluttered with packing crates, cartons of books, overstuffed furniture, a table, and a captain's chair. The bed was in an alcove opposite the galley. Shepherd was browsing through cupboards stocked with canned provisions when Spencer entered the cabin behind him.

"Two nights payable in advance," he announced.

Shepherd put a twenty pound note in his hand and studied him for a long moment before releasing it. "How do I know you still won't tell the authorities where I am?" he finally asked.

"Because I'm a man of my word."

"Just ask anyone who's done business with you, right?" Shepherd said, with a thin smile.

Spencer's eyes flashed with indignation; he whirled to a cabinet, opened a drawer, and removed a pistol.

Shepherd froze at the sight of it.

"I wouldn't be giving you this if I was planning to go to the police, now would I? Come along, take it," Spencer insisted, seeing the terror in Shepherd's eyes. "There are a lot of nasties on the waterfront; too many for my taste. Having this about gives me peace of mind when I'm here working on her. I imagine it might do the same for you."

Shepherd sighed with relief.

The cabbie gave him a set of keys and left.

Shepherd bolted the door after him then, mentally and physically exhausted, he fell face down on the bed and was asleep before the sound of the departing taxi had faded.

20

''**THE MAD DOG AMERICAN** and English whore are leading a barbaric crusade against the Arab world!'' Muammar el-Qaddafi shouted, the twisted veins at his temples throbbing. He stood amid the rubble of his headquarters building, a bulletproof vest strapped around his torso.

A crowd of reporters who had been bused from their hotel surrounded him. Behind them, medical teams scurried to care for bombing victims who were being dug out from the rubble and loaded aboard helicopters that would take them to Al Fatah University Hospital.

"*They* are the two Hitlers behind this act of state-sponsored terrorism!" Qaddafi ranted on, purposely using the phrase from the president's speech. "But they paid for their crimes! Their bombers were destroyed!" He paused dramatically, then cupped a hand over his mouth and leaned to an aide. "Are the children ready?" he whispered calmly—in sharp contrast to his rhetoric.

The aide nodded and, on cue, two gurneys appeared from within the collapsed walls of Qaddafi's home. Each contained a heavily bandaged child.

"The Americans are murderers! *Child* murderers!" he roared, gesturing to the young boys whom he had never seen before in his life. Then he strode toward his tent, which despite several near-misses was still standing.

A phalanx of bodyguards closed in, barring the reporters from pursuing or asking questions, and herded them back onto the buses.

The public relations charade over, Qaddafi entered his tent, where General Younis was waiting along with Reza Abdel-Hadi, head of the SHK, the Libyan secret police. An Akita heeled at his side sprang to a standing position, its tail unmoving and tightly curled.

Moncrieff sat in a chair nearby, still fuming at being left behind

by Larkin. He and Katifa had been fished out of the harbor by a
navy patrol boat.

The tent was in shambles: books and papers littered the woven
floor mats; the steel tent poles had been knocked askew, causing
the billowing fabric to sag to the ground in several places; a support cable on one of the light fixtures had snapped and the long
fluorescent hovered overhead like a ghostly apparition.

The blue cast of the lighting perfectly suited Qaddafi's mood.
"Anything we can do about this?" he asked, having acquired two
essentially useless bombers.

"No, sir," Moncrieff grunted. "The Americans delivered. We
didn't."

"But it was Abu Nidal's doing," Qaddafi protested halfheart-
edly. "Why should we be penalized?"

"No hostages, no ANITA," the Saudi replied with finality. "That
was the deal."

"But the Americans may never even *locate* the hostages, let alone
get their hands on them."

"Then again they might . . ." Abdel-Hadi observed, letting the
sentence trail off mysteriously. The SHK chief was a sullen, ma-
levolent man in his mid-fifties. Dark, dispassionate eyes hid behind
blue-veined lids that rarely blinked. SHK stood for Sahim Hiya
Khurriye, literally Preserver of Life and Liberty; and Abdel-Hadi
carried out his mission with legendary ruthlessness. "Especially if
we help them," he concluded.

"What are you suggesting?" Qaddafi asked, intrigued.

Abdel-Hadi prompted Younis with a crisp nod.

"Moncrieff and the Palestinian woman weren't the only ones
we pulled from the sea last night," the general explained. "We
netted one of Nidal's people too."

The previous evening, the young Palestinian had managed to
shed the heavy cartridge belts that were dragging him to the
bottom of Tripoli harbor, but the gunboat was gone by the time
he surfaced. A Libyan patrol boat plucked him from the oily
waters along with Moncrieff and Katifa.

Qaddafi's eyes flashed at the implication. "He can tell us where
they're taking the hostages," he enthused. "And we can pass it on
to the Americans."

Abdel-Hadi nodded smugly. "He's in solitary. We'll have his
cooperation soon."

"Perhaps some cellmates might help loosen his tongue," Qaddafi suggested, heading out of the tent, the others following after him.

He and Younis strode to the colonel's customized transport-panzer which was parked next to the tent, and headed for Okba ben Nafi Air Base.

Moncrieff, carrying a small package under his arm, boarded a helicopter that was taking injured soldiers to Al Fatah University Hospital.

Abdel-Hadi headed for the military prison on the other side of the compound, the Akita heeled next to him on a short leash. A section of the prison had been damaged during the air strike and some of the inmates were being moved. One of them had broken ranks and was running across the grounds toward the wall that enclosed the compound.

Several military guards were in hot pursuit.

Abdel-Hadi called them off and unleashed the Akita. The powerful canine, heir to centuries of breeding by Japanese emperors who prized their fierce loyalty and killer instinct, sprinted across the grounds. The fleeing prisoner heard the animal approaching and whirled. Without breaking stride the 130-pound Akita leapt into the air, clamped its jaws around his throat, and, with an abrupt jerk of its massive head, shredded it. Then as if it had just fetched a stick, the animal bounded back to its master in search of praise.

The SHK chief patted its head and descended into the bowels of the prison, the Akita padding after him. He strutted through the maze of concrete corridors, waving one of the guards to follow him. His nostrils flared at a vile stench as they entered a small room. The walls were lined with wire cages filled with rats, which went into a frenzy at the dog's presence.

"Brother leader thinks it's time the Palestinian had some cellmates," Abdel-Hadi said to the guard slyly.

THE HELICOPTER circled to a landing at Al Fatah University Hospital. Paramedics rushed forward with gurneys and began removing the injured Libyan soldiers.

Moncrieff climbed out, carrying his small package. He hurried into the hospital, took an elevator to the third floor, and went to a private room at the end of the corridor. Two military guards posted at the door stepped aside as he approached.

Katifa lay peacefully in the bed. Several hours of surgery were required to remove the bullets that had torn her smooth flesh. She had survived thanks to Moncrieff's heroic efforts and the superb medical technology brought in over the years by oil companies, which had raised health care in Tripoli to near-Western standards.

A nurse was adjusting the flow of an intravenous fluid as Moncrieff entered.

"She's doing quite well," the slight fellow said with a reassuring smile. "Aren't we?"

Katifa nodded and forced a smile.

"You'll just have to take my word for it," the nurse teased affectionately, taking Katifa's pulse before leaving the room.

The Saudi leaned across the bed and kissed Katifa's forehead gently.

She broke into a weak smile at the sight of him. "Moncrieff," she whispered in a dry rasp.

"How are you feeling?"

"Frightened," she replied, her eyes dark with concern. "Abu Nidal knows we deceived him. He'll send a hit squad for us. We can't stay here."

"Yes, I know. We'll be leaving soon."

"To where? Beirut isn't safe and—"

"Jeddah," he said, referring to his home in Saudi Arabia. "The arrangements are being made. In the meantime . . ." Moncrieff opened the package he had brought, removed a small pistol, and wrapped her hand around the grip. "Nine rounds, automatic; the safety's off," he went on, tucking in the bed covers to conceal it.

"I love you," she whispered, touched by his loyalty and concern, her spirits bolstered by his presence and the cool steel in her hand. But the moment was quickly marred by thundering echoes of machine gun fire that came back in a chilling rush, filling her with a depressing sense of failure.

Three floors below, Katifa's nurse stepped out of an elevator and hurried down the corridor to a phone booth. He took a slip of paper from his wallet and dialed the operator.

"Yes," he said softly, "Collect; to Beirut, please?"

AT OKBA BEN NAFI AIR BASE, Qaddafi's Transportpanzer came through the entrance gate and rumbled down the main access road, passing the blackened hulks of several SU-22 fighters destroyed in the air strike. Each twisted wreck was centered in a ring of scorched concrete. Those that hadn't been hit were aligned in diagonal rows on the flight line.

Qaddafi scowled at the sight, his head filling with the acrid scent of incinerated space-age plastics and exotic metals that hung in the air.

The TTP continued on to hangar 6-South. Qaddafi and Younis left the vehicle and entered through a personnel door, where an armed guard was posted.

The two F-111 bombers were parked side by side. The needle-sharp radar covers and engine shrouds had been removed. Maintenance personnel crawled over the sleek fuselages. Qaddafi stood between them, head cocked haughtily, envisioning their future exploits; this was his first look at them, and despite the withheld Pave Tack programming key, he was clearly impressed.

The man in charge of maintaining the planes was an East German avionics expert, the resident genius in a growing community of European and Asian nationals Qaddafi had hired to care for his arsenal of hi-tech war machines. The balding, bony fellow was in his glass-walled office conferring with several members of his staff when Younis caught his eye and waved him over.

"Any way we can develop ANITA on our own?" the general asked impatiently when he joined them.

"My technicians are already looking into it," the East German replied through a tiny mouth that barely moved when he spoke. "It's a long shot but it may be possible."

"Do it," Qaddafi shot back. "Give them whatever they need—equipment, personnel. Spare no expense."

"In the meantime," Younis said, brightening, "we'll start training flight crews."

"How long, assuming we have ANITA?" Qaddafi asked.

"It takes an American crew more than six months to become fully proficient. The limited scope of our mission will reduce that considerably; but all training flights will have to be at night, and only at night. We can't take any chances that the planes will be spotted."

Qaddafi nodded thoughtfully. "Were the bombers delivered with a full complement of ordnance?"

"Yes, sir," Younis replied. "We have enough explosive power to turn that Tunisian dam into a pile of sand."

21

IT WAS a gloomy Friday morning in Camp Springs, Maryland. A humid haze heavy with the moisture of coming rain lay over the city like a wet blanket.

Stephanie Shepherd was sitting at her breakfast table staring sadly at a story about the air strike in the *Washington Post* when the doorbell rang.

The children scurried to answer it. Their sorrow had turned to denial; for days now, every time the phone or doorbell rang, they fully expected someone was bringing the joyful news that their father was alive.

Laura opened the door to find an air force driver standing on the porch with several pieces of luggage.

"Mrs. Shepherd?" the driver said as Stephanie arrived. "Right there next to number nineteen," he went on uncomfortably, offering her pen and clipboard. She signed it and led the way inside. The driver put the rumpled bags in the den and left.

The children huddled, staring at them in stunned silence. Their father's things had come home without him and their hopes had suddenly withered.

"Come on, we have to get ready," Stephanie said, referring to a memorial service later that morning. "Grandma and grandpa'll be here any minute."

The children shuffled off, leaving Stephanie alone with Walt's luggage. She hadn't expected his effects would be returned so quickly, and was close to losing her composure. She had no way of knowing that Applegate had expedited their shipment to reinforce the idea that her husband was dead. Her lower lip started to quiver and she hurried from the den, thankful she didn't have the time to go through it now.

T H A T   S A M E   M O R N I N G, the president sat at a desk in his East Wing living quarters, reviewing a speech. The euphoria of punching out a bully had worn off and his mood matched the weather—not because of the hostage debacle, of which he had no knowledge, but because four airmen had been lost. He slipped the file cards into a pocket, reflecting on the grim task that awaited. He'd faced many tragedy-stricken families, but it never got any easier. The chattering rotors of Marine 1 landing just across the grounds pulled him from the reverie.

"I'm afraid it's time," he said to the First Lady, who had just joined him. They exited through a door that opened onto the Rose Garden, where Secret Service agents were waiting with umbrellas, and walked toward the helicopter, passing a surging crowd of White House correspondents.

"Why was the raid carried out at night?" one shouted over the roar of the chopper's turbine.

"Sources say Qaddafi was in his tent just before the attack," another said. "How did he escape injury?"

"Is it true Congress wasn't properly notified?"

"Mr. President? Mr. President," another bellowed, thrusting his microphone at him. "Why did we use bombers based in the U.K.?"

"I can't comment at this time," the president finally said. He continued past them without breaking stride and boarded the helicopter.

The flight to Andrews took just over 10 minutes. Marine 1 was descending over the north end of the air base when the president looked out the rain-streaked window and saw an island of black umbrellas clustered below.

Beneath them were representatives from the departments of Defense and State, the air force, Congress, and the families of the airmen whom, all believed, had died in the raid on Tripoli. Stephanie and her family were seated in the front row along with CIA-provided mourners serving as relatives of the weapons systems officers whose identities the Company had created.

The scream of turbofans rose in the distance as eight F-4D Phantoms streaked overhead, their sonic booms pounding the mourners with surprising force as one of the jets peeled off and vanished in the mist.

The president's speech was an eloquent tribute delivered with heartfelt sadness. There wasn't a dry eye when he had finished.

He left the podium and worked his way down the line of mourners, spending a moment with each, offering his condolences.

"Mrs. Shepherd?" a voice called out.

Stephanie turned to see Congressman Gutherie coming toward her.

"I'm very sorry," he said, clearly saddened.

"Thank you," she replied, forcing a smile as she introduced him to her parents and children.

"If there's anything I can do to help—"

"I'm sure there is, but right now . . ." Stephanie paused and shrugged forlornly, letting the sentence trail off. Gutherie nodded and was about to leave when her eyes came to life with a question. "You think the Libyan government will be cooperative?" she asked. "I mean, about returning my husband's body?"

Gutherie reflected on that dark day six years ago when members of the Iranian hostage rescue team were tragically burned to death, and jocular mullahs brandished their charred bones like war clubs. "You understand," he began, delicately touching on the matter, "the crash, the heat, there's a chance that—"

"He's little more than a pile of ashes?" Stephanie asked weakly. "If that's the case, I want them here—in Arlington where they belong. Where the children and I can . . ." Her voice cracked and she left it unfinished, the sense of loss, of being suddenly cut adrift on unchartered waters overwhelming her.

Gutherie put an arm around her. "State might know something," he said as she wept softly. "On the other hand, Walt's CO might already be into it."

"Will you find out for me?"

"Of course," Gutherie replied, his voice rising over the departing helicopter. "You have his name?"

"Larkin," Stephanie replied. "Colonel Richard Larkin."

22

S H E P H E R D had spent the remainder of the week aboard the barge eating and regaining his stamina. Friday evening, he began work on the next phase of his plan. He wrote his signature beneath his photograph in the newspaper he had taken from the post office; then, he stuffed Spencer's pistol in the pocket of a rain slicker he had found in a locker along with an old sweater and seaman's cap, and went up the cobbled hill to Poplar High Street, where a sign flickering amid the electronic glitter proclaimed: SNAPSHOTS—THREE POSES 1£.

He slipped inside the automated booth and, holding the newspaper flat against his chest, pushed a coin into the slot, and sat rock steady as the strobe flashed three times. The mechanism whirred and the strip of snapshots fell into the tray, ripe with the scent of developer. On his way back to the barge, he found a record shop and bought a blank cassette and fresh batteries for his recorder.

The next morning, he stood in the main cabin of the barge looking about, then reached up and ran a hand along the back side of a ceiling beam; unsatisfied, he examined a hanging lamp and several sections of built-in shelving before finally focusing on the table. It had a round wooden top on an ornate, cast-iron pedestal. He pulled the captain's chair aside and turned the table upside down, then left the barge and crossed the dock to the equipment shed, where he found a piece of old inner tube, a pair of scissors, a hammer, and some tacks, all of which he took back to the cabin. He cut a 4 × 8-inch strip out of the black rubber and placed it flat against the underside of the table. He tacked one end to the wood, then stretched the rubber tightly before tacking the other. He fetched his recorder, set it in the voice activated mode, turned the microphone switch to High, and slipped it beneath the taut rubber sling, which held it securely against the wood. Then he righted the table and sat in the chair to make sure the device couldn't be seen.

"This is Walter Shepherd, Major, United States Air Force, speaking," he drawled in a low voice, going on to recite his serial number. "As you know, I'm supposed to have been killed in the raid on Libya. Well, the truth is, I wasn't. The next voice you hear will be Air Force Major Paul Applegate, military intelligence, who's going to explain what really happened and why."

Shepherd retrieved the recorder and played back his preamble, determining that the level was satisfactory. Then he went for a walk along the waterfront, reviewing the rest of his plan. He returned several hours later to find Spencer waiting for him.

"Your bloody friends from the hotel came by my flat this morning," he said gravely. "It seems they've been tracking down every cabbie who worked the waterfront this week."

"What did you tell them?"

"I said the post office was the last I saw of you."

"Thanks," Shepherd said, relieved.

"Like I said, I'm a man of my word." Spencer stepped to the refrigerator, removed two bottles of Watney's, and popped the caps, handing one to Shepherd. "To your health, Major."

Shepherd stiffened at the remark.

Spencer held up a newspaper in explanation—the one with Shepherd's photograph and signature that he had left in the cabin. Spencer had seen other copies but hadn't made the connection. Seeing it there, seeing it with Shepherd, had driven the resemblance home despite the four days of stubble and weariness that obscured the vibrant face in the picture.

"I imagine you could tell quite a story," Spencer said.

Shepherd nodded. "But I wouldn't be able to prove a word of it. I can't even prove who I am."

"You must know things, I mean, that no one else could; things that'd go a long way to proving—"

"I have to find someone I can trust first."

"What about your embassy?"

Shepherd shrugged with uncertainty.

"Scotland Yard? The military?" Spencer went on. "One of them has to be—"

"*Which* one? I can't afford a mistake. Besides . . ." Shepherd paused, wracked with frustration at the stumbling block that had confronted him all along. "They're all connected. Soon as one gets into it, it wouldn't be long before my 'bloody friends,' as you call them, are all over me." He paused thoughtfully, then added, "I figure the media is my best shot."

"What are you waiting for?"

"My wife."

Spencer questioned him with a look.

"The way I see it, I'm going to get one run at this target," Shepherd explained. "But I've got to be sure who the enemy is and what he's up to, first. I've got a plan worked out and my wife's the key to it. I didn't want to get her involved but there's no way I can pull it off without her."

Spencer nodded. "How long have you been married?"

"Twenty years," Shepherd replied. "Twenty years next Friday." He paused, thinking it through, then asked, "How would you like to help me celebrate?"

THAT AFTERNOON IN LANGLEY, Virginia, Kiley summoned Larkin to CIA headquarters; they went immediately to an audio laboratory in a subbasement where a communications technician was waiting for them.

In the center of the electronics-packed room, a small table stood beneath a high-intensity lamp; centered in the bright circle of light was a pale blue air mail envelope that had been steamed open, a pile of neatly folded bathroom tissue, and an audio cassette.

"You listen to it?" Kiley asked.

"Yes, sir," the com tech replied. "Mostly family chatter; last third's where it gets interesting."

"From the top," Kiley ordered.

The com tech stepped to a console, dropped the cassette into the holder, and pressed the play button.

"Thursday, three April," Shepherd's voice began in an easy drawl. "Real pretty up here, babe. We left the Grand Banks behind about an hour ago. Advance report for touchdown is rain and more rain. Sounds like we're talking weather for ducks. Speaking of water, Al thought you should know that Beethoven used to pour ice water over his—He's waving at me like a matador. Not Beethoven, Al. Be talking to you soon.

"Tuesday, eight April. How is my favorite little gymnast doing? And how's her mommy and brother? I went over to the hospital last night to see Al. He's complaining the pasta isn't al dente, so

I figure he's doing okay. It turns out that little sortie with the Russians was just a warm-up. We've got a real live mission on the boards now. It should be history by the time you get this; so should Qaddafi. I'm real sorry about messing up our anniversary, babe. Like I said, we'll make up for it soon as you get here.

"Tuesday, fifteen April. This is going to shock you, babe; it's going to make you happy too. Don't believe what you've been seeing on TV, don't believe the president, don't believe anybody. I didn't go down over Libya; didn't even fly the damn mission. I'm alive but I'm in big trouble and need your help." Shepherd went on to explain about the attempts on his life, naming Larkin and Applegate. "They're trying to kill me," he concluded. "I don't know what their game is, some kind of conspiracy I guess. I figure our phone's been tapped; they might be watching the mail too. Anyway, if you get this, just come to London as soon as you can. Check into the Hilton and I'll find a way to contact you. Trust no one, no one. Miss you and the kids like crazy. Kiss them for me, okay? I love you, babe, I love you with all my heart."

Kiley and Larkin exchanged apprehensive looks.

The hiss of blank tape filled the silence.

"Fuck," the colonel finally groaned.

Kiley was silent, analyzing the situation. Though Shepherd had quite correctly assumed his phone, mail, and family were being monitored, a man in his position had little choice but to try, the DCI thought. The device CIA had installed in the switching center at Andrews had prevented any contact by phone. It was only natural Shepherd would turn to other means to obtain help, other means that, Kiley now shrewdly realized, could be turned against him.

"I think with some selective editing, this tape can be used to advantage," he finally said, nodding as the idea crystallized. "Can we lose the incriminating information and keep the instructions?"

"No problem, sir," the technician replied. "Just tell me what stays and what goes."

"Good. As soon as we're finished, we'll forward it to Shepherd's wife and let her lead us to him."

"How do we know she won't go to the air force or the media?" Larkin asked. "I mean, the fact that he said to trust no one doesn't rule it out."

"Good point," Kiley mused. "But we have people who can stop her, should she try."

23

GUTHERIE had a speaking engagement after the memorial service on Friday and didn't get back to the office. First thing Monday morning he asked his secretary to call Larkin. Since she had no number for him, she called the Pentagon and got it —his real number, not the cover one in Heyford.

When it came to unconventional missions, the DCI knew preventative damage control had its limits. The dangers of revising military records to support an operative's cover far outweighed the advantages. Kiley had labeled the inviolable rule DDD: documentation destroys deniability.

"No Colonel Larkin, Richard or otherwise, based in the U.K.," Gutherie's secretary announced about a half hour later.

The Congressman's brows went up as she knew they would.

"Quite a guy . . . Vietnam ace, Special Forces," she went on, saving the plum for last. "He works in the White House these days."

"The White House," Gutherie echoed flatly. "What the hell are they up to now?" He was already irritated over executive branch end runs around Congress. The last-minute notification of the air strike on Libya was only the latest affront. They didn't even pay lip service to oversight anymore; and lately, he'd heard rumors that Special Forces personnel working out of the Pentagon were carrying out unauthorized covert activities in a number of the world's trouble spots.

The congressman swiveled to the window and looked out at the Capitol. It was still raining. The flag was heavy with water and hung limply against the pole.

STEPHANIE and the children had spent the weekend at her parents' house in Bethesda. After breakfast, she left Laura and Jeffrey, and drove to her home on Andrews Air Force Base;

her husband's luggage was in the den waiting for her and she wanted to be alone.

She lifted one of the pieces onto the desk and opened it slowly. Her head filled with Walt's scent, which came from within the bag. She savored it, then began gently removing the items, pausing reflectively before putting them on the desk: shaving gear, toiletries, civilian clothing, an old sweater that she crushed to her bosom. She had removed about half the contents when she heard the mail dropping into the box next to the front door.

She paused, welcoming the interruption, and fetched it. Her eyes darted to the pale blue air mail envelope amid the magazines and fliers, darted to Shepherd's bold printing. She returned to the den, opening the envelope carefully to preserve it, then removed the contents, undid the tissue wrapping, and stared solemnly at the cassette. Walt's scent was one thing, his voice another, and she wasn't sure she was ready for it.

The ring of the telephone jarred her.

"Stephanie, you sure about the name of your husband's commanding officer?" Gutherie asked.

"Yes, yes, I am—Larkin. Colonel Richard Larkin. That's what they told me when I called Heyford. Why?"

"I have a feeling something strange is going on," he replied, telling her of his secretary's discovery and of his suspicions that covert activity was getting out of hand. "Did your husband say or do anything unusual lately?"

"Well, come to think of it, he was always good about keeping in touch. This time was different."

"Anything else?"

"I just got a tape from him in the mail. He always sent one before flying a mission. I haven't listened to it yet."

"Why don't we do it together?" Gutherie suggested, hearing the uncertainty in her voice. "Who knows, it might shed some light on this."

Forty-five minutes later the congressman's black New Yorker was parked in Stephanie's driveway and the two of them were in the den. Gutherie put the cassette in the tape player and turned it on.

"Thursday, three April. Real pretty up here, babe," Shepherd's voice began. The engaging charm of his gentle drawl enfolded Stephanie in its familiar warmth. She stared out the window at a stand of budding Aspen as she listened, almost chuckling at the image of an ice-water-soaked Beethoven. Walt's reference to his favorite little gymnast coaxed a poignant smile from her. When he got to Brancato growling over poorly cooked pasta, she had almost put the horrible reality out of her mind. But his remarks about the mission wrenched her back abruptly. Her eyes had filled with tears by the time he promised they'd do something special to make up for their anniversary.

Stephanie shrugged, acknowledging that the tape hadn't shed even a glimmer on the situation, when the selectively edited section began.

"Tuesday, fifteen April. This is going to shock you, babe; it's going to make you happy too. Don't believe what you've been seeing on TV. I didn't go down over Libya; didn't even fly the damn mission. I'm alive but I'm in big trouble and need your help. Come to London as soon as you can. Check into the Hilton and I'll find a way to contact you. Trust no one, no one. Miss you and the kids like crazy. Kiss them for me, okay? I love you, babe, I love you with all my heart."

A rush of adrenaline hit Stephanie with staggering force. Her color returned, a sense of joy spreading over her like a warm glow.

Gutherie was rocked; he stood in shocked silence, staring at the tape player.

"Walt's alive," Stephanie finally said in a stunned whisper. "He's alive, *alive*," she repeated, savoring the word. Her spirits soared, then came crashing down as the implications of the message hit her, hit her hard, and she turned a frightened look to Gutherie. "What do you think happened to him?"

"I have no idea," Gutherie mumbled, the words sticking in his throat.

"You said you thought something strange was going on. You asked me if Walt said or did anything unusual. If you know something, please tell me."

"I did, Mrs. Shepherd. Believe me, I told you everything I know." The congressman stepped to the desk and picked up the air mail envelope. "It came in this?"

Stephanie nodded solemnly, then shut off the tape.

"It was mailed in London the day after the air strike," Gutherie observed pointedly, examining it.

Stephanie bit a lip, holding back the emotions that had welled up, then nodded as the pieces began falling into place. "I didn't pay much attention to it at the time, but I had a feeling something wasn't right."

"What do you mean?"

"Walt wouldn't change bases without letting me know, let alone go a week without calling back. We're a close family; I told you, he always kept in touch." She paused, as a question occurred to her. "Why would the president say he died in the line of duty?"

Gutherie shrugged, clearly baffled. "I'll make some calls; see what I can find out."

Stephanie nodded numbly, struggling to cope with the wrenching swing of emotions; then, her presence of mind returning, she reconsidered. "Wait. Wait, no. I don't want you to call anyone," she said firmly.

"What do you mean? Why not?"

"You heard what Walt said about not trusting anyone. He said it twice; he must have a good reason."

"Mrs. Shepherd, I think you can trust me."

"Don't take this the wrong way, but, under the circumstances, I don't have much choice, do I?"

"Quite true," Gutherie mused. "Of course, it's possible it might have just been a figure of speech."

"No, I know my husband," Stephanie said adamantly. "He's a pilot, a technically precise man; and if he said *no one*, believe me he meant it."

"What are you going to do?"

"I'm going to London; I'm going to do exactly as Walt instructed," Stephanie replied. Then locking her eyes onto his, she added, "And I expect you to do the same and keep this between us."

"I can't say I blame you, Mrs. Shepherd; but it's obvious something's terribly wrong. I can't just ignore it."

Stephanie broke into a knowing smile. "I realize there may be a hot issue here, Mister Congressman," she said pointedly, her resolve strengthening with each passing minute. "Just give me some time to get to London and find out what's going on."

Gutherie winced, unable to deny that the upcoming campaign had occurred to him, and wrestled with the decision.

"A day or two. I'll leave tomorrow," she declared. "Please, I'm afraid for Walt; he sounded so desperate."

Gutherie let out a long breath and nodded.

24

F O R T H R E E D A Y S, the interval between sonar signals had been gradually diminishing.

Following the call from Kiley, Commander Duryea had put the *Cavalla* on a heading for the Middle East and began hunting for the PLO gunboat.

"Lot of ocean out there," he prompted McBride.

"Probably hug the coast all the way to Egypt," the exec offered smartly, assuming the Zhuk would remain in Libyan waters, avoiding the 6th Fleet on station off Benghazi, several hundred miles northeast of Tripoli.

"I'm counting on it. Sixth gets nosy and spooks them, the element of surprise goes out the window and the hostages along with it."

"Any chance she'll port someplace to refuel?"

"Negative. She's carrying two auxiliaries," Duryea replied, having spotted the deck-mounted tanks while berthed in Tripoli harbor. He stepped to his keyboard and typed the word MAFIA. A graphic depicting a line of undersea SOSUS hydrophones was superimposed on the electronic chart of the area.

The MAFIA net cut across the Mediterranean from Sicily to Misratah, 50 miles east of Tripoli. Each cluster of detectors was encased in a huge tank moored to the bottom and linked to an onshore transmitter by fiber optic cables. The hydrophones picked up the sounds of the sea, its inhabitants, and all vessels that crossed or came within several hundred miles of the net. All data was relayed via FLTSATCOM to SOSUS control in Norfolk, Virginia, for computer processing and storage.

Duryea brought the *Cavalla* to periscope-antennae depth and sent the following cable on an SHF channel:

FM: USS CAVALLA
TO: SOSUS CONTROL NORFOLK

REQUEST CURRENT DATA ON ZHUK CLASS PATROL
CRAFT. ASSUME EASTERLY COURSE SOUTH/MED.
MAFIA CROSSED IN LIBYAN WATERS POST 0130/
14APR.

Zhuk was a Soviet Navy classification, which meant the gunboat's
basic acoustic signature—a sound fingerprint created by a vessel's
propulsion machinery and hull moving through the water—was
already in SOSUS computer files. All contacts that fell within
Duryea's parameters were matched to the specimen signature.
The gunboat was identified; its course, speed, and location established and radioed to the *Cavalla*.

Duryea used the BC-10 to estimate the gunboat's current position and plotted an intercept course.

"Come to zero eight seven. All ahead full."

The *Cavalla* was at 90 feet, 65 miles astern of the gunboat, when
Cooperman heard the first sonar echo on the BQS-6 bow array.
Primarily a passive collector, the big spherical transducer had
single-ping ranging capability. Cooperman fed the data to the BC-
10 computer for DIMUS analysis. Digital multi-beam steering pro-
cessed many signals simultaneously, isolating the sharply defined
frequencies, allowing Cooperman to lock onto the unique cavitation of the gunboat's twin propellers.

Now within striking distance, Duryea was waiting not only for
cover of darkness but until an hour when the Palestinians would
be asleep. Then and only then would the team of SEALs attempt
to rescue the hostages. Duryea was hugging the attack scope,
watching the PLO gunboat riding a gently rolling sea, when an
alienlike silhouette entered the command center.

Lieutenant Diego Reyes was a fireplug of a man, his black wet
suit stretched taut over planes of hard-packed muscle. A laser-
honed diver's knife rode his left calf. Born in a Los Angeles barrio,
the cocky Chicano had eagerly traded the world of drive-by shoot-
ings for the calculated violence of covert action.

"Ready to deploy, sir," he reported, as coolly as if announcing
dinner was ready. "They have sentries?"

Duryea nodded and stepped back from the periscope, letting
Reyes have a look. "Take the conn. I'll be in section eight," Duryea
said to McBride, using the nickname that the SEALs—thought
by some to be certifiably insane—had given their quarters.

Duryea and Reyes made their way to a compartment where five men in wet suits were reviewing deck plans of the Zhuk. Pictures of the hostages and cards displaying phonetically printed Arabic phrases were taped to the bulkheads. Like their leader, the SEALs were young, action-oriented, and driven to flirt with death—a team of disciplined killers for whom the time between missions was torture.

"Two sentries," Reyes announced, marking the positions on deck plans. "Piece of cake, right?"

"Right!" the group responded spiritedly.

"Wrong. We're talking religious fanatics here!" Reyes admonished, a slight accent surfacing with his temper. "These ragheads think they're fighting a holy war. Like God's on their side or something."

"Does that mean they go straight to pussy heaven just like us?" a SEAL cracked.

"Yeah, but the word is *theirs* makes ours look like a weekend pass in a convent. These mother fuckers don't back down. If they can't blow you away, they're gonna get their dicks real wet trying. Got it?"

A cacophony of four-letter wisecracks erupted as the team pulled on hoods and diving masks, and followed Reyes up a ladder and through a hatch into the dry deck shelter, mounted on the exterior of the *Cavalla*'s hull. A swimmer delivery vehicle hung from a cradle within. Five feet in diameter, thirty feet long, the black SDV resembled a minisubmarine with three open cockpits. Each had two breathing regulators on flexible hoses that were fed by a common scuba unit built into the vessel. Compartments in its sleek plastic hull contained the standard complement of weapons, rope, grappling hooks, and roll-up boarding ladders.

"Go with God," Duryea said.

"You really think He takes sides?" Reyes asked.

"I've heard it said, He takes the good."

"Then we've got nothing to worry about."

Duryea smiled. He left the DDS, locked the access hatch, and then pulled a lever, opening valves that quickly filled the chamber with ice cold seawater. When the aft bulkhead yawned open, Reyes released the tie-down latches and eased the vessel from its cradle. It emerged into the green-black depths, leaving a graceful trail of swirling bubbles behind.

A thousand yards ahead, the churning wake of the Zhuk's propellers caught the light of a crescent moon that sliced through hazy clouds.

Reyes set the dive planes to neutral and homed the throttle. The SDV accelerated toward the gunboat like a ravenous shark that had just spotted its prey.

Commander Duryea went directly to the *Cavalla*'s communications room and printed out a message:

FM: USS CAVALLA
TO: DCI/KUBARK

TARGET SIGHTED. PROCEEDING AS PLANNED. UNODIR.

The officer on duty scanned it for encoding, got to the sign-off, and questioned Duryea with a look, though he had no doubt of his captain's intent.

"Send it and shut off the radio," Duryea replied, making certain it was clear.

UNODIR—an official U.S. Navy acronym—was pronounced "you know dear" and meant "unless otherwise directed." That the sender's radio had been turned off to preempt countermanding orders was implicit. UNODIRs were favored by submarine commanders, who, unlike their surface counterparts, were often out of voice contact with their superiors. They were most often used in covert operations, which were Duryea's specialty. He wholly embraced the navy dictum that with absolute power came absolute responsibility, and knew that by documenting he had taken action without clearing it in advance, a UNODIR didn't cover *his* ass but those of his superiors.

When Duryea returned to the command center, the SDV was 15 feet beneath the surface, abreast of the gunboat.

Reyes maneuvered into position just starboard of the hull and signaled to one of the SEALs in the aft cockpit, who fired a speargun at the Zhuk's propellers. The dart-sized projectile was tethered to a net stowed in the SDV. As the tether became entangled in the whirling blades, the net was drawn from its compartment and swiftly sucked into them. Made of Kevlar strands—the material that when woven into fabric can stop a bullet—the net gradually bound both props in a knotted bundle of shredded space-age plastic. And it did so gently and silently, disabling the gunboat without the jolt or racket that a chain or explosive device would have made, waking the crew and alarming sentries.

On the Zhuk's bridge, the PLO helmsman was staring curiously at the erratically surging tachometer. He had heard no noise to indicate the boat had struck floating debris; he had plenty of fuel, and no reason to suspect the vessel was about to be boarded. He cut back the throttles and the gunboat soon lay dead in the water.

The aft sentry was wondering why they'd stopped when his walkie-talkie came to life.

"I think something's fouled the props," the helmsman said, deciding he had plowed into a kelp bed. The thick plankton that flourishes along the North African coast often trapped divers and disabled vessels.

The sentry crossed the deck with a flashlight and was about to peer over the transom when with stunning rapidity, a gloved hand thrust upward; a glint of metal flickered in the moonlight; blood splashed onto the deck in explosive spurts. The sentry pitched forward against the rail, clutching at a gaping slash in his throat that had severed his vocal chords, ensuring he couldn't scream.

Reyes was standing on one of two boarding ladders the SEALs had hooked over the stern gunwale. He grabbed a handful of the dying Palestinian's hair and yanked him over the rail into the sea.

Four SEALs followed Reyes up the ladders onto the deck, the sixth remaining behind with the SDV. They separated into two groups and moved up opposite sides of the superstructure toward the bow.

The forward sentry was lighting a cigarette when he heard a short-lived whistle. The barbed, stainless steel arrow covered the distance from speargun to the center of his chest in an eyeblink. He was teeter-tottering, mouth agape in silent agony when three SEALs sprang from the darkness and pitched him over the side.

Reyes was already moving up a short companionway to the bridge. The helmsman was on the radio, trying to raise the aft sentry on the walkie-talkie. He never heard the powerful Chicano slip into the cabin behind him. His last memory was the flicker of light from a loop of hair-thin wire passing in front of his face.

"Grips secured, wrists crossed," the instructor had exhorted with authority born of experience. "Then over-and-pull with a decisive snap; a tactic that when properly executed will neatly sever head from torso."

Any doubts Reyes might have had were quickly dashed by the fountain of blood that erupted from atop the helmsman's shoulders and the sickening thud of his cranium against the steel deck.

Reyes led the way down to the captain's cabin just aft of the bridge. Accustomed to engine vibrations and the rush of water against the hull, the rotund Palestinian had sensed the quiet and awakened. He was swinging his legs over the side of the bunk when Reyes slipped into the cabin, clamped a hand over his mouth, and put a knife to his throat.

"Tell your men not to resist," Reyes whispered tensely in phonetic Arabic.

The groggy Palestinian glanced to the gleaming blade and nodded repeatedly, eyes wide with fear.

Reyes dragged him out of the cabin and down the corridor to where the hostages were quartered. He approached the first cabin slowly, quietly, imagining their relief, their joy at having at last been rescued; he turned the latch, opened the door, and peered inside. It was empty. As was the next and the next. Indeed, all he found were a handful of sleeping seamen, who heeded their captain's warning and offered no resistance.

"They've got to be here!" Reyes barked. "Check the stores and engine room! Look for secret compartments!"

The SEALs proceeded to rip up floor hatches and tear out bulkhead and ceiling panels. They nearly dismantled the Zhuk's interior before finding the blind panel in a passageway, the panel that invisibly sealed the compartment where the hostages were held, the panel that when opened explained why it had been so easy, why the captain had been so cooperative—there wasn't a single hostage aboard.

25

''**C O M E   O N,** the fucking boat never made port!" Kiley exploded when informed about the hostages. He charged out of his chair and circled toward Larkin. "They're not there; they're not in Beirut; what the hell happened? They vanish into thin air?"

"It looks like they were transferred to another vessel en route, sir," Larkin replied, reddening.

"No shit?" Kiley snapped sarcastically. "Shepherd's still on the loose; Fitzgerald is who the hell knows where. Not a very impressive performance, Colonel." He crossed to a sideboard and scooped some ice into a tumbler. "What's Duryea's game plan?" he rasped, spinning the cap from a bottle of well-aged Dewar's.

"He's requested a KH-11 review for openers, sir," Larkin replied apprehensively. He knew the need to search videotapes on which spy satellite data was stored—tapes on which the rendezvous between vessels in the Mediterranean had been hopefully recorded—went to the heart of a gritty dispute between intelligence agencies and would further annoy the DCI. Though CIA could request specific KH-11 surveillance, the storage and analysis of raw satellite data was an NSA function.

Kiley groaned, as Larkin expected, and buzzed his secretary on the intercom. Going outside the Company had always been an anathema to him, more so under the circumstances. "Set up a meeting with Lancaster," he ordered grudgingly. "I need him as soon as possible."

Barely a minute had passed when the DCI's intercom buzzed. "He's available right after lunch, sir," his secretary reported, "but I'm afraid he's insisting it be in his office."

"Fine, fine," Kiley barked impatiently, the gravity of the situation overriding territorial imperatives.

Several hours later, Kiley and Larkin arrived in the Old Executive Office Building across the street from the White House on 17th and Pennsylvania.

Despite his own conservative tastes, Kiley had always found Lancaster's office unbearably stuffy and wasted no time in getting down to business. He made no mention of the air strike or debacle in Tripoli harbor in his briefing, explaining only that CIA had learned the hostages were aboard a PLO gunboat and had been transferred to another vessel, thwarting a rescue attempt. "The bottom line is we need a KH-11 fix on the second vessel as soon as possible."

Lancaster nodded thoughtfully, his dour expression hidden behind a cloud of pipe smoke. The hastily arranged meeting had made him suspect the DCI had been up to something; but being cut out of a hostage rescue operation was well beyond anything he had imagined. "I'll arrange it," he finally said.

"When?"

"Tomorrow."

"Not acceptable," Kiley replied sharply.

Lancaster stared at him blankly for a long moment, drawing on his pipe. "The colonel will be handling liaison?" he finally asked, ignoring Kiley's reply.

Kiley nodded, bristling with frustration.

Lancaster shifted his look to Larkin. "Tomorrow; Fort Belvoir; oh eight hundred," he said, rapid-fire. "My people will be expecting you."

A short time later the DCI's limousine was on the Beltway, heading back to Langley, when the mobile phone twittered. Kiley sat trancelike, letting it ring, his mind fixed on his old friend Fitzgerald and on the infuriating mystery of the hostages' whereabouts.

Larkin saw he was preoccupied and answered it.

"Colonel Larkin . . . Yeah, yeah. You bet I'll tell him." He hung up and turned to Kiley. "Surveillance reports Mrs. Shepherd booked a flight to London. She leaves tomorrow."

Kiley's eyes brightened. "Everything in place?" he asked, savoring the thought that it might soon be over.

"Yes, sir," the colonel replied, thinking it had been weeks since he had seen the old man smile.

26

B R I T I S H A I R W A Y S flight 829 from Dulles made a big looping turn over the Buckingham countryside, coming onto a heading for London's Heathrow International. The time was 2:37 P.M. when the jetliner touched down and taxied to a stop at a terminal 4 boarding ramp.

Stephanie Shepherd deplaned with a carry-on bag, cleared passport control, and hurried down the green-walled corridor for those not involved with customs.

She didn't notice a casually attired man in the crowd assembled behind the barrier. He appeared to be meeting arriving passengers and didn't stand out. Stephanie had no way of knowing that he was waiting for her nor that he would easily recognize her from a CIA-procured snapshot that he palmed.

When certain of her identity, Applegate pocketed the snapshot and nodded to the two Special Forces agents backing him up that he had spotted her.

Stephanie paused to get her bearings, then followed the signs to the taxi queue along the west facade of the building. Moments later, she was tucked inside one of the boxy black cabs heading toward London.

A sedan with U.S. military insignia affixed to the visor came from the restricted parking area adjacent to the terminal. Applegate accelerated around a bus that blocked his view and followed the taxi into the thickening stream of vehicles exiting the airport.

About an hour later, Stephanie checked into the Hilton on Park Lane opposite Hyde Park in London's fashionable Mayfair district. She tried to nap but couldn't fall asleep and spent the remainder of the afternoon reading in the plainly furnished room. Her mind kept drifting and she was staring out the window at the park far below when the phone rang, startling her.

"Hello?"

"Mrs. Shepherd?" Spencer asked, in his mild cockney. He was

calling from a street corner booth, which he had done several times daily for the last three days—a routine Shepherd had worked out in the event Stephanie arrived in London prior to the earliest possible date he had estimated. "I'd like to confirm that you called for a taxi?" Spencer prompted.

"A taxi?" Stephanie answered cautiously. She sensed this might be her husband's way of making contact, but was uncertain how to respond and decided to be truthful. "No, I'm sorry, I don't believe I did."

"Actually it *was* a gentleman who rang me. He gave the name Viper, he did; said to say, Happy anniversary."

Stephanie's heart fluttered, any misgivings she had vanishing. "Oh yes, yes, now I remember."

"Good. The taxi will pick you up at the Hertford Street entrance at precisely six o'clock this evening."

"Yes, six o'clock," she replied, her pulse surging. "Hertford Street. I'll be waiting."

In the room directly below, Applegate glanced to a CIA communications technician and smiled. Shepherd's tape had alerted them to where Stephanie would be staying; she had made the reservation at the Hilton prior to departure, and they had had more than sufficient time to learn which room she had been assigned and tap the phone.

Applegate took the elevator to the lobby, crossing to a bookshop off to one side of the entrance. Its open facade afforded a clear view of the entire lobby area.

"She's been contacted," Applegate said to the agent stationed there, who was browsing casually through a rack of magazines. After reviewing the details, Applegate left the hotel via the Hertford Street entrance and briefed the second agent, who was stationed in the doorway of a building across the street; then he went to his car, which was parked just down the hill, and waited.

Stephanie was excited and shaken by the message from the mysterious caller. She showered, dressed, and, at exactly 5:55 P.M., slipped into a raincoat and went to the lobby.

The agent in the bookshop saw her leave the elevator. He palmed a small walkie-talkie and clicked it on. "Target is moving," he reported softly.

Applegate smiled and lifted the microphone from the sedan's dash. "Hertford Street?"

"Affirmative."

"Okay. Stay on her," Applegate instructed. "The taxi may be some kind of diversion."

Stephanie spun through the revolving door and walked tentatively to the curb. There was no taxi waiting. It seemed like an eternity, though barely a minute had passed before the clatter of a diesel rose and she saw the headlights coming up the hill.

The agent across the street backed into the darkness as the cab rumbled to a stop next to her.

"Please step in, Mrs. Shepherd," Spencer urged. Shepherd's description and Stephanie's clearly anxious demeanor had made her easy to recognize.

"Walt?" she blurted as she opened the door, hoping to find him tucked in the backseat. Her spirits plunged on discovering he wasn't.

"She's getting in the cab," Applegate said into the microphone. "Better move it."

Stephanie pulled the door closed and perched on the edge of the seat. "My husband, he's okay?" she said, leaning anxiously toward the driver. "You've seen him? He's alive?" she went on in a rush.

"He most certainly is," Spencer replied, going on to introduce himself and give Stephanie a note.

Friday, 24 April. Welcome to London, Babe, it began. Stephanie brightened at the sight of Walt's handwriting. In an economy of words, the note confirmed that Spencer was a friend and outlined precisely what she was to do.

"Shouldn't we be going?" she prompted, her heart thumping from the surge of adrenaline.

"Soon as I'm sure we won't be leaving that car behind," Spencer replied, eyeing the rearview mirror.

Stephanie turned to the window and saw two men getting into a gray sedan down the street. As soon as the doors slammed, the taxi drove off slowly.

The sedan pulled away and followed.

As the taxi made its way south on Park Lane, Stephanie was taken by the glittering cityscape, a tableau of centuries-old buildings that defied the soaring towers of glass and steel. Spencer swung east into Piccadilly, taking Shaftsbury through the theater district to the Holborn Viaduct, which bypassed the City, as London's financial heartland is called, angling across the boroughs of East Cheapside and Fenchurch, skirting the forbidding streets of Whitechapel, finally turning north into Bishopgate, where the russet colonnade of Liverpool Street Station loomed like a Victorian backdrop.

"Ready?" Spencer asked, as he cruised to a stop in front of the ornate turn-of-the-century edifice.

"Yes, yes, I think so," Stephanie replied hesitantly.

"You'll do fine. It's that one right there," Spencer said, pointing out one of the many arched entrances. "The one with the big clock."

Stephanie got out of the taxi and approached the facade of finely pointed brick at an easy pace, easy enough to be followed, as Shepherd's note had instructed.

The train station was alive with weekend travelers hurrying beneath the delicate latticework of steel and glass that spanned slender cast-iron columns. The space below the rhythmic vaults was brightened by lush ferns cascading from baskets hanging above the platforms.

Stephanie entered beneath the clock, heading for the endless rows of tracks. She was aching to see Walt, wondering if she ever would, her heart thumping so loudly she could almost hear it over the public address announcements that echoed through the cavernous station:

"Miss Moore, Miss Tessa Moore, please meet your party at track twelve . . . Mr. Colchester, Mr. Nicholas Colchester to a courtesy telephone please . . . Your attention please, the six-forty express to Cambridge will be departing from track eighteen this evening . . ."

Shepherd was on a pedestrian bridge above the Bishopsgate colonnade, his eyes riveted to the arched entrance below the clock. The anticipation had been building since Spencer reported he had made contact with Stephanie.

The clock read 6:34 when Shepherd saw her striding beneath it. His head filled with the memory of her scent; he had an impulse to dash down the staircase and embrace her. The sight of Applegate and the two Special Forces agents snapped him out of it.

For once, Shepherd was relieved to see them. All along, he had anticipated that his adversaries would intercept the tape he had sent to Stephanie, and he had shrewdly counted on their zealous bent for manipulation and deviousness to use it against him. He knew that Stephanie would be surveilled until he had been terminated, knew that her watchdogs would let her lead them to him. Shepherd had made that the cornerstone of his plan. Now he knew it had worked.

On the other side of the station, Stephanie was approaching a row of ticket windows where people were standing in long queues. The two agents following her exchanged puzzled looks as she continued past, not buying a ticket as they expected she might. Applegate was in the lead, deftly slipping between travelers to maintain visual contact with her, when the public address announcer intoned, "Major Applegate, Major Paul Applegate, please come to a courtesy telephone. Major Applegate to a courtesy telephone please."

Applegate stopped walking; no one knew he was there, not Kiley, not Larkin. "Don't lose her," he warned the others as he dropped off to take the call.

He had no doubt it was Shepherd.

The numerous courtesy phone locations eliminated the possibility that Shepherd might be waiting for him. Still, as a precaution, Applegate selected the one near the ticket booths, which was in an open area.

"May I help you?" a woman's voice asked the instant he lifted the receiver.

"This is Major Applegate. I was paged."

"Ah yes, Major," she enthused cheerily. "You have a call; please hold. Go ahead, sir," she said when the connection was made.

"Applegate, this is Shepherd," Shepherd said in a hard, commanding tone. He was curled in a phone booth just inside the colonnade where Stephanie had entered the station. "I don't know what you're up to, Major, and I don't want to know. I wouldn't blow the whistle on you if I did. My point is—"

"Where the hell are you, Shepherd?" Applegate interrupted. "What do you think you're—"

"Shut up and listen, dammit. The point I'm making is you have no reason to kill me. My wife and kids are all I care about. Now, I want you to bring me in; I want me and my family to be given new identities and relocated. You know, like they do with witnesses? That's what I want. You arrange it?"

"I don't know," Applegate replied, caught off guard. "I mean, I'd have to clear it. My people would need assurances that—"

"Then let's meet somewhere and work it out."

"Sure, sure we can. How about—"

"Hard Rock Cafe in Mayfair," Shepherd shot back, beating him to it. "Fifteen minutes." He hung up and hurried from the booth.

"Shepherd? Shepherd, dammit!" Applegate groaned, slamming the phone onto the hook. He began shouldering his way through the crush of travelers in the terminal to the street, then he sprinted to his car and clambered behind the wheel. He was reaching for the microphone to contact the agents when his eyes darted to the rearview mirror, to the face that had suddenly appeared directly behind him.

"Don't move, Major," Shepherd barked, jabbing the pistol Spencer had given him hard against the back of Applegate's skull. "Hands on the wheel and keep them there." He reached around from the backseat, where he had been concealed, slipped his free hand inside Applegate's jacket, and took the Baretta from his shoulder holster.

"What the fuck is this, Shepherd? You said—"

"I lied," Shepherd retorted. He kept his pistol against Applegate's neck and pushed the Baretta into his waistband, then leaned over the seat, grabbed the microphone cable, and yanked it out of the dash. "Get moving. Make a left at the next corner."

"Fuck you; go ahead shoot; shoot me right here."

"Listen up, Major. One of us is going to do the driving; if it's me, you wake up with a nasty lump on your head and an even nastier headache. Your move."

Applegate muttered an expletive, started the car, and drove off into the night.

27

T H E   F - 1 1 1 that had once had AC MAJ SHEPHERD stenciled on the nose gear door was streaking down Okba ben Nafi's south runway at 145 knots when the Libyan pilot eased back the stick and the sleek bomber rose into the balmy North African darkness. Its Vietnam-era camouflage had been painted over with a pattern of soft desert browns; all U.S. markings had been replaced by the bold green square of the Libyan Air Force.

"It would be best if they remained unmarked, sir," General Younis had counseled when Qaddafi gave the order.

"Have you no national pride?" Qaddafi exploded, launching into one of his tirades. "You're too easily cowed by the Americans. Did you know they sold dozens of these aircraft to the Australians? *Dozens.* So who's to say where we got them?" He threw his copy of *The Military Balance* at Younis and added, "Now you know where to go for spare parts."

Younis had no choice but to console himself with the knowledge that the F-111s would be flown only at night.

The two aviators in the cockpit were the cream of a mediocre crop from which Younis had selected four crews. Like test pilots in an unfamiliar aircraft they were coping with a barrage of flight and mission data. Twenty minutes after takeoff, the fast-moving bomber was 250 miles from base and closing on its target.

"Thirty miles," the pilot reported.

"Attack radar engaged," the wizzo replied, eyes riveted to the Pave Tack monitor, as he manipulated the control handle that swings out from the right sidewall.

Qaddafi and Younis were in the tower at Okba ben Nafi with the East German avionics expert, hovering over one of the radar screens, listening to the pilot and wizzo.

SHK Chief Abdel-Hadi sat off to one side, the Akita heeled patiently next to him.

Moncrieff paced nervously behind them. He wasn't thinking

about F-111s, water shortages, or pipelines, but about getting Katifa to Saudi Arabia, where she could safely convalesce. Rejecting
commercial flights as too vulnerable to attack by Nidal's hit squads,
he had gone to his family for assistance and one of the Royal
DC-9s was due to arrive at Okba ben Nafi shortly.

Qaddafi and Younis flinched as the crackle and hiss from the
radio was suddenly broken.

"Twenty miles," the F-111's pilot reported. He pushed the throttles to the stops, beginning a high-speed bombing run designed to
minimize the time that the plane would spend in hostile airspace.

"They should have acquisition by now," the bony East German
groaned, avoiding Qaddafi's angry glare.

"Ten miles," the pilot announced. "Five . . . four . . ."

"Blank screen," the wizzo reported, his eyes darting between
the columns of alphanumeric data.

Younis snatched a microphone from the tower radar console.
"Save the ordnance," he ordered, knowing the bombs would miss
the target—a defunct oil pumping station in the desert, selected
because it was the same distance from Okba ben Nafi as Nefta
Dam in Tunisia.

This was the third training sortie in as many nights and, each
time, despite the F-111's being right on target, the Pave Tack
program invariably wasn't.

"I thought you had this solved," Qaddafi challenged the East
German.

"So did I," the flustered engineer replied. "We've checked
and double checked every sequence point; the data is accurate
and precise; it's the entry key that we haven't been able to
crack."

"We'll just have to wait until the Americans get their hands on
the hostages," Younis counseled softly.

"What about the Palestinian?" Qaddafi demanded, shifting his
glowering eyes to the secret police chief.

Abdel-Hadi's thick brows went up apprehensively. "Nothing.
He has a strong will, and I'm concerned we'll—"

"Find a way to break it," Qaddafi retorted angrily. He was still
smoldering when the pilot of the Saudi jetliner radioed the tower
for landing clearance.

Moncrieff had been paying no attention to the others; now, he
came to life. "They must have immediate clearance," he exhorted
in an urgent tone.

The air traffic controller glanced at Qaddafi.

Qaddafi nodded sharply. Then making one of his legendary mood shifts, he turned to Moncrieff with a warm smile. "Allah be with you," he said, embracing him. "Both of you."

"My apologies for what happened," Moncrieff replied. "I know how frustrating it has been for you." He waited until Qaddafi nodded, then hurried to the elevator. At the base of the tower a waiting jeep whisked him across the airfield.

A DC-9, sporting the Saudi royal family coat of arms on the tail, touched down on the west runway and was directed by air traffic control to the military helicopter port. Two royal bodyguards deplaned, joining Moncrieff, who led the way to a Libyan Air Force helicopter. The Soviet-made Mi-8 lifted off and set a course for Al Fatah University Hospital.

AT ABOUT THE SAME TIME, a battered van came down University Road in the Al Fatah district and turned into a people's shopping precinct. It stopped in front of a market where the nurse who had been caring for Katifa was waiting. He got into the van, joining a two-man PLO hit squad, and directed them the short distance to the hospital.

When reporting Katifa's survival, he had withheld her whereabouts, insisting they meet in Tripoli, at which time he would reveal it in exchange for money.

"She's in room three seventeen," the nurse said as they pulled into the parking lot. "But there are . . ." Before he could finish, one Palestinian had a handful of his hair, the other a knife to his throat.

"Wait, wait," he blurted as the blade nicked his flesh, sending a drop of blood along the edge of polished steel. "You can't get to her without me."

The Palestinians hesitated; they had planned to kill him and keep the money for themselves.

"There are bodyguards—two—outside her room," the nurse went on, shrinking from the blade. "They're heavily armed; but I can get—"

"*You're* going to get us past them?" the Palestinian with the knife interrupted sarcastically.

"No, no, I can get *her* past them. I'm her nurse. I will bring her to you. I will bring her right here."

The Palestinians exchanged looks, clearly pleased at the development, and released him. "Go," the driver said, throwing open the van door.

"My money, please," the nurse said nervously, edging toward the door.

"When we have her," the one with the knife retorted, snapping the blade closed.

"I would have to be a fool to agree to that."

The driver removed a packet of bills from his jacket and grudgingly gave him half of it.

The nurse pocketed the fistful of cash and hurried across the parking lot in the darkness to the emergency entrance. He put the money in his locker and slipped into a lab coat, then went to the administrative offices.

In Libya, medical care, like education and housing, is fully covered by the government and there was no bill to be paid. The clerk knew Katifa was being discharged that evening and her release papers were ready for her signature. The nurse picked them up and took the elevator to the third floor.

Katifa had shed her hospital gown and robe in favor of jeans, turtleneck, and jacket. She was putting her few personal belongings into a bag when the nurse entered pushing a wheelchair.

"Ah, good, you're ready," he said, presenting her with the papers and a pen.

"Is it time?" Katifa asked, puzzled, as she signed them. "I didn't hear the helicopter."

"You're going to the airport by van."

"Are you sure? Moncrieff said a helicopter."

"There must have been a change of plans. He's waiting for you in the parking lot with a van," the nurse replied coolly as Katifa limped to the wheelchair. He helped her into it, slung the strap of her bag over his shoulder, and rolled her to the elevator.

One of the guards accompanied them to the ground floor, where they exited into a lobby area. "Would you take these to administration?" the nurse asked, handing him the release papers. As the guard strode off, the nurse wheeled Katifa down a corridor that led directly to the parking lot. The doors opened automatically and he continued through them without breaking stride, pushing the wheelchair into the night.

Katifa was looking about anxiously for Moncrieff when the Palestinians emerged from the darkness. She gasped at the sight of them, her hand tightening on the pistol in her jacket. She had the element of surprise and decided to keep it, waiting until they were at point blank range before squeezing the trigger. The bullet caught one of the Palestinians in the center of his chest, knocking him back against the van. The other recoiled in surprise, his eyes darting to the smoking hole in the pocket of Katifa's jacket. He was armed but hesitated an instant before drawing his pistol; not because he had qualms about killing her but because Abu Nidal had ordered otherwise, and the weapon in his hand was a pentothal-filled syringe.

Nidal hadn't sent them to kill Katifa but to bring her back to Beirut. Despite her apparent disloyalty, she had written *Intifada*, had fought long and hard for the Palestinian cause; and as her adoptive father, Nidal wanted to hear her side before taking extreme measures. At the least, he would learn what position others who had attended the fateful meeting at Assad's villa in Damascus had taken.

The Palestinian hesitated no more than a second or two, but it was long enough for Katifa to pull the trigger again. He fell to the ground mortally wounded and lay motionless next to his colleague. The syringe dropped from his hand and went rolling across the macadam. Katifa glanced behind her for the nurse, but he had run when the first shot rang out and was long gone. She was getting out of the wheelchair when she heard the rising whomp of the helicopter.

It came in over the hospital at a steep angle and landed in a designated area in a corner of the parking lot. Moncrieff and the two Saudi bodyguards were coming down the steps when Katifa limped into the helicopter's headlights.

"Hit squad," she called out over the rotors.

Both bodyguards produced Uzi machine guns from beneath their jackets and secured the area while Moncrieff helped her up the steps into the helicopter.

Fifteen minutes later they were at Okba ben Nafi Air Base. Moncrieff settled Katifa in the elegant compartment aft of the cockpit as the Royal DC-9 began rolling down the long runway. It lifted off and banked sharply to the east, coming onto a heading for the Arabian peninsula.

T H E   W H I N E of the jet's turbofans was a perfect match to the chilling scream that echoed through the prison beneath the Bab al Azziziya Barracks. It wasn't a short, sudden outburst born of fright, but a prolonged, desperate bellow of excruciating pain.

The Palestinian lay naked on the floor in a corner of a pitch-black cell. He was curled in a fetal position to protect his face and genitalia from further assault by his cellmates—cellmates ordered placed there by Abdel-Hadi, who knew that the solid steel door, which kept the light out, would also keep the hungry rats in.

The young terrorist shivered with fear, listening to them scurrying about in the darkness. Soon, the scratch of claws on concrete quickened. He swept a hand blindly across the floor, batting away the vile attacker; he smacked it aside again and again, until he finally clamped his fist tightly around the snarling rodent's torso. The frantic animal dug its claws into his palm trying to get loose. He smashed it against the floor repeatedly, until blood oozed between his fingers and the crunch of bones had become a pulpy thump. He had just tossed the limp carcass aside when he felt a stabbing pain in his buttock. Razor-sharp teeth tore loose a piece of his flesh and the snarling rat scurried off with its prize as another chilling scream echoed through the prison.

Abdel-Hadi was still smarting from Qaddafi's reprimand when he arrived at the barracks compound. He went directly to the prison and entered an interrogation chamber where a guard was waiting.

"Is that the Palestinian?" Abdel-Hadi asked.

The guard nodded.

"Fetch him," the SHK chief ordered. "We should have a chat before the rats get his tongue."

28

MOMENTS AFTER Shepherd had captured Applegate outside Liverpool Station, Stephanie, who had continued walking to the opposite side of the building, approached the Broad Street colonnade. The two Special Forces agents were following close behind.

Spencer had slowly circled the building in his taxi. Now he spotted her coming from the station and, perfectly timing his arrival, came to a stop just as she reached the curb. Stephanie got in without breaking stride and the taxi drove off.

One of the agents hurried to the street for a taxi, but those for hire were all properly queued on the opposite side of the building. The other agent hurried back through the station in search of Applegate and discovered the sedan was gone.

It was a few blocks away on Middlesex, nearing Commercial Road, when the radio came to life. "Major? Come in, Major," the agent's voice crackled. "She's back in the cab. Major, do you read?"

Shepherd was in the backseat of the sedan, holding the gun on Applegate and smiling with relief at the bewildered voice. As he had planned, Stephanie was safely back in the taxi and he had Applegate where he wanted him. Soon the sedan was snaking between the warehouses; then the drumbeat of cobblestones rose as it started down the winding hill, thundering across the desolate wharves to the barge.

Shepherd prodded Applegate up the gangway into the cabin and shoved him into the captain's chair.

"Let's see some ID," Shepherd ordered.

Applegate scowled, removed his wallet from his jacket, and threw it on the table. It was a large travel type. Along with the usual cash, identification, and credit cards, it also contained his pilot's license and passport.

"You bastard," Shepherd said with disgust, coming upon Applegate's military ID. He had been hoping he would find evidence to the contrary, something to dispell the ugly implications.

Applegate shrugged impassively.

"That won't cut it, Major," Shepherd warned, his drawl thickening with anger and indignance. "If I'm going to die for my country, it better damn well be in my one-eleven. Now you're going to tell me what the hell this is all about."

"And you're going to kill me if I don't," Applegate retorted with weary insolence.

"I might."

"Either way you lose, Shepherd."

"I wouldn't count on it," Shepherd shot back, matching his smug tone. "You ever thought about being a cripple, Major? A paraplegic? Maybe a quad?" He had the pistol aimed at Applegate's forehead; now he began slowly lowering it. "I knew a pilot once; flew over a hundred sorties in Nam without a scratch; he wasn't home a week when he got rear ended on the freeway." The muzzle came to rest against Applegate's kneecap. "Whiplash; paralyzed from the neck down." Shepherd's eyes narrowed to vengeful slits as he squeezed the trigger. The pistol fired, emitting a blinding flash and loud report.

Applegate lurched and let out an involuntary gasp before it dawned on him that the bullet had missed, that Shepherd had purposely moved the gun off line. The bullet blew a hole in the chair, sending up a shower of splinters between his legs.

Shepherd pressed the muzzle against Applegate's knee again. "I asked you a question, Major."

Applegate glared at him.

Shepherd held the look for a long moment, waiting, waiting, letting the tension build, letting the weapon dig into Applegate. The sweat on the Major's forehead began rolling down his face; his mouth turned to cotton, his tongue flicking nervously at his lips.

"Something you want to say, Major?" Shepherd taunted.

Applegate's lips tightened into a defiant line.

Shepherd thought back to that terrifying day in Heyford. The sickening memory of blood and brains that had suddenly filled the air, spattering his face and flight suit, consumed him as he methodically pulled the trigger again.

The bullet creased the inside of Applegate's thigh. He groaned, his hands clutching his pants as blood seeped through the torn fabric from the burning wound in his flesh; then through clenched teeth he finally rasped, "Qaddafi wanted a couple of one-elevens,"

"You gave my one-eleven to Qaddafi?" Shepherd exploded, his eyes ablaze with anger. "Why?"

"I was following orders."

"So were the Nazis. You killed a fellow officer in cold blood; been trying to kill me. I want to know why!"

Applegate's eyes darted anxiously to the gun. "Qaddafi can't make any trouble with them."

"Keep talking, Major," Shepherd snapped, punching the muzzle into Applegate's other kneecap.

"We had a deal put together," Applegate continued, clearly in pain. "Qaddafi didn't hold up his end so we held back ANITA."

"Who's we?" Shepherd demanded. "Who?"

Applegate shook his head no, stonewalling.

Shepherd pulled the trigger and blew another hole in the wood between his legs.

"CIA," the Major answered. "Kiley's been off his nut over the Fitzgerald thing." In nervous bursts he went on to explain how and why the F-111s were delivered to Libya, concluding, "The bottom line is Qaddafi gets one-elevens, the Palestinians get a sanctuary, we get the hostages."

Shepherd gasped. He was beyond being shocked now. A lifetime of unquestioning patriotism had just been destroyed. A few moments passed before he reached under the table and removed the voice activated tape recorder from the sling that held it in place. "Anything you want to add?" he asked in a weary tone, setting it on the table in front of Applegate.

The Major winced at the sight of it and glowered at him in silent hatred.

Shepherd held the look; then hearing the rumble of tires on the wharf, he glanced out the window to see the taxi's headlights cutting through the darkness.

Applegate took advantage of the distraction and leapt to his feet, shoving the table into Shepherd, who went reeling backward, losing his grip on the pistol; it went skittering across the deck along with the tape recorder. Applegate scrambled after the gun, scooping it up on the move. Shepherd took cover behind the bulkhead that separated the main cabin from the galley just as Applegate opened fire.

Outside on the wharf, the taxi came to a stop next to Applegate's sedan. Stephanie and Spencer were just getting out when the crack of gunshots shattered the silence. A bullet struck one of the barge's windows, sending a shower of glass onto the dock.

"Walt! Walt! Oh, my God!" Stephanie cried out, lunging toward the gangway.

Spencer grasped her arm and pulled her behind the taxi as an exchange of shots rang out.

A tense silence followed.

It was broken by the rumble of the barge's old door sliding back. A figure emerged and started down the gangway in the darkness, reaching the bottom before a shaft of light illuminated Applegate's face.

Stephanie paled at the sight of him.

Applegate stumbled across the dock, heading for the sedan, heading right for Stephanie and Spencer, who were crouching between it and the taxi. They froze with terror as he raised the pistol at point blank range. A single crisp report, a blue-orange flash that came from behind Applegate, split the night. The big man stiffened, swayed, and collapsed onto the wharf.

Shepherd lowered the Baretta he had taken from Applegate earlier, and hurried down the gangway. Stephanie let out a cry of joy and ran toward him. He embraced her, his head filling with her familiar scent. They clung fiercely to each other.

Spencer was bent over Applegate's lifeless body. The bullet that felled him was the last of three that had found their mark, and the major was near death.

"He's barely breathing," Spencer announced. "You want me to take him to a casualty room?"

Shepherd considered it for a moment and scowled. "It'd serve him right if we threw him over the side," he replied, gesturing to the Thames.

"You'll be no better than he is if you do that," Stephanie admonished.

"Yeah, I guess," Shepherd said somewhat grudgingly, knowing she was right. "Besides, even if he pulls through, he won't be in any shape to make trouble." He and Spencer took hold of Applegate and loaded him into the backseat of the taxi. "Better say you found him in the street," Shepherd warned before the cabbie drove off.

Shepherd stood there clinging to Stephanie, watching the clattering diesel climb the hill and disappear into the night. This certainly wasn't the first time he had killed, but it *was* the first time he had done it face to face, the first time he hadn't been insulated in his cockpit. He shifted his eyes to a small pool of blood on the wharf and stared at it for a long moment before he led Stephanie up the gangway into the barge.

The cassette recorder was lying on the floor of the cabin along with Applegate's wallet and ID. "It's all right here," Shepherd said, retrieving the recorder. He saw Stephanie's bewildered look and gently put a fingertip to her lips to stem the barrage of questions he knew was coming. "In the morning, okay?" he asked softly. He took her hand, crossed to the alcove, and collapsed onto the bed. They burrowed beneath the mound of wool blankets, their arms and legs entwined, torsos pressed together, breathing in unison and listening to each other's heartbeats.

"The kids with your folks?" he finally whispered.

Stephanie nodded.

"What did you tell them?"

"I said I needed to get away for a few days to put myself back together," she explained, her voice cracking with emotion. "I didn't want to get their hopes up. I mean, I was going crazy. I knew you were alive but I was so afraid something would happen to you before I got here. I . . ." she paused, her eyes brimming with tears. "I love you so much," she whispered.

They clung to each other for hours before their anxiety subsided and their passions rose. Soon they were inside each other's clothing, his hands moving over the familiar swells of her body, hers gently grazing his bruised flesh, soothing the pain, releasing the pent-up tension. Several weeks had passed since they were last lovers, but the intervening events made it seem like an eternity. Grieving one minute, making love the next, they soared to moments of pure joy that crested in an electrifying affirmation of life; then, satiated and wracked with exhaustion, they collapsed into each other's arms and slept.

I N   W A S H I N G T O N ,   D . C . , dusk was falling when one of the Special Forces agents called Kiley from London to report that Shepherd had eluded them and that, after mysteriously vanishing from Liverpool station, Applegate had turned up dead on arrival at The London Hospital. "Better screw the lid down as tight as we can, sir," the distraught agent concluded.

Kiley listened in thoughtful silence, his mind racing through the myriad of moves and countermoves like a chess master. "Maybe not," the DCI finally said, enigmatically. "After forty years in this game, I've learned that sometimes, *sometimes*, the very thing we're trying so desperately to hide is precisely what ought to be revealed."

THE FOLLOWING MORNING in London, a cool, clear dawn broke over the Thames as the waterfront began coming to life, the slow-moving traffic gently rocking the river barge.

The haunting sounds that came through the windows were soon rudely joined by a voice, a familiar voice, a grating voice that drummed at Shepherd in his sleep. No! No, it can't be, he thought, convinced beyond doubt he was in the throes of a cruel nightmare. Try as he might to shut it out, Applegate's voice droned on, the insolent tone filling Shepherd with anger and fear. He suddenly sat bolt upright in the bed, emitting an anguished cry. His eyes wide with terror, he tried desperately to focus on the hazy figure hovering over him.

"Easy, hon," Stephanie said, embracing him comfortingly. "Easy. It's okay, everything's okay."

But it wasn't; despite her presence, despite her assurances, the voice continued.

Shepherd's eyes soon focused on his tape recorder atop a small built-in dresser next to the bed. "The tape," he said with an immense sigh of relief. "You're listening to the tape."

Stephanie nodded, eyes full of compassion and concern, knowing now all that he had been through. She shut off the tape, draped a blanket over his shoulders, and kissed him lovingly; then she fetched them both a cup of coffee from the galley.

"Hard to believe, isn't it?" Shepherd said, sipping from the steaming mug. "Our own people—"

"I know," she replied glumly. "Your commanding officer works in the White House."

"Larkin?"

Stephanie nodded.

"A little detail Major Applegate forgot to mention," Shepherd observed, thinking he was going to need every piece of ammunition and data he had amassed.

He gathered Applegate's wallet, credit cards, passport, and

identification, which were strewn across the floor, and put them in a manila envelope along with his tape recorder and the cassette containing Applegate's account of the conspiracy. He was about to add the strip of snapshots of him holding the signed newspaper when he paused thoughtfully, then fetched a pair of scissors from the galley and cut one snapshot from the strip.

"Hang onto this," he said, giving it to Stephanie. "Anything happens to me you can—"

"Walt," she protested.

"Just in case. You can use it to prove I was alive and well the day *after* the air strike."

They left the barge, got into Applegate's car, drove along the waterfront to Knightsbridge, in London's West End, and parked in a multilevel garage around the corner from the Underground. A sense of exhilaration at having prevailed came over Shepherd as they hurried toward Bowater House, the modern office tower on Knightsbridge Road opposite Hyde Park, where CBS News was located.

CBS was the network of Murrow, Sevareid, and Cronkite, the network that had exposed McCarthy, that had damn near invented electronic journalism and, for decades, had set standards of quality and integrity for the industry. Shepherd imagined the stunned reactions, the buzz of excitement as a dead man walked into the newsroom; imagined the lead story that evening as Dan Rather, with patented, thin-lipped gravity, would reveal the ugly conspiracy to the nation and world.

Stephanie sensed his mood and tightened her grip on his hand as they approached the building, its horizontal bands of gray granite and steel mullions in stark contrast to its Victorian neighbors. At the newstand on the corner of Sloane, Shepherd's eyes darted to his photograph on the front page of the *London Times* and a headline that proclaimed: PILOT THOUGHT DEAD, A DESERTER; KILLS USAF OFFICER.

Shepherd stared at it in disbelief. "Better buy one," he finally said to Stephanie in a hoarse whisper. He led the way to Hyde Park, the seemingly endless expanse of greenery in central London, where they settled on a bench and read the story:

> In a bizarre mix-up that has baffled U.S. Air Force officials, informed sources have told the *Times* that Major Walter Shepherd, reportedly killed during

the raid on Libya, had actually gone AWOL moments before he was scheduled to take off in his F-111 bomber. Believed upset at having to fly a combat mission with a new weapons systems officer, the thirty-seven-year-old veteran of the Vietnam conflict failed to appear on the flight line. The last-minute switch of crews had apparently confused Air Force public information personnel, who referred to the original mission roster when releasing the names of pilots and weapons systems officers whose bombers had been shot down by Libyan surface-to-air missiles. *Times* sources have also learned that last night Major Shepherd allegedly shot and killed Major Paul Applegate of military intelligence, who had tracked him down. Though critically wounded, Major Applegate evidently managed to escape from his attacker and was found unconscious on an East End street by a taxi driver who took him to hospital. However, he expired before casualty room doctors could administer treatment. At press time officials were still trying to piece together other details of the story.

Shepherd looked up from the paper, feeling as if he had been kicked in the groin. "They took it away from us," he finally said, the color draining from his face as he spoke.

"What do you mean?"

"The truth. It threatened them, scared the hell out of them," he said, briefly savoring the idea. "They were terrified someone would find out I was alive before they could kill me. But not anymore. The bastards turned the whole damn thing around."

"So what?" Stephanie replied, undaunted, trying to bolster his spirits. "The story has obviously been planted; the air force doesn't know if it's true or—"

"That's my point. The moment I surface, I confirm it. I'll be arrested, charged with desertion, charged with *murder*; anything I say will be seen as an alibi, as something I cooked up to cover my butt."

"But it's the truth."

Shepherd shrugged. "I can't prove it. I mean, it's all so damned absurd. Who'd believe it?"

"You have the tape—"

"They'll claim I forced Applegate to make it. Hell, the truth is I did. You heard it, so will they. Then they'll say I killed him to shut him up."

"Your word against theirs. What about a lie detector? Wouldn't that—"

"Steph," he interrupted. "Did I fly that mission?"

"No."

"Did I kill Applegate?"

"Uh huh," she replied dejectedly, seeing where he was headed.

"Exactly what they're saying; the rest are shadings, details. The bottom line is I'm looking at a court martial no matter how I slice this. If I lose, I face a firing squad . . ." He let the sentence trail off forebodingly, then added, "Assuming I'm not killed resisting arrest."

They looked at each other forlornly.

"You can't run forever," she finally said.

"And I can't come forward unless I can prove what's on that tape."

"How?"

"There's only one thing I can think of," he said, intrigued by the audacity of the thought. "Get back my plane."

29

THE MORNING AFTER the meeting in Lancaster's office, Larkin drove to Fort Belvoir in Virginia to begin the search for a Mediterranean rendezvous between the PLO gunboat and a second, mystery vessel. The top-security installation where KH-11 data was monitored and recorded was located 10 miles south of Alexandria.

After identifying himself, Larkin was given a security badge and taken to a computer room where a technician waited.

The KH-11 satellite that had been spying on Tripoli and surrounding areas transmitted high-resolution color images by day and infrared images by night to the huge antenna atop the concrete blockhouse. The data was recorded and stored on videotape. Each of the special-sized cartridges covered a twenty-four-hour period.

The technician had a half-dozen stacked next to a high-speed videotape analyzer that was tied into Fort Belvoir's powerful Cray Y-MP supercomputer. The data on the cartridges covered the time between the failed hostage exchange and the discovery that the hostages weren't aboard the gunboat, the time during which they had been transferred to another vessel.

The technician loaded the first cartridge into the analyzer, then programmed the computer to ignore all land-based data, instructing it to search for two vessels side by side in open sea.

Since each frame of videotape depicted a large section of the Mediterranean, the technician further instructed the computer to break the frames down into grid squares and analyze them individually, starting with Tripoli harbor, working north, and east to west. The images were blown up and viewed on a 1,250 line per inch video monitor that provided twice the resolution of a standard television set.

That was two days ago.

Now in the center of the screen two elongated specks stood out against the dark texture of the sea. The technician typed on his keyboard and the infrared image on the monitor began zooming in slowly; the dark specks kept increasing in size until two hazy shapes filled the screen. The oblong blobs were heavily textured but devoid of definitive pictorial detail.

"Might be something," the technician said.

Larkin shrugged, unconvinced; the hostage debacle had plunged him into an angry depression and the news of Applegate's death had made it worse.

The technician typed another instruction. "For our purposes, we can assume those blobs are vessels," he explained. "At super-computer speed—that's billions of operations per second—the image-enhancement program will compare groups of data particles against a library of known shapes, objects, and details. In this case I've programmed it to deal only with seagoing vessels of certain classifications. It begins with the general and proceeds to infinitesimal detail." He nodded to the monitor, where the image had begun gaining definition. In moments the fuzzy details had resolved into the distinct, clearly identifiable decks of two vessels.

Larkin just about gasped when he saw them.

It was so simple, so obvious, so perfect, he thought. He could hardly believe his eyes. There on the monitor was the PLO gun-boat and next to it—goddammit, *connected* to it by a gangway on which the infrared images of cowed men could be seen walking —was a submarine.

"Clever bastards," Larkin said bitterly.

Indeed, while intelligence operatives were searching every slum and hellhole in the Middle East for the hostages, Abu Nidal had shrewdly hidden them beneath the sea. For countless months they had been cruising the Mediterranean's inky depths—and they still were.

A S   H E   D I D   E V E R Y   N I G H T before leaving the office, Bill Kiley was watching the network news. That morning he had paused longer than usual in front of the memorial wall in Langley's lobby. Applegate's death had ruined whatever satisfaction he had derived from neutralizing Shepherd; the thought that another star, an anonymous one, would soon be engraved in the

Georgia marble had intensified his gloomy mood. He was cursing the media's antiadministration bias when his secretary told him Larkin was on the line.

"That's great news, Colonel," he said enthusiastically when Larkin told him the hostages had been located on a submarine. "We can thank the Syrians for this one."

"Syrians, sir?"

"Damn right. Moscow sold them some Romeos a couple of years ago; three to be exact. That explains why Nidal can't make a move without clearing it with Assad first."

"Well, if anyone can find that sub, it's Duryea," Larkin said encouragingly.

"I'm counting on it," Kiley replied, tilting back in his chair, entertaining an idea. "Hold on for a minute." He swiveled to his computer terminal and typed in ROMEO. A directory appeared on the screen. He scrolled through it and found the file he wanted. "How soon can you leave for the Mediterranean?"

"Tonight," Larkin replied, brightening at the chance to get out of the DCI's doghouse and back into the field.

"Good. I have something one of our people picked up that I think Duryea will find useful. It'll be at Andrews when you get there. Stay on top of this," Kiley urged. "Get Fitz the hell out of there for me."

30

THE TURN OF EVENTS had hit Shepherd with devastating impact. He and Stephanie abandoned Applegate's car, took the Underground back to the East End, and returned to the barge. Though the major was no longer a problem, Shepherd had no doubt that along with CIA and the military police, every law enforcement agency in Europe would be on the lookout for him. Despite that, he knew exactly how he would get out of England; however, he had no idea how he was going to get back his F-111, let alone get into Libya.

"We could ask Gutherie," Stephanie suggested.

"The congressman?"

Stephanie nodded.

"I don't know," Shepherd replied, wrestling with it. "How do we know he isn't owned by the CIA?"

"He's their watchdog; chairs the Intelligence Committee. And he's been part of this from the start."

"What do you mean from the start?"

"It was Gutherie who found out Larkin works in the White House," she replied, explaining the circumstances that led to his listening to the tape with her.

Shepherd thought about it for a moment, then nodded. "Okay, but don't tell him any more than you have to." He remained on the barge while Stephanie went up the hill to a phone booth and made a collect call to Washington, D.C.

SEVERAL DAYS had passed since the congressman and Stephanie had listened to the tape. The possibility that the tape would provide him with a high-profile campaign issue had ended abruptly with the reports of Shepherd's desertion and murder of Applegate.

Gutherie had just returned from the Capitol when his secretary asked if she should accept a collect call from Mrs. Shepherd in London.

The congressman nodded emphatically and lifted the phone. "Mrs. Shepherd," he said sadly when the connection was made. "I'm sorry things turned out for you the way they did."

"They're vicious lies," Stephanie retorted sharply.

"I don't understand," Gutherie replied, surprised by her brusqueness and tone. "If that's the case, why hasn't your husband come forward and told his side of it?"

"He can't. Not until he has proof."

"You're with him?"

"We've made contact," she replied evasively. "Can you help him get into Libya?"

"Libya? Why?"

"I don't have time to explain now. Yes or no?"

"It's impossible. They no longer have an embassy in the U.K. Besides, the president's ordered everyone out. Libya is off-limits to Americans."

"What about Tunisia?" she asked, turning to a backup destination Shepherd had selected.

"That wouldn't be a problem. Tunisia doesn't even require a visa for entry. You know, for what it's worth, you might try a place called D'Jerba Island," Gutherie suggested. Just off Tunisia's southeastern coast, the legendary home of the lotus eaters—where Ulysses landed more than 3,000 years ago—had recently acquired an international airport and modern tourist facilities, and was a thriving resort and convention center.

"Gerber, like in baby food?" Stephanie prompted.

"No. It's *D* apostrophe *J-e-r-b-a*," Gutherie replied, spelling it out. "I attended a conference there a few years ago. It's about as close to Libya as you can get without living in a tent; and if I remember correctly, in those days there was a small Libyan Embassy in one of the convention complexes."

"Thanks. I'll pass it on to my husband. It's important you still keep this to yourself," Stephanie cautioned firmly. "You understand?"

"Not really, no," the congressman replied curtly. "Not without knowing why."

"Walt will be killed if they find him."

"If who finds him?" he asked, sensing the issue he sought was still viable. "Come on, what's going on?"

"You were right about covert activity getting out of hand. That's all I can tell you."

"You're not making this easy."

"I just told you they'll kill him. Please."

"Okay," Gutherie said, moved by her desperate tone. "But I can't sit on it forever."

"Thanks."

"I still wish you'd tell me what's going on."

Stephanie wrestled with it in silence for a few seconds, then slowly lowered the receiver onto the hook.

Gutherie heard the line go dead. He was sitting there, staring out the window, when it occurred to him that there was one other person who might know.

S T E P H A N I E returned to the barge and briefed Shepherd on the conversation. He nodded thoughtfully when she finished, then began rummaging through the cartons of books stacked in the cabin. Several were filled with oversized volumes, and one contained an atlas. Shepherd pulled it free, then turned to the map of Tunisia and located D'Jerba Island. "The congressman's right. It can't be more than fifty miles to the Libyan border," he observed, brightening. "Remind me to thank him when I see him."

"That's a promise," Stephanie said, smiling; then her eyes drifted to Applegate's ID on the table, next to a sheet of paper on which Shepherd had been practicing his signature. "Are you sure about using those?" she asked. "He's been in the papers, on TV. It's not a common name; someone might recognize it."

Shepherd nodded knowingly. "But not as easily as they'll recognize mine. Just better odds this way; and I have a couple of ideas how we can make them even better."

They waited until it was dark before they went up the hill to a men's shop on Kerbey and bought Walt some clothes: casual slacks, a sport jacket, shoes, shirts, underwear, and a small travel bag.

Then they split up.

Stephanie headed for a row of shops down the street that sold used books.

Shepherd walked a few blocks to the automated snapshot booth he had used previously. He took three sets of pictures, changing his shirt for each.

Next stop was a self-service copy shop on Montague where he cut a picture from each strip, backed them with scotch tape, and affixed them to Applegate's pilot's license, passport, and military identification. Then, he made color Xeroxes of all three, trimmed the military identification and pilot's license to size and heat-sealed them in plastic at an adjacent machine.

The passport was more difficult: the personal data and photograph were on the inside front cover under a toned laminate. Anything pasted over it would obviously abut the stitching that held the pages; but the matte surface laminate was smaller than the cover, leaving a border around the three edges and the sewn spine.

Shepherd returned to the barge and trimmed the Xerox, coated the back with spray adhesive he had purchased at the copy shop, and positioned it on the inside cover of Applegate's passport over the laminate.

The alteration of all three pieces of ID, which once would have taken an expert forger several days to accomplish, was completed in just over an hour.

Stephanie couldn't find the publication she sought in the used book shops. One proprietor sent her to a shop in Charing Cross that specialized in military publications. There she finally found several tattered copies of a 1969 U.S. Air Force orientation manual for Wheelus Field, now Okba ben Nafi Air Base. After making her purchase, she hurried to a street corner phone booth, settled in with a handful of coins, opened the Yellow Pages to Airlines, and began dialing.

"British Airways, reservations," a cheery voice answered. "How may I help you?"

IN WASHINGTON, D.C., Bill Kiley was packing up the three briefcases he took home each night. The discovery of the hostages' whereabouts had bolstered his spirits; something had finally gone right and he felt like celebrating. He called his wife and suggested they meet at their favorite restaurant for dinner. He was on the way to the elevator with his bodyguard when his secretary caught up with him.

"COMINT just sent this up," she said with a smile, handing him a computer printout. The acronym, shorthand for Communications Intelligence, referred to the department responsible for intercepting electronic communications. Monitoring computerized airline reservation systems was but one of its many activities.

The printout was a list of commercial air carriers, flight numbers, departure and arrival information, and dates; the name Walter Shepherd was next to each.

"Damn," Kiley said admiringly. "He's booked on every flight out of the U.K. for the next week."

"Twenty-seven," she replied. "Departures from six different airports, eighteen destinations."

Good but not good enough, he thought, brightening. Things sure *were* going right.

"Put it on the global net," he instructed. It was just a matter of time now; every airport, every flight would be covered. It didn't matter which one he actually took. Shepherd was history.

31

AFTER INFORMING KILEY that the hostages had been transferred from the gunboat to a submarine, Larkin left Fort Belvoir, taking Route 1 north through Alexandria.

Forty minutes later, he crossed Memorial Bridge into the District. He had plenty of time to stop at his apartment, pack a bag, and catch the late shuttle out of Andrews. The Capitol dome glistened in the late afternoon light as he cut across 23rd to Virginia Avenue and pulled into the garage beneath his high-rise.

He parked in his assigned space and had taken a few steps toward the elevators when a voice rang out.

"Colonel Larkin?" The words echoed off the concrete walls of the cavernous space.

Larkin turned to see a figure coming toward him. Whoever it was cast a long shadow across the oil-stained concrete.

"Jim Gutherie, Congressman from Maryland," the big fellow said, extending a hand. "I need a few minutes of your time, Colonel."

Larkin's eyes narrowed with uncertainty. "I'm not in the habit of holding meetings in parking garages, Mister Congressman."

"Nor am I."

"Then I respectfully suggest you call my office for an appointment."

"I did. Your secretary was reluctant to make one. She said you were leaving the country and wasn't sure when you planned to return."

"That's exactly right," Larkin said, starting to back away. "I'll have her contact you as soon as I do."

"I'm sorry, Colonel. This can't wait."

"I have a flight to catch," Larkin said, glancing at his watch. "Whatever's on your mind, make it fast."

"Major Walter Shepherd."

"Shepherd?" Larkin echoed with a disgusted shrug, hiding his concern. "The guy who deserted and killed that MI officer?"

"Yes. What do you know about him?"

"What I read in the papers. Why?"

"I don't recall them mentioning you were his commanding officer," Gutherie countered sharply.

Larkin was rocked; he held Gutherie's look for a long moment, regaining his composure. "That's classified," he said coolly. "That's all I can tell you."

"I chair the HIC, Colonel," Gutherie replied pointedly. "I'm cleared right into your personnel file: Special Forces, CIA, White House staff—"

"Then you know my sanction."

"I have a feeling you're abusing it."

Larkin seethed and burned him with a look. "Who the fuck do you think you are anyway?"

"The guy who's going to nail your ass," Gutherie retorted, waving to a car behind him. The black New Yorker pulled forward and stopped next to him. "That's a promise, Colonel." Gutherie got in, slammed the door, and the car roared across the garage.

Larkin waited until it had gone up the ramp and disappeared into the night, then went to the elevator.

LE LION D'OR on Connecticut Avenue had the finest French cuisine in Washington; and despite Bill Kiley's brusqueness and penchant for profanity, he had cultured tastes that he preferred to indulge in privacy. He and his wife were at their usual table when the security man slipped behind the beveled glass screen and whispered something to him.

"I'll be right back," he said to his wife. "If the waiter comes, I'll have the escargots and lamb." Then, without further explanation, he walked slowly to the parking lot, climbed into his limousine, and lifted the phone. It was Larkin calling from his apartment.

"How did *he* get into this?" the DCI exclaimed after the colonel briefed him on his encounter with Gutherie.

"I don't know, sir; but he made damned sure I knew he chaired the House Intelligence Committee."

"Don't remind me," the DCI said. "He's a fucking pain in the ass; not the type to let go."

"How do you want to handle it?"

Kiley leaned back in the seat, a vague recollection tugging at his memory. "You proceed as planned, Colonel," he finally said. "Leave the congressman to me."

Larkin fetched his two-suiter, returned to his car, and drove to Andrews Air Force Base. A CIA courier was waiting in the boarding lounge when he arrived. "From Langley, sir," he said, handing the colonel a slim attaché case. Larkin waited until he was airborne before opening it. He broke into a broad smile on seeing the contents. The old man didn't miss a trick.

T H R E E   D A Y S had passed since the team of SEALs discovered there were no hostages aboard the PLO gunboat. Duryea had kept the *Cavalla* on station in the Mediterranean, awaiting data from the KH-11 review.

It was 8:36 A.M. when the communications officer delivered a cable to Duryea's compartment:

KEYHOLE REVEALS CARGO IN QUESTION TRANSFERRED TO ROMEO CLASS SUBMARINE 14APR AT 02:47 HOURS. 344216N/125832E. ASSUME BOAT UNDER SYRIAN COMMAND. MAJOR LARKIN IS EN ROUTE. ROME STATION CHIEF WILL COORDINATE MEETING ON USS AMERICA.

Duryea topped up his coffee, went to the command center computer terminal, and queried the BC-10. Data on the Romeo began printing out across the screen: Diesel; twin screws; top speed 13 knots dived; primitive electronics. A total of twenty built in the late 1950s: five still operated by the Soviet Navy; one scrapped, two sold to Algeria, three to Bulgaria, six to Egypt, and three to Syria.

Discounting the Soviet and Bulgarian boats, which were deployed elsewhere, Duryea calculated a maximum of eleven Romeos could be plying Mediterranean depths—eleven underwater *antiques*, he thought, making a connection.

He went to the sonar room and handed the cable to Cooperman. "Remember that weird contact?" he prompted.

The rotund sonarman shrugged his shoulders. He detected literally hundreds of contacts daily in the heavily traveled Mediterranean; and whatever Duryea was referring to had been long forgotten. "*Which* weird contact, sir?"

"The antique; the one you'd never heard before?"

"When we were closing on Tripoli harbor?" Cooperman sensed where the captain was headed.

"Yeah. I'm thinking it might've been lover boy."

"Stay tuned, skipper," Cooperman enthused, turning to his equipment. Alphas, Charlies, Viktors—the nuclear-powered core of the Soviet Navy were the contacts that stuck; not a thirty-year-old diesel. But now that it had meaning, he knew exactly what to do.

All sonar contacts were stored on magnetic tape. A high-speed search found the one in question. Cooperman put it up on the oscilloscope, then accessed the BC-10 computer. Its magnetic bubble memory contained the acoustic signatures of all Soviet Navy vessels. He retrieved the basic Romeo profile and ran it through the oscilloscope, comparing its pattern of frequencies to that of the recorded contact. Save for minor harmonic idiosyncrasies due to the signatures' being made by different sets of propeller blades, they matched.

I T   W A S just after noon when Larkin's flight touched down on the long runway adjacent to 6th Fleet headquarters outside Naples, Italy.

A CIA driver was waiting when the colonel deplaned with his carry-on and attaché. "We're over here, sir," he said, leading the way to a gray government sedan. "We've arranged a ride in the backseat of an A-six that's being delivered to the *America*."

The Intruder's pilot was ready to go when they arrived on the flight line. Larkin pulled a jumpsuit over his clothing, donned a helmet, and climbed into the seat behind him. Barely an hour later they had covered the 420 miles from Naples to the USS *America* on station just southeast of Malta.

"Ever landed on a carrier before, sir?"

"First time," Larkin replied, unimpressed by the hair-raising tales of landing at 145 knots on a postage stamp pitching in a rolling sea. On the contrary, now that he was out of the DCI's doghouse, he was feeling rather cocky; but he quickly paled, knuckles whitening, as the pilot skillfully brought the Intruder in over the *America*'s fantail. It slammed onto the short runway in a controlled crash and was jerked to a neck-snapping stop by the arrester cable, forever ending any controversy over who had bragging rights among pilots.

Commander Chris Duryea had been ferried from the *Cavalla* a short time earlier. His boat was classified as a hunter-killer submarine and, knowing he would soon be playing underwater hide-and-seek with the Romeo, Duryea had brought his chief hunter and killer along.

"Good to see you again, Colonel," the commander said when Larkin was ushered into the secure compartment in the *America*'s communication bay. He latched onto Larkin's hand, then introduced Cooperman and Reyes.

"As you probably know," Larkin began after the coffee had been served and preliminaries dispensed with, "this is the old man's operational priority; a personal obsession. I made him a promise I'd have some traveling companions when I returned; seven of them to be exact. Any ideas how I keep it?"

"Well, we've been kicking a few around," Duryea replied, signaling Cooperman with a nod.

The sonarman brought Larkin up to speed on the mysterious contact. "Turns out it was a Romeo," he concluded. "Cross referencing location and time of contact with Keyhole data, odds are it's our boy."

"In other words, Colonel," Duryea said, "we can separate the target from any other ship in the Mediterranean; hell, in the world for that matter."

"Then what?"

"Intercept and board," Reyes said in his cocky manner. "We foul the props; force her to surface—"

"Easy does it," Duryea cautioned. "Remember we're talking about a dived boat here. The trick is to incapacitate her without spooking the crew."

"We'll need deck plans," Reyes declared.

"We have them," Larkin replied. He set the attaché on the table and removed a set of drawings, *construction* drawings that went well beyond deck plans to delineate every rivet, hatch, electrical chase, air duct, snorkel vent, and mast. "Compliments of the director."

The group scoured the drawings, determining where the hostages would most likely be quartered; then they searched unsuccessfully for a way to disable and board the Romeo without endangering them.

Duryea was prowling the room, deep in thought. "I think we're coming at this backwards," he finally offered.

"Which means?" Larkin wondered.

"Incapacitate the people, not the boat."

"The people . . ."

Duryea nodded; a growing smile left no doubt he knew exactly how he would go about it.

32

THE THAMES lay long and flat, like a black liquid mirror unstirred yet by the morning's barge traffic.

Stephanie watched as Shepherd dressed and packed his things into the travel bag. A week ago she thought he was dead; now, barely more than forty-eight hours after getting him back, she was losing him again.

"Wish me luck, babe," Shepherd said, embracing her.

"I'll *bring* you luck," she replied, her eyes leaving no doubt she intended to accompany him. She had been up half the night listening to the creak of old timbers, thinking about it, and her mind was made up.

"I thought we said you were—"

"The children will be fine," she interrupted knowingly. "I'm going with you, Walt. I'm going to be with you every minute I possibly can."

Shepherd smiled, clearly pleased by her spirit, which had always captivated him.

The sun was still below the horizon when they left the barge and took the Underground to Victoria Station, just east of Belgravia near Westminister Cathedral, where they caught the 7:10 express to Brighton, the quaint seaside resort south of London.

Just over an hour later they were in a taxi traveling the winding coast to the town of Hove, to a small general aviation airport on the bluffs above the sea. It was well known to American pilots because private planes could be rented there—planes registered in the United States, which meant British flying certification wasn't required.

The rental clerk was a chatty, methodical fellow who, to Shepherd's dismay, moved at a snail's pace.

"Well, that just about covers the formalities, Major Applegate," he said, as he ran the credit card through the magnetic reader and glanced at the display, waiting for an approval code.

Shepherd's heart rate began racing. Had they canceled Applegate's credit card? Was there a code to signify the bearer was a fugitive? Was the computer printer, which had just unnervingly come to life, pumping out an alert? He flicked a nervous glance to Stephanie, who forced an encouraging smile.

Shepherd wasn't keen on using a dead man's credit card but had no doubt it would be more dangerous to use one of Stephanie's, which had his name on it. Applegate had been dead for two days; the chances that the issuing company had been notified and had broadcast a global warning were unlikely. Finally, the clerk jotted the approval code on the form and pushed it to Shepherd.

"Thanks for your help," Shepherd said as he signed Applegate's name.

"My pleasure, Major. Have a lovely holiday," the clerk replied, dropping a set of keys into Shepherd's palm. "Space thirty-eight."

Shepherd and Stephanie hurried from the rental office, following numbers stenciled on the tarmac to a Mooney 252. The four-passenger, single-engine aircraft had unusual stability, crisp sportscar handling, easy to read instrumentation, and was an excellent IFR plane. Cruising comfortably at 200-plus MPH, it burned an economical 12 gallons of fuel per hour, giving it a range in excess of 1,000 miles. It was well suited for the 1,250-mile journey to Tunisia.

Shepherd did a walk-around and soon had the Mooney zipping down the runway, flaps at 10 degrees, throttle wide open, air speed indicator climbing. A sense of relief, of exhilaration came over him as he eased back the yoke. While law enforcement authorities were blanketing airports in London, Manchester, Norwich, Birmingham, and Edinburgh, the plane lifted off, banking south over the English Channel onto a heading for the coast of Brittany.

Private and business aviation was as prevalent in Europe as the United States. Countless aircraft crisscrossed Common Market borders, refueling on foreign soil en route to their destinations. Their passengers were treated no differently than commercial travelers who had disembarked at an airport to make a connecting flight, never officially entering the country or undergoing passport control procedures.

Shepherd's flight plan—basically the same route the F-111 bombers would have flown if France had approved use of her airspace for the raid on Libya—took them on a southeast course past Paris and Lyon to Nice on the French Riviera, where they landed and refueled, then across the Mediterranean, skirting the eastern coasts of Corsica, Sardinia, and Lampedusa to southeastern Tunisia. All but 300 miles of the flight were made over, or in sight of, land.

They spent the time discussing ways to get Shepherd into Libya: renting a boat in one of D'Jerba's fishing villages and making port immediately adjacent to Okba ben Nafi Air Base topped their list, but that area of coastline would undoubtedly be heavily guarded by Libyan patrol boats; an extremely low-altitude flight to a desert landing was a close second, but that would leave him stranded miles from the air base without any transportation; renting a four-wheel drive vehicle and crossing somewhere along the miles of desolate border solved the problem; but in these scenarios and others they had considered, once inside Libya, Shepherd would still not only have to gain access to a high-security air base, but also locate his F-111, and steal it without any guarantee it would be fueled or in flying condition—all without speaking a word of Arabic.

Now, barely more than eight hours after takeoff, the domed mosques and beehive-shaped houses of D'Jerba shimmered above the Gulf of Bougara like clusters of golden pearls in the late afternoon light. The tiny island's mild climate and proximity to the capitals of Europe, Africa, and the Middle East made it ideal for a vacation or business convention.

"There it is, babe," Shepherd said, dipping a wing to give Stephanie a better view. The 197 square miles of palm and olive groves were split down the middle by MC-117, the arrow-straight road connecting Houmt Souk in the north to el-Kantara in the south, where a 5-mile-long causeway linked D'Jerba to the mainland. "An hour's drive to the Libyan border," he went on. "A hundred and fifty miles to Tripoli."

Shepherd came onto a heading for Melita International Airport and radioed the tower. Many private aircraft arrived and departed daily and he received routine landing clearance. He brought the Mooney down to a smooth landing and taxied to a parking area. After tying down, he and Stephanie presented themselves as tourists and cleared passport control without incident.

They took a taxi to the Dar Jerba Hotel, the pride of the island's burgeoning tourist industry. Set on pristine beaches amid swaying palms, it was a sprawling complex: four hotels, convention hall, casino, cinemas, several radio stations, and accommodations for 2,400; a place where two Westerners wouldn't stand out, which was why Shepherd had selected it.

He left Stephanie outside and went to the check-in desk in the lobby with their bags, registering under the name Paul Applegate. He used Applegate's credit card and reluctantly presented the altered passport at the clerk's request. The impeccably uniformed fellow recorded the number in a register, then returned it.

Shepherd didn't like it but he had little choice. He had traveled extensively and knew it was standard procedure in hotels through-out the world to forward the name and passport number of each guest to local authorities. He took some solace in the knowledge that by using Applegate's name and avoiding having Stephanie register, he had prevented the name *Shepherd* from appearing in either hotel or police records.

The bellman led Shepherd through a courtyard to a domed waterfront cottage that resembled a miniature mosque. Stephanie followed at a casual pace a short distance behind; she waited until the bellman had departed, then joined Shepherd in the cottage.

The blazing white interior was bathed in golden light and alive with the delicate scent of lemons and pomegranates carried by sea breezes from nearby groves. They left their bags where the bellman had dropped them and exited via a private deck to the beach.

For about an hour, they walked D'Jerba's sugar-fine sands, re-viewing the ways they had devised to get Shepherd into Libya; then, feeling gloomy about his prospects, they sat on a windswept bluff and watched the sun falling swiftly toward the horizon. Shep-herd was tracing a fingertip through the sand, examining the possibilities over and over, when his eyes brightened with a rec-ollection. "Steph," he finally said, breaking the long silence, "didn't the congressman say there was a Libyan Embassy here some-where?"

"Uh huh. I recall him mentioning it. He wasn't really sure. Why?"

"Let's hope he was right," Shepherd said, a chill going through him at the idea that had surfaced. "If he was, I think I know how I'm going to do it."

"You do?"

"Yes," he replied, becoming more convinced that he had not only found a way into Libya but also into the cockpit of his F-111, he added, "Applegate said the Libyans don't have ANITA, which means they've got a couple of useless bombers. I'm betting they'd like nothing better than to get their hands on an expert."

"They sure would," Stephanie replied; then, her enthusiasm tempered by concern, she said, "But you can't just walk into the embassy and say you know they have them; they're going to ask *how* you know."

"And the minute I tell them, they'll know exactly what I'm up to," Shepherd said, finishing her thought.

Stephanie nodded glumly.

Shepherd ran a hand over his bearded face. "Maybe we're missing something here," he said pensively. "Maybe the key to pulling this off is to just play the hand I've been dealt."

"What do you mean?"

"Anyone who reads the papers knows I'm a fugitive; they also know I'm a one-eleven pilot."

"True."

"So all I have to do is let the Libyans know I'm available; they'll figure out the rest."

"You're still taking a chance by coming forward."

"*I'm* not coming forward," he said with a smile, as the details solidified. "You are."

She didn't know exactly what he had in mind, but she knew he had found the answer. He had that look, she thought, the look that always came over him before a mission, the one that transformed Walt Shepherd to call sign Viper, to that person she didn't really know.

The Libyan Embassy was closed by the time they located it in a colonnade of offices adjacent to the Dar Jerba's convention center, a vaulted building on the far side of the sprawling complex.

Beneath the multicolored Libyan flag in the window was a sign that in several languages proclaimed: LIBYAN PEOPLE'S BUREAU.

Despite years of tension and strict border control, Libya and Tunisia had maintained diplomatic relations. The Libyan People's Bureau, as Qaddafi called his embassies, was located in the capital city of Tunis, but ever anxious to acquire military and industrial technology, he had also established a bureau on D'Jerba to generate contacts with the international businessmen who frequented the island. Hence, the bureau's multilanguage sign and posh interior, elegantly furnished in chrome, leather, and glass, which had been designed to resemble the offices of Western corporations, right down to the personnel.

THE FOLLOWING MORNING Stephanie dressed in the gray tweed suit and black pumps she usually wore to interviews in the District and returned to the embassy alone. She approached the receptionist with a confident stride, identified herself, and asked to see the attaché.

Adnan Al-Qasim was a tall, trim man in his mid-forties who favored conservatively tailored suits, cordovan wingtips, and subdued striped ties. His English was impeccable, as were his French and German. Educated in the United States, he had the look and demeanor of a successful corporate executive.

"I have something of a confidential nature to discuss with you," Stephanie said, taking a seat opposite him; then, shifting her eyes to the office door, which was open, she prompted, "Would you mind?"

"Of course not," Al-Qasim replied genially. He buzzed his secretary and said something in Arabic.

A moment later, the door to the office closed.

"Thank you," Stephanie said. She removed a newspaper clipping from her purse and handed it to him. "Are you familiar with this?"

Al-Qasim took the clipping and perused it from a distance. It was the *London Times* story that branded Shepherd a deserter and killer. "Well, yes, vaguely. I recall seeing something in news reports. Why do you ask?"

"There are a number of reasons. I'll begin by telling you Major Shepherd is my husband and those reports are untrue."

"Well, it's only natural for you to take that position, Mrs. Shepherd. Forgive me if I'm missing something here," Al-Qasim said in a puzzled tone, "but I haven't the slightest idea why you're telling this to me, or why you're in Tunisia for that matter."

"First, it's important you understand why my husband deserted. Bear with me if you will?"

Al-Qasim smiled knowingly. "Since I'm quite certain you're going to tell me, I'll reserve judgment."

Stephanie nodded and straightened in the chair. "My husband took the action he did because no state of war exists between the

United States and Libya, and he thought it was wrong to kill innocent people."

"Indeed, it is," Al-Qasim replied, still not quite sure what to make of her. "I fully agree."

"Then I imagine you would also agree it was his concern for your countrymen that has made him an international fugitive."

Al-Qasim's brows went up slightly at the inference. "It might be possible to make that argument, yes," he admitted grudgingly.

"A concern for your countrymen," Stephanie went on, "that has resulted in his being hunted like an animal who will probably be shot on sight."

"That's most unfortunate, Mrs. Shepherd," Al-Qasim replied, fully aware that she had just quite shrewdly positioned him. "I hope you're not suggesting my government is responsible for all this."

"No, sir, not at all. But under the circumstances, I *am* suggesting that it would be only fair to expect your government to help Major Shepherd if it had the chance."

"Reasonable enough," Al-Qasim said. "But quite frankly, Mrs. Shepherd, fairness and reason aside, I expect it would depend on just *what* my government was required to do."

Stephanie studied him for a moment, acutely aware that she was about to play the card Shepherd expected would get him into Libya. "Before I go further, I must warn you that if what I'm about to say becomes known, if the media should get involved before you go to your people, it could prove very costly not only for my husband but for your government as well."

Al-Qasim nodded, his eyes widening curiously.

"As Major Shepherd's official representative, I formally request that he be granted political asylum in Libya."

33

THE PASTEL-COLORED BOWS hovered tantalizingly close to Jim Gutherie's face. He finally captured one in his teeth and began pulling on it slowly, releasing the blond's breasts from the teddy. She led him to the bed where the redhead, her smooth white skin sprinkled with freckles, lay naked.

Gutherie removed the cap from a felt tip pen and placed the point on a tiny freckle on the redhead's chest. He pulled it slowly, drawing a line over the swell of her breast to another freckle and then on to another and another, creating an intricate network that resembled a sign of the Zodiac; then without lifting the pen, he drew a line down the center of her abdomen, making her shiver, arriving at another galaxy of freckles that splashed across her flesh just above her pelvis. He was zigzagging from one to the next when he paused and gently slipped the pen partially inside her.

Indeed, what had begun as a way to satisfy a purely physical need had gradually led to the living out of kinky fantasies; fantasies that, thanks to the magic of videotape, had been recorded for posterity and delivered to the office of the director of Central Intelligence, where the congressman had been invited for lunch, ostensibly to discuss the work of his committee.

"Turn it off," Gutherie pleaded, mortified.

Bill Kiley watched a few more twirls of the pen before he aimed the remote control at the VCR. "Connect the dots isn't our usual lunchtime fare," he said facetiously. "Of course we don't face the pressure of running for election every two years," he went on, pretending to be sympathetic. "It must be a terrible grind. No sooner do you get elected than you have to start campaigning again. Eleven terms, isn't it?"

"How did you find out about this?"

"Your psychiatrist. You recall we recommended him?"

Gutherie's eyes flared at the implied breach of patient-doctor confidentiality.

"Oh, we would never ask him to compromise his professional standards," Kiley explained. "However, his files are computerized and quite detailed."

"What do you want?" Gutherie asked dejectedly.

"For openers, your pledge to drop all thoughts of pursuing the matter of Major Shepherd."

Gutherie had heard the desperation in Stephanie's voice when she called; he didn't know what was going on but he could imagine. "What have you people been up to?"

"I'll show you," Kiley replied smugly. "I'll show you the kind of tapes we usually watch around here."

He replaced the cartridge in the recorder with the one that had accompanied the Polaroid of Fitzgerald, announcing he had been kidnapped.

Gutherie's eyes darted to the monitor and saw Bassam hanging upside down and naked from the trapeze in Casino du Liban. Kiley advanced the tape to where the terrorists were spinning Bassam on the apparatus; then he zoomed in, presenting Gutherie with a gory close-up of the knife slicing the agent's flesh until the incision completely girdled his waist.

Gutherie cringed, a chill running through him as Bassam let out a piercing scream.

Now two masked terrorists plunged their fingers deep into the incision on opposite sides of Bassam's torso and grasped the flesh tightly in their hands. He let out another agonizing scream.

Gutherie winced as the terrorists tightened their grasp on Bassam's flesh and, with one powerful downward yank, accompanied by a harsh chattering sound, they skinned him alive, peeling the flesh from his torso back over his head in one piece like a sweater. Blood ran in sheets from the exposed musculature of his carcass, which swung back and forth on the trapeze.

Gutherie felt as if he had been punched; he buried his head in his hands, unable to look any longer.

"That's what this is all about, Mr. Congressman," Kiley said. "Brave, selfless men undergoing unimaginable horrors; giving more, *much* more, than their lives."

Gutherie looked up, his eyes vacant and glazed.

"I'm sick and tired of playing by rules that benefit the wicked and penalize the just," Kiley continued. "Sick of turning the other cheek to support this higher moral plane you politicians claim we inhabit. While we're sitting with our hands folded in front of your damned committee, our enemies are literally peeling the flesh from our bones. I hope I answered your question."

"Yes," Gutherie replied in a barely audible rasp.

Kiley took a copy of Stephanie Shepherd's *Capitol Flyer* interview with Gutherie and handed it to him.

"Your favorite journalist was in London with her husband last time we saw her," Kiley declared. "Has she been keeping in touch?"

"What makes you think she'd contact me?"

The DCI handed him several photographs: Gutherie and Stephanie during memorial services at Andrews; Gutherie entering and exiting her home. "I have a list of phone calls if you'd like to see them. We weren't sure what to make of it for a while but you cleared it up for us the other night."

"Colonel Larkin—"

"Name doesn't ring a bell," Kiley said, feigning he was puzzled. "Really, Mister Congressman," he went on, gesturing to the videotape cartridge of Gutherie's indiscretions, "does it matter?"

"What do you want to know?" Gutherie's broad shoulders sloped in defeat.

"Where are the Shepherds now?" Kiley asked. His people in the U.K. had come up empty so he knew Shepherd hadn't taken any of the commercial flights he had booked. He also knew there was one obvious alternative for a pilot on the run. A check of private aircraft rental agencies had quickly turned up the charge on Applegate's credit card. "And don't tell me London," he warned. "We know Major Shepherd rented a plane."

"Tunisia," Gutherie said, trying to decide if he hated himself or Kiley more.

The DCI's brow tightened. "Where in Tunisia?"

"D'Jerba Island," Gutherie replied after a long silence. "She said her husband wanted to get into Libya."

Kiley's face stiffened with concern, then his eyes drifted to Shepherd's file on his desk. He didn't have to open it. He knew the salient details by heart; indeed, any uncertainty he might have had of just how expert Shepherd was when it came to tactical innovation had been swiftly dispelled by recent events.

Shepherd was desperate, Kiley thought; but his actions weren't those of an aimless fugitive. On the contrary, they were the precisely calculated moves of a man driven to disprove the charges with which he'd been unjustly tarred. It was clear he had wisely decided that coming forward and denying them wasn't the answer. Furthermore, Shepherd's desire to gain entry to Libya indicated he had a plan; an objective that, whatever it was, would clear his name if he could pull it off. Kiley ran down the list, putting the pieces together, putting himself in Shepherd's shoes. There was only one thing that could bring the truth to light; one thing that could prove it beyond any doubt—one thing in Libya. After forty years of clandestine gamesmanship, thinking the unthinkable had become a matter of routine and, now, to his horror, the DCI was quite certain he knew Shepherd's objective.

He buzzed his secretary on the intercom. "Get me Colonel Larkin on the *America*."

34

HAZY SUNLIGHT streamed across the Mediterranean, infusing D'Jerba with a pale saffron glow.

Shepherd stood in the bathroom of the waterfront cottage, shaking a can of shaving cream. "Well, here goes," he called out to Stephanie, who was showering.

"I was kind of getting used to it," she replied.

Shepherd filled his palm with the aerosol foam and began lathering it over his four-week growth of beard; he was getting used to it too; but it was time to get back to being Walt Shepherd.

Two days had passed since Stephanie's meeting with Adnan Al-Qasim at the Libyan People's Bureau. It was almost as if she and Walt had taken a long-promised vacation. But despite moments of blissful happiness, despite the romantic pull of the sea and the desire to explore the ancient island, indeed, despite the temptation to just drop out of sight and start life anew, they kept their vigil, remaining within earshot of the phone; and yesterday, when it finally rang, their expectations rose, then quickly plummeted when a room service clerk inquired what they wanted for breakfast.

Now, clean-shaven, his face taut and stinging from the razor, Shepherd sat on the deck outside the cottage. The orientation manual for Wheelus Air Force Base was flopped open on the table in front of him; but his eyes were distant, staring out to sea, lost in the turmoil that had become life.

The phone rang, snapping him out of it.

Stephanie answered it. She heard Al-Qasim's voice and signaled Shepherd as he came in from the deck. "Yes. Yes, I think so," she said to Al-Qasim. "Can you hold on a minute?" She covered the mouthpiece and in an anxious whisper said, "They want to talk."

"Good," Shepherd replied, brightening. "When?"

"Noon. Al-Qasim will pick you up."

"Did he say where we're going?"

"Tripoli."

Shepherd nodded and took the phone from her.

"This is Major Shepherd," he said authoritatively. "I want to impress on you that there will be no media involvement, no announcements; this must be kept quiet. No, it's not a matter of being caught but killed. Do you understand? Good. Noon is fine. I'll be ready." He hung up and turned to Stephanie. His elation and sense of triumph were quickly tempered by the sadness and concern he saw in her eyes, which glistened with the knowledge that from this moment on he would be proceeding alone.

ON THE USS AMERICA, south of the island of Malta in the Mediterranean, a Navy A-6 was hooked to the starboard catapult. The pilot gave a thumbs-up to the launch officer and the Intruder was rocketed from the carrier's deck in a thundering explosion of steam and blue-orange flame. The all-weather bomber dipped slightly, then its twin turbojets sent it soaring in a graceful arc into the azure skies.

"Don't spare the J-4, Lieutenant," Colonel Larkin urged from the backseat as they leveled off.

The pilot pushed the throttles to the stops and the A-6 bolted forward on a heading for D'Jerba.

Several days had passed since the strategy session on the *America*. After hatching the plan to incapacitate the personnel aboard the Romeo, Larkin and Duryea contacted Kiley, briefed him, and requested technical assistance. The DCI was enthused and code named the plan Project Twilight. "I'll get OTS right on it," he replied; the acronym stood for Office of Technical Services, the group at Langley that researched and developed special items related to clandestine activities.

Then Duryea returned to the *Cavalla* to hunt for the Romeo. He knew it would stay submerged, and therefore, unlike the Palestinians on the gunboat, there was little chance the crew could spot reconnaissance aircraft. This meant that ASW Vikings based on the *America* could assist in the search.

Larkin remained aboard the carrier to coordinate the effort. He was in a briefing room mapping out search patterns with Viking crews when Kiley called and briefed him on Shepherd's whereabouts and his suspicion that he was out to retrieve his F-111.

The colonel wasted no time in gathering his things and arranging transportation. The pilot who had ferried him from Naples needed flight time and volunteered.

Now, less than 30 minutes after takeoff, the A-6 had covered the 300 miles to the Tunisian coast and was approaching D'Jerba.

The tower at Melita International didn't receive landing requests from U.S. warplanes very often; but when the pilot informed them he was ferrying a passenger, they had no reason to deny him clearance.

Larkin climbed down from the cockpit and hurried toward the arrivals building. The A-6 taxied for immediate takeoff and return to the *America*.

The time was 10:37 A.M.

"You're with the military?" the woman at the passport control desk asked, not because Larkin's passport noted his military rank, which it didn't, but because his method of arrival had been brought to her attention.

"I'm a technical consultant," he answered, forcing a smile. He'd have preferred to enter the country more quietly; but embarking from a carrier and the pressure of time had left him little choice.

"Why did you come to D'Jerba?"

"To meet my sister and brother-in-law; they're vacationing here. Say, maybe you can help me out." He knew that hotels the world over routinely forwarded data to local authorities and expected she could help him locate them. "His name's Shepherd, Walter Shepherd; I don't know where they're staying. Maybe, you could—"

The clerk shook her head no. "I'm sorry, we're not allowed to give out that information."

"I *could* call every hotel on the island," Larkin said, slipping some bills from his wallet discreetly. "Or you could save me the time."

The clerk deftly palmed the money and turned to her keyboard. "Shepherd, you say?"

"Yes, Walter Shepherd."

"I'm sorry," she said, looking up from the monitor. "I'm not showing a Walter Shepherd."

"What about *Stephanie* Shepherd?"

The clerk shook her head no.

"No one named Shepherd is registered in any of the island's hotels?"

"That's correct."

Larkin shrugged. "I must have been misinformed," he said matter-of-factly, then asked casually, "By the way, are there regular flights to Tripoli from here?"

"Each evening at seven. But Americans aren't—"

"Yes, I know. Just curious. Thanks."

He was crossing to the car rental desk, working the problem, when he recalled that Kiley had said Shepherd used Applegate's credit card to rent a plane. Instead of returning to passport control, Larkin went to a phone booth and called the first hotel listed in the directory.

"I have a business meeting with one of your guests," he said, "but I've forgotten the room number. Yes, his name's Applegate. Paul Applegate."

Larkin called three more hotels before the operator at the Dar Jerba recognized the name.

"He's on the beachfront; cottage forty-seven. Do you wish to speak with Mister Applegate now?"

"No, I have what I need. Thanks."

T H E   T I M E   W A S 11:45 A.M. when the Shepherds crossed the sprawling Dar Jerba complex to the main building. Approximately 15 minutes later a BMW 735 sedan pulled up to the main entrance. Al-Qasim got out and waited beneath the canopy. Like his elegantly furnished offices and conservatively tailored suits, the car was part of the facade to impress international businessmen.

"That's him," Stephanie said, spotting the attaché through the huge panes that enclosed the hotel's lobby. She and Shepherd held each other tightly for a long moment. "I love you, Walt," she whispered, her eyes starting to fill as their lips parted.

"Love you too. We're going to have us twenty more," Shepherd said reassuringly, slipping from her grasp.

Stephanie stood there, holding herself together as he strode into the blinding sunlight, suitcase in his hand. Just like he was going bowling, she thought, watching as Shepherd and Al-Qasim shook hands and exchanged a few words before driving off in the BMW.

After twenty years she still didn't understand him. It wasn't that she couldn't fathom how he lived with danger but why he enjoyed it so much. He was always happiest when flying headlong into a kill-or-be-killed situation, as long as it was a calculated risk. It was as if being able to anticipate threats and create a game plan to counter them made him invincible and assured success. It was a fine theory for the stock market or Super Bowl, she thought; but *this* game wasn't played for profits or trophies—life was the stake.

Stephanie headed for the cottage. Almost a week had passed since she had left Andrews, and her thoughts turned to her parents and children. They were undoubtedly aware of the news reports branding Shepherd a deserter and murderer; now, she could chance calling them to explain.

A   S H O R T   T I M E   B E F O R E,   far across the Dar Jerba's grounds, a Peugeot sedan turned onto the street that paralleled the beachfront cottages. Larkin parked and went to one of the automated information kiosks that dotted the grounds. It contained a house phone. He dialed the operator and asked for cottage 47. When there was no answer, he walked a short distance to the white-domed structure, approaching it from the beach side.

A credit card easily slipped the latch on the sliding door to the deck. Larkin entered the bedroom and began taking stock of the contents: the single suitcase and the presence of only women's clothing and toiletries indicated Shepherd was gone and wouldn't be returning; the navigation charts and instruments on the dresser meant he wasn't flying anywhere.

Larkin was about to leave when he heard the key in the lock, the door opening, and glimpsed Stephanie through an opening in the stucco grillework that divided the interior spaces. She came down the corridor, entered the bedroom, and was crossing to the phone when the door shut behind her. She turned to see a man she didn't know stepping out from behind it.

"Where's your husband?" he asked softly.

A gasp stuck in Stephanie's throat. A tense moment passed before it dawned on her. "You're Larkin, aren't you?" It was a statement; an indictment. "You bastard."

Larkin stood his ground, hand poised to go for his sidearm if necessary. "He's on his way to Libya, isn't he?" His wintry eyes searching hers for a reaction, he saw the evasive flicker and made a move toward the door, further testing her.

"No!" Stephanie shouted, lunging for him. "No!"

Larkin whirled, his suspicion confirmed beyond any doubt now, and shouldered her aside. Stephanie regained her balance and came back at him with a fury; then she froze suddenly as the colonel pulled a Baretta from inside his jacket and leveled it at her forehead.

Larkin held the weapon on her for a long moment, immobilized by her expression. It was different than what he'd seen on the faces of those he had confronted and killed in combat. There was no surprise in *their* eyes, no sudden realization of life's fragile thread. Yet it wasn't the contrast that captivated him, but a nagging memory. He had seen Stephanie's puzzled horror before; seen a woman's eyes wide with terror. Once.

He kept the pistol trained on her as he backed out of the cottage, then holstered it, crossing the grounds to the rented Peugeot.

Shepherd was on his way to Libya; now; *driving* there, Larkin quickly deduced, having already eliminated other modes of transport. The map of D'Jerba provided by the rental agency was on the Peugeot's seat. The tiny island had few roads. The route to the mainland and south to the Libyan border was boldly delineated.

A T   T H E   E N D of the winding causeway connecting the island to the Tunisian mainland, Al-Qasim's BMW hummed with finely tuned precision as he came through the Al Kurnish off-ramp, accelerating onto the two-lane ribbon of concrete that ran along the coast.

"I make this trip with businessmen several times a month," Al-Qasim explained, breaking the silence.

"Why? It can't be faster than flying."

"Oh, it isn't," Al-Qasim admitted, pausing briefly to set up the punch line. "Assuming your flight isn't delayed or canceled."

"I hadn't thought about that," Shepherd said, relaxed by the small talk. "You know the military, everything by the numbers, on a timetable."

"Yes, I'm sure your bombers arrived in Tripoli right on schedule," Al-Qasim said, in a sarcastic tone.

You bet your ass they did, Shepherd thought, resisting the temptation to say it. Playing the role in which he'd been cast, he replied, "I understand how you feel; but there's no need to take it out on me."

"You're quite correct, Major. My apologies."

"Accepted. We were talking about driving—"

"Yes, I was about to say I find it gives me an opportunity to ease a client's anxieties about doing business in my country."

"Well, that's something I can relate to."

"I'm not surprised. It's been a while since I've taken an American across."

"You anticipate any problems?"

"No. Despite current tensions, your oil companies are still well represented, as are your citizens. Many have ignored the order to leave. I'm sure your documents will be ready."

"I hope so. I can't just turn around and go back if this doesn't work out."

"Well, since you mentioned it, Major Shepherd, I didn't think the circumstances warranted political asylum. I forwarded your request to Tripoli only as a matter of routine. To be honest, I was quite surprised when they agreed to it, let alone so quickly."

"I guess they had their reasons," Shepherd said matter-of-factly. He had known all along that the *apparent* circumstances wouldn't qualify him for asylum and realized that Al-Qasim hadn't been told about the F-111s or the need for ANITA. "Thanks for your help."

"You're welcome." Al-Qasim explained that once across the border they would drive to the People's Central Committee Headquarters in downtown Tripoli, where government officials were expecting them.

A DISTANCE BEHIND, Larkin's Peugeot had just left el-Kantara at the southernmost tip of the island and was starting across the causeway, passing Borj Castille, the seventeenth-century Spanish fortress that rose from the tip of a peninsula jutting out into the gulf.

Five minutes later the Peugeot came through the Al Kurnish turnoff onto the coastal highway. Ever since Qaddafi closed the border, the area south of D'Jerba had become a virtual no-man's-land. Once a main conduit between the two nations, the Al Kurnish Road carried only occasional traffic now.

Larkin sat behind the wheel, pedal to the floor, speedometer edging 150 KPH, staring at the empty road ahead, his mind fixated on the confrontation with Stephanie Shepherd, on the memory of the last time he had come that close to shooting a woman.

It occurred several years after his return from Vietnam. He was married at the time and, despite the joy of reunion, the experience of being shot down and hunted in Asian jungles tormented him, straining the relationship. It ended the night he rolled out of bed in the throes of a violent nightmare and went for the pistol he kept in the nightstand. His wife was awakened by the commotion and sat up against the headboard. Larkin saw the movement in the darkness and went for her. He had the muzzle in her mouth and was squeezing the trigger when he saw the terror in her eyes, in her clear blue Anglo-Saxon eyes, and snapped out of it. He had no doubt he would have killed her had they been brown.

A speck on the horizon pulled him from the reverie. He accelerated and quickly caught up to what turned out to be a pickup truck. Larkin pulled abreast in the opposite lane, glanced across to the driver, who was a local and clearly alone, then went flying past.

THE CONCRETE BLOCKHOUSES at the Ras Jdyar border checkpoint were flanked by a chainlink fence that paraded across the bleak landscape from desert to sea.

Al-Qasim waved as he approached. The Libyan Army guard in the security kiosk recognized him and raised the steel gate-arm. The BMW drove through without slowing, continuing across the grounds to the main building beyond.

"We're in Libya now?" Shepherd asked as they parked and got out.

"Yes, safely inside Libya," Al-Qasim said with a smile, leading the way inside.

As the attaché had promised, Shepherd's documents were ready and his entry was handled routinely. In minutes, they had been signed and stamped and, paperwork dispensed with, he and Al-Qasim were on their way.

They were leaving the building when they saw a car approaching on the Tunisian side of the border. It stopped well before reaching the security kiosk. The door opened and Larkin got out. His eyes narrowed and locked onto Shepherd's in a lethal, penetrating stare that, despite the fence and distance separating them, made it clear he was far from beaten.

Shepherd held it unblinkingly.

They glared at each other through the chainlink for a long moment before Al-Qasim broke the tension.

"Do you know that man?"

Shepherd nodded without taking his eyes off Larkin. "His name's Larkin. Colonel Richard Larkin."

"An American—"

"Yes, he tried to kill me once."

"We should be going," Al-Qasim said nervously.

Shepherd hesitated, then broke it off with Larkin and shook his head no. "I'm concerned for my wife."

Al-Qasim raised a brow. "I know the provost of the D'Jerban police quite well. Why don't I call him and ask if he'll look in on her?"

They returned to the main building and Al-Qasim made the call. After hanging up, he forced a smile and reported, "The provost said to tell you your wife is fine."

"What do you mean?" Shepherd asked, apprehensively.

"Well, it seems this Colonel Larkin has already confronted her. The provost said she filed a formal complaint against him. He promised he would notify me as soon as the Colonel was apprehended."

Shepherd eased slightly and smiled at the prospect, then followed Al-Qasim outside.

The Peugeot was gone.

They returned to the BMW to discover an armored, four-wheel-drive vehicle was parked directly behind it, blocking their exit.

Three men in civilian attire were standing next to the matte black vehicle. The two in their twenties had an air of vigilance and intensity. The third was older and sullen with an icy malevolence.

Al-Qasim recognized him immediately.

He flashed official identification and addressed Al-Qasim in Arabic. Shepherd had no idea what he was saying but heard the sharp, commanding tone and saw that the attaché was clearly intimidated. Al-Qasim listened and nodded dutifully, then turned to Shepherd. "Secret police," he said, his eyes flickering nervously, "the *head* of the secret police."

"What? What's going on?"

"You're to go with him," Al-Qasim replied. This was news to him, but he didn't dare question it. Reza Abdel-Hadi's presence was authorization enough.

"This way, Major," the SHK chief ordered in heavily accented English, gesturing to the Soviet-made Krazz. He directed Shepherd into the backseat and got in next to him. A wire screen separated the cab from a windowless compartment where prisoners ostensibly rode.

Abdel-Hadi's Akita was caged there now.

The powerful vehicle lurched forward with a throaty roar, leaving Al-Qasim in a swirl of dust.

"Are we still going to Tripoli?" Shepherd asked.

"Tarabulus," Abdel-Hadi corrected sharply. "We don't call it Tripoli."

"Where in Tarabulus?"

"You ask many too questions, Major," the SHK chief retorted. His dark, purplish lips tightened into a hard line that left no doubt the remainder of the journey would be made in silence.

BOOK THREE

WE WANT A PLACE FOR OUR
BODIES TO BE BURIED IN,
AND A PLACE WHERE OUR
GENERATIONS, OUR
CHILDREN, CAN LIVE AS
FREELY AS OTHER HUMAN
BEINGS.

—YASSER
ARAFAT

35

A THIN SHEET OF SAND was blowing across the runway as a Lear jet with Syrian markings touched down at Beirut International Airport.

The time was 4:23 P.M.

Yasser Arafat bounded down the steps, bracketed by bodyguards. It had been a long day and his khaki twill fatigues had lost their creases. A Magnum revolver slapped at his side as he crossed the tarmac at a brisk pace and entered an armored Mercedes limousine.

Just over three hours had passed since he left his residence near Worldwide PLO Headquarters in Tunis for the 1,600-mile flight. His fear of Israeli hit squads had turned him into a jet-setting nomad who rarely slept in the same place on consecutive nights, deciding at the end of each day where he would stay that evening.

But this night had been planned for weeks.

Indeed, Arafat had been quietly fuming over the failure to exchange the hostages for a sanctuary in Libya. Now that Abu Nidal had been released from the hospital and had had time to convalesce, Arafat would confront him on the matter. Despite Nidal's withdrawal from the PLO and reports of deep personal animosity between the two, they had been playing a shrewd game of good cop–bad cop for years: Arafat the ever reasonable negotiator, piously warning he wouldn't be able to keep extremist factions in check unless certain concessions were made, then throwing up his hands and pointing to Nidal's acts of terrorism as proof whenever they weren't.

The limousine made its way through the city, heading north on the coastal highway toward Casino du Liban. Arafat stared out the window at the tapestry of rubble that resembled ancient ruins. The buildings might have been new, but the ruins *were* ancient, he thought, reminded of Abba Eban's infamous quip, "The PLO never missed an opportunity to miss an opportunity." The hostage debacle was a perfect example and it galled Arafat that the former Israeli foreign minister would be laughing out loud if he knew.

The square-edged limousine pulled through the casino's entrance gates and was escorted by sentries down the long approach road to the arched portico.

Abu Nidal observed Arafat's arrival from a second-story balcony. Soon after aborting the hostage exchange, he was released from the hospital and took up residence here in an opulent suite once reserved for the casino's highest rollers. He looked tan and robust, but he had yet to hear from either his gunboat or the group he had sent to abduct Katifa, and was in a foul mood.

"Were you part of the conspiracy or just blind to it?" Nidal challenged icily when Arafat joined him on the balcony. He knew what was coming and had fired the first volley to gain the advantage.

"Conspiracy?" Arafat flared, his nostrils contracting at the insult. "Assad called you. I was there. So was Qaddafi. You agreed to—"

"*I* didn't agree to anything," Nidal exploded, going on to inform Arafat about the doctored insulin.

"I had no idea," the PLO chairman replied truthfully, concealing he found it bold and rather amusing.

His bull-necked silhouette framed against the sun, Nidal took a moment to regain his composure. Then he asked calmly, "Katifa said I favored the proposal, didn't she?"

"No," Arafat replied without hesitation, pretending he was surprised Nidal had asked. "She made your opposition known, and forcefully so." He had given Moncrieff the ammunition to turn her; Katifa was an ally now; and he saw no reason to contribute to her demise.

"You're certain?" Nidal said, puzzled.

Arafat nodded emphatically.

"But she was the only one who had access to the insulin. She had to be involved somehow," Nidal reasoned. Shaking his head in dismay, he lamented, "I raised her as my own. I can't believe she turned against me."

"The Saudi is quite shrewd," Arafat said slyly. "It's possible it was his doing, not hers."

"For her sake, I hope you're right. She'll have her chance to prove her loyalty when I get my hands on her."

"Since we're drawing lines," Arafat said, holding Nidal's look, "be advised I supported the proposal."

"So the Saudi told me," Nidal replied; then in a tone that left no doubt he found the idea reprehensible, he challenged, "A sanctuary in Libya?"

"Yes, in Libya," Arafat retorted, uncowed. "Our people are scattered, our leaders exiled. Reunification is long overdue. It's time to forsake this patchwork of territories and bring Palestinians together."

Nidal scowled in disgust, his eyes darting to Arafat's elegant wristwatch, visible below the cuff of his fatigues. "Rolex? Cartier? How much? Five thousand? Ten?"

"Close enough," Arafat replied, not the least embarrassed. His wealth—the result of partnerships in several Kuwaiti construction companies—had always been a source of pride; as was the fact that he had never taken money from the PLO or Fatah organizations.

"Perfect copies that keep perfect time can be had for far less," Nidal declared pointedly. "Of course, as someone very bright once said, there is nothing like the genuine article if you can afford it."

Arafat winced and grunted in capitulation.

"And we can," Nidal went on. "We have the currency to bring Palestinians together in *Palestine*."

Several hours later, they were dining in Nidal's suite when he glanced at his watch. "I have to take a call," he explained to Arafat. "Come along if you wish."

Arafat followed him down the main staircase, and through the amphitheater to the backstage communications center where the call from the Romeo came in each evening at 9:00 P.M. sharp.

This routine was dictated by the fact that all submarines, from the most primitive diesel to nuclear-powered missile-launcher, are essentially out of contact with command centers when dived. The most modern are equipped for reception of very low and extremely low frequency radio transmissions to depths of 100 meters. However, these bands lack sufficient width to support voice communication, require the boat move at slow speed, demand special antenna be deployed, and are painfully slow, ELF taking 30 seconds for the transmission of a single character. As a result, most navies transmit submarine fleet orders continuously; and each boat on its own schedule copies all messages, acting only on those addressed to it. To initiate communications, a submarine must either float a plastic buoy containing an antenna or come to periscope-antenna depth, putting one of several radio masts above the water. Voice communications demand the latter.

Like many early model submarines, the 35-year-old Romeo did not have VLF or ELF capability, which meant that when the submarine was dived, Nidal could not contact it at will, via voice or cable. Therefore, each day at this hour, the Romeo came to periscope-antenna depth, her hull just 3 meters below the surface, and contacted him on the gunboat or, as of late, at Casino du Liban.

"This is the Exchequer," the terrorist in charge of the hostages said. "Your currency is secure."

"I may make a withdrawal soon," Nidal said.

"I understand. Can you specify a date?"

"Not yet. But I expect it shall be sometime in the near future," Nidal replied, ending the transmission to prevent detection of the submarine's position.

"What does that mean?" Arafat challenged as they left the backstage communications center and entered the amphitheater, where the trapeze hung ominously in the cold glare of the kliegs. They were walking beneath it when Nidal whirled, his heel scraping in a crusty pool of dried blood.

"It means," he shot back, "that it's time the Zionists in Washington and Tel Aviv felt the full might of the Intifada."

Arafat groaned, dismayed. "The timing is all wrong. The air strike has played right into our hands. It's turned world opinion. Now the *Americans* are being—"

"You never learn," Nidal scoffed angrily.

"*They're* being called terrorists now," Arafat went on in a rush. "The tide is swinging in our favor unless we do something rash and reverse it."

Nidal's lips tightened grudgingly. Arafat had always been an unwelcome but valuable check on his impulsiveness. He was on the verge of accepting his counsel when the radio man appeared.

"The gunboat," the young guerrilla enthused.

Nidal hurried to the radio console and took the microphone. "Yes, yes? Where are you? What happened?"

The captain briefed him on the encounter with the SEALs, explaining that the gunboat had been adrift in the Mediterranean ever since. Unable to repair the damaged propellers or the radio that the SEALs had destroyed before departing, his crew had nearly run out of food and water by the time a Turkish freighter spotted them and offered assistance. He was calling from the freighter's bridge.

Nidal's face dropped as he listened, his expression hardening into an angry mask at the report of the assault. "You're certain they were Americans?"

"Their leader spoke in phonetic Arabic," the captain replied. "A European would have spoken French."

"Yes, and an Israeli would have said nothing. We await your return. Godspeed." His soft eyes were ablaze with anger. He strode boldly onto the stage of the amphitheater, bent to the floor, and scooped up a palmful of dried blood, then held the crumbly, blackish mound out to Arafat, and hissed, "Intifada now."

36

AFTER LEAVING the Ras Jdyar border crossing, Abdel-Hadi's Krazz headed east into Libya on the Al Kurnish Road.

Shepherd sat next to the taciturn SHK chief as the vehicle hurtled toward Tripoli at extremely high speed: first Bu Kammash, then Zurwarah, Sabratah, Az Zawiyah, Janzur; the towns and miles flashed past; a tableaux of boats, fishermen, and drying nets on one side; stunted wheat, cracked irrigation ditches, and farmers bent to plows on the other; and everywhere, children watching and waving with wide-eyed innocence, as would his own, Shepherd thought, wondering if he would ever see them again.

A short time later, Tripoli's rooftops edged the expanse of neon-blue sky. The ornate domes and spired minarets of ancient civilizations were crowded out by the concrete boxes that had sprung up in recent decades.

The Krazz had just passed the People's Congress, a modern structure on the western outskirts of the Old City, when the driver made a right into Al Jala Road, a broad, eucalyptus-lined motorway that angled inland from the coast. It bordered the Christian Cemetery and the people's shopping precinct, cutting through an industrial district to a rural area, where the Krazz negotiated the rows of concrete dragon's teeth that lined As-Sarim Street, and approached the Bab al Azziziya Barracks.

A squad of infantry flanked a Soviet-made tank parked sideways across the entrance, blocking it. Shepherd was looking right down the barrel of the T-55's cannon, its turret positioned to fire on any hostile vehicle that might approach.

The sentry recognized Abdel-Hadi and signaled to the tank with a wave. It roared to life and backed up, allowing the Krazz to enter the compound. Abdel-Hadi's driver snaked around bomb craters and rubble in the unpaved road, coming upon a tent of coarse brown fabric that lay across the earth like an immense, dusty camel.

Abdel-Hadi issued some orders in Arabic to guards stationed outside the tent. They frisked Shepherd, and swept a metal detector over him, confirming he was unarmed. Then, the SHK chief ushered him inside.

Shepherd's eyes darted to the multicolored pattern that swooped overhead, in startling contrast to the exterior. A few seconds passed before he sensed a presence and turned to see Muammar el-Qaddafi slouched inconspicuously behind a plain desk.

General Younis was standing next to him.

Qaddafi's cape was tossed rakishly over one shoulder, his large head cocked slightly to one side, eyes glancing up at Shepherd in a curious stare.

Shepherd smiled thinly and nodded, thinking that the colonel's positioning wasn't accidental, but calculated to allow him to gauge his visitors' stature and intent, and seize the initiative.

Finally, Qaddafi stood and came around the desk.

Shepherd held his ground as the impact of being face-to-face with the notorious Libyan registered. He was taller than Shepherd had imagined; barrel-chested and muscular; his leathery face was stippled by a five o'clock shadow that caught the bluish cast of the fluorescents; his eyes were hard like polished obsidian.

"Major Shepherd," Qaddafi said softly in English, extending a hand. Twenty years ago as a young cadet, he had attended the Royal Military Academy at Sandhurst, England, and was surprisingly fluent when it suited him.

"Colonel," Shepherd said, judging from the handshake and roughened palm that Qaddafi was as strong and physically capable as he looked.

Qaddafi introduced Younis; then, addressing Shepherd, he said, "I have always admired men with the courage to follow the dictates of their conscience."

"I did what I thought was right, sir," Shepherd drawled humbly, playing his part. "I took an oath that I'd never carry out an order I knew to be wrong, and I stuck by it. Our nations aren't at war. My government had no justification for military action." It was killing him to say it but he had little choice.

"You paid a high price."

"It could've been higher."

"I understand all too well, Major," Qaddafi replied, his eyes darting about warily at Shepherd's allusion to personal safety;

then he opened his cape, revealing a bulletproof vest girdling his torso. It was a lightweight Kevlar model with Velcro fasteners. "Now, since we're speaking of price," Qaddafi resumed, somewhat effusively, "the question, as you Americans say, is 'what's in this for us'?"

"A combat pilot," Shepherd said pointedly; an F-111 pilot and you damn well know it, he thought, having no doubt this accounted for the secret police escort and audience with Qaddafi. Indeed, he had counted on it, not only to get him into Libya, which it had, but also into the cockpit of his F-111 bomber.

Qaddafi arched his brows and flicked a look to General Younis, who was standing off to one side. "In other words, Major, you wish to trade your knowledge and flying skills for asylum in the People's Jamahiriya."

"That's correct."

"Be advised, Major," Younis warned, stretching to full height, "we would require *specific* knowledge."

"For example?"

Younis broke into a sly smile. "Just enumerate the systems with which you're familiar."

"Certainly. I have no problem with that," Shepherd replied nonchalantly, not wanting to appear eager. "APQ forward-looking attack radar, APQ terrain-following radar, ASQ digital fire control computer, ANITA—that stands for alphanumeric input for target acquisition—and of course all the standard navigational, avionics, and armament systems, including laser-guided Pave Tack."

"You have a thorough working knowledge of them," Younis prompted, secretly delighted at the development.

"I've been flying one-elevens for over fifteen years, General," Shepherd answered, relieved it was going as planned. "I'm sure we can work something out."

"Well, Major," Qaddafi said in an insidious tone, "I wouldn't take that for granted if I were you."

Shepherd hadn't expected that.

Neither had Younis, who stiffened with concern. He had seen it happen before and dreaded what was coming next.

Shepherd knew the deal he proposed made perfect sense. Was it possible Qaddafi hadn't made the connection? Or had his people developed ANITA on their own? "I'll be more than happy to take you through any one of these systems step by step," he offered.

"That's what bothers me." Qaddafi's eyes narrowed in suspicion, carving deep gorges in his forehead. "I've always found it difficult trusting men who change allegiance so quickly."

"There's been nothing quick about it, sir," Shepherd responded, assuming Qaddafi was testing his resolve. "I've been thinking about nothing else since I was assigned to the mission; and no matter how I came at it, it came up wrong. The truth is, I knew all along I had no choice but to take the action I did."

Qaddafi studied him thoughtfully. "You could be the man you claim, or"—he paused, splaying his hands—"you could very well be a spy."

"A spy," Shepherd echoed; he realized where Qaddafi was headed now.

So did Younis. As he had surmised, Qaddafi's paranoia had hold of him. They finally had their hands on ANITA, and the colonel was about to throw it away.

"Yes, yes, a disgruntled patriot, a man without a country, it's the perfect cover," Qaddafi went on, envisioning the conspiracy. "And not the first time CIA used such a ruse to set up an operative. You see it, Younis?" he prompted, descending further into the abyss. "You see how clear it becomes once pointed out?"

"Well, it's certainly possible, sir; but I don't think this man is an intelligence operative. I—"

"I do," Abdel-Hadi interrupted in Arabic, having long ago realized that *his* power grew along with Qaddafi's paranoia, real or imaginary threats notwithstanding. "Kiley is very shrewd, very clever."

"You deny Kiley is your commander?" Qaddafi suddenly challenged, locking his eyes onto Shepherd's to drive the accusation home.

"Yes, I do," Shepherd shot back, holding the colonel's penetrating stare unblinkingly.

"You deny that this despicable shetan sent you here to assassinate me?" Qaddafi shouted, gripped by the mania that had put Libyan Air Force markings on the F-111s.

"I'm not an assassin, sir," Shepherd replied evenly.

"Liar! He sent you here to kill me because the air strike didn't. Yes, yes. Despite our agreement he conspired against my life and . . ." Qaddafi paused, whirling to face Shepherd again. "Or could it be that he decided to exact vengeance because he didn't get what he wanted? Because we didn't—"

"Excuse me, sir," Younis interrupted in Arabic. He had little hope of reaching him, but thought it best Qaddafi be stopped before revealing the arms for hostages deal. "I really don't think that's the case here. I suggest we give him a chance to—"

"*That* is a matter for our courts," the colonel retorted in Arabic; then in English he said, "Islamic justice is uncomplicated and swift, Major. Murderers are executed; thieves have their hands cut off; political assassins . . ." He let the sentence trail off ominously.

"Why not give him a chance to prove what he says?" Younis suggested gently. "Let him demonstrate this knowledge that he claims he—"

"I have all the proof I need right there," Qaddafi snapped, indicating Shepherd's eyes. He was caught up in a fit of raging madness now, one hand clawing at his wiry hair, the other pointing accusingly at Shepherd. "See? See how he looks at me? Take him away!" he ordered, with an abrupt wave of his hand. "Take this emissary of Satan from my home!"

These last exchanges were in Arabic.

Shepherd had no idea what had been said, but Qaddafi's anger was unmistakable, as was the general's dismay. Suddenly Abdel-Hadi nodded to the two secret police officers stationed at the entrance to the tent.

They cuffed Shepherd's hands behind his back and dragged him outside into swiftly falling darkness.

When they were gone Qaddafi took a few moments to collect himself; then he turned to Younis with a strangely serene expression. "Do you really think he is bona fide?"

"Yes, sir, I do," Younis answered contritely, uncertain if Qaddafi would take offense at the reply.

Qaddafi nodded thoughtfully. "Take whatever steps are necessary to confirm it."

37

HAVING FAILED to prevent Shepherd from entering Libya, Larkin decided to fly to Tunis, where a United States consulate, CIA support personnel, and a secure communications link to Langley awaited.

He drove the Al Kurnish Road back over the causeway to D'Jerba, continuing north on the MC-117 to the airport. The time was 2:34 P.M. when he returned the rented Peugeot.

As the colonel headed for the terminal, the clerk at the car rental desk routinely checked his name against a computer alert that had come in earlier from police headquarters. It had been sent to all car rental agencies, airlines, hotels, and customs in response to Stephanie's complaint. The clerk set the papers aside and called airport security.

Larkin purchased a ticket on the 4:20 flight to Tunis, then went to a phone booth to alert the station chief to his arrival. He didn't see the rental clerk pointing him out to the two D'Jerban police officers.

"Colonel Richard Larkin?"

"Yes."

"Our report states you possess a firearm," one of the officers said, his right hand cradling an Uzi submachine gun that hung from his shoulder.

Larkin nodded and glanced to his left armpit.

The second officer deftly slipped the Baretta from Larkin's shoulder holster and confiscated it.

"Passport, please?"

Larkin reached to a pocket and gave it to him.

"You will come with us now."

"Why?" Larkin asked warily. "What's the problem?"

"Accusations of certain crimes have been made against you," the officer replied stiffly.

Larkin studied him for a moment, deciding. He knew the military mentality all too well; they had orders to bring him in, and neither argument nor resistance would convince them otherwise. "Okay," he said calmly.

After reporting that Larkin had been apprehended, they led him outside to a white Land Rover that had POLICE in French and Arabic on the doors, and drove to police headquarters in Houmt Souk, D'Jerba's capital.

Larkin was taken directly to the provost's office, where Al-Qasim and Stephanie were waiting. There were no line-ups viewed from behind one-way mirrors here; defendant and plaintiff were brought together for direct eye-to-eye confrontation in the Arab manner.

Stephanie stared at him, seething with animosity.

"Is this the man?" the provost asked. He was slender and well-groomed, with a thoroughly professional demeanor. Like many North Africans, he spoke English with a French accent.

"It certainly is," Stephanie replied sharply.

Al-Qasim nodded in confirmation. He had just returned to his office from the border checkpoint when the provost called with news of Larkin's capture.

"Colonel Larkin?" the provost said calmly. "Did you break into this woman's hotel room and threaten her with a pistol as she has charged?"

"Yes, sir, I did," Larkin replied shrewdly, deciding the truth would serve him best. The charges against Shepherd were public knowledge, he reasoned; conversely, *he* was an officer of the law, clearly in the right. "I was sent here by my government to apprehend a fugitive. Mrs. Shepherd was helping him escape."

"You have no legal jurisdiction here, Major."

"I realize that, sir," Larkin said in his most deferential tone. "I intended to contact you but there wasn't time. As you know, Major Shepherd escaped."

"What are the charges against him?"

"He deserted from his squadron and killed an American military officer."

The provost nodded. "In the United Kingdom. Yes, yes, I recall that incident now."

"Being accused doesn't make my husband guilty," Stephanie protested, bristling with frustration.

"His actions speak louder than your words, Mrs. Shepherd,"

the provost intoned. "I'm afraid they tend to undermine any claim of innocence."

"I'm aware of that," Stephanie said grimly, aching to explain; but she knew it was futile, knew from the provost's reply that, as Walt had predicted, appearances were what counted.

The provost shifted his look to Al-Qasim. "As I understand it, you drove Major Shepherd to the border?"

"Oui. Je n'etais pas au courant de ces accusations," Al-Qasim explained, pretending he was bewildered. "Elle a dit que le Majeur était consultant—"

"En Anglais, s'il vous plaît," the provost admonished.

"I didn't know of these charges," the attaché lied with an anxious glance to Stephanie. Diplomatic immunity notwithstanding, involvement in criminal activity could result in his expulsion from Tunisia. "I was under the impression her husband was a technical consultant interested in doing business in Libya."

"Mrs. Shepherd," the provost prompted.

Stephanie studied Al-Qasim for a long moment before answering. "That's correct," she finally said, deciding there was no reason to betray him; then, shifting her look to Larkin, who held it coldly, she added, "*He's* the one who's lying."

"Since we're speaking of deception," the provost said, his tone sharper now, "your husband used false identification to enter Tunisia. Are you aware of *that*, Mrs. Shepherd?"

It was a matter of record. There was no sense denying it, Stephanie thought, nodding resignedly.

"Identification he took from the officer he shot and killed," Larkin added.

The provost's expression darkened, leaving no doubt the remark had the effect Larkin intended. "Are you aware of that as well, Mrs. Shepherd?"

Stephanie's lips tightened in a thin line; then, shoulders slackening in defeat, she nodded again.

"I appreciate your time, Colonel," the provost said after a short silence. "I'm sorry for any inconvenience."

"Not at all, sir," Larkin said, checking the time. "If you have no further questions, there's a slim chance I can make my flight."

The provost nodded and shook Larkin's hand.

The colonel left the office, retrieved his pistol at the front desk, and headed for the airport.

"What happens now?" Stephanie asked apprehensively.

"Having allegedly helped a fugitive to escape, the law requires you be detained," the provost replied; he watched Stephanie's face fall at the specter of imprisonment; then, after a calculated pause, he added, "You'll be released on your own recognizance and remain on the island until your guilt or innocence can be determined. May I have your passport, please?"

L A R K I N arrived at D'Jerba's Melita International shortly after his flight to Tunis had departed. On learning there were no others that evening, he checked into a hotel at the airport and called the U.S. Consulate in Tunis. He identified himself to the CIA station chief and, prompted by the gravity of the situation, he disregarded the unsecured line between D'Jerba and Tunis, and asked the call be routed on a secure net to Langley.

T H E   T I M E in Washington, D.C., was 8:58 A.M.

The DCI had just come from a breakfast meeting with the president when his secretary told him Larkin was on the line.

"You think he can pull if off?" Kiley wondered, on hearing that Shepherd had gained entry into Libya.

"I don't know. Qaddafi isn't just going to let him waltz in there and walk off with a one-eleven. I figure we've got a little time."

"Any ideas?"

"There's a Libyan diplomat who helped Shepherd get in. I think we can use him."

"Can we trust him?"

"I doubt it, but he can be leveraged. He'd look pretty bad if his boy ripped off one of Qaddafi's new toys. We'd be doing him a favor."

"Good." Kiley grunted. "Keep me posted as to—"

The intercom buzzed interrupting him.

"Hang on, Dick." He put the colonel on hold and tapped the intercom button. "Yes," the DCI growled, annoyed at the intrusion. "Oh. Okay, thanks," he said, his tone softening at the message; then he switched back to Larkin and announced, "Arafat's on the tube." Kiley turned on the television with a remote control and searched the channels, finding the PLO leader surrounded by journalists. While Arafat fielded questions in emotionally charged Arabic, a CNN correspondent turned to the camera and reported:

"PLO Chairman Yasser Arafat has just accused the United States of cold-blooded murder. The alleged killing of three Palestinian seamen occurred weeks ago when U.S. Navy commandos assaulted a PLO gunboat in search of American hostages. Arafat was quick to point out that none were found aboard the vessel. Then, in a stunning admission, he revealed that all Americans taken hostage in the Middle East in recent years were abducted, *not* by extremist Muslim factions, who had served as a ploy to deter rescue attempts, but by terrorist Abu Nidal for the purpose of ransoming Palestine. Furthermore, angered by the deaths of his countrymen, Nidal has now accelerated his timetable and demanded a Palestinian state be created in Israel no later than the start of Ramadan, the Muslim New Year. He is threatening to kill one hostage for each day beyond the deadline."

Kiley slumped dejectedly in his chair. "Bastards," he finally said, bitterly.

"Sir?" Larkin said.

"They're going to kill them all if they don't get a homeland in Israel by Ramadan."

Larkin groaned and muttered an expletive.

The DCI sat there in silence for a long moment. "As soon as you finish with the Libyan," he finally said, "you'll have to go see Moncrieff."

"I thought the bastards got him. Where is he?"

"Jeddah. He called last night. He and the lady made it to the family palace; but he's pissed off over being left behind in Tripoli. He wants out."

"I don't blame him."

"Nor I. The trouble is we need an insurance policy on this now; and he's the key to it."

"I understand, sir."

After briefing Larkin on the details, Kiley went to the White House, where the president and his advisers were meeting in the cabinet room to formulate a response to Arafat's announcement. En route, he considered revealing the upcoming rescue attempt but, fearful the news might be leaked to the media, he decided against it.

"Tel Aviv's just told Arafat to take a hike," the secretary of state reported in his methodical cadence. "I gave the prime minister every assurance that we weren't involved in this incident." He swept his eyes over the group and, lowering his voice, added, "I hope I wasn't misleading him."

"No, sir," the CJC replied truthfully.

"Ken? Bill?" the president prompted, picking up on the secretary's lead.

"I authorized no such action, sir," Kiley replied, choosing his words carefully while looking his commander-in-chief straight in the eye. He had Duryea's UNODIR locked in his office safe and if push came to shove, at least technically, he could argue he had been truthful.

"Ditto, Mr. President," Lancaster replied.

The speechwriters were already at work when the meeting concluded. That evening the president went on television, branding Arafat's claims outright lies and denying that the attack on the gunboat ever took place. "Furthermore," he concluded, "the United States does not make deals that reward terrorism and encourage hostage taking; nor will we ask others to do so. We fully support the decision of the government of Israel to reject this outrageous demand. The United States never has and never will negotiate with terrorists."

L A R K I N spent the night at the airport hotel.

In the meantime, CIA personnel at the consulate in Tunis worked with the Saudi Arabian Embassy to obtain a visa, cutting the processing time from the customary weeks to hours. The following morning a CIA courier flew to D'Jerba and delivered the documents to Larkin. Then the colonel went to the Libyan People's Bureau to meet with Al-Qasim. He arrived well after midday and was informed the attaché was hosting a luncheon for a group of German businessmen.

Larkin waited until he returned.

"I have nothing to add to what I said yesterday," Al-Qasim said defensively, assuming Larkin was there to press the matter. "Major Shepherd misrepresented himself and there is nothing I can—"

"More than you know," Larkin interrupted sharply, going on to brief Al-Qasim on Libya's acquisition of the F-111s and Shepherd's intention to steal one.

The Libyan was stunned; he sat in silence assessing the implications. "You're certain?"

Larkin nodded gravely.

"Why should I believe you?" Al-Qasim challenged. "Or any of this, for that matter?"

"Because you're smart enough to realize you have nothing to gain and everything to lose if you don't," Larkin replied pointedly.

Al-Qasim's face stiffened with concern.

"Well," he finally declared, brightening slightly at a thought, "he won't have an easy time of it. The last time I saw Major Shepherd, he was in the custody of the secret police." He took the phone and dialed SHK headquarters in Tripoli. A brief conversation in Arabic followed; then he hung up and, with relief, announced, "Major Shepherd is the unhappy occupant of a cell in Bab al Azziziya prison."

Larkin broke into a relaxed smile.

"I assure you, I'll make sure he stays there."

"*Dies* there," Larkin said in a cold whisper.

38

A DAMP, bone-chilling draft blew through the prison beneath the Bab al Azziziya Barracks on As-Sarim Street in Tripoli.

The maximum-security dungeon was a filthy, windowless hell-hole where men and time passed without notice. There were no dawns, no dusks, only the glare of incandescent lights that burned twenty-four hours a day, and the intricate Arabic graffiti that served as epitaphs for its countless victims.

After his encounter with Qaddafi, Shepherd was taken here by the secret police and locked in a fetid cell. He stood in the narrow concrete box and shuddered as the steel bars clanged shut behind him. He had no idea if he was being held for trial, extradition, or, as the crazed Libyan had cruelly hinted, for punishment via some hideous Islamic ritual. He swallowed hard, fighting a nausea brought on by the putrid stench of human waste that came from a hole in the floor. An eternity passed before he could bring himself to sit on the edge of the filthy cot. His emotions ran the gamut from paralyzing fear to seething anger to an overall numbness. Only thoughts of Stephanie and the children sustained him.

Overhead, a bare bulb, enclosed in a wire cage, threw a pattern of harsh shadows across the cell. A gigantic spiderweb, Shepherd thought, deciding it was a more than fitting metaphor.

He lay awake for hours, finally getting some fitful sleep. The sounds of coughing and defecation woke him. He sat up feeling disoriented: this wasn't an ugly nightmare as he had hoped but a dehumanizing reality. He waited until his bladder was ready to burst before he stepped to the opposite corner, straddled the rancid hole, and urinated.

Moments later, a guard appeared and set a wooden bowl on the floor outside his cell.

"What is this stuff?" Shepherd called after him, eyeing the repulsive contents, which resembled a sponge floating in beige house paint.

The guard ignored him and went about dishing out breakfast to the other prisoners.

"Is bread and camel's milk," a voice called out after the guard had gone.

Shepherd looked up to see a young prisoner with wary eyes peering at him from between the bars of a cell across the corridor.

"Thanks." Shepherd gingerly plucked the chunk of bread from the milk.

"The colonel's own breakfast regimen, they claim."

"Figures."

"You are from U.K.?"

"United States."

The prisoner's eyes narrowed in suspicion as he found the only sensible explanation for an American being in a Libyan jail. "A shetan."

"I don't know what you mean by that," Shepherd drawled, sipping some of the bitter-tasting milk.

"How do you say? An espionage?"

"You mean a spy?"

"Yes, spy."

"No. I'm a pilot."

"Ah," the prisoner intoned, thinking he understood now. "One of those shot down bombing."

"In a manner of speaking." Shepherd decided it was neither wise nor possible to explain. "Where did you learn English?"

"University."

"In Libya?"

"Gaza."

"Israeli?"

"Palestinian," the prisoner replied sharply; then, deciding the slur was unintended, his expression softened and he asked, "You know of Bir Zeit?"

Shepherd shook his head no.

"I study for political science there. Now I fight to liberate Palestine."

"PLO?"

The Palestinian nodded.

"What are you doing in here?" Shepherd asked, unable to imagine why the Libyans would imprison him.

"Exterminating rats," the Palestinian quipped proudly, going on to boast that he had beaten the Libyans and their torture; the rats had torn his flesh but not his will or belief in Islam, which fortified him even in moments of total despair. Like Qaddafi and Abdel-Hadi, the Palestinian had no way of knowing that CIA had learned the hostages were hidden on the Romeo and he steadfastly refused to reveal their whereabouts. The SHK chief had decided to give him a taste of the good life before torturing him further. His rat bites had been cleansed and bandaged, and he had been removed from solitary confinement.

"What do they want from you?" Shepherd asked.

"The place of hiding for American hostages," the Palestinian replied matter-of-factly.

Shepherd hadn't expected that and took a moment to think. "You know where?"

The Palestinian nodded smugly. "But I am not telling to you," he taunted with a cocky smirk. "I stopped them from being released."

Shepherd's eyes narrowed as the ugly truth dawned on him. "You get a perverse kick out of kidnapping and murdering innocent people?"

"No. I fight for my homeland; my people—"

"No. *Armies* fight for homelands. You're a terrorist."

"Yes," the Palestinian replied, undaunted. "Yes, just like Shamir and Begin. Both were once wanted by Interpol. We have learned from the Zionists that rights won't be coming to you unless you take them."

"What rights?"

"To identity as Palestinians."

"You blew that when you started slaughtering women and children."

"Why *not* to kill them?" the Palestinian retorted. "The child will become an enemy soldier; and the woman will bear more."

"I rest my case."

"What is 'rest my case'?" the Palestinian demanded.

"It means, you proved my point. You're nothing more than animals."

"We only want what is rightfully ours."

"You're sure as hell going about it the wrong way."

The Palestinian spat at Shepherd's feet.

"I rest my case," Shepherd countered pointedly.

They stood there, faces framed by the bars, eyeing each other with hatred, finally deciding to tend to their empty stomachs.

Several hours later, a guard came lumbering down the corridor and charged into the Palestinian's cell. The guard, who carried the flabby bulk of a once avid weightlifter, yanked the Palestinian from his cot, hooked a massive arm under his chin, and dragged him off like a sack of grain.

Soon a plaintive wail reverberated off the concrete walls. This was no accident. Abdel-Hadi had purposely located the interrogation chamber within the cell block so the inmates could hear what happened to those who didn't cooperate.

And, indeed, the Palestinian still staunchly refused to give Abdel-Hadi the information he wanted. The cocky terrorist had been stripped naked, his ankles and wrists strapped to a straight-backed chair beneath a blazing spotlight.

"Where are they?" Abdel-Hadi demanded in Arabic, shouting over the high-pitched whine of an electric motor that came from the darkness. "Where?"

The Palestinian stared at him defiantly.

The guard lunged forward threateningly, the whine growing louder in the young terrorist's ears.

"No," Abdel-Hadi said sharply, holding the huge man off. "A rat retreats once its hunger is satisfied," he said to the Palestinian in his gravely voice, "but *this* animal"—he paused, gesturing to the guard—"he never gets enough. Now, the hostages, where are they?"

"Fucking your mother," the Palestinian taunted.

The SHK chief's eyes flared; he turned as if to walk away, but whirled suddenly. The back of his hand connected with the Palestinian's face with a loud smack. Then he stepped aside and nodded to the guard.

The obese fellow grabbed the prisoner's hair and brutally yanked his head forward. He waited before commencing the torture, allowing the unnerving whine to heighten his victim's anxiety.

The young terrorist was trying not to imagine what would happen next when the guard pressed a 2,000-watt hair dryer against the back of his neck. The metal nozzle, modified just for this purpose, produced a disgusting hissing sound as it seared his flesh, sending wisps of smoke curling into the air. The Palestinian writhed in silent agony until the pain and smell overwhelmed him, then he erupted in a blood-curdling yell.

The screams grew louder and longer as the guard went about

blistering more delicate parts of his anatomy. Despite the intense pain, the rough-cut terrorist continued to insist he didn't know where the hostages were hidden.

"Enough!" Abdel-Hadi finally shouted, yanking the power cord from the socket. More than once, he had warned that the Palestinian must be kept alive, a fact their victim had shrewdly deduced when days of torture lengthened into weeks, encouraging his defiance.

The screaming stopped as suddenly as it had started. An eerie silence fell over the prison.

Shepherd was lying on his cot thinking that they had probably killed him when the guard trudged down the corridor dragging the Palestinian behind him. He shoved the naked terrorist into his cell, throwing his clothing after him. Shepherd recoiled at the sight of the man's blistered torso, at the perfectly circular burns covering the body that lay on the concrete floor.

The son of a bitch got what he deserved, Shepherd told himself in an effort to suppress his compassion. But as he watched the Palestinian struggle to all fours and crawl onto his cot, as he listened to the plaintive moans, Shepherd knew that—deny it as he might, as he *had*—he and the Palestinian shared a basic human drive. Despite CIA's insidious conspiracy, which he attributed to the zeal of misguided patriots, his faith in *his* homeland remained intact.

Several hours later, Shepherd was lying on his cot, eyes shut tightly against the glare of the incandescents, when he heard the thud of heavy footsteps coming down the corridor. The huge guard stopped just outside the Palestinian's cell. Had they come for him again? So soon? Shepherd wondered. He was turning onto his side to steal a look at what was going on when he heard the key being pushed into the lock and the metallic creak of the door swinging open. But this time the sounds were sharper and closer. He glimpsed a hulking shadow stretching across the wall above him and broke into a cold sweat.

This time the guard had come for him.

39

ALMOST 36 HOURS had passed since Duryea, Cooperman, and Reyes met with Larkin on the USS *America*.

Upon returning to the *Cavalla*, Duryea began hunting for the submarine that contained the hostages. The coordinates of the submarine-gunboat rendezvous had placed it east of the line of underwater hydrophones that stretched from Sicily to Misratah; but it could be in any of the world's oceans by now. Duryea sent the following cable to SOSUS Control in Norfolk, Virginia, in an attempt to narrow the search area.

REQUEST REVIEW OF MAFIA CONTACTS 14APR TO
PRESENT TO DETERMINE IF ROMEO CROSSED NET
ON WESTERLY HEADING.

In Norfolk, a SOSUS technician immediately went to work on the Illiac-4 processor used to collate and analyze hydrophone-collected data. A powerful system of sixty-four computers in parallel alignment with a one-billion-bit memory, it made short work of Duryea's query.

A short time later, the *Cavalla's* assistant radio operator delivered the reply to the command center:

NEGATIVE. MAFIA NET NOT CROSSED WESTERLY
BY ANY ROMEO WITHIN GIVEN PARAMETERS.

To Duryea's relief, this eliminated any chance that his target had gone through the Straits of Gibraltar into the Atlantic. The Suez Canal to the Red Sea was also a possibility; but the 100-mile journey would have to be made on the surface and would become a matter of record. Duryea discounted it, deciding his target was still in the Mediterranean, somewhere east of the SOSUS hydrophone line.

The eastern Mediterranean was a huge basin, an abyssal plain free of deep trenches and uninterrupted by undersea ridges and seamounts. There were few places where a submarine could hide.

"What do you think?" Dureyea challenged McBride. "If you wanted to disappear, just stay dived and on the move and never be found, where would you go?"

"The Aegean," McBride replied, referring to the sea that bulges northward from the Mediterranean between Greece and Turkey.

Duryea nodded sagely. "Bet your ass; perfect topology, and barely five hundred miles from home."

Indeed, unlike the eastern Mediterranean, the Aegean was a roller coaster landscape of seamounts, escarpments, and ridges interconnecting the Greek islands. Nearly a hundred in number, these formations soared from the ocean bottom and punched through the surface like truncated mountaintops, the underwater terrain rising and falling from Spetses to Hydra to Kithnos, Siros, Mykonos, Paros, Crete, Rhodes, ad infinitum throughout the Aegean. This undulating landscape was the perfect place to avoid sonar detection. Though sound travels through water four times faster than air, and can be detected at vast distances from the source in a contiguous body of water, the island-dotted Aegean was anything but contiguous. Here, despite being equipped with the most sophisticated sonar arrays, a submarine on one side of a narrow island wouldn't be able to detect the presence of a second on the other side. Though just miles apart, neither boat would be aware of the other's presence. Unless, as Duryea and Larkin had decided, one of those boats took advantage of aerial anti-submarine warfare reconnaissance.

ASW aircraft from the 6th Fleet regularly seeded the Aegean with sonobuoys, keeping track of Redfleet submarines proceeding south through the Dardanelles toward the Mediterranean; and in the 24 hours it took for the *Cavalla* to reach its present position 100 miles west of Crete, a Viking from the carrier *America* had been hunting the Romeo.

Flying in an expanding spiral that began near the centrally located island of Naxos, the Lockheed S-3A dropped hundreds of sonobuoys into the choppy waters. The 36-inch-long, 6-inch-diameter cylinders were launched from a 60-cell honeycomb in the plane's underbelly. Lowered in proper orientation to the sea by a tiny parachute, each sonobuoy sank to operating depth and began collecting sonar data, transmitting the coordinates, depth, and bearing of each contact to the Viking by radio link.

Now in an electronics bay behind the Viking's cockpit, the tactical coordination officer sat at his console monitoring the sonobuoys he had deployed. He was switching through the various frequencies when his oscilloscope came alive with a sonar pattern. He patched it into the on-board computer, a Univac digital processor that evaluated data as it was collected, and instructed it to run a comparative signal analysis.

At the same time, 350 miles west of the Viking's position, the *Cavalla* was approaching the Mediterranean Ridge. This rugged undersea mountain range cupped the mouth of the Aegean in a looping arc from the Greek Peloponnisos to the southwest coast of Turkey, skirting the islands of Crete and Rhodes. The submarine was proceeding slowly just beneath the surface at periscope-antenna depth to keep in voice communication with the Viking.

In the captain's cabin just aft of the control room, the soft hum of a computer fan came from a terminal that was tied in to the boat's BC-10. Commander Duryea sat beneath the network of pipes, ducts, and electrical chases that formed the cabin's ceiling, staring at the monitor. He was picking at his lunch while reviewing charts that delineated the treacherous terrain ahead when McBride called.

"ASW contact, skipper."

"On my way," Duryea fired back. He hurried from the cabin, turkey sandwich in hand, and sprinted up the short companionway into the control center.

"Commander Duryea here," he said, taking the phone from McBride. "What do you have?"

"A Romeo, sir," the Viking's tactical coordination officer replied.

"Where is he?"

"Just west of the Turkish channel off Kalimnos." The Tacco recited the coordinates for longitude and latitude, adding, "Course one four zero; depth sixty feet."

"Not exactly next door," Duryea observed, knowing the coordinates put the Greek islands and 300 miles of tricky underwater terrain between the *Cavalla* and the target submarine. "Are you positive it's a Romeo?"

"Affirmative. Acoustic signature comparison verifies," the Viking's Tacco replied, studying *two* frequency patterns that were now tracing across his oscilloscope: the upper being the sonar contact, the lower the computer library profile. "We've seen this guy before, sir. He's been plying the Aegean for a couple of weeks now. Somebody's got him on a tight leash. Every day at twenty-one hundred, he dead stops, comes to periscope depth, and puts up a radio mast."

Duryea's brows went up. "Every day?"

"Affirmative. Twenty-one hundred."

Duryea smiled thoughtfully and filed it away. "Okay, good going," he enthused. "Better get your butts out of there."

"Roger, willco," the Viking's pilot replied, accelerating onto a heading for the *America*.

McBride already had the chart up on the electronic table when Duryea joined him. "Any chance he's heading for the Dardanelles?" he asked, indicating the narrow straits that cut through the northwest corner of Turkey to the Bosporous and Black Sea beyond.

"Not as many places to hide up there," Duryea said. "Why leave the Aegean? I figure he's probably on a random track, snaking between the islands." He turned to his keyboard, and encoded. A pulsing cursor appeared on the monitor, marking the Romeo's position. "Judging from his current position and course, I think he'll proceed until he hits Patmos or Ikaria, somewhere in here, then come to a southwest heading and get lost in the Cyclades," Duryea explained, referring to the group of twenty-seven islands in the center of the Aegean.

"If it's *our* Romeo," McBride countered.

A few minutes later, Duryea was still hovering over the chart table plotting an intercept course when the phone twittered.

McBride scooped up the receiver. "Conn. Yeah, yeah, I'll put him on. Sat-link from Kubark, skipper." He handed Duryea the phone.

"This is the director," Kiley said; the direct voice communication was possible because the *Cavalla* was at periscope-antenna depth to communicate with the Viking.

"Good to hear your voice, sir."

"You won't think so after you hear what I've got to say," the DCI retorted dourly, going on to brief Duryea on the PLO's threat to kill the hostages.

"It may not be as big a problem as you think, sir," Duryea responded, pleased to have some good news to report. "We have a high-potential contact and expect to verify shortly."

"You just made my day, Commander."

"Maybe you can make mine, sir."

"Do my best. What do you need?"

"The status of Project Twilight," Duryea said, using the code name the DCI had given his plan to incapacitate the personnel aboard the Romeo.

"Stand by," Kiley grunted, buzzing his secretary. "I need OTS right away," he growled, referring to the Office of Technical Services. "This is the director," Kiley said when the project administrator came on the line. "I need an ETA for Twilight. You're sure? I'm going to hold you to it." He mumbled, "Thanks," then tapped one of the flashing buttons on his communications console, switching back to Duryea.

"Operational," the DCI reported buoyantly. "You can expect delivery within twenty-four hours."

"We'll be waiting, sir." Duryea turned to his keyboard, typed an instruction, and entered some data. A small window appeared in the upper right-hand corner of the electronic chart table. It read:

02:DAYS
19:HOURS
36:MINUTES
28:SECONDS

—to Ramadan and counting

"When that comes up all zeroes," Duryea said grimly to Mc-Bride, "they start killing hostages."

40

W A T E R E X P L O D E D from the nozzle of the fire hose with incredible force. It caught Shepherd square in the center of his chest and knocked him to the floor of the interrogation chamber. Stark naked, he went tumbling across the rough concrete, the high pressure deluge ricocheting off his body, splattering over the walls and ceiling, and swirling down the rusted drain that Shepherd was certain had carried off the lifeblood of countless torture victims.

The guard clutched the unwieldy hose with both hands, bracing it against his torso, and came at him.

Shepherd scrambled to his feet, trying to elude the ice-cold blast that pummeled him; but the guard's pursuit was relentless. There was no place to hide in the windowless room, no protection from the stinging onslaught. The stream of water pounded Shepherd's body with punishing force, trapping him in a corner. The powerful jet knocked his hands aside and smashed into his groin. He howled in pain, spinning around to protect himself, and yelped as the water surged between his buttocks, trying to penetrate him. Then it slammed into his back, the extreme pressure pinning him flat against the wall. The roar from the gleaming nozzle was deafening. He felt as if he was drowning, certain the high-powered jet would soon be stripping the flesh from his bones.

Suddenly the guard pulled back on the nozzle's cutoff valve. The vicious flow stopped abruptly.

Shepherd slumped against the wall, coughing up water as if he had been pulled from the sea. To his relief, the guard set the hose aside, dragged him to his feet, and directed him to an anteroom where SHK Chief Abdel-Hadi and his two young thugs were waiting.

Shepherd's eyes darted to some clothing on a table, *his* clothing. It had been laundered and folded neatly. When the swarthy guard threw a bath towel at him, Shepherd realized he had just been treated to a shower, Libyan prison style.

The SHK chief watched stone-faced and silent as he toweled off and began pulling on his clothes.

"What happens now?" Shepherd knew from experience it would be a waste of time, but asked anyway. "Am I being extradited, executed, what?"

"What does it matter?" Abdel-Hadi replied slyly. "In your case, they would be one and the same."

The son of a bitch is right, Shepherd thought. If ever two men were soulmates, it was Abdel-Hadi and Larkin; and as he was led through the maze of corridors and security doors—leaving the foul stench of excrement and unwashed bodies behind—the horrid idea that the colonel had gained entry into Libya and would now take custody of him grew stronger with each step.

They went up a concrete staircase to the central processing area where, at Abdel-Hadi's instructions, the officer on duty made an entry in his ledger. Then they went out the main entrance of the prison.

It was mid-afternoon. The sun blazed, unchallenged by a single cloud, the searing heat intensifying the suffocating odor of camel dung. They led Shepherd to Abdel-Hadi's Krazz and opened the door to the prisoner's compartment behind the cab, where the Akita waited.

The powerful canine sprang to a standing position and growled, its black lips curling back to reveal lethal fangs that dared Shepherd to enter. Abdel-Hadi uttered a command in Arabic and the dog backed off. The SHK officers grabbed Shepherd's arms, shoved him inside, and slammed the doors shut.

Shepherd sat on the wooden bench, his face crosshatched with harsh shadows from the heavy wire mesh that separated the prisoner's compartment from the cab.

The two officers got in, followed by Abdel-Hadi, who uttered another command in the same tone he had used with the dog. One of the officers responded by unbuckling a heavy canvas shade that rolled down over the wire mesh, plunging Shepherd and the Akita into almost total darkness. The engine started and the vehicle drove off across the Bab al Azziziya compound.

Shepherd heard the clank of tank treads as the T-55 that was parked in front of the entrance backed up to let the Krazz exit.

He realized they were leaving the grounds. A series of turns, stops, and starts accompanied by the sounds of traffic ensued; the cacophony was followed by a high-speed drive that Shepherd reckoned meant they were traveling on a highway outside the city.

About three-quarters of an hour later, the driver backed off the gas and began down-shifting through the gears. The Krazz slowed and finally stopped.

Shepherd heard a few words of Arabic before the throaty engine came to life and the vehicle started down a sharply curving road that caused him to lean into the turn, followed by another series of sharp lefts and rights.

Throughout the drive, the Akita had been too busy clawing at the steel deck with its huge paws to compensate for the vehicle's movement to pay any attention to Shepherd. Now the powerful animal stood expectantly, sensing the journey was over.

Shepherd heard the engine shut off, the ratchet of the hand brake being applied, then doors opening and slamming closed as the SHK officers got out.

The harsh guttural mumble of Arabic followed; then footsteps approached the rear of the Krazz.

The doors were yanked open.

The Akita lept to the ground and bounded off.

Shepherd recoiled at the sudden blast of light as the officers took his arms and pulled him out. Temporarily blinded, he stumbled, then straightened, squinting to determine where he was, to resolve the amorphous figures that seemed defined by the sharp edges of weapons, of rifles and bayonets. His eyes strained against the whiteness, unable to discern if it was Larkin and a group of government representatives or a firing squad. Finally a compact figure slowly emerged from the haze.

It was General Younis.

Several armed guards were posted behind him.

They stood in an immense hangar on an immaculate, glossy white floor that was boldly slashed by red, yellow, and green stripes used to position aircraft.

"Major Shepherd," the general said, striding forward with a smile.

"General," Shepherd replied apprehensively.

"As you can see, Major," Younis began, gesturing behind him, "it would be to our advantage if you are who you say you are."

Shepherd turned to see the two F-111s parked side by side. He knew the Libyans had acquired them, but was still taken by the sight; indeed, they were the last thing he had expected to see.

"Where did you get them?" Shepherd wondered, knowing Younis would expect him to ask.

"I wouldn't tell you even if I knew," the general replied with a sly smile. "Besides it's hardly relevant to our arrangement."

"Our arrangement . . ." Shepherd echoed flatly.

"Yes, the colonel decided to abide by it."

"Just like that."

"Hardly. As you observed, he has an obsessive concern for his safety that sometimes triggers these 'episodes.' Fortunately, he's quite rational when he comes out of them, almost contrite, at which time we review decisions made under the stress. Sometimes I win; sometimes I lose." He paused and pointed to the Libyan Air Force markings on the bombers. "In your case, he decided to accept your offer to share your knowledge and skills with us."

Shepherd mulled it over, concealing his elation, and decided a challenge was the most natural response under the circumstances. "That's all well and good," he said. "But I'd like some assurances that I won't end up back in that hellhole as soon as I do."

"You have my word, Major," the general said.

"And his?" Shepherd asked, inclining his head toward Abdel-Hadi.

The SHK chief responded with several phrases delivered in sharp, rapid-fire Arabic.

"He said you can be assured that's exactly what will happen if you *don't*."

Shepherd stiffened and nodded resignedly. "Nothing like having a clear choice," he said, reinforcing the impression that they had coerced him.

"I knew you'd make the right one," Younis replied. He and Abdel-Hadi watched as Shepherd crossed to one of the F-111s and began a walk-around, working his way along the fuselage to the nose gear. He crouched to inspect it, then stole a glance at the doors. The vague outline of stenciled lettering that had once proclaimed AC MAJ SHEPHERD was still slightly visible, despite being painted over. A surge of adrenaline went through him. He remained there for a moment, then moved to the adjacent bomber.

"I wouldn't mind seeing a little more tail droop," he observed, indicating the trailing edge of the stabilizers. "I'd have my crew chief fine-tune the flight control system, if you don't mind me suggesting it."

"Not at all. We'd like to hear whatever you have to say, Major," Younis replied, impressed by how Shepherd handled himself. When he had finished the inspection, the general directed him into the office, where his technical staff had assembled with several Libyan flight crews.

"We have flown both aircraft and have a working knowledge of the flight systems, Major," the East German avionics expert said in his clipped cadence. "ANITA is where we stumbled. Unfortunately, none of the codes we developed proved operative."

"Tough without the entry key," Shepherd said, jotting the alphanumeric table on a chalkboard:

A 1	F 6	K 11	P 16	U 21	Z 26
B 2	G 7	L 12	Q 17	V 22	
C 3	H 8	M 13	R 18	W 23	
D 4	I 9	N 14	S 19	X 24	
E 5	J 10	O 15	T 20	Y 25	

"Let's say you want to enter a hundred-and-seventy-eight degrees, fifty-three minutes north latitude. Well, the first digit of each number is encrypted as a simple letter equivalent; the second as a numerical equivalent of that digit written out in Roman letters without vowels; then you alternate as you go. In other words . . ." He wrote on the board:

1 = A
7 = SVN or S = 19, V = 22, N = 14
8 = H

5 = E
3 = THR or T = 20, H = 8, R = 18
N = 14

178/53/N entered as: A:19:22:14:H/E:20:8:18/14

The East German's brows went up. ANITA was neither complex nor brilliant; it wasn't based on top-secret prime numbers or on the polyalphabetic substitution tables commonly used for communications cyphers. Unlike them, ANITA didn't have to withstand enemy interception and subsequent scrutiny by expert code breakers who, working from a purloined cipher, might eventually crack it. No, his technicians had only the Pave Tack entry keyboard, blank screen, and microprocessor with a protected internal entry program that defied them to literally guess what alphanumeric input format it would accept. There were no clues, no intercepted samples to study, only infinite, random possibilities.

When Shepherd finished, Younis produced maps marked with the location of the desert practice target the Libyan crews had been unable to destroy.

They gathered round Shepherd as he encrypted the data, writing the alphanumerics on a programming sheet that he had drawn up; it listed all ANITA functions—longitude, latitude, range, angle of attack, air speed, among others—that the Pave Tack computer required to locate a target and destroy it with laser-guided bombs.

"Encrypting ANITA and entering it is the easy part," Shepherd observed. "*Flying* to it—that's something else. Now the Pave Tack console has two sets of function readouts." He turned to the chalkboard, writing as he continued. "PRESENT—the actual position and attitude of the aircraft in flight, and SELECTED—the target acquisition data. The trick is—"

"Getting the two to match," the East German interrupted. "We're quite aware of the problem."

"There's only one way," Shepherd declared, about to utter the words that he hoped would literally put him in the cockpit of his plane. "Expert instruction. Lots of it. Each crew member has to fly a lot of hours with an expert one-eleven driver next to him."

"I don't doubt it, Major, but as you might imagine, one doesn't place a want ad for one-eleven instructors."

"Now that you're here, now that we finally have ANITA," General Younis chimed in, "I suggest that we reassemble here at eleven hundred tomorrow and plan a mission; a training mission which you and one of our aviators will fly after nightfall."

Shepherd nodded coolly, suppressing his delight; not only would he soon be flying his F-111, but he also would have some time to plan just how he would steal it, how he would overcome the Libyan who would be in the cockpit with him, elude the inevitable fighter escort, and fly the bomber to D'Jerba. "See you on the flight line," he replied in a flat professional tone.

41

M O R E   T H A N   A   W E E K had passed since Moncrieff
and Katifa had escaped from Tripoli and flown to Jeddah, a port
city on the eastern shore of the Red Sea 600 miles south of Suez.
Though Riyadh was Saudi Arabia's capital, Jeddah had long been
the center of banking and commerce, and the royal family maintained a palatial residence there.

Set against a background of craggy mountains, the palace stood
majestically on a bluff above the sea. Its numerous domed buildings were masterful examples of Middle Eastern architecture, re-
plete with intricate tilings and delicate mushrabeyeh latticework.

Katifa had been taken directly to the royal infirmary where she
was attended by court physicians. After a few days they removed
her bandages and prescribed that she swim to rehabilitate and
strengthen her weakened muscles. Prior to discharging her, the
Infirmary's chief of staff—an aging, Harvard-educated physician
who had brought Moncrieff into the world and had no qualms
about voicing his opinion—took Moncrieff aside for a brief discussion.

"What's the problem?" Katifa prompted after the old fellow had
left.

"The Koran," Moncrieff replied, knowingly.

"I don't think I'm going to like this."

"Nor am I," the Saudi said, explaining that the physician had
concerns about where she would be living. Though not radical
hard-liners like their Iranian neighbors, Saudis *were* fundamen-
talist Muslims: women were forbidden to smoke, drive, or drink,
and were strictly segregated from men; they neither worked nor
dined with them, let alone exposed their bodies to them in public.
Even the wives of Western businessmen spent the evening in the
women's quarters while the men dined alone. The idea of Katifa
living with Moncrieff and swimming in the palace pool was un-
acceptable.

Undaunted, Moncrieff arranged for them to move into the royal guest house. Located in Al Hamra, the city's most fashionable area, it was a high-security estate with an immense pool reached by a marble staircase that descended from the main building.

Now Moncrieff sat at a table on a palm-shaded terrace above, watching Katifa's lithe body gliding effortlessly through the water. The instant her fingertips touched the wall, she did a graceful swimmer's turn, her long hair streaming behind her as the momentum propelled her through the sparkling water. She had grown up with political activisim and violence; had *advocated* them; but now, the shock of bullets tearing into her flesh along with her narrow escape from Nidal's hit squad had given her pause. Indeed, though predisposed to reject the privileged opulence of Moncrieff's world, she found the security and the time she had spent with him in this idyllic place more and more to her liking.

Moncrieff had been dividing his time between the guest house and his office in downtown Jeddah. Despite the problem created by Nefta Dam, Libya's Great Man-made River Project was proceeding as scheduled: wells were being drilled and pipeline manufactured and laid, and several other projects were in development as well.

Moncrieff was primarily an intelligence observer; the encounter in Tripoli had been his first and, he had since decided, last field operation. Life was back to normal; and with each day, he was becoming more and more confident that as he had hoped, as he had *conspired*, he and Katifa would be spending their lives together.

"Excuse me, Your Highness," one of the Filipino servants said, pulling Moncrieff out of his reverie. "A Colonel Larkin is here."

"Here?" Moncrieff echoed with a surprised scowl.

"Yes, sir, in the entry. Shall I show him in?"

Moncrieff glanced thoughtfully to Katifa in the pool, then shook his head no. He left the terrace, hurrying through the house to the entry chamber where Larkin was waiting. The colonel wore civilian clothes; he stood next to a magnificently carved fountain that was centered beneath the soaring dome.

"Colonel," Moncrieff said, crossing toward him.

"Good to see you," Larkin replied brightly. Indeed, despite almost a month of wearying travel, his fighter pilot's conditioning had kept him from becoming fatigued.

"I'm sorry we missed each other in Tripoli," Moncrieff said facetiously. He forced a smile and led the way outside, where they wouldn't be overheard. "Really, you should have called," he went on in his British-flavored English as they walked in the gardens that radiated from the domed buildings with geometric precision. "I would have sent a car."

"I barely made my flight," Larkin replied in a bold lie. Yesterday, having been forced to wait until late afternoon to meet with Al-Qasim, he had missed his flight to Saudi Arabia. He spent a second night at the airport hotel on D'Jerba and could have easily called; but he knew Moncrieff was angry and wanted out; he also knew that a royal prince could block his entry into Saudi Arabia with a phone call of his own, and purposely hadn't notified Moncrieff he was coming. "You see Arafat's speech?" he asked, getting to business.

"Yes, I did," Moncrieff replied cautiously.

"It hit the old man pretty hard. But he's worked out an insurance policy and he's counting on you to—"

"I'm out of the loop, Colonel," Moncrieff interrupted. "I told him that."

"I know. We need the lady."

"Katifa?"

Larkin nodded.

"What for?"

"I'd prefer to go through it once. Is she here?"

"Yes. I don't know what you have in mind, Colonel, but the old man briefed me on the hostages. If this has anything to do with the rescue, if it's fieldwork, something dangerous, I'm unalterably opposed to her taking it on. She's just getting back to normal; just starting to enjoy life, and I . . ." He paused, seeing the amused smile that broke across Larkin's face.

"Am I picking up on something here?" Larkin asked.

"Maybe."

"Then maybe you're not the best judge of this."

Moncrieff nodded grudgingly and led the way to the pool area. They arrived on the terrace just as Katifa was getting out of the water. She waved as a servant handed her a towel, then draped it over her shoulders, lit a cigarette, and started up the marble staircase toward them. The bikini did little to hide the freshly healed bullet wounds that dotted her tawny flesh.

"You can thank Nidal for this," Larkin began after Moncrieff had made the introductions. "We had high hopes for this hostage rescue until he threatened to kill them. We still do. But there's no guarantee the *Cavalla* can pull it off before the deadline. The old man figures Nidal won't kill them on the sub because he'd have to dump the bodies at sea. No proof that way; no media hype."

"I agree," Moncrieff said.

"We'd have a chance to stop him if we knew where the executions would be carried out."

"His headquarters," Katifa replied, exhaling a steady stream of smoke. "Casino du Liban."

"You're certain—beyond any doubt?"

"I'm afraid that's not possible with Abu Nidal."

"Then we'll need someone on the inside," Larkin said, leaving no doubt he was talking about Katifa.

"I hasten to point out we're not on the best of terms these days," she protested.

"He tried to abduct her," Moncrieff chimed in. "I briefed the old man. Didn't he mention it?"

Larkin nodded. "He thinks we can *use* it; and do what we did with Yevchenko," he said, referring to a high-ranking KGB officer who, several months after defecting to the West, claimed he had been abducted and held against his will; he subsequently returned to Moscow.

"I recall that incident," Moncrieff said, puzzled at the analogy. "The old man looked like a fool; people thought he had lost his touch, and perhaps more."

"Which thoroughly convinced Moscow that Yevchenko's story was bona fide," Larkin explained with a sly grin. "He's back at Moscow Center now, running his own section; with our blessing, of course."

Katifa thought about it for a long moment and nodded. "I can see how something like that might work," she finally said, "but why should I take the chance?"

"Because you and I both know there isn't going to be a homeland in Israel by the start of Ramadan, this year or any year; and if Nidal kills those hostages, there'll never be a sanctuary in Libya either."

"I think you're wrong. The hostages aren't part of the equation anymore," Katifa explained. "Qaddafi acquired the planes without them."

"Which means," Larkin countered, "he has no incentive to turn over a couple of thousand square miles of desert to anybody."

"Of course he does," Katifa retorted. "You must understand that he wants more than military hardware or water out of this. It's no secret that Arab unity and the destruction of Israel are his goals. A Palestinian sanctuary would be a perfect start; the stature and power he would gain are sufficient incentives to provide one."

"Maybe; but not without ANITA."

"Anita?" she asked, puzzled.

"It's an acronym for a computer entry key," Moncrieff explained. "The F-111s are useless without it."

"And Qaddafi won't get it until we get the hostages," Larkin said.

"There's no other way he can get this entry key?"

"None." Larkin lied, not because he knew Shepherd had already voluntarily revealed them, which he didn't; but because he knew there was a chance the secret police might force him to do so. It was the perfect leverage to manipulate her and he would have used it regardless.

Katifa pondered his reply for a moment, looking out over the grounds and pool that shimmered in the light to the Red Sea beyond. Two thousand years, she thought, two thousand years since Moses parted it, since the Israelis fled the Egyptians; it hadn't even been forty since Palestine was partioned by the British. "Will you excuse us?" she said to Larkin, leading Moncrieff aside.

"He's right, isn't he?"

"Don't do this, Katifa," the Saudi pleaded.

"I don't have any choice."

"You'll be shot on sight."

"No. You just said it yourself. Abu Nidal tried to *abduct* me in Tripoli, not kill me. Believe me, I'd already be dead if that's what he wanted."

"I doubt he would ever trust you again."

"You're forgetting something," she said firmly. "I've been like a daughter to him for almost twenty years. He'll hear me out."

Moncrieff saw the determination in her eyes and knew he had no chance of convincing her otherwise. "I was hoping we had put all this behind us."

"So was I," she said sadly.

42

S H E P H E R D had spent the night billeted in officers quarters at Okba ben Nafi Air Base. He had gotten a good night's sleep, devoured several square meals, and, for the first time in weeks, was feeling reasonably healthy; indeed, the prospect of finally retrieving his F-111 had contributed mightly to his recovery and sharpened state of mind.

"Where's the weight room?" he inquired on arriving that morning at hangar 6-South. He frowned, feigning disappointment when told there wasn't one; in truth, he was much more interested in the physical conditioning of Libyan aviators, than in working out, and was quietly delighted to learn their natural G-suits had gone undeveloped. He spent the day planning a practice mission and reviewing the various flight and attack systems with the East German, his technical staff, and the Libyan flight crews assigned to the F-111s.

Early that evening, after being fitted for flight gear, Shepherd was directed to a locker room where the Libyan aviator General Younis had selected as his first pupil was waiting.

This is the man I have to beat; *kill* if need be, Shepherd thought, as they shook hands and began suiting up: first the Nomex flight suit, then the G-harness that went over it, sheathing calves, thighs, and torso. Made of a double-walled fabric that inflated like a blood pressure cuff during high G-force maneuvers, it squeezed blood from the lower extremities upward to the brain, helping to keep an aviator from blacking out.

Shepherd pulled the last of the zippers that ran up the inseams of the G-suit, then slipped on his flight helmet, closed the visor, and adjusted the oxygen mask. He couldn't remember the last time he had gone a week without suiting up, without flying, let alone a half dozen. It was a strange feeling; strange and distant. He had just raised the visor when he noticed the Libyan take a small pistol and holster from his locker, and strap it to the inside of his left calf below his kneeboard, which held a list of fly-to-points.

They left the locker room, oxygen and G-suit hoses swaying in front of them, General Younis trailing behind.

"Will we have escort aircraft?" Shepherd asked offhandedly, as they crossed the hangar toward the F-111s.

"Certainly," Younis replied. "Why do you ask?"

"I was thinking, if we treated them as bogies we could work on some evasive maneuvers en route to the target," Shepherd explained earnestly. He hadn't wanted to ask, hadn't wanted to risk alerting them; but he knew he would be monitored on radar, knew any unexpected move would trigger suspicion, and needed to keep them at bay for as long as possible. "Our people do it all the time during practice missions."

"Of course," Younis replied smartly. "I expect you to teach our men everything you can, as quickly as you can. Make use of every minute of flight time." He paused, then addressed the Libyan aviator. "You'll be working on tactical evasion en route to the target."

They exited the hangar, striding a short distance through the darkness to the sleek bomber, then began a walk-around inspection in the glare of the work lights that illuminated the area.

"The way we do it," Shepherd said matter-of-factly, making certain he didn't appear too anxious to get into the air, "the aircraft commander does the detailed inspection; the wizzo checks external stores and the like. Mine always paid special attention to the BRUs and Pave Tack pod."

After the inspection, they climbed boarding ladders to the cockpit and slipped beneath the gull-wing canopies. Each had a copy of the ANITA programming sheet Shepherd had made up earlier.

Younis joined Abdel-Hadi and the East German on a platform that was positioned adjacent to the cockpit. They watched intently as the Libyan turned on the Pave Tack computer, and went to work on the NDEP, the console-mounted keyboard, entering the alphanumeric data under Shepherd's supervision. When finished, the two aviators buckled in and latched the canopies closed.

The hydraulic platform lowered and pulled away.

The ground crew coupled a hose from an air blower to the starter breech on the left side below the SOAP door; five minutes later, both engines were over the horn and spinning at 17,000 RPM.

Shepherd lifted the throttles. Fuel flow and ignition were instantaneous. The high-pitched whine sent a chill through him as the blower was disconnected and he began a check of flight systems.

Then the Libyan took the controls. He released the wheel brakes, slowly advanced the thottles and began guiding the bomber through the taxiways toward the runway.

Younis, Abdel-Hadi, and the East German climbed into the Krazz. "Well, we no longer have any use for the Palestinian," Abdel-Hadi observed coldly as they drove off, heading across the air base to the control tower.

They took the elevator to the cab and crossed to the angled windows that overlooked the airfield. Far below, two SU-22 fighters that would escort the F-111 roared down the runway, taking off into the darkness.

"We're on the mark," Shepherd reported moments later, when the F-111 arrived at the top of the runway. He took over the controls, turned onto the center markings, set the brakes, and tested flaps and stabilizers. One at a time, he ran the engines up to full military power, then into afterburner range. "Burners and MIL are optimum," he said. "We're ready to roll."

"You have immediate CTO," came the reply. "Winds are one-four-five at twelve knots."

Shepherd homed the throttles and released the brakes. The F-111 lurched forward and began racing down the long concrete ribbon.

Shepherd's mind was racing along with it, reviewing the moves he had worked out to elude the fighter escort, overcome the pilot, and steal the plane: it would begin with a swept-wing, supersonic TFR dash 200 feet above the desert, which would be followed by the key maneuver, a sudden pull into a high-G afterburner climb. At eight to ten times the pull of gravity, the Libyan's lack of physical fitness coupled with being caught completely unawares would cause him to black out.

"Clueless and useless in the furball" was what aviators called the phenomenon. GLC ambushed the most experienced of them on occasion, lasting as long as 30 to 60 seconds, precious seconds that Shepherd would use to dump the cabin pressure and disconnect the unconscious Libyan's oxygen and G-suit hoses. Deprived of all respiratory support, he would, at the least, remain comatose, allowing Shepherd to disarm him, shoot him if necessary, and take control of the aircraft.

The F-111 was 10 seconds into its takeoff roll now.

The 1,500-foot marker flickered past in a blur.

Shepherd was monitoring inlet pressure, fuel flow and ratio, pounds of thrust, takeoff trim, and air speed. When the latter reached 145 knots, he eased back on the stick, rotating the nose up.

The sleek bomber leapt off the runway and began climbing into the blackness. D'Jerba was a mere 200 miles away; at top speed the F-111 could cover the distance in under 10 minutes.

WHILE THE F-111 streaked skyward, Adnan Al-Qasim's BMW sedan came down Al Jala Boulevard in Tripoli and turned into As-Sarim Street, its headlights playing across the concrete dragon's teeth that lined the approach to the Bab al Azziziya Barracks.

The previous afternoon, after Larkin informed him of Shepherd's intention to steal an F-111, Al-Qasim had quickly realized the matter could destroy him if wrongly perceived; on the other hand, properly finessed, he could orchestrate Shepherd's demise without bringing about his own. Shepherd couldn't very well steal an F-111 while in prison, Al-Qasim had reasoned; so he spent the evening evaluating the situation, deciding it was too delicate to be handled via phone. He called Abdel-Hadi's office and, refusing to divulge his agenda, made an appointment for late the following afternoon. He would be driving executives of a Dutch electronics company to Tripoli for meetings at several ministries and would go to the barracks compound when finished.

Now, on arriving, he presented his credentials to the guard, then proceeded across the grounds to secret police headquarters and asked to see Abdel-Hadi.

"Something came up," the duty officer replied. "He canceled all his afternoon appointments and won't be returning. Do you wish to reschedule for tomorrow?"

Al-Qasim scowled and nodded. "Ten o'clock."

The phone rang.

The officer answered it and jotted down a message, then noticed

Al-Qasim heading for the door and called out, "Al-Qasim. This meeting; it is in regard to what?"

"A top-secret matter, as I explained yesterday."

"It would still be best if I tell Abdel-Hadi something. There's a chance he won't see you otherwise."

"Tell him it's regarding the American prisoner," Al-Qasim replied grudgingly. "He'll know because he—"

"Major Shepherd?" the officer interrupted.

Al-Qasim nodded emphatically.

"He was released this morning."

"Released?" Al-Qasim echoed with apprehension.

"Transferred," the officer corrected, glancing to his log. "Crew quarters; Okba ben Nafi Air Base."

T H E   F - 1 1 1 was streaking high above the desert now, the infinite blackness broken only by the horizon, where a faint amber glow separated sand from sky.

Shepherd was enjoying the incredible silence, the reassuring pressure of the G-suit against his body, and the tingling sensation that was rising in his stomach. He was flying instinctively now; had the moves planned out; had each precious second down cold. He was so close he could taste it: Stephanie, the children, his name cleared, life at long last back to normal.

His eyes darted to the radar screen; two blips were closing on his position. "Looks like a couple of baby-sitters coming in," he observed, enjoying the calmness that had come over him. He was in the zone, in total command; cool, calculating, flying a mission.

Soon distant streaks of light cut huge arcs in the darkness, as the two SU-22 fighters began moving into escort position off the F-111's wings.

"I think it's time for that lesson in tactical evasion," Shepherd said in a friendly tone intended to relax the Libyan. "Hang on."

"You propose to outrun them?"

"Nope. We're going to do something you can't do with any other bomber on earth," Shepherd replied, knowing the maneuver would soften him up.

At that, he hit the brakes—spoilers up, flaps down, throttles back—causing sudden, rapid deceleration. Air whomped against control surfaces in protest; shoulder harnesses dug painfully into muscle.

The SU-22s were caught unawares and went rocketing past into the darkness.

Shepherd trimmed the bomber's attitude and headed for the deck. He leveled out 200 feet above the desert floor, then engaged the terrain following radar.

TFR relied on two low altitude radar altimeters that scanned 1,000 feet ahead. Via a computerized link to the autopilot, the two LARA channels compared data, automatically commanding the aircraft to follow land contours. It emitted an aural tone, beeping on climb, booping on descent. How precisely it mirrored the rise and fall of the landscape was determined by setting a switch on the TFR panel to soft, medium, or hard.

Shepherd set the ride for hard, which meant the bomber would hug the ground, conforming to every rise, ripple, and dip, well below the scanning range of tower radar; then he slammed the throttles to the stops. The afterburners kicked in, belching blue-orange flame and the F-111 rocketed forward.

The Libyan emitted an excited yelp as the acceleration slammed him back into his seat.

"They call this a fighter-bomber," Shepherd said, keeping up the friendly charade. "But just between us, I usually put the emphasis on fighter."

In the tower at Okba ben Nafi, the radar operator straightened in his chair as the F-111's blip vanished from his screen. Younis, Abdel-Hadi, and the East German were staring at it in amazement and concern when the phone rang.

One of the air traffic controllers answered it. "Phone, sir," he said in Arabic, crossing to Abdel-Hadi.

"Who is it?"

"Your duty officer."

"Not now," Abdel-Hadi said, annoyed at the intrusion.

"He says it's an emergency, sir."

Abdel-Hadi scowled and snatched up the phone.

Shepherd had the F-111 in supersonic dash now: wings at maximum sweep, 72.5 degrees; speed Mach 1.75. The TFR began beeping as it detected a sudden rise in the desert floor and automatically, *abruptly*, increased altitude to compensate; the instant the ridge crested the TFR detected the slope and pitched the nose down sharply, hugging the backside of the mountain, the tone booping as it put the plane back down on the deck.

The sleek bomber was nearing the point where Shepherd

planned to suddenly pull into a high-G climb. His hands were poised to move swiftly and precisely, from pistol to cabin pressure dump switch, to oxygen disconnect, to G-suit disconnect when the radio came alive with a sharp crackle.

Several phrases in Arabic followed.

Shepherd recognized General Younis's voice.

"Naam yasidi," the Libyan replied, pretending he'd received a routine instruction. He calmly made a notation on his kneeboard, then deftly reached to the ankle holster just below it, removed his pistol, and leveled the muzzle at Shepherd's flight helmet.

"You will reduce speed, Major," he said sharply.

"Why? What's the problem?" Shepherd asked, hit by a rush of terror-charged adrenaline, his mind racing. He was tempted to carry out the high-G maneuver but realized the Libyan could easily put a bullet in his head before he could.

"The mission is over," the Libyan replied coldly.

Shepherd's heart sank as he nodded, eyeing the pistol, still evaluating, still deciding; then he eased back the throttles and leveled off, coming onto a heading for Okba ben Nafi.

43

THAT SAME AFTERNOON, a U.S. Navy sup-
ply plane took off from Naples and headed south over the eastern
Mediterranean. Several hours later, it circled the 6th Fleet on
station off the west coast of Malta and landed on the flight deck
of the USS *America*.

An orange-vested traffic control officer directed the plane to
an unloading area aft of the superstructure. Crewmen moved in
with wheel chocks and cargo-handling gear and removed a large
container. They wheeled it across the deck to a Sea King helicopter
and loaded it aboard.

The molded plastic container measured 24 inches wide, 36
inches long, and 30 inches deep, and was devoid of markings,
save for a bright red priority routing ticket that read:

ORIGIN: OTS Langley
ROUTING: 6th Fleet HQ, Naples/USS America
DESTINATION: USS Cavalla

As soon as the container had been secured, the gray and white
helicopter rose at a slight angle from the carrier's deck into the
hazy sky and came onto a heading for the Aegean Sea.

THREE HUNDRED TWENTY-FIVE miles
due east of the *America*'s position, the *Cavalla* was 80 feet below
the surface proceeding through a shallow undersea valley in the
Mediterranean Ridge between the islands of Andikithira and
Crete at a speed of 12 knots.

After obtaining a fix on the Romeo's position from the Viking,
Duryea summoned Cooperman from the sonar room.

"See that?" the captain prompted as they studied the track he had plotted on the electronic chart table. "If I'm right, Romeo's going to be proceeding through here about sixteen hundred." He marked a point between two islands on the Romeo's course. "Now, if we're *here* when he is . . ." He marked the *Cavalla*'s course and drew a line between the two marks that was uninterrupted by islands or undersea terrain.

"We have a sonar window," Cooperman said, smiling at the chance to determine if the target was *their* Romeo.

That was hours ago.

Now the *Cavalla* was in position.

Cooperman had the BQS-6 bow array in passive mode listening for cavitation. The sound was made by air bubbles collapsing as they spiraled off the tips of propeller blades and radiated mainly at right angles from the source. Though the submarines were far apart, the *Cavalla* was proceeding at 90 degrees to the Romeo's course, which put the spherical transducer in her bow directly abeam of the target's propellers. Cooperman's ears soon perked at the distinctive hiss; it intensified as the Romeo moved into the window between the two islands. He patched the contact into the oscilloscope, comparing it to the one he had recorded en route to Tripoli weeks before. When identical patterns began tracing across the screen, he called the control room.

"I got him, skipper," Cooperman reported. "It's our boy."

"Good going," Duryea replied. He stepped to his chart table and went about predicting the Romeo's course. Working back from its need to be in Beirut by the start of Ramadan, he calculated when the submarine would have to leave the cover of the Aegean for the Mediterranean and plotted an intercept point. "Even at a prudent fifteen knots we'll be at the IP more than eight hours before lover boy arrives," he said to McBride. "Get Lieutenant Reyes up here, will you?"

"Way to go, skipper," the Chicano enthused when told the contact had been confirmed as the Romeo. "When do we take him?"

"Twenty-one hundred tomorrow; right *there*," Duryea replied, circling a mark on the chart table centered in the basin cradled by Crete, Karpathos, and Rhodes. "That's our intercept point."

Reyes's brow furrowed with concern. "That's open water, sir; he's going to be moving pretty damn fast."

"Big problem, huh?" Duryea asked, deadpan.

Reyes nodded. "He's too powerful to stop and there's no way my guys could stay with him."

Duryea pretended to wrestle with it. "In other words, it would be easier if he was dead in the water putting up a mast."

"Sure, then we could—"

"I'll see what I can do."

Reyes grinned, getting the message. "A dead stop."

"Every day, at twenty-one hundred, Lieutenant," Duryea explained, breaking into a cagey smile. "Like clockwork."

Half an hour later, he was still smiling when McBride took a call from the communications officer. "Chopper from the *America* coming in," he announced.

"Periscope-antenna depth," Duryea ordered.

The Sea King was circling the rendezvous area when the pilot spotted the wake from the periscope. Soon the *Cavalla* punched through the surface, water cascading from her sail in torrents. Several miles to the south, the island of Crete cut a pale triangle out of the sky.

The deck was still awash when an aft hatch, located between the sail and dry deck shelter, which housed the SEALs underwater assault vehicle, swung open. Lieutenant Reyes and several members of his team climbed out and guided the helicopter into position.

While the Sea King hovered, the plastic shipping container was lowered to the submarine by a winched cable. Within minutes, the container was on deck and being wrestled through a cargo hatch into the *Cavalla*'s hold.

Duryea ordered the boat to periscope depth.

The planesmen went to work and the submarine began slipping beneath the surface. It had just leveled off when the phone buzzed.

McBride answered it. "Sonar has a contact on the towed array. Says he's pretty sure it's a Redfleet boat."

Duryea responded with a thoughtful scowl, then crossed to the sonar room forward of the navigation console and stuck his head in the door.

Cooperman was sitting there, head cradled by thick headphone cushions, staring at the frequency pattern tracing across the oscilloscope.

"Twin screws," Duryea observed on seeing it.

"Yes, sir," Cooperman replied, putting the contact through the speakers so the captain could hear the rhythmic hiss. "Coming real fast."

"*How* fast?"

"Forty-plus knots."

Duryea's lips tightened. "I've got a nasty hunch."

"Me too, sir."

Duryea mulled it over, then contacted ASW on the *America*. "Captain Duryea, *Cavalla*," he said. "I need a contact verification." He reported the target's coordinates, concluding, "Request that be a MAD flyover."

The acronym stood for magnetic anomaly detector, a device used to measure disturbances in the earth's magnetic field. In a nonmetallic sea, a large metal object such as a submarine created a significant anomaly. MAD was normally used to locate a target precisely prior to ASW attack, but Duryea had another reason.

Within minutes of his call, an S-3A Viking was launched from the *America*'s starboard catapult. Dusk was falling as it soared over the Mediterranean, closing on the contact. A long tubular probe telescoped from beneath its empennage, like the stinger of a blue tail fly, as it made a low pass over the choppy sea.

"I've got dead needles back here," the Tacco said. "You sure we're on the mark? Hold it," he corrected as the needles began moving off the pins. "I got him now. Barely a wrinkle, though; must be an Alpha."

The extremely low reading left no doubt. Unlike any other submarine afloat, the Alpha's titanium hull and structure left only ferrous fittings and propulsion machinery to create a magnetic disturbance.

In the Soviet boat's control room, Captain Aleksandr Solomatin took a long, satisfied drag on his pipe. His long hunt was over.

The wily Russian hated being bested, hated being fooled by Duryea's false radio transmission and had backtracked through Gibraltar, combing the Mediterranean for the *Cavalla*. He knew he could find it; knew his target's special outfitting sacrificed a degree of stealth; indeed, his sonar technicians were hunting for a unique acoustic signature—a rhythmic whoosh made by the bulbous dry deck shelter atop the *Cavalla*'s hull—that distinguished it from every other submarine afloat.

"Damn," Duryea growled when the Viking's pilot radioed the news. "It's an Alpha—*the* Alpha."

"Man's got an axe to grind," McBride said. "Could cost us the intercept."

Duryea nodded grimly. He loved challenges; loved playing underwater hide and seek; but it was the last thing he needed now. He had the Romeo set up; had the personnel and the technical means aboard to carry out the hostage rescue mission; but there was no way it could commence until he lost the Alpha; no way he could chance Redfleet surveillance or the possibility that the Russian captain might directly interfere with the operation or alert the Romeo. He glanced at the chart table. The clock in the upper right-hand corner of the screen read:

02:DAYS
01:HOURS
18:MINUTES
37:SECONDS

—to Ramadan and counting.

44

A COOL DESERT BREEZE blew through the streets of downtown Tripoli. The time was 9:17 P.M. when three empty buses rolled into the plaza in front of the Al Kabir Hotel on Al Fat'h Street.

The doors hissed open and a Libyan Army officer stepped from the lead bus and strode toward the hotel. He hurried beneath the curved sunscreens and arched window openings that gave the facade the look of a huge pipe organ, and through the angular concrete lobby, where a banner displaying a slogan taken from Qaddafi's infamous Green Book proclaimed: THE PARTY SYSTEM ABORTS DEMOCRACY.

The slogan was one of many that adorned everything from the cellophane wrapper on rolls of toilet paper to the coffee lounge, renowned for its gloomy decor, salty cappuccino, and the crowd of reporters and camera crews who gathered there each night.

The din forced the officer to unleash several blasts on his whistle to get their attention. "Brother leader summons you," he announced.

This was standard procedure; and as they had many times before, the reporters rounded up colleagues and equipment and filed into the bright yellow buses. They had no idea where they were going, what Qaddafi wanted, or if, as was his habit, he would fail to appear.

The convoy wound through the city, leaving a trail of blue diesel smoke in the darkened streets, which were empty of pedestrian and vehicular traffic due to a government-imposed curfew. In less than 20 minutes, the buses turned into As-Sarim Street and were lumbering past the T-55 battle tank and squad of infantry deployed at the entrance to the Bab al Azziziya Barracks. They continued across the grounds, stopping opposite Qaddafi's tent, where squads of soldiers herded the reporters to a podium that had been set up in front of the colonel's sway-backed domicile.

Moments later Qaddafi came through the tent flaps and strode to the podium. His white officer's uniform, bedecked with campaign ribbons, gold braid, and red piping, glowed luminously in the flash of strobes and halogens.

General Younis, SHK Chief Abdel-Hadi, and the Akita followed and stood next to him.

"Once again," Qaddafi began in a self-righteous tone, "the People's Libyan Arab Jamahiriya has beaten the insidious shetans of America. Yes, yes, barely an hour ago, our brave and vigilant forces captured one of the world's most wanted criminals. After deceitfully claiming he had refused to take part in an illegal attack on the Jamahiriya, after deceitfully asking for political asylum and accepting the goodwill and hospitality of the Libyan people, this vile emissary of Satan was caught, red-handed, conspiring to commit murder, larceny, and espionage against them and their leaders." He paused, then nodded to Abdel-Hadi, who snapped his fingers twice in response.

The tent flaps behind Qaddafi parted again.

Shepherd shuffled into view, flanked by Libyan secret police officers. He was gagged and blindfolded; shackles bound his ankles and wrists. He recoiled as Abdel-Hadi brusquely removed the blindfold and the cameras and lights bore in on him.

"Now you will tell the world," Qaddafi addressed the media, "that the People's Jamahiriya has the notorious deserter and murderer, United States Air Force Major Walter Shepherd in custody."

A barrage of questions erupted: "Exactly what did Major Shepherd do to cause your government to file these charges against him?" one of the reporters called out, "Can you be more specific?" another asked.

"No. It is a highly classified matter and not for media consumption," Qaddafi replied with finality, dismissing further queries with a wave of his hand.

Abdel-Hadi and the Akita began walking toward the reporters, who parted as the fierce animal approached. The SHK officers followed, marching Shepherd through the middle of the crowd toward the prison on the other side of the compound. The reporters surged after them but were held back by the soldiers, who forced them to return to the podium where Qaddafi droned on.

The underground prison was ablaze with light when the group arrived with Shepherd. The obese guard was waiting for them.

Abdel-Hadi briefed him in Arabic, then headed down into the prison with the Akita. The SHK officers removed Shepherd's shackles and left him in the huge guard's custody. He marched Shepherd down the staircase, through the security doors, and into the network of foul-smelling corridors to the cell he had occupied previously. It was unlocked. The guard grabbed Shepherd by the back of the neck like a puppet and propelled him into it.

Shepherd maintained his balance and turned as the guard kicked the door closed. It slammed in his face with a deafening clang. The guard stabbed his key into the tumbler and locked it. Shepherd caught sight of the Palestinian peering through the bars of the cell across the corridor. He was standing in a cocky slouch, sporting a broad grin. It vanished when, instead of leaving, the guard turned toward his cell, unlocked it, and went in after him.

The Palestinian resisted, assuming he faced another round of torture. He didn't know that Shepherd had given the Libyans ANITA; that they didn't need the hostages anymore; didn't need *him*.

But Shepherd knew; he also knew that it wasn't torture the Palestinian faced but execution; and that *he* had signed the death warrant.

"You want to know where the hostages are?" the Palestinian taunted in Arabic as the repulsive Libyan dragged him from the cell. "Fucking your mother."

The guard sneered, grabbed a handful of the Palestinian's hair, slammed him up against the bars, and drove a fist into his stomach.

The Palestinian doubled over and wretched.

The big man recoiled, shuffling backwards across the corridor to get out of the way. Nonetheless, the vomit splattered over his trousers and boots. He became enraged, shouting a stream of expletives in Arabic. The Palestinian had been devastated by the blow and was on his knees, clutching his midsection. Just as the guard went for him again, Shepherd impulsively shoved an arm between the bars of his cell and got hold of the Libyan's collar, putting an abrupt stop to his charge; then he yanked back with all his might.

The guard's feet went out from under him. His massive head was much too large to fit between the bars of Shepherd's cell. It smashed into them with a loud crack and bounced off. Shepherd still had hold of his collar and yanked him back again, this time with more calculated intent. The guard unleashed a primal bellow, then his eyes rolled up behind his lids and he crashed to the floor and lay there, unmoving.

The Palestinian sagged with relief.

The pounding of boots on concrete echoed through the corridors.

The Palestinian crawled to the guard and removed the pistol from his holster; then quickly went through his pockets, taking his flashlight and a small zippered pouch that contained his money.

"The keys," Shepherd hissed in a tense whisper, pointing to the chain on the guard's belt, which was just out of reach.

The Palestinian hesitated for an instant, then he unhooked it and put it in Shepherd's palm. Their eyes locked in a brief moment of camaraderie and triumph; enemies bound together by circumstance, they were equals now, just two men fighting to stay alive.

Shepherd let himself out of the cell and tossed the keys to another prisoner as he and the Palestinian took off down the corridor.

Prisoners began pouring into the corridor, engaging the guards who responded to the commotion.

Outside, in front of Qaddafi's tent, the press conference had broken up and the reporters were being herded toward the buses when a siren began wailing. The officer in charge of the infantry shouted an order. The soldiers broke ranks and headed for the prison, leaving the media unattended.

Abdel-Hadi was in the interrogation chamber waiting for the Palestinian, waiting to oversee his execution, when the siren went off; he drew his machine pistol and stepped into the corridor with the Akita.

"Lamarikan wil Phalestineen harbou!" a guard shouted, racing toward him.

Abdel-Hadi stiffened, then crouched to the dog. "Yalla, yalla laoueg houm," he ordered in a tense whisper. "Jib houm."

The huge dog began straining at the leash, dragging Abdel-Hadi through the corridors. The animal had made the journey from Okba ben Nafi Air Base in the Krazz with Shepherd and soon several powerful lunges signaled that it had detected his scent.

The SHK chief removed the leash. "Yalla," he prompted. "Yalla, katal."

The animal raced down the corridor in a frenzy.

Elsewhere in the maze of underground corridors, Shepherd and the Palestinian approached a set of double doors that led to the barracks kitchen; there were no personnel working at this hour. The two fugitives ran past the preparation tables and ovens, following a wall of refrigerators to an open door on the other side, exiting into a corridor lined with trash pails.

Shepherd heard the scratch of claws on concrete behind him and turned to see the Akita bounding toward them. It covered the distance with several strides, then its powerful hindquarters launched it through the air.

The Palestinian whirled with the pistol but Shepherd was between him and the animal, blocking his line of fire.

At the last instant, Shepherd swept a lid off one of the trash pails and used it as a shield, slamming it hard into the charging animal, deflecting it off to one side and past him.

The dog landed on its side with a loud thud and went skittering through the open door beyond the trash pails into the kitchen, its massive paws clawing at the concrete in vain as it slid across the floor. It finally got to all fours and charged again.

Shepherd was lunging for the door to slam it shut and trap the crazed animal inside the kitchen when the Palestinian fired. The dog emitted a pathetic yelp and dropped at Shepherd's feet like a charging rhino.

"What the hell were you waiting for?" Shepherd demanded angrily.

"You were in the way," the Palestinian retorted; then he grinned at a thought that occurred to him and pointedly added, "Maybe I am thinking twice about killing my relative."

Shepherd's cold stare softened; he looked at the dog and said, "Not all animals have that luxury."

They moved off, the Palestinian leading the way to a junction where two corridors intersected.

"Akif," a voice ordered sharply "Akif, ouarmi slahek al ardth!"

The Palestinian stopped in his tracks and turned slowly to see Abdel-Hadi standing in the adjacent corridor, pointing his machine pistol at him.

"Slahek al ardth!" the SHK chief repeated.

The Palestinian complied with the order and tossed his pistol aside.

Shepherd was around the corner in the other corridor, out of Abdel-Hadi's line of sight. He pressed himself against the wall and slowly, silently slid into a crouch, wrapping his fingers around the grip of the pistol that the Palestinian had thrown at his feet. Shepherd waited as Abdel-Hadi advanced toward the Palestinian, waited until he had passed the corner that shielded him, then slipped behind the SHK chief.

"Hold it," Shepherd said sharply, jabbing the pistol into his back.

Abdel-Hadi froze.

The Palestinian wrenched the machine pistol from the SHK chief's hands, then slammed him against the wall. With an angry twist, he screwed the pistol up against the underside of Abdel-Hadi's chin.

The Libyan groaned, eyes bulging with terror.

"No!" Shepherd shouted.

"Why? He is animal, yes?" the Palestinian demanded, his eyes ablaze with vengeance. "Yes?"

"*Yes*, but he's—"

The Palestinian pulled the trigger, firing a burst that blew the top of Abdel-Hadi's head up across the wall in a pulpy shower of gore.

"He was our ticket out of here," Shepherd replied angrily, wincing at the sight, as the sound of the gunfire echoed through the corridors.

The Palestinian shrugged and released Abdel-Hadi, who slid to the floor, painting the concrete with a bloody smear.

They hurried down the narrow corridor to a service door. It opened into a long tunnel that zigzagged beneath the compound.

The pounding of boots rose in the distance.

They went back through the door and waited as the clatter came closer and closer.

Shepherd noticed that the Palestinian was standing near some electrical panels on the opposite wall. He had opened them and was about to throw the circuit breakers, plunging the prison into darkness.

"Hold it," Shepherd cautioned. "I'll tell you when." He listened at the door until he heard the soldiers run past, then cracked it open slightly, waiting while the footsteps died out. "Okay. Now."

The Palestinian pulled the breakers.

The corridors went black.

They used the guard's flashlight to make their way through the pitch-black tunnel to a door that was now unguarded. It was locked.

The Palestinian blew the lock with a burst from the machine pistol. He and Shepherd went through it into an underground garage.

A hulking, canvas-covered vehicle stood alone in the reinforced concrete bunker. They peeled back the shroud, discovering an armored personnel carrier beneath. It was Muammar el-Qaddafi's personal Transportpanzer, the emergency escape vehicle that had spirited him and his family out of Tripoli the night of the air strike.

Shepherd opened one of the thick steel doors in the rear of the hull, and they clambered inside the lushly carpeted troop compartment. While the Palestinian latched the door and climbed to the shielded machine gun turret atop the roof, Shepherd went forward to the cab, got behind the wheel, and turned the ignition switch.

The powerful Mercedes diesel started up with a roar.

Shepherd found a remote control in the cab, and opened the steel doors that sealed the bunker. He engaged the transmission and guided the lumbering 8 × 8 across the garage and up a ramp that led to a street several blocks from the compound.

Shepherd floored the throttle; the eight huge combat tires bit into the tarmac and sent the Transportpanzer rumbling forward to an intersection.

The cross street was a broad eucalyptus-lined motorway that Shepherd recognized as Al Jala Road, the street that the Krazz had taken inland from the coast on the trip from Tunisia. It was poorly lit and deserted. He made a sharp left and accelerated.

A jeep carrying several soldiers rocketed into view behind them. One was radioing to units up ahead. Another manned the front-mounted machine gun and opened fire. The rounds smacked into the TPP's armor-plated hull, sparking aside harmlessly.

The Palestinian swiveled the gun turret around, tracking the jeep as the distance between the two vehicles closed, and fired a sustained burst. The rounds stitched across the hood. The jeep veered out of control and flipped over, spilling the soldiers across the pavement.

Shepherd had the Transportpanzer barreling down the deserted motorway at 65 MPH. In minutes, it had passed the Christian Cemetery, crossed Al Nasar, and was approaching Umar Al Mukhtar, a main east-west conduit that teed across Al Jala Road, which meant the TPP would be forced to turn either left or right.

Several Libyan Army trucks were blocking the right side of the intersection. Soldiers opened fire.

The Palestinian was crouching behind the gunshield, which was clanging like a church bell, raking the street with bullets, the tracers glowing in the night.

Shepherd was about to turn left when a lightweight battle tank, stationed at the People's Congress a short distance away, came rumbling down Bab Qarqarish, machine gun blazing, catching the Transportpanzer in a crossfire. Shepherd steered the TPP across the grounds of the Girl's Military College on Al Mukhtar. He exited onto the Al Kurnish Road, crossed it, plunging down a steep embankment to the beach. Knobby tires churned up the sand as he drove into the surf. The fully amphibious vehicle settled into the sea; then two propellers at the rear of the hull came to life and sent the dark green Transportpanzer into the enveloping blackness.

Shepherd sagged with exhaustion and relief; then he looked back over his shoulder to the troop compartment, and grimaced at what he saw.

The Palestinian was lying on the carpeted floor beneath the gun turret, his shirt soaked with blood.

45

FOLLOWING THE MEETING at the royal guest house with Moncrieff and Katifa, Larkin was shown to the Saudi's study. The regal, book-lined room was equipped with a state-of-the-art computer system, facsimile machine, and secure communications gear. Larkin used the latter and called Kiley at home.

The time in Washington, D.C., was 7:32 A.M.

The DCI had been up for nearly an hour; a cup of cold coffee was at his elbow, red folders and briefing books spread out on the floor around his armchair.

"Good work, Colonel," the DCI replied, relieved that Katifa had agreed to work for them. "How do you plan to handle backup and liaison?"

"The lady's leaving for Beirut tomorrow. I'll do the same and work out of the embassy."

"Not operative," Kiley replied. "Ever since they kidnapped Fitzgerald we've had a hell of a time getting new people in. It could take weeks, maybe months. We'll have to rely on personnel already in place. I'll set it up. She should know the name. Stengel."

"Stengel . . . I'll take care of it."

"Does she smoke?"

"Yes, sir, she does."

"What brand?"

"Those French ones—blue hard pack—Gaulois."

Kiley grunted, making a note of it. "Now, what happened with Shepherd?"

"Libyan secret police locked him up," Larkin answered, briefing him on his meeting with Al-Qasim.

That was twelve hours ago.

Now, after a long day at Langley, Kiley was packing up his briefcases before heading home when—more than eight hours after Qaddafi's news conference—the first wire service report of Shepherd's escape came in.

The lengthy interlude was no accident.

On a direct order from Qaddafi, who thought Shepherd would be quickly captured, the correspondents had been herded into the buses and driven around the city for several hours to prevent them from filing their stories. When it became clear Shepherd had eluded his pursuers, the reporters were returned to the Al Kabir, only to discover the hotel's phone system had mysteriously broken down. Several European reporters eventually made it to their embassies and contacted their bureaus.

IN JEDDAH, Saudi Arabia, the time was 5:16 A.M. when one of the Filipino servants knocked on Larkin's door, waking him. "Excuse me, Colonel. You have a call," he said, explaining it had come in on the secure line in Moncrieff's study and couldn't be transferred.

Larkin pulled on a robe and went downstairs.

"Hold for the director, please," Kiley's secretary said when he came on the line.

"Dick?" the DCI barked. "Shepherd's on the loose."

Larkin groaned, a sinking feeling growing in his stomach. "Do we know how?"

"We're faxing you what we have on the other line."

Larkin shifted his glance to the facimile machine on a sideboard behind the desk, where a single sheet of paper was already emerging from the delivery slot. It was a copy of the wire service report:

REUTERS—SPECIAL BULLETIN—ALL STATIONS.
FUGITIVE USAF PILOT IMPRISONED; ESCAPES

United States Air Force Maj. Walter Shepherd was in the custody of Libya's secret police when he escaped. The prison break occurred during a press conference in which Libyan strongman Muammar el-Qaddafi accused Shepherd of being a CIA operative and claimed his desertion and murder of a fellow officer were part of a cover story to gain entry into Libya. Highly reliable sources in Tripoli report Shepherd and a second prisoner, believed to be a Palestinian national, killed Libyan Secret Police Chief Reza Abdel-Hadi, escaping in an armored personnel carrier.

> The amphibious vehicle traveled a short distance
> across the city to the Mediterranean and when last
> seen was heading out to sea.

"You have it yet?" Kiley prodded impatiently at the silence on the line.

"I'm reading it now, sir."

"I thought this situation was being terminated. What went wrong?"

"I've no idea."

"See what you can find out. If Shepherd surfaces and starts talking before Duryea can make his move, who knows what might happen. We're too close to have anything screw this rescue operation up."

"I'll get on it right away, sir," Larkin replied as the DCI ended the call. The colonel slipped the wire service report into the pocket of his robe and went to the window, which overlooked the Red Sea.

The sun was beginning to creep over the horizon, the low rays catching the flecks of red plankton that floated in abundance just beneath the surface, imparting the legendary crimson glow to the water.

Larkin stood there working the problem; aside from hoping the Libyans caught Shepherd and killed him, there was one base *he* could cover. He knew Shepherd had escaped by sea and that his wife was still on D'Jerba, which was the nearest safe port. He also knew it would take a long time to get there from Tripoli in an armored personnel carrier.

Several hours later, Moncrieff, Katifa, and Larkin were driven in one of the royal limousines to King Abdul Azziz Airport just north of Jeddah.

Larkin's flight to D'Jerba was the first to depart. After dropping him off, Moncrieff and Katifa went to the Middle East Airlines boarding lounge.

"I wish I could think of something to say I haven't said before," Moncrieff whispered when her flight was called.

They embraced hurriedly, awkwardly, acknowledging they had indeed done this before. Katifa felt her eyes starting to fill, slipped from Moncrieff's grasp, and hurried off. He watched her go down the boarding ramp, just as he had that day in Boston five years ago. He waited until the plane had pulled away, then returned to the limousine, certain he would never see her again.

The Boeing 737 flew on a northwesterly heading, crossing Jordan and Syria, to Beirut International Airport, covering the 900 miles in just under two hours.

Katifa deplaned with a carry-on bag and hurried through the shabby terminal to the arrivals ramp.

"Taxi, right here," the dispatcher said, directing her to a vehicle parked forward of the queue.

Katifa climbed into the old Citroen and pulled the door closed. "Number twenty-eight Tamar Mallat," she said, lighting a cigarette.

The cab left the airport and headed north on the express motorway that runs along the broad coastal plain at the base of the Lebanon Mountains.

"Cigarette?" the driver said, holding the pack back over his shoulder.

"I have my own. Thanks," Katifa replied.

"Your brand, isn't it?"

"Yes, it is."

"That's what Mister Stengel thought," the driver said pointedly.

Katifa took the package of Gaulois from him and examined the blue, square-edged box. It was unopened and the cellophane wrapper was intact.

"It contains a radio transmitter," the driver explained. "The unit broadcasts on a dedicated channel that's monitored twenty-four hours a day at the embassy's com center. Casino du Liban is well within range."

Katifa nodded and slipped it into her purse.

The taxi continued north on the motorway to where it branches into several thoroughfares that crisscross the city. The driver took Avenue Camille Chamoun through the Wata and Tallet Khayat districts to the cluster of white stucco buildings on Tamar Mallat.

The street was quiet; a few vehicles lined the curb. Several children were playing as the Citroen pulled to a stop.

Katifa got out and glanced about cautiously, suddenly aware of the pungent scent of cordite, which always hung in the air; then she hurried up the steps of her building. She had noticed the abandoned van across the street; it had been there for months. Like so many of the vehicles on Beirut's streets it was up on blocks, stripped of all usable hardware and parts. Furthermore, like the other vehicles on Tamar Mallat, it appeared empty.

The two men who slipped out the rear door as soon as Katifa

was out of sight had been watching the building through a small window in the van's sidewall.

Katifa was entering her apartment when she heard footsteps behind her and turned to see the Palestinians coming down the corridor. She recognized them from Casino du Liban and knew they had been sent by Abu Nidal. One brandished a pistol. The other swung a Skorpion into view from beneath his jacket.

"What do you think you're doing?" Katifa protested indignantly, as they took hold of her. "What do you—"

"Save your complaints for Abu Nidal," the one with the pistol interrupted.

"Gladly," Katifa replied, relieved. "Casino du Liban was my next stop. Though I didn't expect an escort."

"You have no choice in the matter, believe me."

"Please," she said with disdain, gesturing toward the weapons.

They ignored her remark and, pistol pressed to her side, marched her to their car, which was parked a short distance down the street.

It was late afternoon when they arrived at Casino du Liban. The entrance gates were closed. Heavily armed sentries materialized from nearby cover and surrounded the car, their fierce eyes peering at Katifa in condemnation. One of them opened the door, pulled her from the car, and began searching her. She stood unflinchingly while rough hands ran over her torso and breasts, then up her legs and between her thighs; but she stiffened when the other sentry dumped the contents of her purse onto the hood of the car and began sorting through the contents. He picked up one of the boxes of cigarettes. The flicker of the cellophane wrapper caught her eye.

"The other one is open," she said. She deftly slipped the box from his hand and dropped it into her purse; then she casually took the open pack from the hood, removed two cigarettes, and pushed one between his lips; the other was for herself. He smiled, produced a butane lighter, and lit them both.

When the sentries were satisfied she was unarmed, Katifa put the rest of her belongings back into her purse. Then one of the gates was opened, and the armed escort led her down the long approach road and through the casino to the marina.

The gunboat was tied up in one of the slips. The Soviet-made Zhuk had been towed to an offshore moorage by the Turkish freighter. From there, it had been winched into the marina, where repairs were made to the tangled propellers, gutted interior, and radio.

Now Abu Nidal stood on one of the floating docks supervising as the captain and crew prepared to put to sea. Several Palestinian seamen were stowing stores and ordnance; others were filling the auxiliary tanks with diesel fuel. The terrorist leader heard the sentries coming down the gangway behind him and turned, freezing when he saw Katifa was with them.

"Binti el-amin," he finally said sarcastically, locking his eyes onto hers in a seething stare. "No doctored insulin this time?"

"What? What are you talking about?" she asked, appearing genuinely puzzled. "What's going on? Why were they at my apartment? I don't understand."

"Someone put water in the vials," Nidal snapped, his tone leaving no doubt whom he suspected.

Katifa was silent, as if wounded by the accusation. "How could you even think such a thing?"

Nidal studied her, his eyes boring into her soul. "Then tell me how?" he challenged. "You picked the insulin up and brought it here directly. It couldn't have happened without your compliance."

"Why not? Someone could have easily bribed the pharmacist or arranged to have the vials switched before I picked them up. Believe me, after that meeting in Damascus, I wouldn't put it past any of them."

Nidal took a moment, digesting the reply. "What *about* Damascus?"

"They all betrayed you," Katifa said angrily. "I told them you were opposed to the idea, but they wouldn't listen."

"That's not what Arafat said," Nidal countered slyly, twisting the truth to test her.

"Then he lied," Katifa declared. "It was *he* who favored the plan; he, Assad, and Qaddafi, of course. I suppose Arafat claimed otherwise?"

"No," Nidal replied grudgingly. "He admitted to arguing in favor of it."

"Well?" Katifa said, implying she'd been vindicated. "Why do you think I insisted Assad call you?" she went on in a bold lie. "I was stunned when you reversed your position. But who was I to argue? I looked like a fool; not to mention, I was nearly killed. Frankly, I think I'm owed an explanation."

"Assad spoke with the Saudi, not I."

Katifa stiffened, pretending she was shocked.

"We found out he was in the room below," Nidal explained. "He must have intercepted the call somehow."

Katifa shook her head, dismayed. "That bastard," she said with as much acrimony as she could muster. "Well, at least now I understand."

Nidal mused, then gestured she follow as he strolled down the dock toward the gunboat. "How did you escape from Tripoli?" he asked rather offhandedly.

"With the Saudi," Katifa answered, knowing Nidal was trying to catch her in a lie. She had little doubt that the nurse had reported back to him and that like a clever trial attorney, Nidal knew the answer before he asked the question. "I recuperated and left Jeddah as soon as possible."

Nidal was weighing her reply when the gunboat's captain appeared at the railing. "We're ready to cast off," he called down to them.

"Good luck and Godspeed," Nidal called out over the throb of the engines, as the Zhuk put to sea. Then, turning to Katifa, he challenged "Why should I believe you?"

"Why else would I have come back to Beirut?" she responded spiritedly; then she let her posture slacken, and stared at him like a hurt child. "I haven't forgotten who raised me," she said, her voice quivering with emotion. "Have you, Abu-habib?"

Nidal's expression softened.

"Nor have I forgotten who taught me to fight," Katifa went on. "I've spent my life fighting to liberate Palestine, and I intend to continue."

Nidal nodded and broke into an enigmatic smile. "You'll have a chance to prove it soon," he said, glancing off to the gunboat, which was vanishing in the afternoon mist.

46

THE THYSSEN-HENSCHEL TRANSPORT-
panzer rode very low in the water—which came up to the bottom
of the divided windshield—putting the eight huge tires and two-
thirds of the hull beneath the surface. This made for a low visual
and radar profile.

Shepherd had turned the running lights off and proceeded on
a northerly heading in almost total darkness save for the pale glow
of a crescent moon. It was approximately 150 miles to D'Jerba.
At a maximum water speed of 10 MPH he figured the amphibious
vehicle could be safely inside Tunisian waters by dawn.

The Palestinian was alive but unconscious and breathing labo-
riously. He had been struck in his left arm and chest; Shepherd
deduced that one lung had been punctured. He lifted him to the
bunk built into the customized interior, propping his body at an
angle to prevent blood that might be leaking into his chest cavity
from collecting around the undamaged lung and encumbering
its function; then he began searching the storage lockers for first
aid gear. In the process he found food, clothing, weapons, walkie-
talkies, and maps. He disinfected and bandaged the wounds as
best he could and returned to the cab.

The TTP was outfitted with extensive navigation equipment,
similar in nature to aviation electronics, and Shepherd had had
little trouble activating the TTP's autopilot and surface search
radar systems. The latter, a RASIT surveillance unit, was mounted
on a hydraulic arm above the roof and had a programmable inner
defense zone.

Shepherd followed the coastline, staying close to shore to elude
the Libyan Navy's coastal patrol, which was confined to deeper
waters. He had no way of knowing it was a small, thinly spread
fleet of seven vessels, two of which had been hauled out for routine
maintenance, leaving five to cover more than 1,400 miles of coastline and a dozen major harbors. He used the light that came from

vehicles traveling the Al Kurnish Road atop the palisades, and the light from the numerous towns it connected as guideposts to measure progress and plot his position.

Several times during the night, the surface search radar picked up small vessels putting to sea from fishing villages along the coast. Shepherd studied the blips tracing across the screen until he was certain the vessels were going about their business.

Now, nine hours after Shepherd had first driven the Transportpanzer into the Mediterranean, it was nearing the Libya-Tunisia border and the imaginary line that extended seaward for three miles. The maps he had found indicated that just east of it, on his side of the border, a peninsula of rocky shoals and sandbars jutted into the sea.

A short time later, as dawn broke over the Mediterranean, he spotted the whitecaps and rolling breakers that heralded its presence. He changed course and was angling further out to sea to circle the shoals when he heard loud, guttural wheezes coming from the compartment behind him.

Shepherd put the TTP back on autopilot and went aft to check on the Palestinian. The young terrorist had rolled over onto his stomach and his condition was clearly the worse for it. Shepherd was adjusting his position when the RASIT unit started beeping, indicating a vessel had penetrated the envelope he had set.

A thousand yards to starboard, a Libyan Navy patrol boat was cruising the imaginary Libya-Tunisia border. Like her sister ships, the aging British-made vessel carried primitive surveillance electronics that were supplemented by lookouts.

The seaman in the bow spotted something moving on the surface; something boxlike and low to the water, clearly not a fishing vessel. He used a walkie-talkie to report the sighting to the bridge.

A moment later a spotlight on the patrol boat's mast came to life and sliced through the early morning darkness, reflecting off the Transportpanzer's two rectangular windshields, which sat atop the water like the eyes of a huge frog.

The beam of light swept past, streaming through the windshield into the cab, then again as the Libyan on the spotlight glimpsed the TTP and swept back.

"All ahead full," the Libyan captain ordered.

The patrol boat's diesels roared to life and the vessel began closing on the target.

Shepherd had the Tranportpanzer's throttle to the floor; and though it could do 65 MPH on land, its sluggish pace in amphibious mode was no match for the 20 knots the patrol boat could make at sea. Shepherd was trapped: gunboat to starboard, steep palisades to port, rocky shoals forward, Libya aft. Then it struck him—the long journey on water had him thinking boat; but *this* boat had wheels.

It also had stealth.

Shepherd reached to a bank of six switches on the console and threw them in rapid succession. A rack of dischargers mounted on the left side of the hull began belching thick smoke. It streamed behind the Transportpanzer, spreading rapidly over the water like heavy black fog.

Several Libyan seamen ran to the machine gun mounted in the patrol boat's bow; but by the time they were ready to fire, they had nothing more than a wall of billowing smoke for a target.

Shepherd spun the wheel and aimed the TTP at the rocky shoals, heading directly for a rippling patch of calm water between the breakers, which he reckoned was a barely submerged sandbar. A rolling swell crested and broke against the side of the Transportpanzer, knocking the 50,000-pound vehicle about like a piece of driftwood. Shepherd fought the wheel, trying to keep from being smashed against the rocks that thrust upward from the boiling surf.

The patrol boat proceeded through the smokescreen, closing the distance; but the instant it emerged into the clear, the captain was forced to reverse his engines to avoid running aground.

The Transportpanzer was still partially submerged when it finally made it through the breakers to the sandbar. The eight huge tires began biting into the hard-packed sand and rock beneath, driving the vehicle up the underwater gradient. Shepherd kept the pedal to the floor. The needle on the speedometer jumped to 20 MPH, then 30 as the TTP crawled out of the sea and accelerated across the peninsula.

The Libyan gun crew fired several bursts as the patrol boat backed away from the barrier, and began to circle the shoals; but soon the TTP was a distant speck safely inside Tunisian territorial waters.

Shepherd proceeded north, keeping the Tunisian coastline in sight. Several hours later, a squared superstructure rose on the horizon. The hulking profile turned out to be the ramparts of Borj Castille, at the southeasternmost point of D'Jerba Island.

The rectangular Spanish fortress was perched on the tip of a desolate finger of sand that split the sea. A dense forest of trees and tall marsh grass had grown up along its north wall.

Shepherd beached the lumbering craft, driving it deep into the thickly grown cover to conceal it, and shut the engines down.

The Palestinian's wheezing filled the silence; he was gasping for breath now, barely clinging to life.

Shepherd took the money pouch that the young terrorist had confiscated from the Libyan prison guard. Before leaving the TTP, he raised the steel hatches over the window openings, letting fresh air circulate through the compartment, then made his way through the marsh grass and trees and along the wall of the castle to the beach, continuing on about a half mile to the coastal road.

L A R K I N ' S flight from Jeddah landed at D'Jerba's Melita International airport at 9:58 A.M. having gained an hour due to the change in time zones. Since leaving Washington, he had flown to Naples, then on to the USS *America*, D'Jerba, Jeddah, and now back to D'Jerba. The bone-wearying schedule and change of time zones had finally taken their toll and the colonel was running on pure adrenaline now. After deplaning, he picked up a rental car he had reserved and headed for the road that paralleled the shore-line. It ringed the tiny island without a break as did the broad, flat beaches, which were free of rock caves and dunes, free of hiding places. Larkin began driving south, scanning the shallows and open stretches of sand for the Transportpanzer.

S H E P H E R D had walked about a mile down the road when he noticed a telephone service line coming from one of the poles that lined the shoulder. It led to a small structure perched on a hill overlooking Borj Castille. The castle was one of the island's tourist attractions, and the masonry structure turned out to be a souk, a cluster of vendor stands where food, souvenirs, and local crafts were sold.

The souk was closed now, rarely opening before noon, if at all, this early in the season; but the phone in the booth next to it hummed when Shepherd lifted the handset. He kept thumbing coins into the slot until he got a dial tone and called the Dar Jerba Hotel.

In the beachfront cottage, the phone jarred Stephanie from a fitful sleep. She squinted at the sunlight streaming in from the deck, then to the clock on the nightstand.

It read 10:27.

Late the previous evening, she had heard an English-language broadcast on one of the hotel's four radio stations about her husband's capture and escape. The upsetting news had kept her up most of the night; it was after 5:00 A.M. when she finally fell asleep in her clothes.

Stephanie lunged across the bed and grabbed the phone.

"Hello," she answered in a dry, anxious voice.

"Babe, it's me," Shepherd said.

"Walt," she exclaimed, bolting upright. "God, oh, my God; are you okay?"

"Yes. I made it back to D'Jerba. Someone escaped with me; he's badly wounded." Shepherd replied in a rush of words, glancing apprehensively at several cars that passed on the nearby road.

"Are you sure you're all right?"

"I'm fine; but he has to get medical attention soon."

"There must be a doctor in the hotel. I'll—"

"No, no, I don't want anyone but you coming here. You'll have to rent a car," he instructed, giving her directions to the castle. "Got it?"

"Uh huh," she said, jotting them down.

Shepherd glanced anxiously at another vehicle that roared past. "As fast as you can. Okay?"

"Okay. Oh, listen . . ." Stephanie paused, hearing a click on the line. "Walt? Walt, you still there?" He had already hung up; she pressed the disconnect button, then dialed another room in the hotel. "It's Stephanie," she said, her voice filled with urgency. "Walt just called . . . Yes, yes, he is. Meet me in the lobby at the car rental desk." She hung up, went into the bathroom, and washed her face, then hurried from the cottage.

Shepherd was following the road back to Borj Castille when a reflection coming from the overgrowth caught his attention. It was the Transportpanzer's flat rectangular windshield. He realized that despite being concealed in the marsh, the TTP was clearly visible from the high vantage point provided by the road, as was the broad swath it had cut through the tall grass, which pointed to it like an arrow.

Shepherd left the road, taking a shortcut down a steep bluff, then made his way through the marsh grass to the Transport-panzer. The round trip had taken almost two hours. He entered through the rear hatch and was heading to the cab to move the TTP to more secure cover when he paused, struck by the silence.

The laborious breathing had stopped.

Shepherd hurried to the Palestinian's side and checked for vital signs. His eyes were fixed in a blank stare, pupils dialated and unresponsive. He had no pulse and no heartbeat. His skin was pasty and cold.

Shepherd sagged defeatedly and stared at him for a long moment; then he shouldered the young terrorist's corpse and carried it from the vehicle, pausing to pull a foxhole shovel free of the snap latches that held it to the TTP's hull. He made his way through the towering marsh grass to a small clearing, where he lowered the Palestinian to the ground and started digging. The moist topsoil quickly turned to rocky, hard-packed stratum that resisted each thrust of the shovel. Shepherd stopped and changed the orientation of the adjustable blade, locking it at a 90-degree angle to the handle, which enabled it to be used like a pickaxe. He worked slowly, methodically, his mind adrift—excited that Stephanie would soon join him, depressed over his failure to re-trieve his F-111, and at a loss to cope with the implications.

"Make it big enough for two, Major," a man's voice said, snap-ping him out of his reverie.

Shepherd looked up to see Larkin emerging from the wall of grass that encircled him, pointing a pistol at his head. The colonel had continued driving along the coast until he came upon Borj Castille, easily spotting the Transportpanzer from the road.

Shepherd held Larkin's icy stare in silence. "Are you following orders too, colonel?" he finally taunted. "Or do you just get a kick out of killing your own people in cold blood?"

"I have my reasons, Major."

"The hostages?" Shepherd asked sardonically.

Larkin nodded. "Two for seven; it's an acceptable kill ratio in any war."

"You didn't even get one."

"We got their location," Larkin countered sharply. "They're being rescued tomorrow. Keep digging."

Shepherd hadn't expected that; he weighed Larkin's reply for a long moment before he began hacking at the earth with the shovel, his mind racing, searching for a way to use it as a weapon. But the colonel was standing too far away; Shepherd couldn't come close to hitting him with it. He had been digging for about 15 minutes when Stephanie's voice shattered the silence.

"Walt? Walt, where are you?" she called out from somewhere within the thicket of trees and tall grass that surrounded the clearing.

Shepherd froze at the sound; he had hoped her arrival would distract Larkin long enough for him to somehow gain the advantage.

"Answer her," Larkin ordered in a tense whisper. "Answer, dammit," he insisted, threatening him with the pistol.

"Walt?" Stephanie called out again. "Walt, you hear me? Where are you?"

"Over here," Shepherd finally shouted in reply.

Larkin's attention was riveted on the thicket; then he heard a rustling behind him. His reflexes dulled by jet lag, the colonel was a split second slower in reacting than he otherwise might have been. He turned just as a figure lunged out of the marsh grass and swung a tire iron at Larkin's head. He saw the movement out of the corner of his eye and ducked, causing the bludgeon to graze its target and strike his arm instead, knocking the gun from his hand.

Larkin went after it. As he scooped it up and whirled to fire, Shepherd took several quick steps toward him and swung the shovel like a baseball bat, swung it with all his might. It struck Larkin with a sickening thud; the sharp, V-shaped end of the blade buried itself deep in the center of his chest. He emitted a muffled groan and stiffened, his weapon leveled at Shepherd; but the life went out of him before he could fire and the pistol fell from his hand. Shepherd jerked the shovel. It came loose and Larkin went over backwards. Shepherd let out a long breath and turned to the man who had come out of the marsh grass.

It was Brancato.

Shepherd stared at him in stunned silence, his mind racing with questions as Stephanie emerged from the thicket and wrapped her arms around him. They clung to each other for a long, silent moment. Then Stephanie's eyes drifted to Larkin and the Palestinian. She cringed at the grotesque sight, prompting Shepherd to lead her through the marsh grass to the Transportpanzer. Brancato followed.

"Al," Shepherd finally rasped as they arrived, his voice hoarse from exhaustion. "Al. God, what the hell—"

"I kept hearing about what a great time you were having," Brancato replied wryly.

Shepherd stared at him numbly, appreciating his attempt at levity but beyond response.

"Like I told Stephanie," Brancato went on, "I was still in the hospital when that desertion bullshit hit the fan. I tried calling a couple of times but couldn't get her. I finally reached her dad; he told me you guys were here. I got in last night."

Shepherd nodded, his eyes adrift with uncertainty. "How did you know Colonel Larkin was here?"

"There's a car parked back there. This was on the seat," Stephanie explained, producing a rental folder. The bold printing across the top proclaimed: LARKIN.

Shepherd took another foxhole shovel from the TTP's hull. He and Brancato left Stephanie behind, returned to the clearing, and finished the job Shepherd had started. They dug in silence, burying Larkin and the Palestinian side by side.

"Steph fill you in on what happened?" Shepherd asked as they walked back to the Transportpanzer.

"Yeah, I listened to that tape too," Brancato replied. "Unbelievable." He paused thoughtfully, then asked, "You know about Ramadan?"

Shepherd shook no.

"They're going to kill the hostages."

"Bastards. When?"

"One a day starting tomorrow if they don't get a homeland in Israel. Which everyone knows they ain't."

"Larkin said there's a rescue in the works."

Brancato brightened. "Let's hope he was right."

Shepherd nodded grimly. "You know, when I found out what this was all about . . ." He paused and shook his head in dismay.

"I know what you're thinking," Brancato offered, sensing the irony. "You would've been the first guy to put it on the line for them."

"What military officer wouldn't?"

Brancato nodded emphatically. "What now?"

Shepherd shrugged, wracked with exhaustion. He slumped to the ground, his back against one of the TTP's huge tires. "Go get my plane, I guess."

"No, no, don't say that," Stephanie protested.

"Why? Nothing's changed." Shepherd groaned forlornly. "I still can't prove my story; I'm still on the run. I don't see that I have much choice."

"One thing's different . . ." Brancato said, letting the sentence trail off.

"What's that?" Stephanie asked.

"He won't be going in alone."

Shepherd shook his head no emphatically. "No. No way. This one's mine."

"There are *two* names stenciled on that one-eleven."

"*Al*," Shepherd admonished.

"Name the Italian wizzo from Bensonhurst who won't take no for an answer?" Brancato challenged.

Shepherd thought about it for a moment, then broke into a tired smile.

47

AFTER PICKING UP the Soviet Alpha on sonar, the *Cavalla* remained on course and spent the night proceeding beneath the choppy Aegean to the area of open sea cradled by Crete, Karpathos, and Rhodes, where Commander Duryea planned to intercept the Romeo. He had purposely zigzagged en route to test the Soviet boat's intentions.

The submarine was completing the maneuver when Cooperman called from the sonar room. "I just picked up the Romeo on the bow array, sir," he reported, having already conducted an acoustic signature comparison that removed any doubt. "Range seventy-five miles. ETA our position twenty-one hundred."

Duryea glanced to his watch. "Seven hours."

"Aye, sir."

The captain turned to his chart table and marked the Romeo's position. It had embarked on its journey to Beirut and was just emerging from the Cyclades between Thira and Anafi. "Where's the Alpha?"

Cooperman switched to the towed array. The fingertips of one hand were dancing over the AEP keys, palm of the other working the TD ball. "Bearing one eight zero, range eight miles," he replied, confirming the Soviet submarine was closely tailing the *Cavalla*.

"Stay on both of them," Duryea ordered softly. He hung up and turned to McBride. "Romeo's right on schedule," he said with mixed emotions.

"And the Alpha?"

"Still right on our tail," Duryea replied, clearly annoyed. "What do you figure our Redfleet friend thinks we're doing out here?"

"Based on our course and configuration"—McBride said, referring to the dry deck shelter atop the *Cavalla*'s hull—"he's got to be thinking we're going through the Dardanelles into the Black Sea to do some serious snooping around his bases."

"Which means he'd be expecting us to try and lose him," Duryea said, thinking aloud, his eyes riveted to the Romeo's course and the point of intercept he had drawn on the chart table. "What if we proceed due east to the Turkish channel?" He drew a line across the Aegean, past the intercept area, to the easternmost chain of islands: Lesbos, Chios, Samos, Lipsi, Leros, Kalimnos, Kos, Nisiros, Tilos, Hakis, and Rhodes, which ran in a tight north-to-south line. "At first, it would look like we're running for cover; but I bet Alpha's captain just might notice we've come onto a course that's an alternate route to the Dardanelles."

McBride nodded and smiled.

"What would he do? Pursue or leapfrog?"

"Leapfrog," McBride answered.

"Why?" Duryea asked, in a professorial tone.

"Because the terrain is dangerous and sonar's totally useless in there. I'd sprint ahead and be waiting for us at the mouth of Dardanelles."

"Me too."

"Once we lose him," McBride said, picking up on Duryea's lead, "We can circle Rhodes, sprint back to here"—he indicated an area in the Mediterranean south of the Crete-Rhodes gap—"and be waiting for Romeo when he moves into the Med. Even at top speed, which he'll never make through that terrain, he couldn't get there before we . . ." He trailed off with a scowl, realizing he had overlooked something in his enthusiasm. "Only one problem—"

"We blow the twenty-one hundred intercept," Duryea said.

McBride nodded grimly.

Duryea thought about it for a moment, then brought the *Cavalla* to periscope-antenna depth, and went down the passageway to the communications room.

T H E   T I M E in Washington, D.C., was 8:46 A.M.

Bill Kiley was in a breakfast meeting with his staff when his secretary informed him Duryea was on the line. He left the French Room and went to his office across the corridor to take the call.

Duryea briefed him on the situation. "We have the Alpha set up," he concluded, "but we can't lose him in time to carry out the rescue as scheduled."

Kiley groaned. "When were you planning to make your move?"

"Twenty-one hundred today, sir. Romeo stops and comes to periscope-antenna depth each day at that hour," he went on, anticipating the question. "We're tracking him on sonar now, but I'm thinking we lay back and tail him until twenty-one hundred tomorrow."

Kiley paused, briefly calculating the time, then winced. "That's three hours before the deadline."

"Yes, sir, I know; but based on Romeo's need to be in Beirut by Ramadan, we can predict his course and position with a high degree of accuracy."

"Any options?" Kiley pressed. "Any at all?"

"Other than ignoring the Alpha, no."

"What's the down side if you do?"

"The Alpha spots us making the move, warns the Romeo, and the crazies kill all the hostages."

"Better to chance cutting it close than chance losing them all," Kiley calculated glumly.

"Yes, sir."

"Good luck, Commander," Kiley said, ending the call.

Duryea hung up and glanced to McBride. "All ahead full," he ordered, putting the new plan into action.

THE FACADE of the National Commercial Bank headquarters in downtown Jeddah glowed pale mauve in the twilight, the triangular shaft of white marble rising majestically from reflecting pools, giving it the illusion of being twice its height.

The time was 7:10 P.M.

Moncrieff had spent the day in his twenty-fifth-floor office. He made several phone calls to distant time zones where the business day was just commencing, then left for the day, taking the high-speed elevator to the lobby. His heels clicked on the polished marble as he crossed to an exit that led to a ramp where a Mercedes limousine with the royal crest on the door was waiting.

The Saudi had been working long days in anticipation of the period of reduced productivity during Ramadan; it also helped keep his mind off Katifa's return to Beirut. He was preoccupied with the details of several projects and had reached the limousine before realizing the chauffeur was behind the wheel instead of poised to open the door for him. He scowled and opened it himself, climbing into the backseat.

"I thought Ramadan commenced tomorrow," he said face-tiously, referring to the shortened work hours.

"Don't move," the Palestinian replied sharply as he turned in the driver's seat and leveled a pistol at Moncrieff's forehead. Two more Palestinians emerged swiftly from the darkness and got in, flanking him. The limousine was the only vehicle on the ramp at this hour and they had had little trouble overcoming the chauffeur.

Moncrieff tensed and glared at them as they drove off in the darkness, heading north on Al Madinah Road. There was no need to ask who they were or what they wanted, nor any need to fear for his life; he knew he would already be dead if they had intended to kill him.

One of the Palestinians held a pistol on Moncrieff as the other produced a hypodermic syringe and, with practiced ease, stabbed the needle through Moncrieff's trousers into his thigh, depressing the plunger.

Within five seconds the Saudi was unconscious, and a piece of duct tape had been stretched over his mouth.

The limousine angled east to Andulus Street, leaving the city, and headed north into the desolate terrain that bordered the Red Sea. Twenty minutes later the driver turned onto a dirt road, following it to a rocky slope that tumbled toward the surf below.

A flashlight blinked in the darkness, where two more Palestinians were waiting. The Pentothal had plunged Moncrieff into a deep state of unconsciousness and he offered no resistance as they strapped him facedown to a stretcher; then they carried him to a cove at the base of an outcropping, where the refurbished gunboat was anchored. Once aboard, the stretcher was taken to the compartment where the hostages had been concealed.

The captain ordered Moncrieff be covered with blankets and posted an armed guard inside the compartment; then he closed the hidden bulkhead, returned to the bridge, and gave the order to cast off.

The twin diesels rumbled to life and the rust-stained Zhuk cut through the water on a heading for Port Taufiq and the Suez Canal 600 miles north. The Red and Mediterranean seas were at nearly identical levels and the man-made waterway that joined them had been built without locks, providing swift passage, especially for small vessels.

After setting his course, the captain radioed Casino du Liban. "Cargo aboard and en route," he reported when Abu Nidal came on the line.

"When do you estimate delivery?"

"Within thirty-six hours."

"Very well." Nidal clicked off and glanced to his watch. It was 7:51 P.M; more than an hour before the Romeo was due to check in. He left the communications center, his head tucked between his shoulders like a turtle's, deep in thought.

D U R Y E A had proceeded due east through the southern Aegean, with the Soviet Alpha on his tail, for more than eight hours. This was hazardous terrain. The bottom was a craggy range of seamounts and escarpments, the passage between them made all the more difficult by the crosscurrents that surged like underwater rivers.

Now the *Cavalla* was north of Rhodes, approaching Simi, when the Alpha's captain figured it out. "The Turkish channel," Solomatin mused, hovering over his chart table. "The Turkish channel to the Dardanelles."

"Continue pursuit, Comrade Captain?" his starpom wondered.

"Through that topology?" Solomatin admonished, detecting his eager tone. "Remember what happened to Borzov?" he asked, referring to a colleague who ran his boat aground in a Swedish fjord a decade earlier. "He has been captain of a desk in Polyarnyy ever since."

Indeed, as Duryea had predicted, Solomatin decided to avoid hazardous pursuit and sprint northward on a parallel track toward the entrance to the Dardanelles.

"Alpha's dropping off, sir," Cooperman reported.

Duryea sat deep in thought. The whole thing would fall apart if the Alpha's captain hadn't really gone for the fake but was just playing a clever game of hide-and-seek; and the numerous hiding places the terrain afforded made it hard to be sure he wasn't. Duryea contacted ASW on the *America* and requested a flyover.

"We've had an S-3A tracking him since we made that MAD run," the ASW duty officer reported. He put Duryea on hold and contacted the Viking in flight; 30 seconds later he came back on the line. "Viking reports he just changed course and is sprinting north."

"That's what I want him to do. Make sure your guys let him know they're up there," Duryea instructed, deciding ASW harassment would further convince the Alpha's captain he was endangering the *Cavalla*'s mission and encourage the leapfrog tactic.

"We'll keep a blowtorch to his tail, sir."

The *Cavalla* entered the Turkish channel and curled, not north around Simi toward the Dardanelles, but south around the eastern tip of Rhodes, sprinting at 25 knots into the Mediterranean on a southwesterly course. It covered the 150 miles to the new intercept point south of the Crete-Rhodes ridge in just under six hours, arriving an hour ahead of schedule to pick up the Romeo.

Duryea lifted the phone. "Sonar? Conn. Anything?"

"No, sir. I just did a sweep. We're in clear water."

Duryea pursed his lips thoughtfully. "It's probably taking Romeo longer to proceed through that terrain than I thought. Hang in there."

For the next hour and a half Cooperman sat in his compartment, listening to the sounds of the Aegean. Most of the ferries, hydrofoils, and fishing vessels that ran between the countless islands were stilled at this hour and he was left with the melodic swish of an immense school of sardines riding the fast-moving current.

Duryea kept the *Cavalla* on station, nudging slowly northward into the gap between the islands. He had a cool, patient temperament, which served him well when it came to waiting, to letting a situation develop. But this one didn't; his target never showed. The Romeo had to be out there somewhere. It lacked the speed and stealth to elude him. Despite logic, despite technology, he was haunted by the hollow feeling that the Romeo had somehow managed to get past him and was on its way to Beirut.

48

''I HATE TO SAY IT, BABE, but you better get back to the hotel," Shepherd suggested when Stephanie briefed him on her run in with the D'Jerban police. "Just do whatever you were doing before I got here."

She protested but knew he was right and drove back to the Dar Jerba in the car she and Brancato had rented.

Shepherd, who had been up almost thirty-six hours, spent the afternoon in the Transportpanzer sleeping.

Brancato had spent it thinking.

A pink-tinged glow still hung over the Gulf of Bougara as Brancato made his way through the towering marsh grass to the road. He drove Larkin's rented sedan to the far side of Borj Castille, circling to a flat outcropping of rocks that jutted out into the sea. He rolled down the windows, put the transmission in neutral, released the handbrake, and started pushing.

"Good idea," Shepherd intoned, joining him. He had just awakened and his eyes were still a little glazed.

They got it rolling and pushed it off the edge into the sea. The interior quickly filled with water and it disappeared beneath the surface with a tired gurgle.

"When do we go into Libya?" Brancato prompted, as they returned to the Transportpanzer and brought several cans of touajen, a North African version of lamb stew, to life in the tiny galley.

"The sooner the better; but we're looking at a very narrow window. They only fly the one-elevens at night."

Brancato nodded sagely. "We get there too soon and the machines aren't fueled; too late and they've gone flying. How do we travel?"

"We have a choice—wheels or wings."

"Wings? What kind of aircraft?"

"Mooney two fifty-two. But I vote for wheels," Shepherd said.

"Why drive when you can fly?"

"For openers, the Mooney's at the airport. Just getting our hands on it would be risky; and even if we could, the one-elevens are based at Okba ben Nafi, which means we'll be flying right into the teeth of their radar and SAM installations—without weaponry, electronic jamming gear, or TFR. Even if we defeat the perimeter radar, we'd still have to land out in the desert, which puts us in the middle of nowhere without ground transportation."

"Yeah, and anywhere on or near the air base they'll be waiting for us when we touch down."

"With that," Shepherd went on, indicating the Transportpanzer, "we have weapons, armor, and wheels. Besides, there are all kinds of goodies in there: radios, handguns, clothes, food. And whether we're in the middle of the desert or driving across the air base, that thing looks like it belongs."

Indeed, Qaddafi had specified his escape vehicle be unidentifiable as such, and the Transportpanzer's exterior was of basic military finish and unadorned.

"Take yes for an answer," Brancato pleaded genially. "Okba ben Nafi's on the Mediterranean. We can shoot right down the coast and—"

"Not so fast," Shepherd interrupted. "I had a run-in with one of their patrol boats. They know what I want; they might be waiting for me to come back."

"So we take the scenic route," Brancato suggested. "Must be maps in there."

Shepherd nodded.

Brancato set the bowl of stew aside and made his way to the cab. A rack of shallow drawers, like a dentist's tool cabinet, was built into the console between the seats. Each contained a set of plastic laminated sector maps labeled in Arabic. It took Brancato a few minutes to find the revelant charts, which he laid out across the console. They were for Qaddafi's use and clearly delineated not only the terrain but also the location of Libyan military outposts in the desert, as well as border patrol zones.

"See this area here," Brancato said as Shepherd joined him. "There isn't a road, town, or military outpost on either side of the border for miles. We can leave soon as it gets dark, work our way south along the coast in the water. Then we cut inland about here and make our way through the desert. If we cross the border between these mesas and head due east, it'd put us right on a beeline for Okba ben Nafi."

"Lot of ground to cover," Shepherd cautioned, digesting the plan. "And it has to be done at night. You have a fix on mileage?"

Brancato studied the chart for a moment. "Hundred seventy-five max."

"How many in water?"

"Forty, give or take."

"Twelve hours of darkness," Shepherd said, thoughtfully, "figure average speed—water, desert—twenty miles an hour; doable."

Brancato nodded. "What about fuel?"

"Tanks are still more than half full," Shepherd said, checking the gauges for the two 50-gallon tanks, which gave the TTP its 485-mile range. "The days are getting longer," he went on, glancing outside where the sun was still hanging on the horizon. "It doesn't get dark now until after nineteen hundred. We'll have a lot of time to kill once we get there."

"According to these, there's a patch of heavily forested terrain around this oasis about thirty miles south of the air base. We can hang out until, say, eighteen-thirty, then start moving in. It'll be dark way before we get anywhere near Okba ben Nafi."

"Okay, we go tonight."

Brancato tilted his head thoughtfully. "Or we wait a day and go tomorrow night."

"Tomorrow? Why?"

"Name the holy month that celebrates the victory of Muslims over the Makkans at the battle of Badr *and* commemorates the revelation of the Koran?"

"Something tells me we're talking about Ramadan, again," Shepherd answered.

Brancato nodded. "Starts tomorrow. It's similar to Lent. Muslims fast; they work shorter hours; businesses close early; and there's lots of churchgoing. Their state of mind would be working for us; they'll be less vigilant; less aggressive; *and* there'll be less of them around. And since they can't eat until sunset, they'll be busy chowing down about the time we're making our move on the air base."

"Not these guys," Shepherd countered. "Qaddafi's pushing them hard, real hard."

"We still have to get there. It can't hurt."

While Shepherd considered it, Brancato added, "Besides, you look kind of crummy. An extra day's rest would do you good."

"Sounds like you have all the angles figured."

"Yeah," Brancato said, with a thin smile. "Right up to where you radio the tower for clearance in Arabic."

49

THE ROMEO'S mysterious disappearance had pinned the *Cavalla* in the Crete-Karpathos-Rhodes gap. Duryea had sent a cable to Kiley at CIA headquarters, briefing him on the situation. Several hours later he received a terse reply:

REQUEST VOICE COM ASAP. CITE DIRECTOR

Duryea immediately brought the boat to periscope-antenna depth and deployed a radio mast, then went to the communications room and contacted the DCI.

"I had Romeo's twenty-one hundred wake-up calls put on surveillance priority," the DCI began. "Keyhole made an intercept last night that sheds some light on why he didn't show. I'm cabling you a copy of the translation." He nodded to his secretary, who activated a fax machine that was patched into the phone line.

Seconds later, a fax machine in the *Cavalla*'s communications room came to life. The duty officer took the pages from the delivery tray and handed it to Duryea.

ROMEO: This is the Exchequer. This is the Exchequer. Do you read?

NIDAL: Yes. Go ahead.

ROMEO: Your currency is secure. We are proceeding with arrangements for withdrawal as planned. Do you confirm?

NIDAL: No. The terms of the transaction remain in force but I want to postpone withdrawal for forty-eight hours.

"What do you think Nidal's up to?" Kiley prompted.

"I don't know, sir," Duryea replied, scanning the cable. "Do you have Romeo's location at the time the transmission was intercepted?"

"The southern Aegean," Kiley replied, reciting the coordinates, which confirmed the Romeo had started to Beirut and stopped at 2100 hours to contact Nidal at the point where the *Cavalla* would have intercepted. "ASW follow-up indicates he backtracked to the Cyclades."

"For what it's worth, sir," Duryea said, clearly relieved, "there's no way Romeo can make it to Beirut by the deadline now."

"I don't find that at all comforting, Commander," Kiley growled. "Nidal doesn't make idle threats. He promised to execute a hostage by Ramadan and believe me, he'll find a way to do it."

"They'll have to get past us first, sir."

Kiley grunted, far from mollified, and hung up.

Duryea returned to the control room and kept the *Cavalla* on station for the remainder of the day, waiting for the Romeo. Twenty-one hundred came and went without any sign of it. It was almost midnight when he glanced to the countdown clock in the upper right corner of the electronic chart table. It read:

    00:DAYS
    00:HOURS
    01:MINUTES
    14:SECONDS

Duryea watched until it read all zeroes.
Ramadan had begun.

THAT SAME EVENING, on the southeastern tip of D'Jerba, the glow of dusk was fading to star-dotted darkness as the Transportpanzer rolled out of the marsh grass and past Borj Castille into the sea.

Shepherd and Brancato proceeded south, following the distant causeway to el-Kantara on the mainland, then continued along the Tunisian coast in light surf. They made their way past Zarzis, then cut through the inlet at Bin Qirdan, heading inland across the calm waters of the bay.

Several hours later they guided the Transportpanzer through the rolling breakers onto the beach, crossed the Al Kurnish Road into the desolate, southernmost part of Tunisia, and set off across the desert, well west of the Ras Jdyar border checkpoint.

As the charts had indicated, there were no roads here, no towns in this harsh land that defied even the iron will of desert nomads to inhabit it.

They traveled 30 miles south, then angled east toward the Libyan border, entering an unpatrolled area of steep sandstone palisades that formed a natural barrier between the two nations.

Brancato left the Transportpanzer and went ahead on foot to scout the area. The TTP's halogens illuminated the craggy terrain as he made his way along the base of the ridgeline to a spot where the vehicle could climb the near vertical wall. He guided Shepherd into position, ensuring that the front tires were properly aligned with a narrow canyon he had found on the charts, and returned to the cab. Then, Shepherd shifted the Transportpanzer into the lowest gear and eased the throttle down slowly.

The eight independently driven tires bit into the crumbly surface, sending rooster tails of sand into the air as the TTP accelerated toward the ridgeline and began its ascent. Capable of scaling a 70 percent gradient, it steadily fought its way up the slope onto a desert plateau of parched scrub brush and windburnished sand. Libyan sand.

It was just after midnight.

The Muslim holy month had begun.

Okba ben Nafi Air Base lay 130 miles due east.

A B U   N I D A L had spent the evening in his suite at Casino du Liban, monitoring news broadcasts for signs of a response to his ultimatum. It was a futile vigil.

At precisely midnight, he shut off the radio and television, turned toward Mecca, and fell to his knees, touching his forehead to the ground; joining Muslims throughout the Middle East, he recited to himself the traditional call to prayer for the start of Ramadan as prescribed by the Koran.

> God is greatest. God is greatest. I testify there is no god save God and that Mohammed is the apostle of God. Up to prayer, up to salvation, prayer is better than sleep. God is greatest. God is greatest. There is no god, but God.

Then he took a vial of insulin from the small refrigerator in his suite, shot the medication into the roll of flesh at his abdomen, and went to bed.

The following morning, the sun streamed across the Mediterranean with customary brilliance.

Katifa had kept to herself, spending time in her quarters, which
overlooked the marina and entrance road; this allowed her to
quietly monitor arrivals and departures. Now she heard the throb
of diesel engines and went to the window. Far below, the gunboat
was nosing into one of the concrete slips. Crewmen were throwing
housers to Palestinians on the dock, who lashed them to pilings.

Abu Nidal strode down the gangway from the casino. Perfect
timing, he thought, glancing at his watch. Washington, D.C., was
seven hours behind Lebanon and he had planned that the first
hostage would be executed and delivered to the United States
Embassy in Beirut *not* immediately upon the onset of Ramadan
but midway through the first day. This ensured sufficient time
for the media—who had been notified in advance and therefore
would be present to witness the gruesome discovery—to write and
transmit their stories, photographs, and videotapes for the evening television news programs.

Nidal watched as the blanket-covered stretcher was carried from
the gunboat and down the gangway; then he followed it across
the dock to the casino.

Katifa left the window and locked her door; then she took the
unopened pack of cigarettes from her purse. She quickly removed
the cellophane wrapper, hinged the top, and removed the foil
closure, revealing the radio transmitter beneath: black plastic fas-
cia, minuscule anodized microphone grille, and antenna—which
she telescoped out before pressing the single control button. In
a tense whisper she said, "Tell Mr. Stengel the first hostage has
arrived. I repeat, the first hostage has arrived at Casino du Liban."
She compressed the antenna, closed the top, and slipped the pack
into her jacket pocket.

Later that afternoon she was summoned to the amphitheater.
Nidal was standing on the stage surrounded by several dozen
guerrillas. The crowd of young men and women parted as Katifa
approached. She felt the weight of their eyes, then sensed a figure
hanging from the trapeze apparatus above the stage. It sent a
macabre chill through her.

"The deadline has passed; long passed," Nidal announced. "We
have had no response to our demands. It is time for Intifada to
become more than just a word that the Western media uses to

add spice to their headlines; indeed, it is time for the person who gave our uprising its name to give it meaning."

Nidal took a knife from his pocket and snapped the blade open. "The weapon that killed your brother," he said, offering it to Katifa.

She stepped forward, knowing that, this time, she had little choice but to play out the scenario.

The instant her fingers closed around the knurled grip, the kliegs came on, illuminating the trapeze with a blast of cold light. And there directly in front of her, hanging upside down and naked, his legs lashed to the ornate, velvet-sheathed apparatus, was Moncrieff.

Katifa recoiled and gasped. "No! No!" she shouted in an anguished plea, the knife slipping from her hand.

Nidal smiled slyly and picked it up. "Now, loyal daughter," he said evenly, "you will tell your brothers and sisters why you are really here."

Moncrieff's eyes widened; he squirmed on the apparatus and muttered something from beneath the tape that was stretched across his mouth.

"You wish to speak?" Nidal taunted. He grasped the tape and tore it from his face.

The Saudi screamed in pain. Blood oozed from his lips where the tape had stripped them raw. "Don't . . . don't tell him," he groaned.

Katifa winced, averting her eyes. The thought of what would happen next made her skin crawl. She shuddered as Nidal put the point of the blade to Moncrieff's waist, and flicked his wrist, sending the first half inch of gleaming steel into the Saudi's flesh. Blood oozed from the cut and ran along the edge of the blade. Nidal looked sideways at Katifa. "Why are you here?" he prompted, as the group of young Palestinians closed in around her.

"No," Moncrieff protested through painfully clenched teeth. "Don't tell him."

"His life for information?" Nidal prompted. "Why did you return? What are you doing here?"

Katifa's lips tightened as she wrestled with it.

"No, they'll kill me anyway," Moncrieff warned.

"I guarantee it if you don't," Nidal hissed coolly.

"Please take him down from there." Her voice cracked with emotion. "Please. I'll tell you."

Nidal nodded to the guerrilla who was working the controls. The apparatus slowly lowered Moncrieff to the stage. He lay there, bloodied and exhausted, staring up blankly at Katifa, who had rushed to his side. Nidal brusquely pulled her to her feet and took her to the communications room backstage.

"I'm listening," he said, glowering at her.

"The Americans," she replied haltingly. "They, . . . they wanted to know where the hostages were going to be taken for execution."

The implication dawned on Nidal. "They're planning a rescue?"

"Yes."

"Here?"

"The submarine."

"They know about it?"

She nodded apprehensively.

"When?"

"I don't know. I don't."

Nidal was shaken but he knew the Exchequer would have contacted him at the first sign of trouble. He cursed that he had no way of initiating communication. The time was 6:14 P.M.

In two hours and forty-six minutes, the Romeo would check in and Nidal would warn him.

50

S H E P H E R D and Brancato had spent the night driving the Transportpanzer across the bleak landscape of the Libyan desert. They crossed four north-south roads en route. The first three were narrow, little-used ribbons of macadam broken by drifting sand. The last was Pepsi Cola Road, a motorway connecting Tripoli and the industrial city of Ghariyan 75 miles to the south. It was primarily used by trucks ferrying raw materials and finished products to and from the factories.

Shepherd brought the Transportpanzer to a stop about a quarter of a mile from the road. They waited until the pinpoints of distant headlights couldn't be seen in either direction, then continued their journey.

The time was 7:14 A.M. when they arrived at the patch of heavily forrested terrain Brancato had spotted on the maps, and concealed the TTP in the cool shade of a stand of cedars and pines nourished by a nearby oasis.

Okba ben Nafi Air Base lay 30 miles due north.

"You sure you want to do this?" Shepherd asked as they shrouded the Transportpanzer with a camouflage net they had found in one of the storage compartments.

"Hell of a time to ask."

"We can wait until dark, turn right around and—"

Brancato shook his head no. "*I* can."

Shepherd shrugged forlornly and stretched out on the ground beneath the trees, exhausted. "I mean the chances of pulling this off are pretty damn remote."

Brancato nodded, then sat opposite him.

"I just keep thinking about Steph and Marie and the kids. No sense both of us—"

"And my dog. You forgot my dog."

"Al, I'm serious," Shepherd said in weary protest.

"So am I. If I don't run him, nobody does. Marie said he put on ten pounds while I was in the hospital. I miss him, you know? I mean, jogging every morning with those big paws padding along next to me, slobbery mouth drooling all over everything. God, it's just . . . I don't know, there's a bond there. Of course I'm the only one who understands him. Really, he'd be lost without me. You ever see a dog laugh? This dog laughs—at jokes. I was thinking of trying to get him on David Letterman, but he's . . ." Brancato paused and laughed to himself.

Shepherd was sound asleep.

They spent the day taking turns sleeping and rummaging through the compartments, removing the items they would use —handguns, walkie-talkies, military clothing among them.

As the sun began dropping toward the horizon they removed the camouflage net and started the Transportpanzer rolling across the desert.

About an hour later darkness had fallen, and Okba ben Nafi loomed in the distance, a dusty mirage enclosed by an endless chainlink fence topped with razor wire.

Brancato directed Shepherd to a desolate corner of the airfield, well beyond the end of the runways. Shepherd let the TTP inch forward until the leading edge of its angled snout was flush against one of the pipes that supported the miles of chainlink; a little more gas and the 40,000-pound vehicle began advancing, gradually bending the pipe toward the ground until the adjacent sections of fence lay flat against the sand and the eight huge combat tires rolled over them onto the air base.

Shepherd kept the running lights off until he left the sand for a paved road that cut across the taxiways with geometric precision. Soon the ribbed texture of sheetmetal hangars marched to the horizon. The TTP rumbled past them in the direction of hangar 6-South, where the F-111s were housed.

Shepherd and Brancato exchanged anxious looks at the sight of one of the bombers. It was being towed through the open sliders onto the tarmac for its preflight check. They circled the hangar toward the personnel entrance, which was guarded by armed sentries.

IN BEIRUT, a chilling scream echoed through Casino du Liban's marble corridors. It was Katifa's scream; a scream of horror and forlorn protest. Upon returning to the amphitheater, she discovered Moncrieff once again suspended upside down above the stage. As the Saudi had suspected, Abu Nidal had no intention of sparing his life. On the contrary, as the terrorist leader had planned when postponing the Romeo's departure for Beirut, *he* would be the first hostage executed and delivered to the United States Embassy.

Now Katifa stood but several feet from Moncrieff. Two women held her arms; one of the men clutched fistfuls of her hair, keeping her from looking away. But as Nidal slowly inserted the knife into the cut he had made in Moncrieff's flesh earlier, Katifa struggled free, smashed an elbow into the face of one of the women, and went for Nidal. The guerrilla who had hold of her hair yanked backwards, stopping her abruptly, and brought the grip of his pistol down hard across the side of her head. She screamed and fell to the floor, unconscious.

The next scream was Moncrieff's.

B E N E A T H   T H E   A E G E A N, the *Cavalla* was concealed behind a basaltic ridge that crested just north of the Crete-Karpathos gap.

Cooperman had the BQS-6 bow array in passive mode, using the computer-linked DIMUS program to separate frequency ranges, when he heard the faint hiss on his headsets. He straightened in his chair, pressed a hand to an earphone, and was soon listening to the telltale beat of twin propeller cavitation; he ran an acoustic signature comparison, then buzzed the control room.

"Lover boy's heading for Beirut, skipper," he reported. "ETA our position twenty-one hundred."

"You're positive it's him?"

"Ac-sig's a perfect match."

Duryea turned the conn over to McBride and went up the companionway to the SEALs' quarters on A-deck. The bulkhead adjacent to the door still displayed the pictures of the hostages; the one opposite was covered with the construction drawings of the Romeo.

Four salvage/rescue valves on the exterior hull had been circled in yellow and numbered. They allowed air to be injected into an incapacitated submarine to save the crew and/or float the vessel, and were spaced out the length of the hull in the event bulkhead doors had been closed, sealing off compartments. On another drawing, the salvage hatch forward of the sail, through which divers could enter the vessel, had been outlined in red. Passageways leading to compartments where the hostages might be quartered had also been marked. The plastic shipping container from the Office of Technical Services at Langley was on the floor in front of the drawings. Lieutenant Reyes was sitting on it, refining his plan, when Captain Duryea came through the joiner door.

"Target coming in, Lieutenant."

A thin smile tugged at the corners of Reyes's mouth. "Showtime," he called out to the members of his team, who came surging into the compartment in response. The SEALs went directly to their equipment lockers and began suiting up as Reyes opened the shipping container.

The interior was divided into a six-section egg crate. Each contained a steel pressure vessel, delivery hose, and valve assembly. Reyes removed one from its cushioned sleeve. Painted bright yellow, it resembled a scuba tank; but its gaseous contents would have a far different effect on human consciousness.

Halothane was a general anesthetic that acted on the central nervous system. Commonly used for surgical procedures, the odorless gas was a benign compound with negligible aftereffects. It induced a deep state of unconsciousness within 30 seconds of inhalation.

The SEALs prepared with an economy of movement and conversation. They had already rehearsed every step of the mission; each man had his assignment; each knew individual scuba tanks would be used and carried in standard two-bottle rigs with the tank of halothane.

"Black fitting goes in the regulator, yellow in the sub; black in the regulator, yellow in the sub," Reyes recited, making certain no one had inadvertently connected the wrong hose to his breathing apparatus. "I don't want any of you guys getting off on this stuff."

"I'll wake you just prior to launch," Duryea joked, heading for the communications room.

The time was exactly 7:54 P.M.

AT OKBA BEN NAFI AIR BASE, a sentry stationed outside hangar 6-South noticed the Transportpanzer approaching. It drove past him and rumbled to a stop near the personnel entrance, where another sentry, cradling an AK-47, stood guard.

Two Libyan military officers exited the massive vehicle and strode boldly toward him. Both wore desert camouflage fatigues, sidearms, maroon berets, and sunglasses; security badges were clipped to their pockets. Two gold stars and an eagle on their epaulets identified them as aqids, or colonels. The sentry snapped to attention and saluted. The officers returned it and entered the hangar through the personnel door.

Once inside the hangar, they proceeded down a corridor lined with offices. Though normally staffed with technicians and clerical personnel, most were empty since the workday had been short-ened due to Ramadan, as Brancato had predicted.

In the life-support room, two Libyan aviators who were about to fly a practice mission in the F-111 were at their lockers suiting up when the door half-opened. A colonel appeared, snapped his fingers, pointed to the aviator nearest the door, and gestured authoritatively that he join him outside. The Libyan stepped into the corridor, the door closing behind him. The last thing he re-membered was a rustle of clothing before Brancato, who was concealed behind the door, brought the grip of a pistol down hard across the back of his head.

Boldness, conviction, and the element of surprise.

Boldness, conviction, and the element of surprise.

Boldness, conviction, and the element of surprise.

The instructor at survival-training school had drummed it into all his pupils and now Shepherd and Brancato knew why. They repeated the scenario with the second aviator, then dragged both back into the life-support room and stuffed them inside empty lockers.

A short time later, on the tarmac just outside the hangar, the crew chief and assistant crew chief, who were preparing the F-111 for flight, heard the ear-shattering clang of a fire alarm. They left the plane, hurrying through the hangar into the cor-ridors outside the life-support room and offices, where smoke billowed.

Shepherd and Brancato, suited up in flight gear from the life support room, were concealed in an ordnance storage bay nearby. As soon as the Libyans had passed, they slipped into the hangar and split up: Shepherd headed for the F-111 on the tarmac, Brancato for the one still in the hangar, intending to destroy it via a built-in self-destruct mechanism. Activated by setting a delayed-action timer in the cockpit, it would literally fry all the electronics, avionics, and weapons systems.

Inside the life-support room, flames were roaring up a wall from the trash barrel in which Shepherd and Brancato had started a fire before pulling the alarm. The Libyans were battling the blaze with extinguishers. A sentry who had also responded to the alarm heard a pounding from within a steel locker. He discovered one of the Libyan aviators, who had regained consciousness. A brief exchange sent the sentry dashing down the corridor toward the hangar.

Brancato had just reached the bomber and was about to climb the ladder to the cockpit when he heard the hangar door opening behind him. He whirled, pistol in hand, and opened fire. The sentry went down. Brancato spotted another Libyan through the glass panel in the door, who was running down the corridor toward the hangar. He fired several shots, shattering the glass. The sentry kept coming. Brancato left the hangar, running toward the F-111 on the tarmac.

Moments earlier, Shepherd had crouched to the main landing gear and reached up inside the wheel well, removing a khaki-colored can that contained a starter cartridge. Manufactured by Morton-Thiokol, it was a slow-burning explosive device used to start the engines when pneumatic blower units weren't available. Shepherd had a far better reason for using it—the standard pneumatic start took 5 minutes; a cart start took 20 seconds. He opened the left side SOAP door and inserted the cartridge into the starter breech, moistening the pins with saliva to ensure electrical contact; then he secured the door and went up the ladder to the cockpit.

Shepherd already had the battery turned on and the starter switch in cart when he heard the gunshots and saw Brancato running from the hangar. He lifted the throttle on the number one engine, sending voltage to the starter breech and fuel to the engines simultaneously. The cartridge exploded, ballistically winding the engine to start speed.

Brancato was climbing into the cockpit as the pursuing sentry neared the bomber. The Libyan paused and jacked his AK-47; then, uncertain about blasting one of Qaddafi's prized F-111s with the machine gun, he dashed to the ladder that lay against the fuselage and started climbing.

Brancato reached over the side of the cockpit and fired his pistol. The bullet hit the Libyan in the center of the chest with tremendous force and knocked him backwards. The ladder went with him, saving Brancato the task of shoving it aside.

The tachometer had just ticked 17,000 as Brancato dropped into the seat next to Shepherd. "I couldn't pull the plug," he said. "They were all over me."

"We'll just have to find another way," Shepherd said with a thin smile as he started the bomber rolling.

While guiding it through the darkness, they went about hooking up oxygen and G-suit hoses and plugging in com-cords. By the time they had finished, the air that was being forced through the second engine by the plane's forward momentum had the turbine winding at high speed, and Shepherd lifted the throttle, starting it.

"Master arm on," Shepherd said, throwing the switch that energized the bomber's weapons systems. "Manual release; select two and seven."

"Manual; select two and seven," Brancato echoed, reaching to the stores select panel in the right console. The plane was approaching the top of the runway as he pressed the numbered keys, arming the Mark 82 bombs that hung from pylons below the wings.

IN BEIRUT, television camera crews were waiting outside the U.S. Embassy when a van turned into Avenue de Paris. As it went past, two Palestinians, faces masked by kaffiyehs, pushed a rolled carpet out the sliding door onto the macadam. Marine sentries cordoned it off and radioed for a bomb disposal unit.

Minutes later, the specially attired and equipped crew came from within the compound. They carefully unrolled the richly colored Persian that once graced a suite in Casino du Liban, discovering Moncrieff's skinned carcass inside.

Soon after, in the embassy's communications center, the dedicated radio channel crackled to life.

"Tell Mr. Stengel that Abu Nidal knows about the rescue operation," Katifa reported in a shaky voice. After Moncrieff's execution, she had been carried to the basement and locked in a stone-walled cavern that had once been the casino's wine cellar.

She regained consciousness several hours later and, fighting to shut out the memory of the horrifying events, took the cigarette-packaged transmitter from her jacket. "I repeat, Abu Nidal knows about the rescue operation."

"What action does he plan to take?" came the reply.

"I don't know."

"Do you know if the submarine has been warned?"

"No, it hasn't. Nidal can't make radio contact until nine o'clock."

T H E   T I M E in Washington, D.C., was 1:05 P.M.

Early that morning Bill Kiley had awakened to news reports of Moncrieff's kidnapping. Some fishermen had found his abandoned limousine on the banks of the Red Sea; the chauffeur's corpse was in the trunk. A short time later the U.S. Embassy in Beirut relayed the message that the first hostage had arrived at Casino du Liban, and the DCI knew to his horror just *how* Nidal proposed to carry out his threat.

Now the DCI was in his office, waiting for the rescue mission to commence when his intercom buzzed.

"CNN's on the line sir," his secretary said. "They want to know if you're interested in commenting on a special bulletin they're about to air."

Kiley turned on the TV; an anchorman reported that a Saudi businessman had been executed and delivered to the U.S. Embassy in Beirut; the letters *CIA* had been carved in what was left of his naked corpse.

"No," Kiley hissed, infuriated. "Get the embassy."

"They're calling on the other line, sir."

"Why does the media always know before I do?" Kiley bellowed into the phone. The Beirut station chief ignored the tirade and briefed him on Katifa's message. The DCI was convinced beyond doubt that if the Romeo was warned prior to the rescue attempt, all the hostages would be executed.

Kiley left his office, went to the communications center in the subbasement, and commandeered one of the technicians and his console. "I need Captain Duryea on the *Cavalla*. Flash priority; voice channel; code red."

The com-tech doubted that the *Cavalla* had a radio mast or buoy deployed but tried a voice channel anyway, to no avail. Next he typed up the alert and cabled it. "No acknowledgment, sir," he said, failing to get the signal tone that meant it had been received.

"We've got fifty million bucks worth of radio equipment in here and you can't reach a submarine?" Kiley snapped. "This is an emergency. Find a way!"

"Yes, sir," the harried technician replied. He sent the same cable on several bands with the same result. "Still no response, sir."

"Which bands have you tried?"

"UH and VHF, sir. ELF would take an hour just to—"

"What about HF?" the DCI demanded, referring to the high frequency band, commonly used for intrafleet communications. "You try that?"

"No, sir."

"What are you waiting for?"

"That's an unsecured net, sir."

"I don't give a damn what it is. Lives are at stake here! Lives. Do it!"

Moments before the DCI had arrived, a printer in an adjacent room had come to life. The technician had torn off the incoming cable and was in the process of routing it to the DCI's office when she glimpsed Kiley through the glass partition. She retrieved the cable and went through the door into the communications room.

"From the *Cavalla*, sir," she said, delivering it.

Kiley eased slightly, assuming it would acknowledge receipt of his message, but to his dismay it read:

TWILIGHT PROCEEDING AS PLANNED; UNODIR.

Kiley paled; the UNODIR meant the *Cavalla*'s radio had been shut off. His mind raced frantically in search of options and found one. "Get me the fleet admiral on the *America*," he ordered the com-tech. "Come on, come on." He was on the verge of losing control.

AT OKBA BEN NAFI AIR BASE, Shepherd had the F-111 barreling down the runway: blow-in doors open, wing-sweep at 16 degrees, flaps at 25, slats down, spoilers up, and throttles homed, disregarding the angry voices of control tower personnel coming over the radio. Brancato muttered an expletive and shut it off as Shepherd rotated the nose up and the bomber leapt into the darkness. Shepherd immediately banked right, aligning the bomber with the hangar where the second F-111 was still housed. His eyes were locked on the HUD, where light spilling across the tarmac far below moved onto the cross arrows of the optical gunsight, then he pressed the red button on his control stick, pickling off the preselected ordnance.

Two Mark 82 low level attack bombs dropped from the BRUs. The arming wires set the fuses and deployed tiny parachutes that slowed their descent to the target, giving the F-111 time to exit the area prior to impact.

Shepherd pulled the stick back slightly and pushed hard left, putting the aircraft into a high-G turn as the two 500 pounders turned the hangar and the remaining F-111 into a fireball. Shepherd leveled off, keeping the plane at low altitude, well below the range of Libyan air defense radar.

"Piece of cake," Brancato hooted.

"Yeah, the hard part comes next," Shepherd said, heading directly over Tripoli toward the Mediterranean, which was the quickest route out of Libyan air space.

"What're you driving at?"

"We're coming out of Tripoli with Libyan markings and an outdated transponder code smack into the Sixth Fleet's front yard," Shepherd replied, concerned that fleet commanders might mistake the F-111 for an attacking Libyan jet and launch interceptors or surface-to-air missiles to destroy it. "Better pull up your HF buttons and see if anything's going on."

"Fleet common, eagle-one," Brancato responded, switching on the high-frequency radio to monitor fleet operations. "Usual ops chitchat," he reported. "Sounds quiet otherwise."

Shepherd was just starting to relax when the radar, scanning on open priority, skin-painted a raw return. The lack of an IFF symbol next to the blip left no doubt it was hostile. "Bogie at six miles," he announced, realizing it was one of the Libyan SU-22s that had taken off earlier to escort the bomber.

Brancato fine-tuned the attack radar scope, targeting the interceptor. "Okay, I got him. He's jinking onto our nose . . . five miles . . . four."

"Select fox one, fox one," Shepherd barked, referring to one of four Aim-9 Sidewinder missiles carried on sidemounts affixed to the outboard pylons.

"Fox one," Brancato echoed, his eyes now glued to the moving target indicator, the graphic aviators call the death dot, which was chasing the SU-22's signal. "Okay," he said as the MTI became fixed on the blip. "He's locked up. He's locked up."

"I've got a tone," Shepherd said, pickling it off.

The Sidewinder rocketed from the mount with a loud whoosh and left a fiery 1,900 MPH trail in the darkness. Seconds later a distant explosion lit up the sky.

ON THE USS AMERICA, the fleet admiral was being briefed on the situation via radio by Kiley. He was puzzled by the DCI's desperate tone and use of the HF band, unaware that the com-tech had been bullied into using it to contact the *Cavalla* and had unthinkingly remained on it when calling the carrier. "Excuse me, sir," the admiral interjected softly, "but it behooves me to point out that we're on an unsecured channel."

"I don't care what we're on, Admiral," Kiley snapped. "My point is, the only way to stop Nidal from warning that Romeo is to take out his headquarters."

"You're suggesting an air strike?"

"Damn right."

"That's an act of war, sir," the admiral replied warily. "It will require a declaration by Congress or a direct order from the president. I have neither."

"You have a direct order from the director of Central Intelligence, dammit!"

"I understand that sir, but . . ."

THE F-111 was streaking low over the Mediterranean on a heading for D'Jerba when Brancato, still monitoring the HF band, switched it to Shepherd's headset. "Hey, listen to this."

"Then do it, Admiral," Kiley's voice demanded. "Target coordinates are three four/zero one/five two, north; three five/three eight/two zero, east. Got it?"

"Yes, sir, I do," the admiral replied. "There's nothing I'd like better than taking out that son of a bitch, believe me; but I'm forced to—"

"Nidal's already killed one hostage! If Casino du Liban isn't turned into a parking lot by nine o'clock, they're all going to die! All of them!"

"I'm sorry, sir," the admiral replied, agonizing over the decision. "I can't order an air strike on another nation without proper authorization."

"You're not attacking a nation, you're taking out a terrorist stronghold! Paint a hammer and sickle on one of your A-sixes and get on with it."

"Sir, I'd fly the mission myself if I could, but under the circumstances I respectfully suggest there is no point in carrying this conversation any further."

Shepherd and Brancato exchanged looks. No discussion was necessary. On Brancato's nod, Shepherd made an abrupt change in course. While Brancato went about transposing the coordinates to ANITA for entry into the Pave Tack computer, Shepherd climbed into cloud cover 13,000 feet above the sea, pushed the throttles to the stops, and swept the wings back to 72 degrees.

The F-111 bolted forward on a heading for Beirut.

The mach gauge swiftly climbed to 2.5.

Soon the sleek bomber was streaking through the pitch blackness at 1,650 MPH. At 28 miles a minute it could cover the 1,225 miles in under 44 minutes; and though Tripoli was geographically aligned with Western Europe—almost 30 degrees latitude west of Beirut—both cities, along with the Greek Islands, were in the same time zone. It was 8:11 P.M.

AT CIA HEADQUARTERS, Kiley left communications and went to the lobby, clutching the UNODIR; he stood gazing at the memorial wall, seized by an overwhelming sense of failure and depression. Push would soon come to shove. Technically, the UNODIR would cover him, but the responsibility was his, and he took no solace in it. He returned to his office, went to the wall safe behind the Chinese screen, and encoded the combination on the keypad. The safe held cash, top-secret code books, a standard CIA issue pistol, and numerous red file folders. Duryea's first UNODIR lay atop a pile of cables. Kiley removed it, leaving the safe open, and went to the shredder next to his desk. The first UNODIR went into the laser-honed blades with a precise whirr, spilling in ribbons into the burn bag below. He fed in the second; then, his hands shaking uncontrollably, he took the Polaroid of Fitzgerald from his desk. "I'm sorry, Tom," he said, eyes glistening with emotion.

ON THE *CAVALLA,* the SEALs had suited up, clambered through the hatch into the dry deck shelter atop the *Cavalla*'s hull, and settled in the SDV's cockpits.

Duryea sealed the hatch and filled the DDS with seawater. Reyes opened the aft bulkhead but, instead of piloting the swimmer delivery vehicle into the depths, he waited until the Romeo was abeam of the basaltic ridge that concealed the *Cavalla* from its sonar.

Now with the sound of the Romeo's propellers and diesels to mask the noise of the launch, Reyes turned on the hydroelectric propulsion system and the SDV, its searchlight piercing the cobalt depths, rocketed into the Aegean in pursuit of the submarine.

The plastic-hulled vessel and its six passengers offered imperceptible profiles to radar and active sonar; furthermore, by approaching directly aft in the submarine's blindspot, Reyes ensured any ambient sound would blend with that made by the Romeo itself. He guided the SDV into position below and behind the hull as it began slowly surfacing to periscope-antenna depth in preparation for contacting Abu Nidal.

The time was 8:41 P.M.

FIVE MINUTES LATER in Casino du Liban, Nidal clambered down the grand staircase from his quarters and strode purposefully through the gaming room and amphitheater to the backstage communications center.

"Have you tried communicating with the submarine?"

"No, sir. Exchequer never calls this early."

Nidal bristled with frustration at the limitations of submarine communications and the Romeo's archaic system, which ruled out any contact with the vessel when submerged. "Isn't it possible that he has already surfaced and is waiting until twenty-one hundred to initiate communication?"

"Yes, sir," the radioman replied apprehensively.

"And if he is, doesn't that mean *we* could contact *him* right now?"

The radioman nodded. "It is also possible his transmitter is turned off."

"Try anyway."

"Come in, Exchequer," the radioman said into his microphone.

"Come in, Exchequer. Do you read?" To Nidal's consternation, there was no reply. The radioman tried several more times with the same result.

T H E   F - 1 1 1 was streaking down the center of the Mediterranean 175 miles north of the Egyptian coast.

Shepherd was keeping a wary eye on the systems caution panel, where the sensor that monitored the bomber's skin temperature was flashing intermittently, indicating heat buildup would soon begin to affect various parts of the airframe and electronics.

"Time to go, six plus thirty," Shepherd said, pressing the front of his helmet against the HUD cushion to steady his vision. They were approximately 250 miles from the target as he put the plane into a dive. At 1,500 feet, he began pulling out, easing onto level flight barely 200 feet over the sea; then he reached to the center console, activated the terrain following radar, and looped a forefinger around the paddle switch on the backside of the control stick. This was a safety device that, if released, would automatically and instantly put the plane into a 4-G climb should the TFR malfunction.

The bomber was in all-out supersonic dash now, its speed and altitude making it virtually impossible for Lebanese defense radar to skin-paint it.

"What do we have left?" Shepherd asked.

"Four GBU-fifteens, on three through six."

"Three through six, it is; let's ripple them off."

"Select three, four, five, and six," Brancato echoed, punching in the data. "Ripple salvo."

"We're approaching the mark," Shepherd intoned, eyes riveted to the rapidly changing data on the video display system—longitude, latitude, altitude, angle of attack, air speed, and time to release. "TTR two plus thirty," he announced, watching the latter count down.

Brancato thumbed a button on the attack radar console. The Pave Tack pod rotated out of its bay in the F-111's belly and began scanning the terrain below.

"One minute," Shepherd said, scrutinizing the VDS as he punched the ECM button, releasing chaff and flares into the bomber's slipstream.

Brancato's eyes were riveted to the two images on the multi-systems display, where the alphanumerics and the infrared image of the sea were visible. Soon the craggy Beirut coastline moved into view.

"Thirty seconds," Shepherd said. "Twenty . . . ten . . ."

"Target acquired," Brancato replied seconds later as the columns of alphanumerics coincided and the image of the casino moved onto the crosshairs. He used the control handle to align it, then locked on and hit the laser button. A pencil-thin beam of red light pulsed from the Pave Tack pod, sliced through the blackness, and locked onto Casino du Liban.

Shepherd turned over control of the bomb release mechanism to the computer, keeping the pickle button depressed, as the time to release counted down.

At all zeroes, four GBU-15s automatically rippled off 3-6-4-5 from the BRUs and began tracking on the laser.

Shepherd put the bomber into a sharp toss to avoid the upcoming explosion, but the gimbaled Pave Tack pod rotated on its mount, keeping the pulsing laser locked on the casino. The bombs lined up nose to tail like lemmings and began following it to the target.

T H E   T I M E in Beirut was 8:57 P.M.

Abu Nidal was hovering over the communications console, awaiting the Romeo's call when he heard the telltale whistle and froze; seconds later, the first bomb scored a direct hit on the marina, blowing the floating gangways and 50-ton gunboat to pieces. He was dashing through the amphitheater when the second hit.

An avalanche of equipment—the catwalks, lighting grid, winch unit, and cables of the trapeze apparatus—fell from the rafters, knocking him to the floor. He became entangled in the velvet-sheathed cables and was struggling to free himself when the third and fourth bombs came through the roof of the adjacent gaming room, where the drums of Semtex plastique and crates of ammunition were stored. They erupted in a series of massive explosions that sent a roaring fireball into the blackness above Casino du Liban.

Below, in the wine cellar, Katifa huddled in a corner as the earth shook with the terrifying fury of a castastrophic quake. The last thundering explosion shattered the stone walls that entombed her, pummeling her with debris. She heard the roaring fire and felt the rising heat and then a draft. She crawled from beneath the rubble and along the floor through the smoke, following the cool air to a section of wall that had been blown away and went out the gaping hole onto the hillside, stumbling down the steep incline to the beach.

Another blast ripped through Casino du Liban.

Katifa felt the shock wave and whirled at the sound. She stood there at the edge of the surf, the choppy surface a patina of pulsating red-orange reflections, and watched as the roaring inferno consumed what little was left of the legendary gaming palace. Her thoughts came in a numbing rush. In a matter of months she had lost her brother, her lover, and the man who had raised her. She had lost them all; and for what? Indeed, the most painful part was that they were gone and she really didn't quite know why. Her eyes welled and sent tears rolling down her cheeks. She remained there for what seemed an eternity, feeling hollow and terribly alone, before she slipped away in the darkness.

BENEATH the surface of the Aegean, the Romeo was dead in the water at periscope-antenna depth. Fifty feet astern, the SDV was approaching in line with the engine and props, and away from the bow-mounted sonar. In the submarine's control room, the Syrian captain stepped back from the periscope and snapped up the handles. "Down scope; raise the antenna mast."

Exchequer, the Palestinian in charge of the hostages, crossed to the radio room, accompanied by the captain.

"Ready to transmit," the radioman reported.

The Palestinian watched the time count down and, as always, nodded at precisely 2100 hours. The operator turned on his radio and handed him the microphone. "This is the Exchequer," the Palestinian said in Arabic. "This is the Exchequer. Do you read?" The speaker crackled and hissed with dead air. He swung a baffled look to the radioman. "You have your transmitter on?"

"Of course," he replied, equally puzzled. "One of the amplifiers may have blown a fuse." He crouched to an access panel and went about removing it.

Outside, underwater searchlights slashed the black depths as the SEALs left the SDV and swarmed like foraging sharks over the Romeo's hull. One SEAL went with Reyes to the access hatch. Four swam to preassigned rescue valves.

Each affixed a suction-mounted handhold to the hull, then reached to the yellow tank on his back and unfurled the delivery hose. It terminated in a flexible plastic fitting that had been perfectly mated by OTS engineers at Langley to the valves on the Romeo's hull, enabling the two to be coupled quickly and silently.

It was 9:08 P.M. by the time the hookups were made and each man had flashed his light, signaling he was ready. Reyes returned the signal and the SEALs simultaneously opened the valves, gradually releasing the halothane into the submarine, permeating compartments from bow to stern.

"The transmitter is functioning perfectly," the radioman reported, feeling the effects of the halothane and shaking his head to clear it.

"Perhaps Beirut has had a power failure?" the captain offered. It happened often in the war-ravaged city and made perfect sense.

"What about their emergency generators?" the Palestinian countered.

The radioman slurred an unintelligible reply and slumped forward over the console.

"What is the matter with him?" the Palestinian asked, turning to the captain, who was bending over the radioman with concern when the phone buzzed. A machinist's mate reported that several seamen in the engine room had passed out; others were becoming groggy.

"What is happening?" the Palestinian demanded, feeling lightheaded and faltering as he spoke.

"Carbon monoxide," the captain deduced, turning back to the phone. "Check the exhaust system; there must be an internal leak somewhere." He paused, shaking off a growing drowsiness, then turned to the helmsman. "Surface and open all . . ." He bit off the sentence when he saw him hanging over the controls.

Outside in the frigid water, Reyes was poised over the salvage hatch, timing the halothane. He waited an extra 30 seconds before opening the hatch. Water poured into the air lock below. He and the other SEAL slithered inside and pulled it closed; then they pumped out the water, opened the interior hatch, and dropped into the Romeo, continuing to breathe through their scuba gear to avoid being affected by the anesthesia that hung in the air.

Seamen were lying on the deck, slumped in chairs, hanging over their equipment. One of the Palestinians who had been guarding the hostages stumbled toward them and fired a wild shot from a pistol. Reyes pulled the trigger on his spear gun. The barbed dart stabbed into the terrorist's chest, driving him backwards. The lieutenant made his way through the passageways, checking compartments as he went, finally coming upon the hostages in the ward room. All seven were on the floor; all were chained to bulkheads; all were sleeping like babies.

THE MASTER CAUTION LIGHT on the F-111's instrument panel was on steady. The supersonic dash had burned fuel at an incredible rate and it was dangerously low as the bomber streaked over the Mediterranean.

"Israel? Cyprus?" Brancato asked. "What do you say?"

Shepherd considered it for a long moment. "I say either one would blow the whole thing, if you know what I mean," he finally replied.

Brancato nodded emphatically. "Where else?"

"How about *America*? The USS *America*."

"Oh, boy." Brancato blanched at the prospect of a night landing on a postage stamp pitching in a rolling sea.

Shepherd contacted the carrier, identified himself and the aircraft, and requested a clear to land.

"You say a one-eleven, Viper-Two?" the *America*'s air ops officer replied incredulously.

"Affirmative. I'm lightweight; we carry a tail hook and have arrester experience."

"Not on seven-hundred-foot runways. Suggest you divert to Haifa or Nicosia. Do you copy?"

"Negative," Shepherd replied. "We'll never make it. We're too close to flame out."

"Ditch, Viper-Two. We'll fish you out."

"Negative. I don't have time to get into it. Tell the admiral mission accomplished and give him these coordinates if he needs convincing," Shepherd replied, going on to recite the coordinates for Casino du Liban.

Moments later, the admiral came on the radio. "Major Shepherd?"

"Yes, sir. May I ask if you know who I am?"

"Affirmative, Major. What the hell are you doing up there in a one-eleven anyway?"

"Bringing it home to clear my name, sir."

"And you took out that target along the way?" the admiral said, his tone a mixture of hope and disbelief.

"Yes, sir; in an aircraft with Libyan markings out of Okba ben Nafi. I suggest we have little to gain by revealing that U.S. military personnel were in the cockpit."

"I agree. We have you on radar; we'll put up an A-six to talk you down."

"That's a copy, sir. Thank you."

A short time later the Intruder came up in the lane off the F-111's left wing. "Okay, Air Force, I'll take you all the way in," the pilot said in a calm, reassuring tone. "The name of the game here is overshoot. You can always bolt, get back in the pattern, and make another approach. Copy?"

"Copy."

"If fuel permits," Brancato chimed in, grimly.

"You'll pick up the glide slope at two miles, six hundred feet. We usually beam up a computer graphic as a guide. Since you're not equipped to pick it up, you'll have to eyeball it. What's your air speed?"

"Two three zero," Shepherd replied as the carrier's lights rose at the edge of blackness far below.

"You want to be at one four five when you get there; flaps should be in take off, slats extended, gear down, hook down . . ."

Shepherd called out the moves as he made them. A hard pull on the yellow and black handle dropped the arrester hook from the fairing beneath the tail.

"Okay, there's an optical landing system on the port side of the runway area. That's the left for you Aardvark drivers. It has three lights: a yellow one called the ball and two green ones."

"Yeah, I see it."

"Good. The idea is to keep the ball centered between the greens. That keeps you in proper orientation to the glide path. The landing signal officer on deck is going to ask you to call the ball—if you can see it."

"Copy that."

"Okay. Keep the angle of attack indexer on-speed and stay on center-line. Soon as you see the drop lights dive for the deck."

"That's a copy," Shepherd replied.

"I got him," the LSO said over the radio. "Three-quarters of mile, you're on the glide, Viper-Two, just right of the line. Call the ball."

Shepherd dipped the left wing slightly and aligned the plane with the center of the carrier's runway, trying to time his approach to the rise and fall of the deck. "Ball," he said sharply, as the yellow light popped into view between the greens; but just as suddenly it was gone; all the lights were gone! He and Brancato were staring at an onrushing wall of black steel.

"Too low, too low, Viper-Two," the LSO cautioned evenly. "More throttle."

Shepherd hit the gas and clicked the nose up.

Still the wall of blackness.

"That's it," the pilot of the Intruder said. "Now time it; time the heave—better, much better."

"Concur," the LSO said. "Looking good."

Shepherd and Brancato were convinced they were about to fly headlong into the carrier's foot-thick hull when the ship fell into a valley between two swells, revealing the drop lights and deck beyond.

Shepherd pulled the stick back, slammed the throttles to the wall, and hit the speed brake.

The sleek bomber slammed onto the 700-foot runway in a controlled crash, missing the first two cables. Shepherd got the nose down on the deck just as it bounced over the third and went careening toward the sea; finally the arrester hook snagged the fourth cable and the plane jerked to a neck-snapping stop at the end of the runway, within spitting distance of the edge.

Shepherd and Brancato were thrown forward, harnesses digging into their shoulders against the sudden deceleration, then back as the plane settled down. They sat there in stunned silence watching the deck crew running toward them; then they started to laugh.

51

T H A T   E V E N I N G in the United States, network news programs reported the story of the hostages' rescue, crediting CIA with discovering their whereabouts and revealing that the rescue operation was carried out by submarine-based Navy SEALs; no mention was made of the Casino du Liban bombing. Indeed only the fleet admiral on the *America*, Brancato, and Shepherd had knowledge of the vital role it had played in the rescue. The following morning, newspapers the world over carried similar stories. The headline of the *Washington Post* read:

AMERICAN HOSTAGES RESCUED.

Two other stories on the front page were relevant and worthy of attention. One was headlined:

CIA DIRECTOR KILEY COMMITS SUICIDE

> The body of Director of Central Intelligence William Kiley was found in his Langley office early last night by a security guard making rounds. Reliable sources have told the *Post* that death was caused by a self-inflicted gunshot wound to the head. A suicide note found on Kiley's desk revealed that he wrongfully believed a mission to rescue Americans held hostage in the Middle East had failed, causing him to become despondent over their execution, which he deemed inevitable under the circumstances.

The second story, a smaller one at the bottom of the page, was headlined:

LIBYAN BOMBER DESTROYS PLO STRONGHOLD.

52

AFTER LANDING on the carrier, Shepherd's F-111 had been towed to one of the *America*'s elevators, taken below decks, and concealed beneath a shroud. There was no thought given to refueling and flying on to England due to the plane's gross weight, which made catapulting off impossible. While the carrier steamed for Naples, an F-111 crew chief and team of technicians were flown in from England. They retracted the bomber's pivot pins and removed the wings. The evening that the *America* made port, the disassembled aircraft was trucked to a nearby air base, loaded aboard a military transport, and flown to Lakenheath for refurbishing.

In the meantime, at the fleet admiral's request, Brancato and Shepherd were discreetly flown back to Washington, D.C., for military debriefing.

The Joint Chiefs were stunned by Shepherd's story.

He explained that after bombing Casino du Liban, he and Brancato had realized nothing would be gained by making the arms-sanctuary-hostage conspiracy public. The Chiefs agreed. Before adjourning, a decision as to how Shepherd's re-emergence would be explained was made.

Immediately thereafter, the Tunisian government was informed via diplomatic channels that the charges against Shepherd had been proven false and dropped, and Stephanie was allowed to leave D'Jerba.

A week later, at Andrews Air Force Base, inside the gray brick house on Ashwood Circle, the Shepherds were packing for the move to England when the door bell rang.

Stephanie answered it.

"Congressman Gutherie," she said, a little taken aback at the sight of him towering over her on the porch. "Come on in. Good to see you."

"You too. I hope you won't be offended when I tell you I'm here to see your husband."

"He's in the den," she said with a smile, leading the way between the shipping cartons. "Excuse the mess."

Shepherd was removing the military memorabilia from the walls and packing it for shipment. Laura was helping him, Jeffrey playing amid the cartons.

"I want to thank you for your help," Shepherd said after the introductions had been made and the children directed outside. "What can I do for you?"

"Well, after all you've been through, maybe there's something I can do for you," Gutherie began. "As chairman of the Intelligence Oversight Committee, I see a lot of reports, hear a lot of rumors, and lately, well, there's been a lot of speculation on the Hill that you had a hand in the hostage rescue."

"Thanks. That's very generous of you," Shepherd replied, smiling, "but people in Washington are always speculating."

"Not true?"

"No. I'm afraid it isn't."

"Really," the congressman said. "I mean, I've even heard that the mysterious Libyan bomber that took out Nidal's stronghold bore a striking resemblance to a United States Air Force F-one-eleven."

Shepherd shrugged and feigned he was baffled. "Well, anything's possible, I suppose. But as far as I know, there aren't any one-elevens stationed anywhere near the Middle East."

"So I understand. The reason I'm asking is because many of my colleagues think some recognition is clearly in order for those who participated. I've even heard talk of COMs," he said, referring to the Congressional Medal of Honor.

"Good. I couldn't be more pleased. I think the men who carried out that mission are more than deserving, Mister Congressman. I urge you to support whatever recommendations are made."

Gutherie nodded thoughtfully, then smiled. "Well, Major, you know the truth, and just between us, I think I do too. I can only conclude you're declining recognition because it would force you to reveal the details of your recent experience, and you've been ordered not to do so."

Shepherd shook his head no. "I don't know where you got that idea, but it couldn't be further from the truth."

"You'll have to forgive me if I appear a little dense but I'm confused. You were reported killed over Libya and eulogized by the president. That same day, in this room, Mrs. Shepherd and I listened to a tape, a tape of *your* voice that indicated you were alive, the victim of some unspeakable conspiracy."

"Yes, she told me about that. And I want to thank you again for assisting her in a most difficult time."

Gutherie smiled at Stephanie, then turned his attention back to Shepherd. "I'd like to pursue this a little further, Major, if you don't mind?"

"Not at all, please."

"Several days after we listened to the tape," Gutherie resumed, "Mrs. Shepherd called me from London and asked that I help you get into Libya. She said that my concerns about unauthorized covert activity were justified. She was desperate and refused to tell me more because she feared for your life." He paused, glanced at Stephanie, and asked, "Is that a reasonably accurate account of our conversation?"

Stephanie nodded.

Gutherie challenged Shepherd with a look.

"I've never known my wife to lie," Shepherd declared, putting his arm around her waist.

"Thereafter, you were branded a deserter and murderer and—"

"By the news media, yes. As a public figure, I'm sure you'll agree just because it's in print doesn't mean it's true."

"Does it mean you're confirming Colonel Qaddafi's assertion that the media was used to put forth what we might call a cover story? That you were a participant in this operation and not its victim?"

"Please understand, I don't mean to be difficult. All I can tell you is I participated in a military operation at the behest of our government," Shepherd replied, reciting the story he had worked out with the Joint Chiefs. "Upon its completion I was assigned to serve with the Forty-eighth Tactical Fighter Squadron in England"—Shepherd paused and gestured to the boxes and disarray—"if we ever get packed."

Gutherie nodded and forced a smile. "If I may, Major, I'd like to take another moment of your time, to impress on you that the people you're protecting, whoever they are, are extremely dangerous; loose cannons who had their own agenda, who circumvented democratic procedures and operated outside the law."

"You'll have to take it on faith that I'm not protecting anyone, Mister Congressman."

"Major Shepherd, I'm going to be forthright with you. I'm not sure anymore where you fit into all this; but be advised, it's my job to see that those involved are brought to justice and I intend to do just that."

"Since we're being forthright, I can assure you that they *have* been brought to justice," Shepherd said, reflecting on Kiley, Larkin, and Applegate, all of whom were dead. "Though I'm not so sure justice was properly served."

"What do you mean by that?"

Shepherd paused thoughtfully before answering. "Well, Congressman Gutherie, I guess, if I owe anyone an explanation, it's you. Now, off the record, and I mean I'll deny I ever said this if I hear it repeated, these men you speak of—whoever they are— their methods *were* wrong, I grant you that. They were zealots. They broke all the rules. God knows they put me and my family through hell, and I certainly don't condone their actions. But there was no personal gain involved for them." Shepherd paused briefly, then added, "On painful reflection, I don't think their motives were any different than yours or mine."

"I find that very hard to accept, Major."

"Well, it might be easier if you try looking at it from their point of view."

"What are you suggesting?"

"That right down to their last breath, they had no doubt, no doubt whatsoever, that they had given their lives in the service of their country."

Gutherie didn't expect that; it stopped him; stopped him cold. "Thanks for your time, Major," he said uncomfortably after a long silence. He let out a long breath, shook Shepherd's hand, then nodded to Stephanie, and left.

"You think he'll ever understand?" Shepherd asked as he enfolded Stephanie in an embrace.

"I don't know," she replied softly, her cheek nestled in the curve of his neck, her face aglow with the love and pride she felt for him; then she leaned away so he could see her eyes and said, "But *I* do."

Dinallo, Greg

Purpose of evasion   Cc. 1